D1596524

ALL THE
COWBOYS
AIN'T GONE

ALL THE COWBOYS AIN'T GONE

A NOVEL

JOHN J. JACOBSON

BLACK STONE
PUBLISHING

Printed in the United States of America

First edition: 2021
ISBN 978-1-79995-566-5
Fiction / Action & Adventure

1 3 5 7 9 10 8 6 4 2

CIP data for this book is available
from the Library of Congress

Blackstone Publishing
31 Mistletoe Rd.
Ashland, OR 97520

www.BlackstonePublishing.com

To DJJ, DPJ, MPJ, and JKJ—blessings undeserved. SDG.

There comes a time in every rightly constructed boy's life when he has a raging desire to go somewhere and dig for hidden treasure.

—Mark Twain

PART ONE

CHAPTER 1

As the sun climbed into the dazzling South Texas sky, a young boy sat astride his mustang pony on a low bluff. Looking eastward in the early morning light, he could see a plume of white smoke.

The boy wore the chaps and spurs of a drover, though the last major cattle drive in Texas had been in 1885, three years ago. His blond hair, which he wore long in imitation of his father, hung out below his "sombrero," as he liked to call his range hat. Slung over his shoulder were a small Comanche-style bow and quiver. His mother wouldn't let him take his .22 caliber rifle out by himself until he turned twelve, three long months from now.

It wasn't unusual for him to ride out early and watch the new day awaken. If asked why he did so, he would say, also imitating his father, "I like gettin' out and see what's stirring with the new day, while it's still fresh and wild. Before its newness gets marred by the events of the day." Although riding out early wasn't unusual for him, this wasn't a typical morning for young Lincoln Smith.

He had heard the train even before he saw it, and as the dark iron locomotive came into view, pulling its four cars and caboose, his temper flared. He didn't know whether to spit or cry. He spurred Rocinante, or

"Rosy," as he called his pony, into a dead gallop toward the train. Directing her with his legs, he nocked an arrow on his bow. When he got within forty feet of the locomotive, he loosed the arrow at its smokestack, then quickly nocked another arrow and shot the iron beast again, reloaded, and shot once more. The engineer and the fireman in the locomotive didn't know what to think at the first arrow; then they started yelling and cursing at him. Lincoln would have chased the train farther and shot more arrows, but he had made his point. Besides, if he didn't get back home by eight o'clock, he would have another kind of problem to deal with—his mother started his school lessons then and she didn't tolerate tardiness.

Mrs. Rachel Smith, Lincoln Smith's mother, was just getting up. Leaving her bedroom, she found the fire already burning in the fireplace, and the front door slightly ajar. She walked over to the window and looked outside. On the porch steps, she saw her son sitting with his head in his hands, mumbling something. It wasn't all that unusual to see him talking to himself, but sometimes his passionate imagination did cause her some concern.

All of a sudden, he sprang up. Grabbing his bow and quiver, he ran off toward the side of the barn. Rachel leaned over, trying to see what he had run after, but he disappeared around the back of the barn. Then she heard a canine yelp.

"What have you been doing out there?" she asked him a few minutes later, when he walked into the house.

"A coyote was sneaking around the barn. It's the one that's been trying to get at the chickens. I hit him in the flank, and my arrow stuck. But my bow's too dern small and I didn't bring him down. I need a real bow, or else you ought to let me take my rifle out."

"What did I tell you about using that word?" his mother scolded, bothered more by his language than by some chicken-filching coyote.

"*Dern* isn't really cussing," the boy said as respectfully as he could, while still making what he considered a valid point.

"It's close enough," his mother said. "If you can't think of a better word, you'd best say nothing at all. Speech like that is a sign of a poor vocabulary. And take off your spurs when you're in my house. I don't want you scuffing the floor or the furniture."

"Yes, ma'am," Lincoln said, frowning slightly. He sat down on the chair by the front door and removed his spurs. A gift from one of his father's old Texas Ranger friends, the spurs were among his most prized possessions. They were compact and light and had silver conchos on the metal heel band, and the polished-steel rowels had seven points. But what Lincoln liked best about them was their age and the experiences they had behind them.

"And don't forget to remove your hat while you're at it," his mother said as he was hanging the spurs next to the bootjack by the door.

Lincoln walked over to the table where they would shortly be starting his lessons. He took off his hat and laid it gently on the table, crown down and brim up, the way you were supposed to care for a quality hat. His father had special ordered it for his eleventh birthday, nine months back. This Stetson wasn't one of the new, fancy models that a dude from San Antonio would wear, but an old "Boss" model made from 100 percent beaver. The crown, higher in the back, was shaped with a fold down the middle, and one on either side—the style of the old Hanna outfit that used to run beef down along the Nueces River, a dozen miles away. Lincoln was almost as proud of his Stetson as he was of those spurs.

After they had eaten breakfast and cleared the table, Mrs. Smith sat down with the boy to start his lessons. She had brought a small stack of books to the table, and a slate with three differently colored pieces of chalk. She pulled a book of seventeenth-century poetry from the stack but didn't open it. Instead, she took two small pasteboard-backed books from her apron pocket and handed them to him. She tilted her head down just so she could look reproachfully up at him from beneath arched brows. "I found these on your reading table this morning. You know I have concerns about what you're filling your mind with."

"Yes, ma'am. This one's about Wild Bill," Lincoln said, using one of the books to keep the second one covered.

"I can see whom it's about," his mother said. "I like you reading, just not trashy stuff like this." She was quite proud of her son's enthusiasm for reading, even though his taste in literature wasn't yet what she hoped for.

The book had a gray-and-white cover with a highly imaginative interpretation of Wild Bill with a bowie knife in one hand, fighting off a bear, while shooting a couple of bandits with a six-shooter in the other hand. Lincoln put the books down, and his left eye twitched, as it tended to do when he was concerned or thinking serious thoughts. The twitch was a result of getting launched off his pony while trying a daring new trick that one of his young Indian friends was trying to teach him.

"Yes, ma'am, but it ain't trashy," he said, feeling duty bound to show his loyalty and defend his hero. "Pa was a friend of Wild Bill's and he says this book's somewhat accurate. Pa says Bill was one of a dying breed and that there's not many like him anymore. That's high words, coming from Pa."

James Butler Hickok, better known as Wild Bill, was actually only his third-favorite hero. But third was a lofty position on the boy's list of heroes. Had it been a male who used "trashy" in reference to Wild Bill (and said male's age might not have mattered much), there would have been minor bloodshed. But just as Lincoln didn't cotton to anyone speaking ill of Wild Bill, neither would he tolerate anyone—himself included—behaving disrespectfully to his mother. He would have said it was "against the code" to speak rudely to any woman, let alone his mother. But no man in South Texas would be fool enough to do that. For he would have had to answer not only to Lincoln but also to his father, Marshal Wesley Smith, Lincoln's number one favorite hero, who was not a man to be trifled with.

"I was referring to the quality of the writing, not to Mr. Hickok himself," Mrs. Smith said. "If what you're reading teaches you to say *ain't* instead of *is not*, then it most certainly is trash as far as I am concerned. I'm not speaking about the man, but about grammar and vocabulary. I happen to have met Mr. Hickok on a few occasions myself. Indeed, he was gallant gentleman."

"It was twelve years and two months ago, on August second, that McCall shot him in the back of the head," Lincoln said, setting the books down and standing up. "Shooting in the back is about as low-down as you can get. McCall was a coward and a dern weasel."

"Lincoln, what did I tell you about saying that word! Your foul language isn't going bring back Mr. Hickok—or, for that matter, the old times you so long for."

Lincoln sat back down, feeling just a little sorry for himself. "This book," he said after a few moments, "calls Bill 'a knight chivalric of the western plains,'"—pronouncing *chivalric* properly, with the accent on the second syllable. Lincoln enjoyed the old books of questing knights almost as much as he liked his Western novels, some of which claimed that their heroes were the true heirs of the old knight-errantry. "I admire that," he went on. "Pa's like that too, ain't he? If I could have only been born earlier, I could have been like them too."

"Well, you weren't. It's 1888, and what you need is a modern education if you're going to face the changes that are coming, and they are a-coming."

"It was the dern railroads that started the decline," he answered, recalling proudly his attack on the locomotive earlier in the morning. Lincoln detested machines in general and had a particular bitterness toward trains, whose coming had brought the hunters who butchered the buffalo. They had also put an end to the big cattle drives before he ever got the chance to go on one.

"Now, Lincoln," his mother said, growing stern, "I'm not going to tell you again. If you don't stop saying *dern*, I'm going to wash your mouth out with soap."

Lincoln sat up straight, realizing he had gone a notch too far. "Yes, ma'am, okay," he said, "and I won't say *ain't* no more—anymore. I will try harder to talk good."

"But it's not *that* book I'm most concerned with. It's that other one you're trying to hide underneath it."

She took up the books, set the one about Wild Bill down, and showed him the other one. On its cover, in gray-and-white tones, was a soldier carrying a rifle, with bandoliers crisscrossed across his chest, a cap with cloth hanging from the back to cover his neck, a long tunic that went almost to his knees, blousy trousers tucked into calf-high boots, and a wide sash wrapped around his waist. The title read, *Légion Étrangère: The French Foreign Legion—The Place That Time Forgot.*

"This is not the kind of book a boy your age should be reading. I've heard that they're a bunch of criminals and cutthroats. And there is no place that time forgot. You're just going to have to get used to it."

"Besides jewel thieves, it also says it's where fallen princes and broken-hearted lovers go."

"Lincoln, running away from your problems is not the way to get over them."

"But, ma'am, if I might say so, I do wish I could have been a Texas Ranger or even a scout. I would rather have been a scout for the Seventh Cavalry—for *Custer*, even—than to have been born now." He tried to smile and give the impression he was keeping a good attitude. But Lincoln wasn't great at hiding his emotions.

His mother moved closer to him, smoothed his hair, and looked him in the eye. "There's a story your pa once told me when I got to complaining about something or other. It's a little off-color, but I think it's time you heard it."

"What's *off-color?*"

"It means it's not all that dignified. But it has an important lesson just the same. I think you're old enough to hear it now. It's about a cattle drive, so I'm sure you'll like it. Some old outfit was taking a herd up to Dodge City, and as I think you know, there was an unwritten rule on cattle drives to always extend the hospitality of a meal to anyone who happened to ride up to the chuck wagon at mealtime—even to stragglers.

"There was also another unwritten rule that a cowboy on a drive was never supposed to complain openly about the food. Not only was it bad manners"—this *manners* bit was Mrs. Smith adding her own touch to the tale—"but if he did, the complainer would be bound to clean the dishes and the pots and pans for the whole outfit. And this applied especially to stragglers.

"So during this drive, at suppertime, up rides a straggler and says, 'Howdy, boys. Something sure smells invitin'.' And as was only proper, the boys extended to him a meal. Well, the next day, just as they're starting to eat, he rides up again and says something like 'The aroma was just too much for me.' And for the next three days, he's there at suppertime, saying something of the same nature.

"Well, this abuse of their good manners started to get to the cowboys, and they had a discussion and came up with a plan. An hour or so before supper the next day, they gathered a bunch of ripe horse biscuits."

"I've never seen a horse biscuit. What do they look like?"

"You have seen them; you see them all the time. They're, you know, they're what horses leave behind."

"You mean horse turds?"

"Yes, but I would rather not use the word. That's why I call this story off-color, and I don't want you repeating it in mixed company. Understand?"

"Yes, ma'am. Did Pa really tell you this?"

"Yes, he did. And I took a good lesson from it too, and so can you. The cowboys gathered up a bunch of these fresh horse biscuits and gave them to the cook, and the cook put a little flour on them and some spices and then fried them up nicely. Of course, for cleanliness' sake, he used a separate frying pan from the one he was using for everyone else's dinner"—again he suspected this was his mother's own touch—"and sure enough, in no time at all, up comes the straggler again, looking for a free meal.

"So the cowboys greet him and are all friendly like, and one of them gets up and says, 'Friend, here, let me get you a plate of these dumplings. Special recipe—sure are tasty.'

"They fix him a plate of the special-recipe dumplings, and the straggler digs in and takes a big bite.

"'Ah, horse biscuits!' the straggler cried, spitting out the vile concoction. 'It's horse biscuits!' he repeated, spitting again. He looked up and saw the whole crew of drovers with their eyes fixed on him. After a moment, with something less than a smile, he said, 'But good! If these aren't the best horse biscuits I ever had, I don't know what are.' He thanked them for the meal and rode away, never to bother those folks again."

"Ma, that's a great story! It ought to be in a book."

"But what is the lesson you think I want you to learn from it?"

"I don't know; there aren't any more cattle drives. Maybe, don't take handouts?"

"The lesson is that real cowboys—and people with character, in general—don't complain, even if they *have* something to complain about. And I'd take it a step further: if there is something worth complaining about, *do* something about it. Applied to you, though things aren't the way you'd prefer, there are still going to be plenty of adventures; they're just going to be different. You're just going to have to use your imagination to find them."

It was going to take Lincoln some time to think all this through. He knew that his mother was a smart woman, and he tried to give her opinions a chance. He did like the idea of a person doing something about the things they didn't like. What that straggler did, for instance, was just to get up and leave.

The old clock on the brick mantel above the fireplace started to gong; it was eight o'clock. "I'm going to get another cup of coffee," Mrs. Smith said, "and then we'll start your lessons."

CHAPTER 2

A few minutes later, they started Lincoln's schoolwork. Mrs. Smith, a teacher by training, had taken on the responsibility for the "modern education," as she called it, of her only child. After graduating from Vassar College in New York five years after the end of the War Between the States, she had come to Texas to visit her parents. Her father had been a Union brigadier general in the war and, at its end, was given the command of Fort Sam Houston, outside San Antonio, where former Texas Ranger Wesley Smith had recently become marshal. Though their backgrounds were considerably different, the thirty-year-old marshal and twenty-three-year-old Rachel Clark were quickly smitten with each other. A year later, they married. But it wasn't for another six years, after a difficult birth, that Lincoln was born, who would be her only child. Now her great passion was the education of her precocious son.

And Lincoln *was* demonstrating a certain precociousness, not only in a few of his school subjects, but also in a few areas she wasn't so excited about. He was developing a tendency to be very protective of the honor of the people, things, and ideas he cared about. His feelings about the hero of the book she had caught him reading was an instance of this. Another was his latest black eye, still visible even though it was a week old. He had received this badge of honor while brawling with five lads of similar age.

One of them had made disparaging remarks about the person Lincoln was named after—fighting words.

Naming their Texas-born son after the great leader of the North had been his unabashedly Yankee mother's idea. His father, reared in the North-siding New Mexico Territory and having been a scout in Kit Carson's brigade of the Union Army, went along with the name. He figured that growing up in a former Confederate state, with Lincoln for a name, would probably add a little jalapeño pepper to his son's personality. He himself had had to deal with something similar. After the war he had wanted to ride with the Texas Rangers, and the Texas Rangers were in Texas. He had his share of skirmishes with some of the more hardheaded Lone Stars. Eventually, he won the respect of almost everyone who knew him, either by beating the tar out of the insulter or by outfighting, capturing, and, in some cases, killing the desperadoes and Comanches who were robbing and killing their fellow Texans. Lincoln was going through a little of the same process, though now, having grown to the age of eleven, he fought less about his Yankee roots and more about other points of honor.

But despite all Lincoln's distractions, he was showing real promise in a number of his school subjects, which was very important to his mother. Her challenge was first to engage his imagination. This morning, they were going to practice elocution. Lincoln wasn't overfond of it, but she wisely approached it through some older English poetry she knew he liked.

In the poetry book she pointed to some lines from Andrew Marvell, and said, "Read this stanza, slowly and with the proper intonation."

He began reading:

> "At my back I always hear
> Time's winged chariot hurrying near:
> And yonder all before us lie . . ."

He paused, interrupted by galloping hoofbeats outside, approaching fast. "Ma, someone's in an awful big hurry," he said, beginning to rise.

She restrained him and stood up. But before she got to the window, boots clomped on the wooden porch, and a rapid knocking sounded on the door.

"Pardon, ma'am, for interrupting your schooling," said the deputy marshal standing at the door, "but is the marshal in? It's real important."

The deputy, an older man with gray whiskers, suddenly realized he still had his shabby slouch hat on and quickly removed it.

"Hi, Mr. Beale," Lincoln said, running to the deputy and sticking out his hand.

"Howdy, Linc," the deputy said, shaking his hand but without the playfulness he usually showed Lincoln.

"No, Charlie," Mrs. Smith said. "He went out early this morning after a gambler who got rowdy in town last night. Is everything all right?"

Lincoln blurted out, "Some man was snoring so loud in the room next to him that the gambler shot at his wall and blew off his big toe."

"Hush, boy," his mother said.

"It's Humberto Hill," the deputy said. "He's out of prison and got himself a gang already, and they're out for trouble. They burned the Duncan farm last night. You know Hill's got it in for the Marshal."

"And Wes was just complaining how it was getting so dull around here," she said.

"Them's dangerous pistoleros, ma'am," the deputy said. "I think it best you and Linc get into town soon as possible, at least till Wes gets back."

"Charlie, it's '*they are* dangerous pistoleros,' not *them's*," Mrs. Smith said.

"Ma'am, by rights they are," Deputy Beale said.

"We're going to finish Lincoln's lessons first," she said. "I'm not going to drop everything and run into town every time there's a little commotion around here."

"Ma'am, I would hurry if I was you. I need to warn the Reeds too. I'll ride by here on the way back. I know that's what Wes'd prefer." The deputy put his hat back on, tipped it, and hurried out.

A few moments after getting back to Lincoln's lesson, they heard the report of a rifle.

CHAPTER 3

A half mile from the ranch house, six men carrying rifles walked their horses up to the fallen body of Deputy Beale. Raúl, the youngest and lowest in the pecking order, jumped from his horse and took the dead man's hogleg revolver from its holster, then went through his pockets. He found three dollars, some change, and an old watch and handed the loot to the leader of the group, Humberto Hill. Hill put the pistol in his saddlebag and the money in his pocket. He opened the watch and looked at it, then shook it, banged it on his saddle horn, and put it to his ear. He threw it back at Raúl. "Damned thing stopped," he said. They started toward the Smiths' ranch house.

Mrs. Smith had gotten up and was looking through the front window. She couldn't see anything unusual, but she didn't doubt that serious trouble was afoot out there. She said to Lincoln, who was just behind her, "Get me your pa's rifle. Hurry, now."

Lincoln grabbed a chair and pulled it over to where the rifle hung in a gun rack, above the stone mantel. Standing on the chair, he took the rifle down. It was a custom version of the classic 1866 .44-caliber Winchester. Its polished blue-steel barrel was five inches longer than the traditional version, and its fore band was silver with gold fillings. The initials *WS* were engraved on both sides of the black-oak stock.

Lincoln also took down a box of cartridges and had the rifle loaded in seconds. He then brought it to the window, but rather than give it to his mother, he tried to edge her out of the way. "No, Lincoln," she said. "Give it to me, and you keep back."

"Ma, it shoots low and to the right," he said.

"I know how it shoots," she said, taking it from him. "Now, you stay down, you hear?" She looked back out the window and cocked the rifle.

Marshal Smith didn't get back to San Antonio until a little after noon. He had caught up with the gambler about twenty miles outside town and took him back without any resistance. Back in town, before the marshal had even dismounted, the old man who kept the jailhouse hurried out and told him the news that Hill and his gang were seen in the area. He also told him about the burning of the Duncan ranch and that Deputy Beale hadn't returned from riding out to warn the local ranches. Leaving the trigger-happy gambler handcuffed and in the jailer's care, he took off toward his ranch, eight miles from town.

A few miles away, he could see wisps of smoke rising from behind the low hills in the direction of his ranch. Panic lodged like a lead weight in his stomach—something he had never experienced, even in his worst gun battles against Comanches and outlaws. Without slowing his horse, he pulled the Winchester carbine from its scabbard.

Riding over a hillock, he could see in the distance that the crossbeam at the ranch's entrance had been pulled down. Moments later, when he passed it, he saw five or six bullet holes in the *WS* branded into the wood of the crossbeam. A hundred yards beyond lay the smoldering ruins of his house and barn.

Reaching the house, he leaped off his horse. In the front yard lay a dead body. Another was sprawled facedown on the porch steps. Both had been shot with a large-caliber weapon.

No one could have lived through the fire that destroyed the house. All that remained were the stone fireplace, chimney, and the old brass clock on the mantel.

He ran inside, frantic, looking for any sign of his wife or son. There was no trace of anything human, alive or dead. He walked to the fireplace and placed both hands on the mantel. Trying to calm his racing mind, he rested his forehead on the still-warm brick. After a moment, he looked up and noticed that the old brass clock was still ticking. In a rage, he slammed it off the mantel, shattering it on the smoldering ground.

CHAPTER 4

By the time Marshal Smith camped down that night, he had followed the tracks of Humberto Hill and his gang for close to forty miles. He would have gone farther, but first he had needed to go back to town to get two fresh mounts, more ammunition, and supplies. This cost him less than an hour. He worked fast. In town, no one volunteered to go with him. He wouldn't have taken anyone, even if there were a man he trusted to be cool, brave, and decisive in a fight. And no one had tried to talk him out of going after the gang alone.

He asked to have the body of Deputy Beale, whom he had found while cutting sign in the area around the ranch, properly cared for and buried. Other than that, he didn't say much to anyone, or they to him. His anguish and simmering rage were well understood.

As he was mounting up, the old widow of a Ranger, who had died in a gun battle twenty years before, brought him biscuits and dried meat bundled in a handkerchief. She knew something about what he felt. He thanked her as well he could and rode off, picking up the Hill gang's trail just south of his ranch.

Following their tracks had been easy enough. He was an experienced tracker, and the outlaws had taken scant pains to hide their tracks. He was convinced that his wife and son were still alive. He had found their fresh boot prints in the ranch yard, and their saddles and tack had been taken from the barn before it was burned. And the hoofprints around the ranch yard and on the trail were clear: one rider leading two unmounted horses, a rider alone, and four other riders, two of whom were probably his wife and son.

Humberto Hill was taking them on an old rustlers' trail that ran south-southwest from the ranchland outside San Antonio and into Mexico, crossing the border just south of Piedras Negras. Smith knew the trail and the area well. He had ridden it many times in his days as a Ranger, chasing bandits and cattle thieves who were running to refuge. In those days, the Rangers didn't often cross the border after outlaws. But on this occasion, there was no question. He would need to cross.

He also believed that this was exactly what Humberto Hill was counting on him to do. He was certain Humberto had taken his wife and son to lure him into a weak and vulnerable position. Hill was smart enough to know he wouldn't have much chance in anything approaching an equal fight. He would need to get Smith into a situation, preferably on the other side of the border, where he could use terrain and strength of numbers to exact his revenge.

As Marshal Smith lay in his bedroll that night, close to his small fire of mesquite sticks, he tried to take his thoughts off his family by pondering how Humberto would move against him. The man thought himself smart and tried to do things with an air of style, which complicated trying to anticipate him. Hill was the son of a Mexican woman and a former corporal in the Army of Texas. As things were getting nasty with the events leading up to the Alamo massacre, Corporal Hill bolted across the Rio Grande to Villa Acuña, where he took up with the future mother of his son. Not long after, the corporal got caught cheating at cards in a Mexican cantina and was impaled on the machete of an irate campesino. He hadn't met with a lot of good-will down there in the first place, since the Coahuiltecans didn't hold Texans—even deserters—in very high regard.

Marshal Smith knew Humberto's story as well as anyone. Though the kid never got to know his father, he got a constant stream of stories from his mother about his very special *papá norteamericano*—his charm, his good looks, and especially his intelligence. His mother was quite honored to have borne a child by a gentleman of noble English descent, as Corporal Hill had told anyone who would listen. Growing up with such a special heritage had no doubt played a part in Humberto's lofty opinion of himself.

After Humberto and two of his half brothers robbed a bank in San Antonio, Rangers Wes Smith and Henry "Frenchy" LeBeau had caught up with them at a saloon in Crystal City, where Humberto wanted to stop because he fancied one of the floozies there. It was sheer arrogance to stop on the Texas side of the river; it was cowardice and folly when he had his brothers charge out the front of the saloon, trying to draw the Rangers' attention while he slipped out the back.

Smith was the Ranger covering the front of the saloon, and when Humberto's brothers came charging out with guns blazing, he had little recourse but to shoot them. On the other hand, Humberto did show some smattering of intelligence when, at the saloon's rear exit, he found himself looking down the twin barrels of Ranger LeBeau's shotgun. He surrendered without firing a shot. Humberto had sworn vengeance on Smith for killing his brothers. And he had probably spent his nine years in Huntsville Prison planning every little detail of how he would do it.

The marshal had no doubt that Humberto would try something tricky. The conventional way would be to draw Smith into a place where all the advantages would be Hill's, like in the narrow trail going up the steep-sided arroyo just past the Río Caliente in Huaxuquilla. That would be a perfect spot for an ambush. But Humberto Hill thought himself a savvy hombre. The more Smith thought on it, the more he was convinced that Hill would want to try something novel. Wes didn't know what, but he was going to be ready.

The next morning, as the eastern chaparral began to lighten, Lincoln Smith was already wide awake. Last night, the gang's sleeping provisions for him and his mother had been to bind them hand and foot and let them use the bedrolls that had belonged to the men his mother shot. Humberto had allowed them to have their hands tied in front of them, at least. He wanted them well rested, for they had ridden hard all day and were about to do so again.

Last night they had crossed the Rio Grande a little before dusk and camped behind a bluff that rose above the river's southern bank. From the top of the bluff, in the light of a three-quarter moon, one could see the river and a fair distance across the plain that ran out into Texas. Humberto had a lookout posted there all night, changing every two hours, watching for any movement and listening for any sound of Marshal Smith approaching.

While the rest of the camp slept, Lincoln's mind raced, trying to think what he could do. He had heard the men talking in Spanish—apparently, it never occurred to them that he might know the lingo tolerably well. Once they got deeper into Mexico, some of them would circle back on his father, who was sure to be following them by now. These were desperate men, and Lincoln knew he had to be careful if he tried anything. But his father was coming, and he had to find a way to warn him.

Lincoln didn't have much experience with real-life outlaws, but he had heard lots of talk of the old days and of his father's run-ins with a number of them. And he had read a great many adventure books. He tried to remember whether any of the stories he knew had a situation similar to this, but he couldn't think of anything that might apply.

Then he thought about the discussions he'd had with his father about strategy and tactics. Most of the battles in the War Between the States were more or less undisguised frontal attacks. His father had taught him that the war proved that the frontal attack was a poor tactic, a big waste of life. Far better to use stratagems and other subtler maneuvers. The Reb general Stonewall Jackson, his father had said, was a master of this kind of thinking, and if he had lived, the war might have turned out differently. His father had also said, referring to Stonewall, that you could respect a man even if you didn't agree with him.

Lincoln racked his brain for ideas. He thought of the pirate story, how the captives put messages in bottles and threw them into the sea, hoping someone would find and read them. He didn't have pencil or paper, but he found a stick and tried to make his father a picture in the dirt next to where he had been sleeping. He had just completed drawing four stick men on horses and was about to draw two of them breaking off from the group, when Humberto walked back from relieving himself behind a cholla cactus. He was carrying Marshal Smith's rifle.

"What you doing, whelp?" Humberto hissed, walking up and seeing Lincoln try to erase the image in the dirt. "Drawing pictures for your *papá* to find?" he said, and feigned smacking Lincoln with butt of the rifle. Lincoln hardly flinched, but his mother, who had awakened, threw herself between them. Humberto roared with laughter. Then he scraped the ground with his boot, ruining what remained of the drawing and kicking sand in their eyes.

Lincoln dived for the man's legs to tackle him, but Humberto danced around and then whacked Lincoln with a solid blow across the side of his head with the buttstock of the rifle.

"You villain, he's only a child!" his mother cried out, grabbing the boy to keep him from lunging back at Humberto.

Lincoln didn't lunge, but he wouldn't let his mother hold him either. He glared at Humberto. "A man with any honor wouldn't kick dirt in a woman's face," he said. "You don't have any honor and you don't have any code." This was about the worst thing Lincoln could think to say of a man.

The rest of the gang, now wide awake, howled with laughter. "The only code I got," Humberto said, not laughing at all, "is that I'm going to kill your *papá*—an eye for an eye. I got to keep you two alive, my aces in the hole, until I get him, and then *you're* going to be the other eye."

"We'll see how brave you are when my pa gets hold of you," Lincoln said. "He's coming, and you don't stand any more chance against him than a rattler against a roadrunner. You'd need a whole army against him. He's the best shot in Texas and the best tracker and the bravest—"

"Yeah, yeah, I know he's coming," Humberto interrupted. "I just wish he'd hurry up. Now, you get ready to travel," he said, brandishing the rifle butt at Lincoln again.

"You best be careful with the rifle," Lincoln said. "General Grant gave that to my pa. And if my pa asks him, he'll send a whole battalion down here after you." He said this knowing that the former president had died three years earlier.

The gang laughed again, though a little nervously this time.

"Yeah, and I got this here pistol from General Santa Ana," Humberto said.

His gang didn't laugh at this joke. They looked at each other, as if puzzling over where Humberto had got his gun.

Soon they mounted up and were ready to ride. Before they left, Humberto said to Lilo Bustos, the member of the gang he seemed to consider the most reliable, "Wait on the bluff until you see Smith coming and take this watch," he said, handing the watch to him. "Remember the time you see him. I want to know how far he is behind us. You should be able to see him two or three miles out from the river and you better not let him see you. Ride after us as soon as you spot him and know it's him. We'll wait for you on Mesa Castillo. *¿Entiendes?*"

Lincoln didn't think Lilo Bustos looked too excited about having to wait by himself anywhere near the vicinity of Wes Smith. But since Humberto would kill him if he disobeyed, the decision was easy. He headed for the lookout spot while the rest of the gang took Rachel and Lincoln deeper into Mexico.

CHAPTER 5

Marshal Smith was up and following their trail at the first gray hint of dawn. He figured they were still at least four hours ahead of him, and he wanted to make up much of that time today. It was good that he had two strong mounts, for he was going to be riding hard into the evening.

About four hours later, he crossed the Rio Grande into Mexico, and shortly after that, came upon the camp where Humberto Hill and his gang had stayed the previous night. He dismounted and investigated it, careful not to trample any possible clues to what the gang was up to.

Reconnoitering the campsite, Smith poked the remains of the campfire with the toe of his boot. A small curl of smoke rose from the still-warm coals. Over where the horses had been hobbled, he picked up a piece of horse dung. It had barely dried. He figured he was now about two hours behind the gang—close enough that he had to start being especially attentive. He found and followed the trail leading up to the lookout spot on the bluff. Some of the boot prints were fresher than those down at the camp, and from the length of stride, the man had been in a hurry to leave.

Back at the camp, about twenty feet from the fire, he found a place, big enough for two to sleep, where the ground had been cleared of pebbles and twigs. Close by were the highest density of what he had determined were his wife's and son's boot prints. Just in front of this patch, the tuft grass was trampled hard, as if there'd been a little scuffle.

But what interested him most were the tracks of Lincoln's young mare, over where the horses had been hobbled. Wes had bought the mustang yearling for Lincoln's ninth birthday, almost three years ago. Lincoln had raised and trained her, and though he was an accomplished rider even before then, his real education on a horse had been with Rosy, the filly mustang that his father had bought him when he was nine. His father had taught him some Comanche horsemanship, which he himself had learned as a Texas Ranger. Recognized as the best horsemen on the plains, a Comanche could drop to the far side of his galloping mount, with one heel over its back and his bow arm through a sling braided into the mane, and shoot arrows, deadly at thirty yards, from under the horse's neck, protected from enemy bullets by the horse's body. For practice, Wes and Lincoln used to direct their horses without using the reins. Lincoln had become quite skilled at making his horse sidestep and back up Comanche-style. What Smith saw here were the tracks of two or three sidesteps and backings. While Lincoln was mounted, waiting for the party to ride, he had apparently made Rosy do this maneuver facing the opposite direction of the rest of the horses. He could easily have made it look as if the horse were just acting up.

The clincher was that this same pattern occurred on both sides of the trail. It seemed that Lincoln was trying to tell him to beware of someone breaking off from the group and coming at him from the side. It could also mean he was going to be attacked on both flanks. Marshal Smith wasn't sure of its exact meaning, but he knew his resourceful, imaginative son, who was warning him of some sort of doubling-back maneuver. He was forewarned. Now he just had to be ready for it.

Humberto, his three men, Rachel, and Lincoln had been at their camp on the top of Mesa Castillo for only an hour and a half when Lilo Bustos rode up, his horse lathered and breathing heavily. The sun had just set, and they were sitting around a small mesquite fire. One of his men was cooking a pot of beans.

"*Viene rápido,*" Lilo said as he swung down off his horse. "*Seis u ocho millas atrás. Tiene dos caballos fuertes, y nos sigue casi sin parar. Este hombre sabe adónde va.*"

Lincoln caught the gist of it. His father was trailing them by six to eight miles and coming fast, with two strong horses. Humberto went to his saddlebags, stashed under a creosote bush with his saddle and Smith's Winchester rifle, and took out a spyglass. He and Lilo walked to the edge of the butte, which offered a broad vista of the desert below. Humberto swept the glass over the expanse of parched grass, ocotillo, and prickly pear. After a few moments, he grunted. "I see him," he said. "The damned fool's camped and has lit a fire. He doesn't want to chance riding up the mesa in the dark. Figures this is where we're waiting for him."

"The gringo is loco to come alone," Lilo said. "We have him four to one and we can choose the ground."

"Ah, he comes alone because he is the great Wes Smith," Humberto said, closing the spyglass. "The fool! I'd just as soon shoot him in the back."

Humberto and Lilo walked back to the fire. "*Apúrate, Oso,*" Humberto said to the well-fed man who had cooked the beans and was now wolfing down a second plateful. "You're moving out in ten minutes with her and the brat. You will ride with the moon."

Humberto took a small pouch of money from his saddlebag. He also grabbed his rifle scabbard and Smith's old Winchester. He walked back to Oso and grabbed the plate from him. "You're done," he said, flinging the beans into the chaparral. "Take the woman and kid to Ramona. You should get there by sunset tomorrow. Here." He tossed Oso the pouch of money. "Give it to Emiro Fernández, who will hide you till I get there."

Oso swallowed his mouthful of beans and put the money in his vest. "I will not fail," he said.

"Ride another three hours tonight before you camp. Keep them tied all night. If you let them get away, I will find you and feed your ears to the coyotes."

"I will not fail," Oso repeated. "I will wait for you in Ramona."

"And here," Humberto said, thrusting Smith's rifle at him. "I couldn't hit a barn with this if I were standing inside it. I'll sell it in Ramona."

It was close to midnight, and the fire at Marshal Smith's camp had burned down to embers. He had made his bed next to the fire, and his horses were hobbled next to a mesquite thicket twenty feet away. The camp was quiet and still in the light of the almost full moon that had sunk a third of the way down the western sky.

Smith had made his bed, but he wasn't in it. He had wrapped his blanket over some catclaw and juniper boughs and propped his hat convincingly over where his head would be. From forty feet away in moonlight, it looked like a body sleeping by the fire. He lay low behind the mesquite thicket in front of the horses, scanning the dark for any movement, listening for the slightest out-of-place sound.

He was betting that Humberto Hill would make his move tonight. He had made camp early and built a campfire that would be visible from the mesa. He hoped Humberto would see his camping here as reluctance to risk the steep, narrow trail up the mesa in poor light. Attacking him tonight would suit Humberto's penchant for "style" and his need to be thought smart. In Smith's experience, a lot of outlaws' blunders came from bravado and a need to reassure themselves of their own cunning.

After an hour or so, Smith noticed one of the horses raise her ears. Looking through the bushes, he eased his pistol out of its holster and strained to listen. A few moments later, off to his left, he heard the snap of a trodden mesquite bean. A breath later, to the right, he heard the *snick* of a revolver hammer being cocked. A few seconds of silence elapsed. Smith resisted the urge to thumb back the hammer of his Colt .44, lest he alert the ambush party.

After more seconds of silence, from both sides of the camp, the flash and crack of pistol shots filled the air. Twigs and gravel kicked up around the bedding, and little wisps of blanket wool flew into the air as the bedroll took eight or nine direct hits.

When the shots ceased, two men stepped out of the darkness on opposite sides of the camp. With their pistols leveled, they cautiously approached the "body." The one to Smith's right kicked at the bedroll, and a piece of catclaw clung to his boot. In a fury he kicked it again, and a couple of juniper branches skittered across the camp.

"I couldn't sleep," Smith said, stepping out of the darkness.

Both bushwhackers spun toward him. He fired two quick shots, hitting each of them in the chest. One went down. The other staggered backward and fired another shot, missing badly. Smith fired twice, and he collapsed to the ground. The first man to fall reached for his pistol, which had fallen a foot from where he lay. Smith shot him in the shoulder, then ran to him and grabbed him by the shirtfront, shaking him and screaming in his face, "Where are they!"

Blood trickled out of the bandito's mouth, and his eyes rolled back. Smith flung him back down and ran to the other fallen shooter. "*¿Dónde están?*" he said, grabbing him by the hair. "Where's Humberto? *¿Adónde llevó a la mujer y al muchacho?*"

The dying man tried to speak, then went limp. Smith shook him, yelling, with no result. Standing over the second dead man and breathing hard, he realized he had emptied his revolver and started reloading cartridges from his gun belt.

Then something smashed him in the back, and he heard a gunshot. Staggering forward a few steps, he fell to his knees, still trying desperately to reload the big Colt. Another shot hit in his left shoulder, and another in the back of his right thigh. He dropped his pistol and fell on his side.

"The great Marshal Smith," Humberto Hill said, walking out of the shadows. "The great Marshal Wesley Smith has finally come to the end of his trail."

Smith scrabbled for his pistol, a few feet from where he lay sprawled in the dirt. Humberto walked over and kicked it out of reach.

"I'm going to take my time killin' you."

"What have you done with them?" Smith rasped.

Humberto kicked him in the ribs, then rolled him onto his back and pointed the gun at his face. "Beg, Marshal. I want to hear the great marshal beg."

"Tell me what you've done with them," Smith said. "Just tell me if they're still alive."

"What difference is it to you? You're going where you sent my brothers. When you get to hell, send 'em my regards." Humberto grabbed him by the shirt and, pulling him close to his face, pushed the pistol muzzle hard against Smith's temple.

"Now start begging."

While Humberto taunted him, Smith's right hand slipped down inside the top of his stovepipe boot.

"Beg, Wesley, be—"

As Smith jabbed the knife deep into Humberto's left side, there was a cracking sound as the blade crunched through a rib, puncturing the bandit's pancreas and Celiac artery. Humberto's pistol went off, the bullet smashing the bone on the outside corner of Smith's left eye socket.

Smith pushed him off, crawled to him, and put the knife to his throat. "What have you done with them? Where are they?" Smith bellowed as blood from his eye wound dripped over Humberto's face. "Do one decent thing in your life. Tell me what's happened to them."

"They're dead," Humberto mumbled. "I killed them two hours ago."

Smith stabbed him again, then again. He staggered to his feet but could barely stand. He staggered forward a few steps, dropped the knife, and collapsed on his little pile of juniper boughs.

CHAPTER 6

Oso was hot, thirsty, hungry, and tired, but he was still glad Humberto had chosen him to take Marshal Smith's woman and son to Ramona ahead of the others. He had known they planned to kill the marshal last night, and even though they outnumbered him, and Humberto's plan seemed smart, not being part of that plan was fine with Oso. There could always be a stray bullet. Or, worse, Humberto could have asked him to do something dangerous, like sneak up on Smith while he slept. And that was not something Oso would have wanted to do. Humberto had a knack for making others do the risky work.

But Oso was taking his job of bringing the woman and boy to Ramona seriously. He had no doubt that Humberto would cut off his ears and feed them to coyotes if he let the prisoners escape. The only question was whether Humberto would do it before killing him or after. He tried not to think about it. He was going to get the job done.

It was a hot day, even for October, and they had been riding four hours without a break. The night had passed without incident, though he hadn't managed to get much sleep. Not too much farther ahead was a good waterhole with some shade that would be good for a short siesta.

After another half hour's ride, Oso could see the little copse of salt

cedar lining the far bank of a small pond. After they drank, he would tie
the woman and kid against one of the trees, then relax in the shade close
to the bank.

He would not tie them up so tightly this time. Last night they had
complained and whined about the ropes until he had to drink half the
bottle of mescal he had stashed in his saddlebag just to fall asleep. The
boy had called him names and taunted him with words he mostly didn't
understand, except for "fat." That one he had heard before. He didn't care
what the words meant; he just hoped the boy would be quiet enough to
let him sleep this afternoon. He wanted to save the rest of the mescal for
tonight.

At the waterhole, Oso slid his considerable mass off his horse, a big
chestnut gelding with its best years behind it, and let it drink. Then he
pulled the Texas lawman's rifle from its scabbard and walked over to a large
clump of watercress just above the pond. Pushing aside the bright-green
plants, he drank his fill from the limestone spring feeding the pond. He
took his time while Rachel and Lincoln sat astride their horses, with their
feet tied to the stirrups.

Eventually, Oso got up, untied their feet, and crudely helped them
dismount. Then he retied their ankles in a loose hobble, leaving enough
slack that they could shuffle to the water, but not enough to let them run
or mount a horse.

"Drink," he said. "There is no more water until we get to Ramona."

Rachel and Lincoln knelt at the spring and scooped water into their
mouths.

"Bring my canteen," Oso said to Lincoln, grabbing his arm and
squeezing it hard. Then he patted his pistol. "And don't get brave."

Lincoln shambled over to the drinking horses as Oso dunked his face
in the water, trying to soothe the throbbing. He would not drink quite so
much of the mescal tonight, if his prisoners would only be a little quieter.

"This what you want, mister?" Lincoln said.

Oso raised his head from the water just in time to get wacked under
the jaw by the nearly-full canteen.

The blow knocked Oso facedown and motionless on the muddy bank.

"You did right," Rachel said, taking Oso's pistol from its holster and confirming that he was out. "Your pa would be real proud of you. Now let's get him tied up before he comes around."

A few minutes later, Oso was bound hand and foot to the thickest salt cedar growing by the pond. As long as the sun was high, he would have all the shade he wanted. Lincoln filled their canteens from the spring and hung them from their saddle horns. He also strapped his father's rifle to his saddle. Then Rachel and Lincoln Smith mounted up and rode off, seeking to avoid Humberto and his gang on their way back to Texas.

PART TWO

CHAPTER 7

TEN YEARS LATER

Lincoln didn't want to go, but he also didn't want to disappoint his mother. From what he could determine, a college education wasn't good for much. He wanted to go to Taos, to spend time with some of his father's old friends, hunting elk and bear and bighorn sheep in the southern Rockies. As something of a compromise, he got to choose which school to attend. Her first choice was Harvard, where her brother had been educated. But it was too close to a big, ugly city, and Lincoln would have none of it.

After Harvard, she had suggested the college that recently opened just south of San Francisco. She had thought he would enjoy going west. But when Lincoln discovered that the founder, Leland Stanford, was a railroad man, he categorically refused.

He ended up choosing Dartmouth College, in a thinly populated area of western New Hampshire. What settled it for him was that part of its charter was for the education of Native Americans. His best friend in San Antonio was half Comanche and, sometimes, Lincoln felt he had more in common with Henry Stormcloud Parker's people than with his own. He also liked, as his mother had emphasized, that the area was similar to where much of the action had happened in Cooper's *The Last of the Mohicans*, one his favorite books.

He'd been at Dartmouth now for about three months. He *did* like the terrain well enough. But he would have taken the plains of his childhood any day over the New England forests. Not that the plains were necessarily more beautiful—during a dry spell, they became a vast expanse of sunburnt barrenness. But he liked the loneliness of the plains and the way they made him feel small, as if he could stand on a rise and see to the end of the earth. Here, his chief complaint was that all the dern trees blocked his view.

But even here, in these eastern woodlands so different from his Texas plains, he still liked "gettin' out and see what's stirring with the new day, while it's still fresh and wild, before others get a chance to mar its newness." He had wandered a couple of miles from campus, and he wasn't paying much attention to the animal sign he usually looked for. Though he had a class later in the morning, he wasn't paying attention to the time either. A few days before, at a cotillion with the neighboring women's college, he had been considerably disconcerted. He passionately ached for Anna Flagler, whom he had danced with three times at the ball.

He remembered from his reading that someone as deeply in love as he ought to be carving a poem about her on a tree trunk. He would have to make do with a couplet, for in the back of his mind, he had a notion that he should be getting back to campus soon.

With all that was going on in his head, he was having a hard time focusing on the poem. He had carved an *A* when a bird burst into song. Scanning the branches above him, he saw a small bird with a yellow rump. He didn't know what kind it was, but it looked and sounded a lot like the yellow-breasted warblers that would come up from Mexico and nest in the old oak grove not far from his house.

That old grove had been important to him. It was nestled along both banks of a shallow coulee with a creek running through it. As a kid, he would go there to be alone and to act out scenes from the books he read. There he had been a knight and jousted with other chivalry, stern and stout foes all, well represented by the old trees. There he had pledged his troth to a lady after he had prevailed in a tournament, the last knight standing— though only barely, because of his wounds. In that live oak grove, he had ridden with Kit Carson and Wild Bill and with the Texas Rangers. After losing his father, he had taken on and killed the whole Humberto Hill gang there, saving his father so that they could ride together in his imagination. And later, when he was older, he would hunt there and afterward read or just loll in the cool shadows of the trees, listening to the warblers' song.

Then one day in the spring of '98, a year or so before he left for college, he had ridden over and found the area fenced off. A dirt road had been plowed through the coulee, and heavy machinery hauled in. The trees had been cut down and even the stumps dug out. Workmen were busy erecting a large wooden scaffold, which supported a long steel pipe down the center. This was the first oil well that Lincoln had ever seen. And it wouldn't be the last. He hated them, the machines they powered, and the machines used to build them.

The bird continued its morning song, but Lincoln scarcely heard it. He was aching for all his old dreams: the cattle drives, the Texas Rangers, the times of the mountain men such as his great-uncle and grandfather. And these thoughts always brought him around to his most painful loss of all: his father, who somehow represented the passing of everything Lincoln really cared about.

After standing there in his little reverie for he didn't know how long, he looked up and realized that the bird was gone. He remembered his class and quickly checked his old pocket watch. Without even pausing to put it back into his pocket, he started running.

The class Lincoln was going to be late for was his chemistry laboratory. It met three days a week at nine in the morning. He didn't like the class and wasn't doing well in it. In his three months at college, he had already been late five times. One more tardy arrival, and he would fail the class. He had a little over two miles to go in less than twelve minutes. And first, he must stop off at his dormitory and get his lab jacket and lab book.

By the time he got to the new brick science building, even though it was a chilly October morning, he was dripping with sweat. Fortunately for Lincoln, the workbench he shared with his lab partner was in the back row of the lab. As quietly as a Comanche stealing a horse, Lincoln slipped through the back door and slid unobserved into his chair.

"Lincoln, you are so lucky," whispered T. J. Williams, his lab partner and roommate.

"Tempus fugit," Lincoln whispered back, breathing hard. "Sometimes even when you're miserable. Have we started the project yet?"

"Not yet," TJ said. "He's giving us the safety precautions. Did you read the lesson?"

"Some of it," Lincoln said. "It gave me a great idea."

"I thought you hated chemistry," TJ said.

"I do, but I found something useful. It talked about the way they use this magnesium something-or-other to make big flashes, like when they're taking a photograph."

"Right," TJ said. "You mix magnesium with potassium perchlorate, an oxidizer—that's what we're doing in class today. It's even more powerful than potassium nitrate, which is the oxidizer they use in gunpowder."

"Yeah, well, you know that girl I met the other night at the cotillion?" Lincoln said. "It's her birthday today, and tonight I'm going to make her a giant flare out of this stuff, outside her dorm window, for a birthday surprise. Like a giant candle on a birthday cake."

"You're crazy!"

"It ought to get her attention, at least, and show her how I feel."

"Well, you better listen to what old man Rodgers is saying. We're only supposed to use a tiny bit of it. If you mix it wrong, he says it's real unstable."

"Aw, hell, I've got plenty of experience with gunpowder. My pa and his Ranger friends used to load their own cartridges."

Whispering together in the back of the room, they missed some of what Professor Rodgers was saying.

It was lucky for the class that Lincoln and TJ's desk was in the back of the lab. By the time the tray containing the magnesium and potassium perchlorate reached their desk, only about eight grams of the mixture remained. Lincoln and TJ were supposed to measure out five-eighths of a gram each and return the tray to the professor's desk in the front of the lab.

When the tray got to Lincoln, he began scooping out a few extra grams for Miss Anna Flagler's birthday surprise. What he hadn't heard while he was gabbing with his friend was Professor Rodgers's warning against letting any moisture at all touch the substance. Still warm from his two-mile run to the lab, Lincoln didn't notice the drips of perspiration that had trickled down to his wrist as he held the tray.

Lincoln was correct in thinking that the magnesium and potassium perchlorate mixture would produce a big flash, but he had underestimated it.

When Lincoln's wrist grazed the powder, after its initial fizzle, he saw TJ dive for cover. Then the tray erupted into a huge white flame that rose all the way to the ceiling. The flame also engulfed the wooden lab table where Lincoln and TJ had been sitting, along with all the papers and books on it. The explosion knocked what was left of the smoldering mixture onto the floor, catching it on fire as well. The fire licked up the side of a desk where several dozen manila folders of lab reports were stored vertically in a wooden file sorter. From there, the flames had a short reach to the lab's beadboard ceiling.

The initial explosion knocked Lincoln out of his chair, but he recovered quickly and realized that all his classmates were in danger of being burned alive. Somewhere in his mind, he had the idea that he was made for situations such as this.

"Now, none of y'all panic," he said in a composed yet commanding voice. "This is really not all that big of a deal. Just make your way single file out of the room. There, that's it. No running, now."

Most of the students did seem to be following his commands, getting outside without a lot of shoving and shouting. Professor Rodgers seemed cool and composed as he directed the students out of the room, then went out in the hall and started ringing the fire bell.

"Doggone it, Archie, play the man and stay calm," Lincoln said to a frantic student from Boston whom he had gotten to know from his French class.

By the time he had all the students out of danger, he could see that the fire was getting out of control. He had to do something fast. Throughout the semester, while Professor Rodgers droned on about acid-base titrations, Lincoln had spent hours staring at the ceiling and the large suspended water pipes with their several branches running to the wash basins in the corners of the lab.

He knew what he needed to do. Leaping onto a desk that wasn't burning yet, he grabbed a chair and smashed the water pipe overhead, at its junction with another pipe. The junction broke, and water gushed out. He then went to the other corners of the room and did the same. Water sprayed everywhere, and soon, the fire was mostly under control except for a portion of the ceiling. Leaping onto another desk, he smashed another pipe and directed the water surging out of it to the burning section. This was more fun than he'd had all semester.

Lincoln's worst burns didn't come from the explosion, though it did singe his hair and take his eyebrows down to stubble. The burns on his face would probably leave no scars. His worst burns, on his left arm and hand, came from warding off a falling piece of ceiling. He was having such a fun time squirting out the fire with the broken water pipes, he didn't notice the burns until afterward.

The campus doc made him stay overnight in the hospital, where TJ and Professor Rodgers visited him. Professor Rodgers forgave him and actually managed to laugh at the episode. The dean of students and the college provost also visited him, and they didn't share Lincoln's or the professor's accepting view of the adventure. The day after Lincoln was released from the hospital, he was on his way back to Texas. The college had generously offered not to hold him responsible for the damages if he agreed to leave immediately and never come back.

He never did get to give Anna Flagler her birthday surprise, but he sent her a note via TJ, describing what had happened and dedicating it all to her. She responded by sending flowers to his hospital room, with a note that burning up the chemistry lab for her was the most romantic thing anyone had ever done for her. She encouraged him to write her and invited him to visit that summer at her home in Florida.

CHAPTER 8

Down on the battlefield—actually, a polo stadium—ten mounted Sioux warriors surround three dismounted cavalry soldiers. Planted in the midst of the soldiers is the battle flag of the US Seventh Cavalry. The soldiers fire their carbines at the Indians, protecting the flag at all costs. The Indians are kicking up a great deal of dust and making a lot of noise, war whooping and shooting at the soldiers. After a few moments, only five warriors are still mounted, and only one soldier left standing. The last soldier is hit, twirls in a half circle, drops his rifle, and falls to his knees. With one hand, he grabs the battle flag to keep it from falling, with the other hand draws his pistol, valiantly defending the flag.

Out of the other side of the arena rides a soldier wearing a buckskin jacket, his yellow hair flowing out from under his cavalry hat. One of the five Indians breaks off and chases "Custer." These two, Custer and Crazy Horse, ride around the arena doing mock battle, firing their rifles at each other. Then Custer parries Crazy Horse's lance with his saber. Custer loses his saber and, frustrating Crazy Horse's efforts to kill him, does a series of riding tricks: swinging under and around his horse's neck, bounding off the ground up and over the saddle to the other side and back again, standing on the saddle, reins in hand, jumping over Crazy Horse's repeated lance thrusts.

At the battle flag, the four warriors have dismounted and are shooting at the soldier defending the flag. He is hit three more times and finally falls over. The battle flag starts to fall. Custer, seeing this, rides up, leaps off his horse, and catches the flag before it can touch the ground. Holding the flag in one hand, he takes the saber from his fallen comrade and defends the flag. The last man standing. Numerous shots strike him, and puffs of smoke pop off his chest. Despite these wounds, he kills two more Sioux warriors with his saber. As Custer collapses, he firmly plants the flag of the Seventh Calvary in the ground.

The two dismounted Indians approach him, knives drawn, intent on taking his scalp. But Crazy Horse rides up and commands them to stop. He dismounts and approaches Custer's body. Picking up the saber, he lays it reverently on the fallen colonel's chest. The three remaining warriors jump on their horses and ride away, whooping and doing tricks of their own as they depart.

After a few moments, Crazy Horse comes riding back, leading Custer's horse. Custer jumps up and, as his horse comes near, leaps onto its back. He does a few more tricks; then he and Crazy Horse ride out of the stadium.

Though Lincoln hadn't visited Anna Flagler the summer after his expulsion from Dartmouth College, he wrote to her with fervid protestations of his love. Now, thirteen months later, on a pleasant afternoon in southern Florida, she and some friends, home for Christmas vacation, had just witnessed Lincoln's performance as Custer in Bronco Buck Burke's Wild West and Tranquility Show.

During the show, Lincoln had been so distracted by thoughts of seeing Anna later that evening that he almost thrust the pointed flagstaff through his own foot. Now he and his best friend from childhood, Henry Stormcloud Parker, the warrior who had just "killed" him on the polo field a half hour ago, were standing outside the tent of the show's proprietor. Along with Lincoln and Stormcloud, the rest of the show's employees were also there. Bronco Buck had called an "all hands" meeting. It was to begin right after the show's performance, but Buck was late in making his appearance.

Although it had a number of quality acts and performers, Bronco Buck Burke's Wild West and Tranquility Show wasn't a first-line outfit like

Buffalo Bill's. It was 1899, and the time of first-line Wild West shows was fading. It was a respectable third-line show, though, maybe even a second. Lincoln and Stormcloud had been with the show since its inception in Austin, four months earlier. The backers had hoped to find an untapped market of nostalgia for the Wild West in the smaller cities.

They had started out doing three-day stands as they moved east. But at Memphis, they had had to cut the show down to two performances per city. Hoping to draw a wider audience, Bronco Buck tacked on the name "Tranquility Circus" and added some penny-dreadful Western drama, a magic show, and some cancan dancers. By the time they got to Charleston, they were down to one show per city. As late fall came on, the show went south. They did shows in Savannah and a few towns in the Florida Panhandle. But these drew meager crowds.

Reading in a letter from Lincoln that his Wild West show was in Florida, Anna had persuaded her daddy to arrange a performance on the grounds of his Palm Beach hotel. Though it was a balmy December afternoon and the show had been well advertised, the paying customers had barely outnumbered the show's employees.

"What do you think this meeting's about?" said Stormcloud.

Lincoln didn't answer, only half-hearing his friend's words.

"There's not a whole lot left he can cut out," Stormcloud said. "He wouldn't cut our wages again, would he? Lincoln?"

Lincoln gave him a pitying look.

People liked to call Henry Parker "Stormcloud," not only because it was the translation of his Comanche name, but because it was the polar opposite of his personality. Most of the time, he was steady, mild mannered, practical, and businesslike—in short, everything that Lincoln was not.

"There weren't more than fifty people in the stands," Stormcloud went on, "and half of them were that girl and her friends."

He had changed out of the breechclout, fringed leggings, wig, and feathers he had worn in their reenactment of Custer's Last Stand. He wasn't Sioux, so he wasn't wild about playing Crazy Horse, but with his wig and the way he rode his pony, he looked authentic enough. Lincoln hadn't changed out of his Custer outfit.

When Lincoln didn't respond, Stormcloud gave him a slap on the shoulder. A small cloud of dust stirred up from his elk-skin jacket. "Lincoln, do you have an idea of what might be going on here?" Stormcloud asked, louder now. "I don't feel good about this."

"I think I am so much in love with Anna Flagler that I'm about to bust," Lincoln said.

"I told you to look out with that one," Stormcloud said. Tall with an olive complexion, he generally fared well with the ladies and had at least some insight into what made them tick. He had tried to help his friend with wooing tactics and, at other times, warn him of looming disaster in his pursuit of certain women. But Lincoln never listened. "You haven't said more than thirty words to her in person. Her letters are a joke—no one, even you, talks like that. I'm telling you, Linc, she's not for you. She's toying with you."

Lincoln just sighed.

"Do you think maybe he sold the show?" Stormcloud said, giving up trying to warn Lincoln about Anna.

"Who?" said Lincoln.

A few moments later, the flap door of the tent opened, and two large men in dark suits and bowler hats came out. After a few moments, Bronco Buck followed. He wasn't wearing the old Stetson that usually covered the bald crown of his head, now beading with sweat. The shoulder-length gray hair hanging down the sides, and his gray goatee gave him a similar appearance to Buffalo Bill, though perhaps with less of the latter's dignity. But this afternoon, Bronco Buck was just trying to hold on to what little dignity he had left.

"Well," he finally said, raising his eyes to his waiting employees, "this ain't easy for me, and it ain't going to be easy for y'all neither. But I'll shoot straight with you. I always tried to shoot straight with you. This is trail's end for us. Trail's end. The bank's gone and shut us down. I can't make payroll. They're taking everything—even my wagon. Tonight's the last night. That's it. I am very regretful, but there ain't nothing I can do about it. It's all gone. I've lost everything. They're even taking Hector." Unfortunately, Buck had included his prize white gelding as collateral for the show. He was having a hard time holding back his emotions.

"I am truly sorry I couldn't a done better for you." He turned and went back into the tent. The two men in bowler hats remained outside.

There were only a few surprised murmurs and grumbles from the now-jobless employees. Perhaps, they had seen it as inevitable. Most were happy just to have been part of the show and to have kept it going for as long as they did. And Florida wasn't so bad a place to winter.

Whereas Stormcloud's disposition was usually controlled and practical, Lincoln's tended toward volatile. Hearing that they had just been stranded without a job thirteen hundred miles from home, Stormcloud was concerned that his friend might let loose with some of that volatility now. But Lincoln, with his head tilted slightly to one side as if listening to distant music, still had that same faraway look. Then, in a delayed reaction, he shrugged his shoulders, turned, and bumped into Stormcloud.

"Oh, sorry, pard," he said. "Didn't see you there."

"Are you okay?" Stormcloud said. "I don't want you to be concerned. Things are going to work out."

"Concerned?" said Lincoln. "How can I be concerned about anything right now? My heart's full as that ocean out there is with water. I have only about"—he pulled out his old pocket watch and flicked open the cover—"sixty-five minutes till I see Anna." He didn't even notice that he and Stormcloud were now the only ones left in front of Bronco Buck's tent.

"Linc, I'm warning you, you don't have anything in common with her. She's trouble if I ever saw it."

"No, Stormcloud, you're wrong. She's as true as the air I breathe and as constant as the sunrise."

"Well, what are we going to do, then?" Stormcloud wasn't going to waste his breath arguing. "We just lost our jobs."

"Nothing! Anything! I don't know; I don't care! I've got other things on my mind right now. Won't you just take care of it, please?"

Stormcloud sighed and rolled his eyes. He was used to handling all practical matters in their friendship. Lincoln wasn't very good with money, nor was he good at taking care of the complicated little details necessary for modern city life.

"We have a decent stash of money," Stormcloud said. "We should be okay if we're careful with it. We could stay down here till spring. And if we want to work, there's a couple of circuses down here we could get on with. They always need good riders."

"Whatever you say, pard," Lincoln said. "I'll go along with whatever you decide. Did I tell you what she said to me?"

"What did she say to you?"

"Never mind. It's sacred."

"*Sacred?* I better take your temperature."

"Yes, sacred. I only wish there were some way I could prove my love to her."

"Yeah, too bad there's not some Saracen whose head you could hack off and leave on her doorstep."

"Stormcloud, you just don't understand. They just shut down our Wild West show. Almost everything I care about is gone or going. If I'd been born a hundred years ago, or a thousand, it would be different. But now Anna is my only solace. If I have her, I don't care if I lose the last job in the world. I don't care if they build a thousand oil wells back home—well, actually, I do, but I could handle it. I can go on 'cause the love of true hearts is constant. It doesn't change."

Just then, Bronco Buck left the tent and, escorted by the two bowler-hatted men, walked off toward the hotel.

"Well, maybe true love doesn't change," Stormcloud went on, "but there ain't much of it around. I've seen you like this too many times before."

"You're wrong about Anna, and I must ask you not to talk about her like that anymore."

"I'm not wrong, and you'll see," said Stormcloud, turning to leave. "I'll see you back at our tent. I've got to figure out where we're going to be sleeping after tonight."

"You're a real friend," Lincoln said with a sigh. "I forgive you. I appreciate you looking after where we're going to stay." He looked at his watch again. "Now I got to knock the dust off and get spruced up to go see Anna."

CHAPTER 9

At his tent Lincoln cleaned up and changed his clothes, though what he put on wasn't a whole lot different from what he'd been wearing. He spent about fifteen minutes recopying two poems he planned to give Anna that evening.

He took another look at himself in the little mirror hanging by the tent's entrance and went off to the area behind the tents, where he kept Rocinante.

Other than Bronco Buck, Lincoln was the only one of the show's performers allowed to bring along his own mount. Rosy had been with him since he was nine, when she was a yearling filly. "No way I'm letting her miss out on the fun we're going to have," he had said when expectations for the show were still high. But what really persuaded Mr. Burke was the riding tricks Lincoln could do with her.

When Lincoln got to the roped-off, grassy area where Rosy grazed, she was gone. He walked around and found one of the groundskeepers and asked whether he had seen his horse. He said that after a train came by making a lot of noise and blowing its whistle, he saw a big gray horse running off toward the hotel. "That was about a half hour ago," the groundskeeper said.

Lincoln quickly found and pursued Rosy's tracks. They led toward the back of the hotel, over by a gazebo where he and Anna had spent some time before the show. As he walked on, he saw a girl in something pale blue and lacy moving in the bushes bordering the lake and gazebo. Thinking it might be Anna, he came closer.

After a few moments, he determined that it was indeed Anna. He decided to sneak up and see what she was doing, and maybe surprise her with his early arrival. From tree to tree, he slipped through the perfectly manicured parkland.

As he moved closer he saw her talking to three people who were standing in the bushes. They were three of the same people who had been with her at the show. Creeping closer, he hid behind a large palm tree. A giggling female voice said, "It would be so embarrassing if we get caught." Anna hushed her, saying, "Just be still and quiet, and he won't notice a thing. And, Randolph, you stay down and be quiet too. You better not spoil my performance. I tell you, he's the silliest boy in the world and acts like he's in some medieval romance."

One of the other girls said, "That sounds better than the way most of the boys I know act."

"Oh, hush, and just be still," Anna said, cutting her off.

Lincoln backed away from the gazebo, and his left eye didn't twitch once. A good distance away, he slid down at the base of a big elm tree. His heart felt as if a herd of buffalo had just stampeded through it. He was too confused and stunned to do much of anything. He should have listened to Stormcloud. His heart ached, then he would start to feel angry, then his heart would ache all over again.

Then he remembered Rosy, whom he had known much longer than Anna Flagler and who had shown him a great deal more loyalty. There were a lot of noisy mechanical things out and about these days that she, like him, was not especially fond of. He needed to go and find his true friend.

CHAPTER 10

About four hours later, Lincoln came back to his tent. Inside, in the light of a lantern hanging from one of the tent poles, Stormcloud was lying on his cot, reading a book.

"About time you got back," Stormcloud said, sitting up.

Lincoln had dirt smeared in his hair and on his face, in the Comanche fashion of grieving. It was something he and Stormcloud used to do in games when they were younger, mourning the imaginary death of one of their band. "You don't look so good."

Lincoln tossed the small brown-paper-wrapped parcel he was carrying down on his cot. He sighed deeply and sat down.

"She give you the ax already?" Stormcloud asked. "I told you to look out with that'n. I could see it coming a mile away."

With his eyes down, Lincoln just shook his head. After a moment he said, "No, Stormcloud, that's not it. It's way worse. Something really bad happened."

Stormcloud put the book aside and, standing, said, "What happened?"

"Rosy got run over. It was one of those dern electric trolley cars."

"Oh no, not Rosy!" Stormcloud walked over to Lincoln and put his hand on his shoulder. "I am so sorry, Linc."

"What a day! I lost my job, lost my girl, and worst of all, I lost my horse."

"That could be a record even for you, old chum."

"Yeah, well, at least now I know what I'm going to do next," said Lincoln, picking up the parcel he had tossed on the cot.

"I've been thinking about that too. There's a couple of options, but my favorite is, we go to Alaska this summer. I hear people calling it the 'Last Frontier.'"

"Too dern cold. And just you watch, by the time we get up there, they'll be starting to pump that slime out of the earth just like they are back home. I'll have none of that, thank you. I'm telling you, sucking all that stuff out of the ground's going to make the dern earth cave in."

"Then what are you going to do?"

Lincoln unwrapped the parcel. Inside were two pasteboard-bound books, both with colorful pictures of soldiers on the covers.

"The French Foreign Legion—that's what I'm going to do," he said, tossing Stormcloud one of the books. "Going to North Africa, to be precise."

"You used to have one just like this," Stormcloud said, picking up a book and looking it over, "but the cover wasn't in color."

"Same book, just an updated version. I wanted to join back then, now I'm going to. It's where the brokenhearted go to get over their misery."

"Let me see if I understand this. Your horse gets run over, so you're going to join the Foreign Legion? That's about the biggest non sequitur I've ever heard, even from you, a man of non sequiturs."

"It makes perfect sense to me."

"Well, okay, you lost your job, and a girl made a fool out of you—just like I said she would—but aren't you overreacting just a little?"

"How is it overreacting?"

"Listen, the other thing I was thinking about—let me explain. You know they're offering me a scholarship at the college in Austin. I was thinking that after spending the summer in Alaska, I would take the scholarship. I think it's time for me to quit my gallivanting and get on with my life."

"Sorry, I already tried that," Lincoln said, displaying the scar his laboratory experiment had left on the back of his left hand. "You know what happened to me at Dartmouth."

"So because of this"—Stormcloud raised the book—"you're joining the *Foreign Legion?*"

"That's exactly what I'm doing. I'm getting as far away from this crazy country as I can."

The book's title read, *Légion Étrangère: The French Foreign Legion—The Place That Time Forgot,* and on its cover was a legionnaire in full regalia: white kepi with the white cloth hanging down in back to shade the legionnaire's neck, blue tunic, white blousy trousers wrapped at the waist with a red-and-blue sash, rifle, bandoliers full of cartridges, and, of course, saber.

"I read that book when I was a kid," Lincoln said. "The Foreign Legion. Not only brokenhearted lovers go there, but disgraced princes, and jewel thieves who want to lie low. It's full of those kinds of people. It's where you go when you want to forget and be forgotten."

"Lincoln, you aren't really serious," Stormcloud said.

"It's about the only place left for people like me. There, a man's worth is determined by what he does. They don't even ask you what your name is, and no one dares ask you about your past, because the guy asking is liable to get stabbed in his sleep. It's part of their code—they do have a code, at least—and they stick by it. And they aren't getting crowded out by a bunch of machines and dandified dudes and double-dealing women either."

"You can't believe every crazy thing you read in these kinds of books," Stormcloud said. "This one's about as realistic as those cheap Westerns you still read."

Lincoln picked up the other book. Its title was *The Foreign Legion—Time's Misbegotten Children.* "I found this one too," he said, leafing through it until he found the page he was looking for. "It's a new one. Listen to this,

> 'Goodbye, my ship's a sailing,
> Let no tear fall upon thy cheek,
> Time's scythe ravages not the Foreign Legion,
> In Zanzibar, Mur, and Sidi Bel Abbès.'

"Do you hear that? That's what I've been looking for my whole life—the place that time forgot." He thumbed through a few more pages. "And listen to this. This is their motto: 'Let come what may, though outnumbered ten thousand to one, the Legion does not surrender.' "

That one simple dictum, "the Legion does not surrender," seemed to Lincoln, in that moment, a monumental thing, a great and glorious relic. It was nothing less than a distillation of, to use his father's term, "the old code." It was not only the passing of the old code, but the obsolescence of the very concept, that made Lincoln so forlorn about the modern world. In those five words, all the blurred longings of Lincoln's life seemed to coalesce into something solid and clear. It reflected what he had seen, or at least heard and read about, in the lives of his father and others he admired, whether real or fictional. It suggested a world where men were expected to live by certain simple standards—a world he had tried to reclaim but could not find, because it had passed away. In the recesses of his mind, Lincoln had concluded that in this new world, it was impossible to be a true man anymore. So he had made his decision. He would go to a place where he still could. He would join the Foreign Legion.

"Okay, I agree," said Stormcloud, "it's a good motto. But not good enough to send me to North Africa."

But Lincoln wasn't listening to Stormcloud anymore. He had been launched into a new reverie. At the moment, he was now seeing a palm-lined oasis in the midst of the blazing sun and blistering desert sands. A swarm of black-robed Tuareg tribesmen were attacking the oasis. The bodies of his comrades lay all around him; he was the only legionnaire left alive.

"Well, it's a good motto," Stormcloud said. "I like it good enough."

Lincoln didn't answer.

"But not good enough to send me off to some forlorn desert to get killed in."

Lincoln shut the book and looked up at Stormcloud. "What's in this book might not be a hundred percent factual, but don't you see the poetry in it? It's the *idea* of the place that's important. The ship is sailing into this mythical place that is unscathed by time's ruthless brutality. And even if the place is scathed, they never surrender, never give up. Can't you see I was born for this? The Foreign Legion is my destiny!"

"Zanzibar is in the Indian Ocean, off East Africa, and I have no clue where Sidi Bel-whatever-it-is and Mur are. But they aren't mythical places; they're far away and probably deadly. Linc, you're setting yourself up for another big letdown if you think this is going to be the answer to all your—"

Lincoln cut him off. "Sidi Bel Abbès is in Algeria. I looked it up. And Mur—listen to this. Mur is a small, ancient country way to the southwest of there, and it's just recently been opened up to western countries. It'll be like going back two thousand years. Just imagine, the people, the sights, sounds, smells, snake charmers with cobras rising out of baskets, wild camel-mounted Tuaregs charging as you take cover behind a sand dune. And they fight on racing camels that can run forty miles an hour. And the warriors carry scimitars—long, curved cutlasses that can slice off your head with a flick of the wrist. They have flies there so big and savage, they eat whole horses, and there's even crocodiles, and the weather is so nasty it drives legionnaires mad with something they call *le kafir*, because it's so hot, it 'would make your bloomin' eyebrows crawl.'"

He was quoting one of the few modern poets he appreciated, with, to his thinking, a fair imitation of a Cockney accent. "That's actually India that Kipling is talking about, but it applies to North Africa too."

Stormcloud gave a weary shake of his head. "Well, there's crocodiles here in Florida—alligators, anyway—but I can see that wouldn't interest you. You're loco, you know that, don't you? And your mother's going to kill you."

This gave Lincoln pause. His mother was his one reservation.

"She has her school to take care of," he said, referring to the school she started after she lost her husband. One of her first students after Lincoln was Henry Parker, who also proved to be among her best. "And she has all the money she needs, with what her brother left her. I'm not getting any younger, and I have to do what I have to do. If you aren't coming with me, she'll have you to look after her as well." After reflecting a little more, he added, "And I'll write to her once a week, besides."

"I'm not going with you. I followed you here on this crazy lark, and now I'm going back to Texas to be a lawyer. Our trail forks here."

"Well, if I don't ever make it back, I leave all my Old West books back home to your future son," Lincoln said, with some of the dramatic flair that came so naturally.

CHAPTER 11

The constant clack and sway of the train was getting old. Lincoln hated trains, and he had been on this particular one for five hours after coming aboard in Baltimore. But now he was nearing the end of this leg of his journey. The train had just passed a sign that read, New York City: Nine Miles.

He and Stormcloud had parted two days earlier. Lincoln hadn't put much effort in trying to talk his old friend into coming with him. He didn't feel great about leaving his mother, but he liked the idea of someone brave and reliable being around to look after her. Stormcloud, on the other hand, had used every argument he could muster to get Lincoln to change his mind, but his efforts were futile. Once Lincoln got something stuck in his imagination, there wasn't a whole lot anyone could do to dislodge it.

Lincoln had grown maudlin at their farewell. He not only told Stormcloud he would leave all his old books to Stormcloud's future son, he also said that if there was a true woman left in the world, and he happened to find her, he would name his first son Henry, after his childhood friend.

Lincoln had started his journey to "the place that time forgot" with a series of trains that would take him to New York City. From there he would catch a ship to Marseille, and from there another to North Africa.

The ship from New York to Marseille departed at one a.m., January 1, 1900—an auspicious time, it seemed to Lincoln.

The train pulled into Manhattan's Grand Central Station, and Lincoln gathered his cowhide satchel and his father's old buffalo rifle—all that he was taking with him. Leaving the train, there was a veritable combat of pushing and shoving to get out and join the celebration of the new century.

New York City astounded him. What he had seen of the East Coast had repulsed him, but this upped the stakes. The train station was crowded with ridiculously dressed people dashing about like a bunch of jackrabbits with their tails on fire. Everyone appeared to be trying to outdo one another in appearing sophisticated and fashionable. And everyone was in a prodigious hurry.

Walking through the train station, Lincoln was quite a sartorial contrast to the duded-up city folk. He looked much the way his father must have looked at twenty-one. Under his fringed elk-skin jacket, he wore a dark calico shirt with button-down pockets. His blue army riding pants had the gold stripe down the outer leg and a black leather belt with a Seventh Cavalry brass buckle. His pants were tucked into tall black leather stovepipe boots with Chihuahua spurs fixed on the heels. An old beaver Stetson, like the one he had worn as a boy, was pulled down low on his forehead. Under his hat, at the back of his neck, his blond hair curled over his collar. Slung over his shoulder was his old rifle. In his satchel, he carried a few changes of clothes, incidentals, and several pounds of books.

People turned and stared at him as he walked through the station. Passing a small crowd of youths, he heard a few whispers and giggles, especially from the girls. He knew he was starkly out of place and time, but he didn't mind the stares. It just strengthened his resolve to escape from their world. Meanwhile, he rather enjoyed the feeling of being an alien and a stranger.

Outside the station, he looked for a conveyance to take him to the docks. A line of the newfangled horseless carriages stretched down the street. Lincoln looked the machines over in disgust, then scanned up and down the street for anything horse drawn.

Three cabbies in overcoats and gloves stood talking and smoking and trying to stay warm in the cold night air. Seeing Lincoln, a tall one with a pockmarked face said, "I thought we got rid of them when we got rid of the Injuns." Lincoln ignored the insult and continued looking for a more suitable ride.

"How about a ride in my motor, young man," said an older cabbie smoking a very short cigar. "This little gem will do twenty miles an hour on the flat."

"I'd as soon ride a polecat," Lincoln said.

"They're the latest thing," the cabbie said. "A few years, everyone will have 'em."

"I'm not interested in what everyone's going to have," Lincoln said. "I would be obliged if you could direct me to a conveyance that doesn't run on slime sucked out of the ground—you know it's gonna make the dern earth cave in."

"Suit yourself," said the cabbie. "We make the cloppers wait down the road. But I'd get you where you're going twice as fast."

"I'd just as soon go twice as slow," Lincoln said and walked off.

About a quarter mile down the street, he came to a horse-drawn carriage. The old driver was asleep in the front seat.

Lincoln coughed a couple of times to no effect, then said, "Excuse me, sir, but can you take me to the docks?"

The driver woke, startled and confused to see a rifle-toting frontiersman standing in front of him. "New Year's Eve is kinda crazy in that part of town, son," he said, taking off his cap and rubbing his bald head. "You just might fit right in. Old Dutch don't take much to all the commotion, but I can get you in the neighborhood."

"Your horse and I are in full agreement." Lincoln put his rifle and satchel on the back seat and got in the front.

As they clopped along, the sidewalks filled up with more and more people. The cabbie looked over at Lincoln a number of times, trying to figure him out.

"That's a fine-looking old horse you got there," Lincoln said, trying to engage the old-timer. "Musta' been something in his prime."

"You know your horses, sir. Old Dutch just turned eighteen, and he was a good 'un. Still is—just gets a little spooked by all the noise." The driver gave his fare another appraising look. "If you don't mind me asking, what's a fella like you doing in the big city?"

"I was in a Wild West show. Born in Texas, just died down in Florida—the show did, that is. Bank shut us down."

"Not much interest in them shows anymore," the driver said. "Country's changing so fast, it's hard to keep up."

"I've never been one for keeping up," Lincoln said. A motorcar raced by, honking its horn, and he nearly jumped out of his seat at the sudden racket. The horse sidled, but the cabbie managed to keep him on the road.

"Them motorcars 'bout put me out of business," the driver said.

"*Those* motorcars," said Lincoln.

The driver looked over at him again, even more confused. "So you catching a boat back to Texas?" he asked.

"It's changed back there too." Lincoln shook his head sadly. "First it was the railroads, then the telegraph and electric wires, and now all the pumps making all that noise, sucking the slime up out of the earth that those dern motors burn. Then you got your bankers, lawyers, lying politicians—why, I'm getting as far from this whole crazy country as I can."

Another motorcar raced by, blaring its horn, its goggled driver looking like a giant beetle. This time Lincoln barely jumped.

"Oh, I was meaning to ask," he said after settling back down. He reached into his shirt pocket and pulled out a piece of newspaper. "You heard of this place, Captain Ahab's? It's supposed to be down by the docks." The advertisement showed a picture of a man with a beret and a spade beard standing before Niagara Falls. The caption above read, "The World-Famous Daredevil Frenchy LeBeau Conquers the Niagara."

"Sure, I know it. It's down on the waterfront, right by where you're going. Pretty rough place though, 'specially on New Year's Eve. There's a lot of friendlier places I could recommend."

"Nah, if this is the real Frenchy LeBeau, he was a friend of my father's."

As they rode on, the throng grew larger and more boisterous until the street finally became impassable. The driver pulled over, and Lincoln jumped out and walked around to pay him. As he did, a motorcar swerved around him, blaring its horn.

"You got to watch them things," the cabbie said as Lincoln stepped down from the running board. "The waterfront's three blocks down, straight ahead. Ahab's is down to the left a half block or so."

Lincoln paid him and grabbed his things.

This was a far more diverse crowd than at the train station, and many of these people had been drinking. He got jostled against tweed-suited businessmen and strangely attired women with oddly small waists and bulbous leg-of-mutton sleeves, but also Arabs, West Indians, Europeans speaking in unknown tongues, Chinamen with their hair in a long braid, East Indians, and even a couple of legionnaires, whom he tried to follow but quickly lost in the crowd.

Farther on were organ-grinders with dancing dogs, old Civil War veterans on crutches, a fortune-teller's tent, whores, pimps, reeling drunks, and a band of demonstrators carrying a sign that read, Workers of the World Unite. The buildings of the block were decked out with ribbons and banners and, up in the air above the crowd, a hot-air balloon with a large sign that read, Welcome to the Twentieth Century.

As Lincoln got closer to the docks, his mood began to change. It wouldn't be long before he was on his way, but to what, exactly? Whatever awaited him across the ocean, he couldn't say—only that it would be nothing like this. That was something he had no doubt about.

CHAPTER 12

Lincoln finally got through the crowd, to the relative calm of the docks. It was also much darker here. A large tramp steamer was moored along the quay. Across from the dock, a row of seedy bars lined the street. One had, above its door, a carved figure of a sailor with a wooden leg, and in the window was a poster like the advertisement he had from the newspaper.

He paid the two bits admission, handed his satchel and rifle to the surprised coat-check woman, and went in. Inside it was lit with the new incandescent lights—mandatory now in New York public buildings because of their reduced fire risk. From somewhere out in the cloud of tobacco smoke, a tinny piano was banging out loud and rowdy ragtime music. The place was packed with tough-looking men and tougher-looking women. A long bar, three or four deep with customers trying to get a drink, stretched the entire length of one wall. Opposite the bar, an elevated stage looked out at maybe twenty tables. A thick purple curtain embroidered with mythological scenes of winged cherubic Cupids aiming arrows at a bacchanalia below them hung down from before the stage.

The tables were mostly filled, but Lincoln managed to find an empty chair near the end of the stage. He sat down after asking a woman whether it was taken. She seemed flattered that Lincoln had chosen to sit beside her and didn't seem to mind his attire. But then, fashion didn't appear to be a big priority in this establishment. She found a glass and poured him a beer from the pitcher at the table. Lincoln drank it and then ordered another pitcher for the table as they waited for the show to begin.

Before long, a woman wearing an A-frame sign over a skimpy glittery circus outfit stepped in front of the curtain. On both sides the sign read, The Taming of the Niagara, by Frenchy LeBeau. She sauntered up and down the stage, showing off the sign and her legs.

The crowd greeted her with whistles and catcalls. After a few minutes, the piano music stopped, and the woman went back behind the curtain. Taking her place was a man in a top hat and a four-button suit that made his shoulders seem huge and square. He raised both his hands to quiet the crowd, but just then someone at the bar started chanting, "Fren-chy! Fren-chy! Fren-chy!" and clapping his hands in time with the chant. Soon the whole place had joined in the clapping and the chorus of "Fren-chy! Fren-chy! Fren-chy!"

Finally, the announcer succeeded in quieting the crowd. "Ladies and gentlemen," he said in a singsong voice, "he has generaled in the armies of France. As a Texas Ranger in the Wild West, he has been the doom of desperados and Comancheros. He has captained with the North-West Mounties."

"General in the French army, my arse!" yelled a gray-haired gentleman with rotted teeth and a yellowish scar from his ear to his lip. The crowd howled with laughter, followed by more whoops and catcalls.

Lincoln didn't think this was funny, and he didn't like the disrespect the crowd was showing. His eye began to twitch; he gripped his mug of beer tightly. He glared at the man with the scar, trying to catch his eye.

The announcer, maintaining perfect poise, quieted the crowd. "Having tamed the frontier and the territories, he has now challenged nature herself, taking on the mighty and merciless Niagara."

"It better be good or *we're* going to tame *him*!" hollered a young gent with a patch over one eye and a tattoo on his neck. The rowdy crowd joined in with wild laughter.

Lincoln was growing more and more disturbed by the crowd's general lack of decorum. He was contemplating getting up and punching the young upstart in his good eye, when the announcer continued, "Ladies and gentlemen, from Paris, France, the world-famous Frenchy LeBeau, and the taming of Niagara Falls."

The crowd cheered as the curtain rose on a stage set of a waterfall, made by long strips of blue and white cloth swaying over an imitation cliff. Below the falls, a blue cardboard river, topped with several large white balls of cotton, seemed to churn and flow.

Above the falls, chin cocked slightly upward, hands resolutely on hips, chest expanded in an air of courageous dignity, stood Frenchy LeBeau. He, too, was dressed in circus togs: black tights, a white shirt with blousy sleeves, and a black cape. In his late fifties, he wore a black spade beard, and longish black hair under a red beret. The same woman who had come out earlier now stood beside him, the sandwich board gone and her circus outfit showing to greater advantage.

Lincoln was fairly certain it was the real Frenchy LeBeau. Seven years ago, just after Lincoln turned fourteen, Frenchy had stopped in San Antonio on his way to California, to look up the family of his friend and former brother Ranger, Wes Smith. Frenchy looked pretty much the same except for his outfit, and the beard and hair that had turned from gray to black.

Frenchy raised an arm and cocked his wrist in a flamboyant theatrical gesture. The crowd grew silent, not wanting to miss a word. "Few have assailed the mighty Niagara and survived," he intoned with a French accent as false as the cheap perfume on the woman sitting next to Lincoln. "This is a basic barrel—no special reinforcement on the outside, no special protection on the inside." He hefted the large wooden tun beside him, showed it to the audience, then placed it on the edge of the waterfall. "The secret is ballast— ballast on the bottom, and light straw on top. Elegance in simplicity."

"Ah, you're full of bilgewater," yelled a short, wiry man with the look of the sea about him, who had stood on a chair.

"You got straw, all right—in your *head*," said a woman of a nice complexion but missing several teeth, standing by the bar. Lincoln bit down on his lip and tried to keep his eye from twitching.

Frenchy loaded three good-sized rocks into the barrel. Then, with his female assistant's help, he climbed in. Standing inside, he waved to the crowd.

A thunder of boos and jeers and laughter followed as Frenchy finally squatted down in the barrel, and his assistant piled straw on top of him. Then she fastened the lid.

A drumroll came from offstage and rose in a steady crescendo. Finally, the assistant, with some difficulty, rocked the barrel onto its side. She paused a moment and then, in a dramatic gesture, kicked the barrel over the falls.

It rolled down a ramp obscured by the false falls and splashed to a stop in the false river as two buckets of real water were tossed high in the air from behind the stage.

The top of the barrel came off, and out crawled Frenchy LeBeau. He struck a pose with a triumphant attitude, a few wisps of straw stuck in his beret, and hefting a large dead fish held high above his head.

But the audience didn't cheer. It erupted in a loud cacophony of boos and hisses and oaths and started throwing vegetables, many of them no longer fresh. Frenchy, rather than be offended, luxuriated in the abuse.

Lincoln jumped up and launched onto a man who had just nailed Frenchy with a rotten yellow squash. Lincoln knocked the man onto the next table, spilling beer all over the patrons seated there. They sprang up, knocking over someone at the table behind them and spilling beer all over them as well. One of the men at this table punched one of the men from the other table, who stumbled into the table behind him. In this way, the mayhem spread, with people throwing fruit not only at Frenchy but at each other, and dousing whomever they could with whatever beverages were at hand. The whole club broke out into an admirable brawl.

Two men at the table Lincoln landed on grabbed him and threw him back onto his original table, smashing it, and Lincoln fell into the arms of the woman he had been sitting with. She pushed him forward, toward a man who was charging him with his head down, like a bull. Like a good matador, Lincoln sidestepped, but then another man attacked him from the side. The woman who had been sitting with Lincoln smacked this man with a pitcher, whereupon the woman sitting with him flung the contents of a beer mug in her face. She, in turn, pushed the other woman backward onto another table, spilling all its drinks.

Lincoln had been knocked toward the short-but-tough seafaring man who had made the bilgewater reference. He had just felled a swarthy man twice his size with a chair to the head. Lincoln hit him with an uppercut that fazed him some but didn't knock him down. The swarthy giant, who was on his feet again, picked up the small man and threw him across the room, where he crashed against the piano without noticeably distracting the piano player.

Then someone came flying at Lincoln from the side, driving Lincoln and himself onto the stage, close to where Frenchy stood with his fish. Getting up, Lincoln hit this man with a left-right combination, knocking him off the stage.

Lincoln turned and saw Frenchy standing there staring at him, looking irritated. "What do you think you're doing!" Frenchy said, his accent gone.

"I'm defending my father's friend," Lincoln replied.

"For crying out loud, don't you know they *pay* me for taking this abuse? It's all part of the show, but it ain't supposed to turn into a riot."

There was now total mayhem in the bar. In every direction, people were diving and jumping and falling onto each other. Women pulled hair and doused each other with drinks and swung mugs and pitchers. A man jumped on the stage and attacked Lincoln with a chair. Lincoln ducked the chair and threw a roundhouse that knocked his attacker right back off the stage.

"Is this the sorry pass that an authentic hero of the West has come to?" Lincoln said to Frenchy.

"Times have changed, kid. A man's got to do the best he can with the cards he's been dealt."

The little seafarer, having pushed away from the piano, jumped onstage and took a swing at Frenchy. Frenchy ducked, and Lincoln belted the man in the jaw, causing him to twirl in a slow circle. Frenchy, who was still holding the big fish, swung it by the tail, knocking him off his feet in mid twirl, backward into the cardboard river.

"Who'd you say you were?" Frenchy asked Lincoln.

"Lincoln Smith, Wes Smith's son."

A man charged at Lincoln, who knocked him off the stage and then dived onto him, smashing one of the few tables left upright.

The small man who Frenchy knocked into the river still had some fight in him and staggered toward the ex-Ranger. Frenchy knocked him into the river again with the fish, and this time he didn't get up. Frenchy then jumped off the stage to help Lincoln with the three men who had him at a disadvantage. Frenchy knocked one of them down with his fist. Lincoln dropped another with a three-punch combination, and the other with a left uppercut that the man never saw.

Frenchy grabbed Lincoln, who was starting to follow up on the last man he had hit, and studied his face. "Thunder and lightning!" he exclaimed. "Last time I saw you, you weren't but a pup."

A man sneaked up behind Frenchy and knocked him down with a chair leg. Lincoln flattened him, but then someone else broke a chair over Lincoln's head. He went down and didn't get up.

CHAPTER 13

Lincoln lay unconscious on a cot in Frenchy's dressing room. He had a large red welt on his forehead and smelled like the dead mackerel that someone had tossed on his face after blindsiding him with a chair. Frenchy sat across from him, studying his face and thinking melancholy thoughts about his younger days riding with Lincoln's father. The door of the dressing room opened, and Belle, Frenchy's female assistant, flounced in, carrying Lincoln's satchel and rifle. She shoved the rifle at Frenchy's chest and threw the satchel at Lincoln but missed, hitting the side of the cot. The satchel caromed off, disgorging a few books, a denim shirt, and Lincoln's boat ticket.

"Get out of here," Frenchy growled at her. "This kid and I are almost kin."

"He cost us a hundred and fifty dollars tonight, and it's coming out of your share." She slammed the door as she left.

Frenchy looked the rifle over. He rubbed his hand over its black-oak stock and the carved initials of his old friend. After a minute or so, he leaned the rifle against the wall and gathered Lincoln's scattered possessions off the floor. He looked over the boat ticket, then the books. Along with the two Foreign Legion books were *Knights of the Table Round* and *Chivalry in the Old West*.

As Frenchy thumbed through one of the Foreign Legion books, Lincoln stirred. He put his hand to the goose egg on his forehead. "Oh, what time is it?" he groaned.

"Take it easy, you got plenty of time," Frenchy said, handing him his steamship ticket.

"Where's my rifle?" Lincoln said, bolting upright on the cot.

"We got your things; it's there," Frenchy said, pointing it out. "That's the old piece General Grant gave your pa, ain't it? My, my, that were probably thirty years back. You've kept good care of it. It's still one beautiful firearm."

"That's about all I got left of his—that and this old watch," Lincoln said, taking the watch from his pocket and putting it to his ear.

Frenchy sighed deeply. After a few moments, he said, "Well, I see you got his same taste in books."

"Yeah, I guess I do." Lincoln smiled. "You know, my ma used to tell me stories of your and my pa's adventures. By the way, it's *was not*. You use *were* when there's a plural subject."

"Your ma was always correcting Wes just like that."

"She'd box my ears if I used bad grammar."

Frenchy shook his head, marveling at where the time had gone. "She ever remarry?"

"Nah, she never really could accept that my pa was dead."

"Used to call him 'The Man Who Can't Be Killed.' I always thought maybe he went off to Argentinia or someplace like that when he thought you and your ma was dead. Like Butch and Sundance did."

"Argentina. No, I don't think so. My ma ran notices in the papers down there." Lincoln opened his watch and checked the time. Then he put it back in his pocket and started repacking his satchel.

"So you're going off and joining the Foreign Legion. Some lady been trampling on that young heart of yours?"

"It's true modern ladies don't seem to appreciate certain of my qualities, but that's not really it. These times and I just don't seem to be mixing so well."

"No more damsels in distress, so you have to go around saving old friends of your pa's."

"I just wish I could have been born when the West was young."

"Son, the Old West is gone, the East Coast has pretty much gone insane. If I were a little younger, I'd hitch up and take off with you."

"I thought, you having been a French general and all, you might be able to tell me what to expect. Maybe even recommend me to someone."

"I hate to tell you," Frenchy said, handing the Foreign Legion book to Lincoln, "but I never was in the French army. It's just a stretcher I got in the habit of telling. Matter of fact, the only thing French about me at all is my name, which I took from my stepfather. Real name's Herbert Throckmorton, which I chose to discard for obvious reasons. And don't go repeating that."

Lincoln laughed. "Don't worry. Where I'm going, no one uses their real names anyway."

"Yeah, that's what I read in the books," Frenchy said. "And that it's a place where brokenhearted lovers go, and those who want to forget and be forgotten."

"Yeah," said Lincoln, standing and shaking Frenchy's hand. "The place that time forgot."

"Well, son," Frenchy said, a world-weary look in his eye, "I'm not so sure you can count on everything you read in those books."

A half hour later, in a biting wind, Lincoln walked up the gangplank of an old French steamer bound for Marseille. About three-quarters of the way up, he heard behind him a sudden barrage of fireworks, and the approving roar of the crowd. He turned and watched the colorful patterns exploding in the sky and listened to their bursts mingle with the noise of the celebration. He stayed there for a while, blowing into his hands and contemplating what the new century had brought with it, and hoping with the optimism of youth that he was leaving it behind.

CHAPTER 14

For the first time in his life, Lincoln was thankful that his mother had made him study French. Stumbling through that old French grammar book and plodding through those boring French novels now seemed worth it. On the voyage to Marseille, he had bombarded the crew of the French steamer with all sorts of questions about *La Légion Étrangère*. His accent wasn't great, and he missed words when they talked fast, but he got his questions across and understood most of their answers. What they told him whetted his sense of adventure even more. The Legion was not a place for the faint of heart.

They had come within sight of Marseille on a bright, cold afternoon after fourteen days at sea. As they approached landfall, they passed the *Château d'If,* the small penal island that loomed ominously a mile out from land, at the mouth of the harbor. Lincoln couldn't recall for sure, but he thought it was the place where the hero had been imprisoned in *The Count of Monte Cristo.* He had tried to confirm it with a few of the crew, but they hadn't even heard Alexandre Dumas.

As the ship entered the harbor, on a high, rocky cliff stood immense old Fort Saint-Jean, still looking vigilant in its whitewashed austerity, guarding the port. Below it, rows of yellow-and-white buildings with terra-cotta roofs lined the slopes leading up from the docks. Even though the city lay across the Mediterranean Sea from North Africa, its Moorish influences were everywhere present. The very breeze seemed to whisper of romance and adventure, filling him with a sense of exhilaration that he hadn't felt since he was a kid.

Indeed the city had witnessed the Spanish wars against the Moors. Here, in the eleventh and twelfth centuries, the knights of Charlemagne and their sons had drawn swords against the Saracens. And the Crusaders, perhaps even Richard Lionheart, had passed through here on their way to and from the Holy Land. But Marseille was even older than that. The once-small village lay on the ancient road from Rome to Spain and then on to the English Channel. In this place, Julius Caesar and his legions had camped two thousand years ago.

And this was just the beginning of Lincoln's journey. Soon he would be seeing things even older and more exotic.

That night he stayed in a reasonably clean hotel a half mile from the docks. The room and the food were remarkably inexpensive. After checking in and having dinner, he walked the city for hours. In the shadow of the old fort, he found the Foreign Legion recruiting office, which was closed. He would come back early the next morning and start his life as a legionnaire.

The next morning, he changed his remaining dollars into francs. He had read of the legionnaires' meager pay and also that having a bit of extra cash was a big benefit to a new recruit just learning the ropes. In Florida he had sold his saddle and everything else that he didn't absolutely need—keeping, of course, his rifle and a few books. With the money he had taken with him from Texas and the pay he hadn't spent from Bronco Buck's Wild West Show, he had managed to salt away a decent grubstake. It ought to last him a year if he shepherded it wisely.

It was about a mile walk from his hotel to the recruiting depot at the north end of town, a block away from Fort Saint-Jean. The depot was situated in a run-down area toward the end of *La Canebière*, the major boulevard running parallel to the sea. The big old white stone building looked like an ancient Roman mausoleum. Several flags flew out in front.

As Lincoln turned up the street and approached the depot, a crowd of men stood around in front. He walked on the opposite side of the street and stopped to have a discreet look.

The sign on the front of the building said in French, English, and German: Recruiting Depot—The Foreign Legion. Below this, again in all three languages, were the words New Recruits Welcome. As he stood there, ready to take the most important step of his young life, he almost didn't notice the two men leaning on the wall of the building behind him.

"Well, Johnny," said a voice behind Lincoln, "looks like another one's going down, like a dogie to the slaughter."

"Downright pity, pard," a different voice replied, "'cause there's something in the lad that looks almost respectable. That rifle he's totin', though, ought to do for a rogue elephant, like the one almost trampled you in Burma."

Lincoln turned around to have a look at the two men. Both were probably in their early forties. One was tall and broad shouldered, at least six feet three, and had the self-possessed look of someone who didn't frighten easily. He had a sunburned, ruddy complexion and was clean-shaven except for a long and bushy mustache of the sort that cowpunchers used to wear. Indeed there was something of the American West about him, even though he was dressed in dark-brown corduroy and a newsboy cap.

The other was short, about five feet seven, but Lincoln wouldn't have wanted to say that to his face. He was tightly muscled, especially in his arms and chest, and dressed like his companion. He wore his mustache in the fashion of a debonair British military officer, but he didn't really look like an officer. He seemed too scrappy and independent. He had even more of that just-as-soon-spit-in-your-eye look about him than his companion.

Just then a Frenchman strode up to Lincoln and greeted him like a long-lost brother. "Monsieur, monsieur," the Frenchman said, hugging him in the unintimate manner that seemed customary among the French. He proceeded to address Lincoln in broken English with an odd bit of French thrown in. "You have come to join *La Légion Étrangère*; this is very good. You have come to the right place. I am pleased to introduce myself. I am Jean-Pierre Bolware. There are many important things for you to know about the *La Légion Étrangère* before you join, and it is good you have found a friend to advise you."

"What, exactly, do I need to know before I join?" Lincoln said, not really taking a shine to the unctuous fellow.

"I am a poor man," said the overeager Frenchman, "and for my services, I must ask a slight fee."

"Enter the wolf," said the shorter of the two Americans.

"More like a sheep in wolf's clothing," said the taller one.

"Well, all right, Johnny, but he'd be a poor mangy sort of sheep," said the short man.

The Frenchman had now linked his arm through Lincoln's and was trying to lead him across the street, away from these two.

"Jake, you can't let it happen to the child," said the tall man.

"Well, then, I'll play the Samaritan," said his friend, "for our uncle's sake. I believe the lad just might be kin." And with that, Jake, the smaller of the two, ambled casually up to them. Grabbing the Frenchman, who was several inches taller than he, by the nape of the neck, he gave a squeeze.

"Ah-h," the Frenchman groaned, letting go of Lincoln and cringing under the strength of the grip.

"You run along now, and keep your stinking hands off the cousins from the homeland," Jake said and gave the man a shove that sent him stumbling away.

The tall American walked up to Lincoln, who didn't know what to make of what had just occurred. "I'm Johnny," he said, "and this here who just kept your bacon out of the frying pan is Jim, but his friends call him Jake."

"Would you mind telling me why you did that?" Lincoln said. "I'm fixin' to join up, and maybe he had some information that would be useful. Mighta' been worth a few francs."

"Would have been about the worst money you ever spent, friend," said Johnny, "and you woulda' had a poor return on your investment. You appear to have a trusting heart, which is a risky thing around these parts."

Even though they wore city clothes, Lincoln was pretty sure they were from the western United States, but that wasn't all he liked about them. "Well, I guess I'll listen to what you have to say," he said. "My name's Smith." He had already thought about what name he was going to use in the Legion, where it was common practice to use a *faux nom*. Anonymity was one of the things the Legion offered to a man who wanted a fresh start. A person's identity was kept secret unless volunteered, and inquiring too deeply into a fellow legionnaire's past could result in blows or worse. But with a name like Smith, Lincoln figured he had all the anonymity he needed.

"'Smith'—that's original," said Johnny. "Jake, our new friend here is Smith."

"The pleasure is ours," Jake said. "Do call me Jake." And they both shook hands with "Smith."

"As I said, I'm here to join the Legion, and this here's the recruiting depot, isn't it?"

"Well, it is and it isn't," Jake said. "As a matter of fact, we're joining up too, but as the wise man adviseth, we've done ourselves a little investigating first. What we've discovered is that going through those doors would have been the sorriest mistake we ever made."

"Pards, if you'll excuse the interruption, I think the sensible thing would be if we continue this discourse a bit farther from the premises," Johnny said. "There's still hostiles about."

The Frenchman whom Jake had sent packing had now gathered a half-dozen layabouts from in front of the depot. He was talking to them while darting vengeful looks at Jake and Johnny.

"I think Long John's suggestion prudent, though the numbers are in our favor," said Jake. "But I reckon a ruckus this close to the fort wouldn't pan. Let's amble down and find us a cup of that good French coffee and see if you ain't convinced by the time we're done. If not, we done our best for our countryman."

"I guess I can spare a few minutes," said Lincoln. He didn't like the looks coming from Monsieur Bolware and his crowd either.

CHAPTER 15

They walked away together, and little Jake gave the loiterers about the fiercest look that Lincoln had ever seen from a human. The look seemed to physically push them back about three feet. Johnny gave them a smile that, in its way, was just as menacing. The group backed up and didn't appear interested in following them.

After a couple of blocks, they found a small café. Taking seats at an outside table, Johnny positioned himself so he could keep an eye down the street they had walked up. Jake sat looking the other direction.

"*Café* for us *trois*," Jake said in a sort of make-do pidgin French to the dour-looking waiter who came to their table. The waiter deigned to take their order and left.

"Jake," said Johnny, "from the way our young friend here forms his hat, I'd have to say that the wind that blew him here is from down South Texas way. If I ain't mistaken, it's the way some of the outfits down there used to wear 'em."

"Why, I do believe you're right," said Jake. "And he does have a bit of the windblown look about him, like ourselves."

"That's a compliment, by the way, coming from Jake," said Johnny to Lincoln.

"I was reared outside San Antonio." Lincoln was impressed. Anyone who could recognize what part of the country you were from, just from the way you formed your range hat, couldn't be all bad. "Recently, I've been around the States some. Things are pretty much gone to pot back there. You probably wouldn't recognize the place."

"It's possible," said Jake. "We've been away for a spell."

"You boys punch a few cows in your time?" asked Lincoln. "But maybe up north? I hear there's a little of that still going on in Wyoming and Montana."

"We was both top hands when we was youngsters," said Jake. "And you hit the bull's-eye, pard. We're both children of Montanee, God's own country. Near twenty years since we left. Been seeing the world a bit."

"Yep, you're talking to a couple of regular tumbleweeds," Johnny said. "And we got a bit more tumblin' to do before we're done, I reckon."

The waiter brought their three cups and placed them unceremoniously on the table. The cups were small without handles. The coffee was strong and black, with at least a quarter inch of grounds settled to the bottom of each cup. The waiter didn't leave until Jake had paid him.

"We'd offer you more," said Johnny, "but we're a bit constrained in the doubloons department. Fact is, like you, we figured we'd travel on the Legion's nickel, till we discovered that we still had a fair jaunt ahead at our own expense."

"I'm obliged for your hospitality," Lincoln said, "but I'd like to know what you're talking about. What would have been so bad about hooking up with old Frenchy back there?"

"Well, nothing much," Jake answered, "other'n that depot would have sent you to about the worst place on God's green earth, in the worst army, under the worst officers, with the worst pards, and under about the worst conditions."

"No place at all for a fine American cousin of ours," Johnny said.

"But . . . that's the enlistment depot, isn't it?" Lincoln asked. "That's what the sign said and what they told me at my hotel."

"That would appear to be the appearance of things," Jake said, "but one of the things you'll learn soon enough is that it's best to take some time before you bet a pile on appearances. 'Cause likely as not—and Big John will back me up on this—when it comes to money, women, fightin', wars, armies, women, treasure, and women, appearances can be deceiving."

"What he's saying," said Johnny, "is that there's more than one way to join the Legion, and after investigating into the matter, joining up through that station isn't the preferred way gentlemen the likes of us should be inclined to choose. You see, that depot is run by some old former swab captain from the French navy, who is now the recruiting colonel for the Legion's Second Regiment. And the Second Regiment is stationed in Madagascar, an island oven on the equator that is billy hell if ever there was such a place in this life. No one with any sense would want to suffer the next five years in that place, though he wouldn't likely survive near that long. If you've heard of old march-or-die Madagascar, that's the place. You see, you enlist here and you're on your way there, by all accounts a place worth avoiding.

"But word has got out about the Second Regiment and Madagascar, and the recruiting business for it is turning into a run-out claim. So our colonel here, being a former swab, is using some of the recruiting techniques of old Bonaparte's navy—'pressing,' as it's known. Your Frenchman back yonder was just the swab colonel's effort to reel in a recruit. A considerable number of youngsters, right on the verge of taking the plunge, start having the old second thoughts—cold feet, as the saying goes. Your Frenchman there would have steered you in, right on the spot, after telling you all the glories of the place, before you had a chance to change your mind. And would have taken a few of your doubloons for the favor, as well. If you flinched, he would have tried to get you sauced on *aguardiente* or arrack or whatever they use around here to get you blind drunk. Or worse, he would have knocked you on the head and dragged you in. We seen it happen yesterday to a couple of unsuspecting Italians, who, being Italians, probably deserved it."

"Well, I didn't come here to go to Madagascar," said Lincoln.

"The lad has some sense," said Jake.

"Now, if you," Johnny went on, "and we, for that matter, were to go straight to Sidi, that's the place where they recruit for the First Regiment. And the First Regiment is where gents such as ourselves ought to be throwing in our lot."

"And why's that?" asked Lincoln.

"It ain't that there's not going to be a bunch of scamps and lowlifes there too, like in the Second Regiment—"

Lincoln was sorely tempted to correct his use of *ain't*. It was a bad habit he had learned from his mother. Instead he said, "Scamps and lowlifes— not your fallen princes and brokenhearted lovers? I guess in the books it's just poetic license."

"It could be, but then, I ain't sure what that is," said Johnny.

Jake grinned. "Translation: not only don't he know, he don't even *suspect*."

"It doesn't matter," said Lincoln. "Pardon the interruption."

"The First Regiment," Johnny continued, "is somewhat more respect-able than the Second, on account of most of its officers ain't French. But still there'll be all types—true men and scamps, and worse'n scamps. Just like anywhere."

"From what we hear though, they're someone to ride the river with in a fight," said Jake.

"To tell the truth," Johnny said, "there are some who might consider me and Jake a bit on the scampish side ourselves, but that depends a lot on the situation and on your definitions."

"When it comes down to the old code," Jake said, "there ain't nobody truer than my ol' pard here, and I usually try to follow suit."

"Jake is about as full of frijoles as any man I knowed," said Johnny. "But there ain't no man alive you would rather have next to you when the chips are down. He's about as solid of a citizen as they come." Johnny gave Jake a slug on the shoulder for emphasis.

"Them's almost fightin' words, beanpole," Jake said.

"You best be glad they ain't, short stuff."

"He's the only man dumb enough to call me that, and that's only 'cause I'd have to stand on a ladder to flatten him."

No doubt about it, these were Lincoln's kind of people. Despite their crustiness and their banter, there was something solid and reliable about them. His father used to use the term "solid citizen" as a high compli-ment on a man's character. And it wasn't a reference to civic behavior. Just having the term in their working vocabulary impressed him. He felt they were the kind of people he'd want around when the heat was up.

"As I was saying before Jake's bosh," Johnny said, "the big difference in where you enlist is where you end up. You enlist here, it's Madagascar; enlist in Sidi Bel Abbès, it's Mur. And Mur is the place me and Jake plan to do our legioning. And we'd recommend you do the same."

"Mur!" Lincoln said, "I've read about Mur. That's why I came and that's where my sights are set."

"Mur is the place, all right." Here Johnny stopped and looked at Jake. "What do ya think—is Smitty here our man?"

"He appears a natural-born member of the tribe," Jake said.

"Okay, then, what we're going to tell you now is top secret, but we're going to tell you anyway, seeing as you're a pard from the homeland, and we know we can trust you by the way you wear your hat."

"Speakin' 'bout hostiles . . ." Jake said, looking up the street. The Frenchman he had squeezed, along with about eight others, had just come around the corner and posted themselves a couple of storefronts away, across the street.

"They just don't know what's good for 'em," Jake said.

"Best not to get riled," Johnny said, looking down the other end of the street. "They could have backup." From that direction, two French policemen came around the corner. "Them gendarmes could be in league with them. If we end up arrested, we'd be off to Madagascar before you could say . . ."

Three nuns came around the corner and were walking up the sidewalk. " . . . Before you could say three Hail Marys," Johnny went on.

"Them Frogs need a lesson in manners," Jake said.

"Pull your horns in, pard," Johnny said. "I know you could whup 'em, but we can't afford a row, and we got a boat to catch." Johnny stood up and walked to the nuns, greeted them, and started making pleasant conversation with them. He seemed quite comfortable talking with women, even nuns. They might even have blushed.

"I guess John's right," Jake said, getting up. "We best wiggle on." Lincoln grabbed his things, and the three of them walked away and down the street with the nuns.

CHAPTER 16

"We're going to level with you and put our cards on the table," Johnny said. They were in their room, in a hotel considerably less expensive than the inexpensive one where Lincoln had stayed the night before. Leaving the café, they had strolled along with the nuns to an old church a few blocks away. After a few minutes of kneeling in the pews, they left through a side door and made it straight for the hotel. Apparently, the pressing crew had not seen them.

Johnny had finished packing his rucksack and sat down in one of two chairs at a small table. Lincoln sat in the other chair. Jake was taking more time packing, wanting to make sure his other pair of pants was folded with nice creases in the legs.

"We'd been in the south of Egypt, not too far from the first cataract, looking for treasure," Johnny went on. "That was about two years ago. Our quarrying had turned up dry and things were heatin' up in that part of the land, since the Mahdi, as he was called, and his dervish army was on the warpath again. We came back to Cairo and were in some gin palace there, where a lot of embassy guards and soldiers went to quench their thirst. We got to talking with some big German sergeant who works for some big-noises in their embassy. He had just got back from this place Mur that we had never heard of. Well, after a few rounds of the local firewater, he starts blabbing about the place. See, he has heard his ambassador and the other stiffs talking. And they're saying they're about to win some big construction project there, and all of them are going to be moving there soon. But then he says, kind of confidential like, that the real reason they're going there ain't to build this dam they're proposin', but that the country is full of riches and treasure, and Germany is going to make some kind of pile off her. And he says he'll be choked if he ain't goin' to get his share of it. That's what the German said. Ain't that right, Jake?"

Jake had finished packing and was over at the window, with the curtain pulled back slightly, looking out onto the street. He moved away from the window and took a seat on the bed. "Sure enough, I believe he said the place is 'floating in wealth.'"

Johnny got up from his chair and walked over to the door. After unlatching the lock, which may or may not have held if someone tried to force it, he checked the hallway.

"So you see," Johnny went on after relocking the door and returning to his seat, "things started to get interesting to us 'cause huntin' for treasure is one of Jake's and my lines of business. So we set about investigating the matter ourselves. And sure enough, the place appears to be a pearl. There's all sorts of old stories and legends about it. But the point is not if they brought their riches with them when they came there centuries ago (which we happen to doubt), or if they discovered them there, which is more probable. The point is not *how* the riches got there, but that they're there. According to one account, mounds of gold, rubies the size of plums, and diamonds as big as grapes."

"But the Germans didn't win the contract," Lincoln said. "The French did. I've done some reading about it myself."

"That's the truth, all right," Johnny said. "About a week after that first talk with the sergeant, it was announced the French got it. And the Germans got all in a lather, protesting and crying cheat, and half the embassy got sacked. But there was nothin' they could do about it. So not long after that news, we see the Hun sergeant again, and as he knows that treasure finding is of interest to us, he wants to talk. He says he's got something he wants to sell us 'cause it's no use to him anymore, 'cause he ain't goin' to Mur. So he plops down this old map in front of us, which shows the location where he says there is treasure to be found. He said he bought it from some old Murian when they was there making their proposal. The map is old, made on a sheepskin, and had some words we couldn't read at the time. We seen our share of this kind of stuff before, but this one looked the McCoy.

"But we wanted to know, if he was so sure it was good, why didn't he just quit the army and go find his treasure as a civilian? That's when he told us that Mur won't let just anybody into the country. As long the Germans won the contract, he was in, 'cause he was going to be stationed there. But now that the Germans were out, there was no way he could get in, even if he deserted the army—which he would consider if he thought he could get in. This seemed to us to make his story even more credible, and the map more interesting, especially at the price he was willing to part with it for. So after some negotiation by Jake, who is good at that kind of thing, we bought the map.

"Then this is the kicker. Jake and I was learning all we could about Mur and making plans and figuring how we was goin' to get in. And about two weeks later, the Kraut sergeant finds us again and is all hot to buy his map back. He won't say why, though we press him pretty hard. He just says that things might change and he figures he'll be getting back there soon enough. And to get it back, he's willing to pay twice what we paid him for it. This told us a lot more about the map than any amount of his swearing about how good it was mighta' done."

At this point Jake pulled from inside his shirt a leather wallet that hung down from his neck on a leather cord. He took from it a carefully folded piece of paper and handed it to Johnny, who smoothed it out on the table and patted it affectionately.

"Now, as I said, we have some experience in this line of business, and the first thing an experienced fella does when he gets a map is make a copy of it, for the obvious reasons. And this here's ours."

"So this is why joining the Legion through Sidi is so important to you?" Lincoln said.

"We told you we was going to shoot straight with you, and we are. That's the plain truth of it. If me and Jake are going to discover some of that treasure, the only way we're going to do it is to join the Foreign Legion and get ourselves stationed in Mur. And the way we are going to do that is to enlist not here, but in Sidi Bel Abbès.

"But even if you don't throw in with us, you don't want to join the Second Regiment and end up in Madagascar. Everything we said about that outfit is true. The First Regiment is who you want to be doing your legioning with."

"When we join, we'll be taking our legioning seriously," said Jake. "There'll be no shirking our duty, which, as you'll learn, is to your partners in arms and ain't to France. We ain't no shirkers; it wouldn't be the honorable thing. But on the side, we mean to do some treasure findin'."

"And after discussing it fully," Johnny said, "we came to the conclusion we needed to take on another partner in our escapade. By our reckoning, this is going to be a three-man job. And after studying the matter, we think you're our man."

"Well, I must say I'm flattered," Lincoln said. "But how do you know? You've known me all of two hours."

"That's not quite right," Jake said. "We've been keeping our eye on you since you got in yesterday afternoon."

"You've been following me around since *yesterday*?"

"Yes sir, since you came by the depot," said Jake.

"We've been lookin' for a pard and been keepin' an eye on the station," Johnny said. "It was clear you was from Texas, and that was a good start. And from the way you dressed and handled yourself, you looked like a man we had a certain amount in common with. After that we wanted to make sure you didn't get pressed till you understood the facts."

"As the wise man sayeth," said Jake, "the clothes oft revealeth the man, or something such."

"And packing a custom '66 Winchester gives you a certain standing, as it more than likely has a tale or two behind it." Johnny added, "That is indeed a fine piece you're carrying."

"As John said we wanted to make sure them Frogs didn't get you till we had a chance to enlighten you about the situation. That dinner you had last night coulda' fed a troop."

"You about walked us out yesterday, following you around," said Johnny.

"But we do appreciate your enthusiasm," said Jake. "Reminds us of ourselves when we was younger—not that we ain't still."

"Well, I'll be," said Lincoln. "I got to admit, it's a bit maddening."

"What, getting followed?" asked Jake.

"No, being so daft I didn't notice it."

"Me and Johnny have some experience at being scarce when we want to."

Lincoln laughed. "Well, I don't know what to say! But I did come to join the Legion, not to go treasure hunting. How much would it cost me, anyway, to join in with you?"

"Why, we figure one-third of what we originally paid for the map," said Jake. "Actually, we sold it back to the Hun sergeant since we had our copy. But we figure that would be a fair enough ante up."

"Jake got him down to twenty-three British pounds, which is a hundred and fourteen US greenbacks and forty-eight cents. So your share would be thirty-eight dollars and sixteen cents."

"That's nothing," Lincoln said with a laugh. "If that map's any good, it's worth a lot more than that."

"That is the truth," said Johnny. "But as we wasn't counting on any traveling expenses once we got here, that amount should get us to Sidi comfortable enough."

Lincoln went to the window and brushed aside the grimy curtains and looked outside, more to take a moment and think things over than to check the street.

"Well, you've done me a service, steering me away from enlisting here," he said, turning from the window. "And I'd consider it an honor to travel with you to Sidi. Why don't you let me pass you the money and you can keep my share of the map? If you hit your strike, you can pay me back, though I won't hold you to it."

Both Johnny and Jake's expressions sank as if they had been called greenhorns by someone they respected.

"What's the matter with that?" asked Lincoln.

"It's like this," Jake said. He stood and picked up the map. "We may cut a fine line on certain things on occasion, but we do have the code. And taking handouts ain't part of it. We'd be honored to take you in as a partner, especially since, even young as you are, we reckon you're part of the breed. We do appreciate your offer, but we can't take it."

"I understand," said Lincoln after pausing a moment. "I can't guarantee I'll be able to do anything with you or for you once we get to Mur. I may be of no use at all."

"All we ask is that you do what you can," Jake said. "We wouldn't ask you to do nothin' you didn't feel comfortable doin'."

"If this doesn't beat all," said Lincoln. "I guess, then, I'm one-third partner of, of . . . *What* am I one-third partner of?"

"Why, could be millions or could be camel flop," Johnny said. "But it sure should be interesting."

CHAPTER 17

Jake and Johnny had already found the Italian steamer that would take them to the port of Béjaïa in Algeria. It would sail with the tide at three that afternoon. They wanted to lie low until then, since it was possible that the pressing crew would be on the lookout to send them to Madagascar. But they needed to pay for their berths, buy some supplies, and, as Jake insisted, "Have a hearty last meal on the continent." Even at his size, Jake was, according to his partner, a healthy eater.

They spent another hour in the hotel talking, which is to say, Johnny and Jake regaling Lincoln with stories of their travels. Lincoln soaked it up. Since joining the merchant marine twenty years ago in San Francisco, they had been to Hawaii, Australia, Siam, Burma, India, and Tahiti, where they picked up some ability with the French language. After leaving the merchant marine, they spent more time in the East Indies and Southeast Asia, doing a little "soldier-of-fortuning." From there, Johnny said, "The gold fields of South Africa called, and we did some poking around diamond fields there too." When it looked as though there might be another war down in South Africa, they headed for Egypt, where some recent discoveries had gotten their interest. As Jake put it, they were not yet rich with money, but they were millionaires in experience. Lincoln agreed with them, and he thought the latter more valuable anyway.

The ship leaving that afternoon would take them to Béjaïa, on the North African coast. From there they must find some kind of passage, traveling 180 miles through dangerous foreign territory, to Sidi Bel Abbès, the worldwide headquarters of the French Foreign Legion. After enlisting at Sidi, they still had to travel another 150 miles southwest to Mur, but this part of the journey, since they would then be legionnaires, would be at the Legion's expense.

Lincoln had suggested buying a cabin on the steamer rather than going steerage, but Johnny and Jake were adamant about conserving their resources. They didn't know what they might be facing down the trail, and might need it for a little *baksheesh*. Johnny explained that most of the world ran on *baksheesh*, which was a bit like "greasing the old palm, 'cept somewhatly legal." It didn't take much to convince Lincoln to go steerage. That would probably be more interesting anyway. And in a few hours, he would be on his way to North Africa.

They ate their meal, which was more like two meals or even three, then bought their boat tickets and necessary supplies without incident, and arrived at the docks a half hour before the ship was to sail. As they approached, they caught sight of the Frenchman named Bolware, who had tried to help Lincoln enlist that morning. Standing just behind him was a small mob of unsavory-looking fellows. At a gesture from Bolware, they all moved in front of the gangway, blocking access to the ship.

"Looks like we got ourselves a sending-off party," said Johnny. "I count thirteen of 'em. Thoughtful of them, ain't it?"

"Thirteen makes it a little fairer," said Jake.

Johnny and Jake looked up and down the dock but saw no policemen. "Too many witnesses for the gendarmes to be in cahoots with 'em," Johnny said, peering up at the ship, where an audience of seamen was looking over the rail. "I believe they've done some miscalculating. This is nothing more than a warm-up for Jake here."

Lincoln glanced over to Jake, who looked deeply focused, as if he were intent on solving a chess problem. "Why don't you let me handle it?" Johnny said to Jake. "I don't want you to risk hurting your hands when we might need them for polishing jewels."

"Nope," said Jake. "I don't like that Frenchy's attitude, nor his looks neither. I'll be careful."

"Ain't no use arguing with him," Johnny said to Lincoln. "If they'd let you and me pass, we could watch it from up on the deck and get a better view."

What happened next was a marvel.

Jake took off his pack and coat and handed them to Johnny. Then he walked up to within about six feet of Monsieur Bolware. Lincoln put his satchel and rifle down and took off his coat too, and started after Jake, but Johnny put out an arm and stopped him.

"Aren't you going to help him?" Lincoln said.

"I don't get involved in this type of thing unless there's a difficulty, which, in this case, I highly doubt. I wouldn't want to hurt nobody. Now, watch and learn why it's not good to rile Jake Burns."

Jake walked up face to face with Bolware, who was about five feet in front of his henchmen. "You best be scattering in a hurry," he said in his pidgin French. "I'm going to count to ten and then you better be gone; otherwise, I'm not responsible for your health." He also employed some sign language to make sure he was understood, one of the motions being to put his two hands together and then separate them vigorously, and another being to slice his index finger across his throat.

Lincoln wasn't sure they understood what Jake had said. So he took a few steps up and expressed Jake's sentiments a little more clearly. "My friend asks you," he said in his considerably better French, "to please get your reeking carcasses out of our way before he thrashes you all to within a few inches of perdition and then throws you into the sea. You do not know whom you are dealing with. This is Jake Burns, former lightweight champion of the world." Lincoln was pleased with his interpretation and hoped his friends had caught it and didn't mind this slight embellishment.

"How'd you know Jake was a champion?" said Johnny. "He don't like to boast, but when we was in England, he whupped Jack McAuliffe, though it was only an exhibition."

Upon hearing Jake's challenge, the French gang had fallen back a couple of steps, but their leader didn't. That was his first mistake. And on hearing Lincoln's words, they fell back a few more steps, and two of them actually broke off and ran away. Then Bolware turned and snarled something at the gang, and they stepped closer, though not boldly.

Jake began to count, "One, two, three . . ." Lincoln didn't bother to interpret.

Jake strode up to Bolware and hit him under the chin so fast that he was arcing backward through the air, halfway to the water, before his gang could react. Only about eight of them moved toward Jake. By then Bolware had splashed down below the quay, and Jake was bestowing his focused attention on the others.

As the eight moved forward, they made the mistake of forgetting that Lincoln was now at their flank. And when three of the eight moved on Jake, Lincoln couldn't hold himself back. Johnny reached out and tried to stop him, but not very hard.

By this time Jake had sent the next three into the water and was dealing with three others who had the bad judgment to come at him even after seeing what he did to their fellows. Jake was a combination hitter— two or three left jabs, then a wicked right cross, hook, or uppercut. Not a haymaker like some amateur, but from close in, using the power of his hips. He delivered his three- or four-punch combinations in less than a second. One such flurry for each of the three assailants proved ample.

The two remaining Frenchmen were slightly behind the three attacking Jake, pushing them forward but also inadvertently making escape difficult. Lincoln ran at them full speed and bowled them over the edge of the quay. Unfortunately, his momentum carried him over too, and he fell the twenty feet to the water. He surfaced in time to see Jake send the last three Frenchmen flying. They splashed down not far from him.

The next thing Lincoln knew, loud cheering erupted from the ship's deck. Up on the quay, Jake and Johnny were looking over the side, laughing and shaking their heads but also making sure the Frenchmen in the water didn't act up with Lincoln so near. But the thought seemed not to have occurred to the Frenchmen.

The seamen on the ship dropped Lincoln a life ring and hauled him out of the water, straight up onto the deck. Johnny and Jake grabbed all their things, and shortly the three of them were aboard the ship that would take them to Africa.

PART THREE

CHAPTER 18

Suleiman, the king of Mur, had two main reasons for choosing France's bid over Germany's for building his country's hydroelectric dam. The first was that Germany had demanded certain exclusive trading privileges with Mur, whereas France had a much more flexible position. The second—and this was of preeminent importance to Suleiman—was that France promised to complete the dam in two years rather than the Germans' three.

Suleiman had many virtues. He was courageous, decisive, and intelligent, and he had a great paternal love for his people. But patient he was not. He had a hard time understanding why anything in the era that had produced electricity, internal-combustion engines, and airships should take three years to build. And after his son, Prince Kamak, had convinced him of his need to modernize the country by bringing electricity to it, the king wanted it immediately.

His intense interest in the dam's progress included weekly visits nine miles up the river valley from his palace. Of course, his bodyguard and entourage, which included the French ambassador, had to join him on these excursions. This was something of an irritant to the French ambassador and the French engineers, since these interruptions didn't help in meeting the completion schedule.

Despite Suleiman's "help," the dam was nearing completion. The formal dedication ceremony was to take place in just two weeks. In that ceremony, the king would have the privilege of pulling the switch that would bring electricity to Mur, allowing the little kingdom to take a major step toward becoming a modern nation.

The king had just completed his weekly review of the dam's progress. He and his entourage had left the dam's deck and walked to the motorcar waiting to take him back to Mur. He, Ambassador Montier, and Prince Kamak seated themselves in the back seat of the king's new Daimler. A Murian driver sat at the car's controls while the driver's assistant stood in front, ready to crank the starter. The vehicle was one of eight that had been built last year. It was almost identical to the topless model made for Lionel Rothschild, aside from the eighteen inches of added legroom for the back seat. The king was a large man who didn't like to be confined.

At a signal from the motorcar's driver, the king's bodyguard of six mounted Murians started down the dirt road following the river valley. The signal gave the riders a head start, necessary to prevent the car from running into the horses, which had happened. After letting the guards get about fifty feet ahead, the driver gave his assistant another signal. The assistant cranked the starter four or five times. It backfired loudly and started belching a cloud of oily white smoke. The assistant ran around and jumped in the front passenger seat, and the car pulled away. Four mounted legionnaires, France's contribution to the party's security, followed at a safe distance.

"If what Monsieur Montier's engineers tell me is true," the king said to his son, "everything will be ready for the ceremony." The king didn't need to speak so loudly, for after the Daimler's blustery ignition, it didn't make more than a mild putter.

"Only a month behind schedule," Prince Kamak said to Ambassador Montier. "I must commend you and your engineers. But, Father, if you please, I will reserve my congratulations until the dam is finished and our country has electricity. You are satisfied that what remains to be done shall be completed on time?"

The king and his son presented quite a sartorial contrast. Suleiman still preferred his long, flowing Murian robes, bound at the waist by a wide leather belt that accommodated a variety of bladed weapons. The prince, but for his darker complexion, might have been mistaken for a European. Indeed, the French ambassador and Kamak were attired quite similarly in their fashionable light woolen suits.

"Cosmetic touches on the dam's surface are, to my understanding, all that is left," said Ambassador Montier. "The turbine is already operational."

"Cosmetic touches?" said Prince Kamak. "I hope our choice of contractor does not prove to have been based on French aesthetics over German attention to detail."

"I am sure the king's choice will prove correct," said the ambassador.

The king smiled. He was used to Kamak's gibes, since the prince had favored the Germans for the project.

"Time will tell, will it not?" said Kamak.

The king's party had descended from the hills below the dam and was now driving on the high plain that stretched out to the edge of the desert. A mile in the distance, guarding the way up to the dam, Suleiman could see Fort Flatters. Built two years ago, it now housed the First Regiment of the French Foreign Legion, here to protect France's investments in the region.

"You may send your guard back to the fort," the king said to Ambassador Montier. "There is no need for them to escort us the rest of the way." It was another four miles back to the gates of the walled city, and the king thought it ridiculous to have so many guards in the first place.

"They wouldn't obey me if I told them," said the ambassador. "They are under strict orders from Major Athos to accompany us back to the palace gates."

"Major Athos!" the king huffed. "He's like an old woman with his caution and fretting."

"There are many, Your Highness," the ambassador said, "who would find it quite amusing to hear one of the Three from Camarón likened to an old woman. He is known to be one of the bravest men ever to wear a legionnaire's kepi."

"I have told him, and the other two as well, what I think of their obsession to watch over me."

"The recent disturbances by that sect are a concern for them," the ambassador replied. "And, if I may say so, Your Highness, for me as well."

"There is more danger from Tuaregs and slave traders in the desert than from the followers of Thanatos here. They are nothing more than a few toothless old primitives who do not like my hydroelectric marvel."

At the mention of the dangers of the desert, an expression of concern came over the ambassador's face.

"Is that why the Three from Camarón are not accompanying us today?" asked Prince Kamak, noticing the change in the ambassador's countenance. "I assume, Monsieur Ambassador, they are escorting your daughter on her journey from Sidi Bel Abbès?"

"Yes, but if you are unaware, it was your father who insisted on it."

"I was unaware. But, Father, how gallant of you!"

"I would have gone myself if I could have," the king said. "I sent them as an indulgence, to relieve their boredom."

"I do look forward to meeting the mademoiselle," the prince said. "It is my understanding she is a remarkable young lady and, I believe, something of a scholar?"

"She's a headstrong girl. I would that she had stayed in school in Paris."

As the ambassador said this, they came in view of the ancient walled city. Behind the high whitewashed walls, the king's palace stood out, the largest and most majestic structure among many smaller domed buildings. Just east of the city wall stood the remains of an ancient Murian temple. Above it floated a hot-air observation balloon that Prince Kamak and his archaeologist associates were using in their excavation of the site.

"She will probably pester you to death about the temple you're exploring," the ambassador continued.

"I am afraid she would be terribly bored," Kamak replied. "The scientific approach to archaeology is painstaking and slow—antithetical to the romantic imagination. I doubt that she would share my excitement in finding a good shard of pottery."

The ambassador chuckled. "Nevertheless, be warned."

The king's party drove through the city's rear gate, newly enlarged to admit an automobile. Even so, they still must take a route to the palace that avoided the old narrow lanes built thousands of years before Gottlieb Daimler's marvelous invention.

The escort and the king's car pulled up to the arched rear entrance in the ten-foot wall surrounding the palace. "That will be all," the king said to the legionnaires who had ridden behind the motorcar. "And peace be upon your children."

The sergeant in charge gave Ambassador Montier an inquiring look. After a glance around, Montier nodded to the sergeant. The legionnaires turned their horses and rode away.

The six Murian guards dismounted and, after tying up their horses, stood in formation at the side of the gated entryway.

As the king stood to leave the car, a loud, high-pitched warbling sound came from behind the car. From the palace stables, four black-robed men with shaved heads ran toward the king, screaming in a shrill tremolo as they came. Two carried long, curved scimitars; two carried spears.

The six Murian guards broke formation and ran up, forming a line in front of the car, drawing their swords. At about eight paces, one of the dervishes hurled his spear. It sank deep into a guard's chest. As the dervishes ran on, the five remaining guards broke their line and charged them. A dervish impaled one of the guards on his spear, but as he did so, another guard's scimitar slashed halfway through the spearman's neck.

The king's first reaction had been to push his son and Ambassador Montier to the floor of the car. Then he drew his sword in one hand and a dagger in the other and, with surprising dexterity for a man his age and size, leaped out of the car. Running into the melee, he sliced a dervish's arm off at the elbow, then silenced the man's screams with a dagger to the heart.

The dervish who had thrown his spear drew a dagger from his belt and threw it end over end at the king, striking him in his left shoulder. Ducking a sword stroke, the king yanked out the dagger and plunged it into the dervish's liver.

In a matter of seconds, all four dervishes were dead. So were four of the king's guards. Ambassador Montier and Prince Kamak were still down in the back of the car. The king's driver and assistant had fled.

Then, behind the king, came another war cry. From out of the shrubbery along the palace wall ran a single dervish, spear held high. Twenty paces from the king, the assassin drew back his lance. A pistol shot rang out, and the dervish crashed to the ground, his spear landing a few feet in front of the king. Another shot rang out, and the fallen body twitched and went still.

"My father, as I have told you," Prince Kamak said soberly, standing in the back seat of the car, "it would behoove you to equip yourself with one of these." He held a semiautomatic Mauser Broomhandle pistol.

A few moments later, the four legionnaires came galloping back. The king, ignoring his wounded shoulder, was inspecting the bodies of the dead dervishes. The robe of one had come undone. On his bare chest was the tattoo of a man's body with the head and tail of a crocodile.

CHAPTER 19

It was a three-day sail across the Mediterranean from Marseille to Béjaïa. Knowing that their berth on the steamer did not include meals, Lincoln and his new friends had bought enough supplies to last the voyage. Their quarters in steerage were dank and dark, and they had just enough room to spread blankets on the floor in the little corner allocated to them. None of them was afflicted with "Neptune's revenge," as Johnny called it. "Old cowboys gen'rally don't get seasick," he said. "I reckon if you've spent a fair amount of time rolling in the saddle, it ain't a whole lot different from rolling on a ship."

There may have been some truth in this, since Lincoln hadn't had any trouble on the voyage over from New York either. Johnny and Jake, who had spent many years traveling by sea, seemed quite at home on the ship.

"Reckon I'll be taking the first watch," said Johnny as they settled down in their quarters that night.

"That's good of you, John," said Jake. "I'll take the next two. Our young friend here may need the extra sleep, case he wants to go swimming again once we reach Béjaïa."

This wasn't the first allusion the two of them had made to Lincoln's little dip in the harbor at Marseille. But growing up with the name Lincoln in a former Confederate state had thickened his skin, and he could take as much ribbing as he could give. "I had no idea those Frenchies would give way so easy," he said. "It was dern hot out, anyway."

Jake laughed and gave Lincoln a friendly slug on the arm. "It's going to be a parcel hotter where we're going and with a lot less water. But I suspect you're going to do fine."

"But I can't have you taking my share of the watch. I wouldn't want you getting irritable for lack of sleep. You really think we need to set a watch? I mean, it's not as if we have a whole lot worth stealing."

"That rifle of yours got to be tempting to any thief with an eye for firearms," said Johnny, "but thievin' ain't the chief concern. It weren't no smile of providence that tussle Jake had with the Frogs on the dock. It was viewed by most of our shipmates."

"Why," said Lincoln, "I'd think anyone who saw it would ponder hard about tangling with us."

"These boys ain't French lubbers," said Johnny. "They'd be a bit more seasoned. And there's sometimes a foolish pride among seamen when it comes to fightin'."

"Don't know if it's pride or just plain old dullness of intellect," Jake said.

"Point is," Johnny went on, "they might see us as a challenge. Maybe, maybe not. In uncertain territory, always best to keep a lookout posted. Can't afford to go underestimating your foe. If the Greeks'd had lookouts, there would have been no Trojan War."

At first thought, Johnny's illustration didn't make a lot of sense, but then Lincoln supposed it was probably true: if the Greeks had been on the lookout, Paris wouldn't have been able to make off with Helen, which would have averted the Trojan War. "You have a point there," said Lincoln.

"You bet," Johnny said. "Beware of Greeks bearing gifts."

Now Lincoln wasn't sure he was following Johnny's illustration after all. But he did get the main point, the need for alertness—a feeling that was growing more palpable to him the closer they got to Africa. They were approaching a strange and foreign land, and he could imagine that it was ruled, or at least influenced, by strange and foreign gods. The sultry air held a note of the exotic, but also of danger. The swarthy seamen who spoke in strange tongues, the uncommunicative other passengers, the very spirit of the ship all seemed to be saying, *Danger lurks*. But Lincoln was too excited to be frightened. He was so keyed up, he stayed awake reading by candlelight even after he had stood his two-hour watch.

The next morning he was up at daybreak and wanted to go explore the ship. Johnny, who had the watch, didn't think it wise for him to go wandering alone. After waking Jake, they took a small breakfast of dried fish, hard cheese, and harder biscuits. Then, toting their goods, they went topside.

The old steam freighter had a large smokestack, and three large sails that would be hoisted when the winds were right. The ship, the *Purgatorio*, had been christened in 1837, and its steam plant had been replaced three times since. Lincoln wanted to find out everything he could about it, and, after wandering the deck under the scrutiny of the ship's first mate, he wanted to explore its lower decks. Johnny and Jake advised him on the imprudence of this, and Lincoln acquiesced.

They stayed topside, enjoying the sea breeze and the morning sun till it got too hot, and soon they headed back belowdecks. On the way, the cook's mate met them with a message from the ship's cook asking them to stop by the galley. In the galley, which was fairly roomy compared to the tight quarters in the rest of the ship, they met the cook, who sat in a chair, drinking from a mug that perhaps contained coffee.

"Ah, my American friends, do come in," the cook said, getting up from his chair with some difficulty. He was old, remarkably skinny for a cook, and spoke passable English in a German accent. His sinewy arms were heavily tattooed, and he had the look of the sea about him. He had three cups already out on a fold-down table and offered his guests coffee. Once he had poured and handed them each a cup, he pulled a bottle from a cupboard and offered them a pour. "A little grog in the morning to steady you for the day?"

Johnny and Jake accepted, but Lincoln passed.

"I'd venture you are on your way to join the Legion," he said, "though, if I am not mistaken, your objectives do not necessarily involve the glory of France. By all accounts, something is stirring in the desert past old Sidi, and I am interested to know what you may have heard."

Lincoln started to say something, but Johnny quickly and smoothly cut him off. "Mate," he said, "I got to confess we'd just as soon stay out of the politics. We're natural-born fightin' men, and from what we've heard, there's a lot of good, clean, honest fightin' needed down in those parts."

"Kinda runs against our pedigree, the slaving still going on in those parts," Jake added. "But wouldn't mind hearing what you've been hearin'. We do like to be informed."

"You are telling truth, then?" asked the cook. "You have not heard the rumors?"

"Do we look the type that'd spin you a yarn?" said Jake.

The cook paused for a moment, looking them over. "Well, *he* doesn't," he said, pointing to Lincoln.

"It would be good to hear what you have heard," said Lincoln, "I'd like to know what I'm getting myself into."

"There's trouble down there for sure," answered the cook, "with a bunch of religious zealots getting out of hand. And those who I am not proud to call my countrymen are displeased about being passed over in favor of the French . . ." Here he paused and, more quietly, added, "Because there is treasure of a sort down there."

"Well, we're just Americans lookin' for a good fight and don't really concern ourselves with those kinds of things," said Jake.

"And wouldn't understand them if we did," Johnny added, finishing his drink and getting up.

Jake and Lincoln got up as well and, after thanking the cook, took their leave of the galley.

Later, Johnny said he doubted that the cook believed a word they said. He also would bet cash to cow chips that the cook hadn't let on half of what he knew.

"Yep," Jake said, "it 'pears we just might be onto something."

They didn't have a lot to do when they got back to their berth. Lincoln went back to the book he'd been reading. Johnny asked what was so interesting.

"This is about the history of where we're going," Lincoln said.

"Educate us, then," said Johnny.

"You sure you want to hear?"

"We're all ears," said Jake.

"Well, the Barbary Coast—that's where we're heading first. The area has been a hive of pirates since before the time of Ulysses. Barbary pirates plagued Caesar's fleet and pestered sailors even down to Nelson's time. I don't know as much about them as I do about the pirates of the Spanish Main—that's basically the Caribbean, and those pirates were mostly English—but most of the ones here were Moors and used broad curved cutlasses, like shortened versions of Arabian scimitars, called *yataghans*."

"My oh my, John," said Jake. "We got ourselves a partner who's a scholar too."

"Listen to this," said Lincoln, thumbing back a few pages, "'Africa has magic in its very name. Old Homer will tell you that it was Africa's enchanted shore that grew the lotus, whose sweet fruit caused travelers to lose even the memory of their native land—the strongest memory of all. It was in Africa that Herodotus placed the Garden of the Hesperides, whose fruit Hercules was to gather, and the palace of the Gorgons, through whose great gates Perseus was to force his way.'"

Lincoln interrupted himself to say, "This is all from the old Greek writings. 'There, too, was the country of the Garamantes, where, said Herodotus, the cattle were obliged to walk backward as they grazed, because their great horns curved in front of their muzzles. In Africa, said Strabo, are the leeches seven cubits long'—a cubit's about a foot and a half—'big enough to drink the blood of twelve men; while, if you believed Pomponius Mela, Africa is the home of satyrs, fauns, and strange beasts that dwell among the crags of lost Atlantis and howl to see the sun rise and set.' And listen to this, Stabo goes on and says, 'From Africa came travelers' tales of great one-legged creatures that could outrun gazelles; basilisks, whose breath would melt the hardest stone; dragons, prodigies, and fabulous monsters. Pliny found nothing surprising in such reports and put forward plausible reasons to explain why new species of animals were a natural result of conditions in Africa . . .'"

"I can buy beeves havin' to walk back'ards to eat," interjected Johnny, "but no man—one- or two-legged, is outrunning no gazelle."

"Let him go on," said Jake. "If we're to be ranchers someday, the more we learn about livestock the better."

Lincoln looked up from his reading, not even trying to conceal his enthusiasm. "That's where we're going, gentlemen. Can you *believe* it? And then Alexandre Dumas says some modern doctor discovered an animal that was part cow and part donkey. And also, listen to this, 'The scientific world acknowledged that a new variety of rodent, the horned rat, had been discovered in Africa—a charming little animal whose existence was suspected by Pliny . . . and has now been established beyond doubt.'

"That's what the great Alexandre Dumas has to say about North Africa. He also wrote some of my favorite books, like *The Three Musketeers*."

"He said they have rats with horns on 'em?" asked Johnny, taking off his hat and running his hand across his head. "You mean, like a steer with horns, but this is a *rat* with horns?"

"Now what's so hard about that?" Jake said to Johnny. "You seen your share o' horned toads, haven't you? What's so different about a horned rat?"

"Yeah, well, maybe they're kinda the same," said Johnny, apparently still wrestling with the concept of a rat with horns.

Lincoln put his book down. "I can't wait to get there. I've been waiting my whole life to do something like this."

"You've been waiting all your life to see a *horned rat*?" asked Johnny.

"No, I've just wanted to go to a place where everything is strange and new and it's like what you felt seeing everything the first time."

"I thought you wanted to go where everything is old," said Jake.

"Yes, I want to go to a place where everything is so old it looks new."

"Oh," said Jake, now rubbing the top of his head.

A little later Johnny was in a pensive mood. "Now I'm okay with an animal that is half cow and half mule," he said quietly to Jake, not wanting to wake Lincoln, who had finally closed his book and nodded off. "But a rat with horns is giving me trouble."

"John, you got to keep an open mind," Jake replied, having almost dozed off himself. "It did say it right there in the book."

"I ain't buying it."

"Well, I'm going to make myself a little tiny lariat out of twine, and if I see one of them, I'm going to lasso it like I would a itty-bitty steer. I mean to get me one."

"Are you ready to put your money where your mouth is? I got a sawbuck says you don't."

"You're on, pard. Matter of fact, maybe we could breed 'em when we get our ranch. Might be a real business there."

"I ain't breeding no horned rats at our ranch. They'd have to be big as chickens to have enough meat to make it worth our while."

"You got a point there," Jake said. He didn't often concede anything in an argument to Johnny, but he did here, almost. "Course, maybe they are big as chickens—you know, like a muskrat."

"You know something," Johnny said after a few moments, having tired of the subject, "you got to 'preciate our new pard's attitude. He's not like them that make you feel like you need a bath after listening to their whining and complaining. That's just the kind of attitude we need if we're going to find us a treasure."

"Oh, I agree," said Jake. "I purely do. I just hope our young pard keeps that sunny attitude once he's had his first truck with the Sahara."

CHAPTER 20

The afternoon following the attempt on King Suleiman's life, Ambassador Montier sat in his office in the palace, pondering the trouble that was brewing in Mur. The first two years since the French came and began building the dam had been peaceful—he could almost say *pleasant*, but for having to deal with the king's eccentricities. Then, in the past two months, this cult of religious fanatics had surfaced. The king had insisted they were an archaic sect that could not pose any real trouble. But the failed assassination attempt—which the ambassador had to consider an attempt on his own life as well—had shaken Suleiman out of his complacency. Then, this morning, only barely awake from his troubled sleep, he had gotten the news that Jaffar, the king's chief vizier, was missing and unaccounted for since last night. And to add to his worries, his daughter was coming. And she was two days late in arriving.

The king would recover from his shoulder wound, which didn't appear to be serious. At least, this was the prognosis from the king's Murian physician, if that was the right word for the old man the king called "the wisest leech in all the desert." Treating the king's shoulder, he had scrubbed it with hyssop and za'atar, then anointed and bandaged it with a mixture of rue, aloe, and onycha. During the scrubbing, Suleiman had roared like a wounded lion.

After the attack, the ambassador, though physically unscathed, had not slept well. And now what kind of trouble had his strong-willed daughter gotten herself into? He hadn't wanted her to come at all. When she insisted, he had sent the Three from Camarón to escort her on the final leg of the journey, through the desert from Sidi Bel Abbès. The route was ordinarily dangerous enough with thieves and brigands roaming the area. But recently, he had gotten reports of a band of Tuareg slave traders in the region, and this concerned him greatly. It even concerned the king.

Unable to sleep, Montier had finally sent for the king's physician. The old man gave him a potion of mandrake root and poppies.

He had awoken late this morning from a strange dream-filled sleep to learn that not only had his daughter and the Three still not arrived, but the king's vizier was missing. As he sat at his desk, still groggy from last night's sedative and pondering whether to send the Legion column in search of his daughter, someone started banging on his office door.

He took the wet compress from his forehead and put it in the desk drawer. "Enter," he said.

The Legion adjutant who served in the palace hurried in. "The mademoiselle and the Three have arrived," the adjutant said. "I have conveyed your wish that they report immediately."

"At last! Thank you, Lieutenant. Is everything in order with them and my daughter?"

"She appears to be well. She's an enthusiastic young lady and doesn't stop asking questions. She has asked if I could arrange a tour for her and her companion."

"Companion! I didn't authorize . . . What kind of companion?"

"A middle-aged man, monsieur. I believe he is some kind of scholar. He wears a suit that is too small for him."

"Is he French? What kind of Frenchman wears an ill-fitting suit?"

"I agree, sir, most strange. But he is indeed French, sir."

"Ah, just what I needed, someone else to look after. But at least she's safe. Do make sure that she and the Three see me as soon as possible."

The adjutant left, and a few minutes later, Amanda Montier burst into her father's office. She had in tow a graying bespectacled man who wore a dusty and, indeed, poorly fitting suit. Behind them entered three Legion majors—the Three from Camarón.

"Oh, Father!" the attractive young woman exclaimed, rushing into the ambassador's arms. Dressed in a fashionable riding habit of jodhpurs, a tailored jacket, and riding boots with spurs, she didn't look too worn from her journey. "Are you all right? We heard about what happened yesterday."

After mutual assurances that each was safe and unhurt, the ambassador's voice grew stern. "You know I am not pleased with you. It was my strong desire that you stay in Paris with your studies. There has been trouble here of late, and now this attempt on the king."

"I know you didn't want me to come. But I just had to be here with you if you are in danger. And besides, I am so interested in Mur, I want to learn everything I can about everything. And since I knew you wanted me to stay at my studies, I decided to bring them with me. This is my tutor, Professor Pleitan. He is a great authority on ancient North African history and archaeology."

The professor walked up and bowed formally. Montier barely acknowledged him.

"I am sure we are going to have such a grand time here," Amanda said.

The Three from Camarón were still standing a few steps inside the room. Long ago, the Legion had bequeathed to the three heroes, and only survivors of the battle of Camarón, the names of Dumas's musketeers. Now the burly legionnaire of Levantine descent, known as Porthos, swung the office door shut with a bang. Montier thought him aptly named, for his fiery personality had certain similarities to the fictional musketeer.

"Sir," said the legionnaire known as Athos, "it is important that we get a full briefing of yesterday's events immediately." Tall, grim, bearded, with a patch over his left eye, he spoke American English. "And what is this about Jaffar going missing?"

Just then another knock came at the door. The ambassador nodded to Porthos, who opened it. Prince Kamak entered the room, with a grave look on his face.

"Monsieur Ambassador," he said, "I am sorry to interrupt you, but I have some information regarding the king's vizier, which I thought you would like to hear at once." He then acknowledged Amanda with a bow of his head and the others with a glance.

"Why, yes, of course" said the ambassador. "Prince Kamak, may I present to you my daughter, Mademoiselle Montier. You are familiar with Majors Athos, Porthos, and Aramis, and this is Professor . . ."

"Professor Pleitan," Amanda filled in.

"Welcome to our humble country, mademoiselle," said Prince Kamak. Amanda offered her hand to the prince, who took it and gallantly kissed it. He acknowledged the Three again with a slight nod. There followed an uncomfortable few moments of silence.

"Well, what is this news?" the ambassador said.

The prince gave a short but concerned glance Amanda's way. Aramis, the tallest and slenderest of the Three, said in his Oxford accent, "Sir, perhaps it would be best to let the mademoiselle and the professor get some rest from their journey."

"Yes, yes, indeed. My dear, off with you, now. I'll see you at dinner."

"I don't need rest, Father. Who is Monsieur Jaffar?"

"Mademoiselle," said Athos in the commanding voice so natural to him, "this is Legion business."

Amanda hesitated, then kissed her father and left with the professor in tow, clearly not happy at being left out of the conference.

After she and her tutor had gone, the ambassador offered a seat to the prince, who accepted, and to the Three, who declined. "Please, Prince Kamak," the ambassador said, "what news have you for us?"

"An hour ago," Kamak replied, "the king's vizier was found dead outside the city walls. The cause of death has not been determined, but on his face was an expression of extreme anguish and terror. He was stripped to his waist, and carved on his chest was a bloody figure that appeared to be a man with the head and tail of a crocodile."

"Are you saying that he, too, was one of these religious fanatics?" the ambassador blurted with none of his usual diplomatic self-possession.

"No," said the prince. "He was one of my father's most faithful servants. It was apparent that the followers of Thanatos had carved their mark on him, sending a bloody message."

"Ambassador," Athos said, "we need to hear what has been going on since we left, including details of the attempt on the king's life and all that is known about Jaffar's disappearance and murder."

"It was last week, just after you left," the ambassador said, beginning to pace about, "that these new signs of the sect began to appear. Before that, there were only rumors and no real evidence that they even existed." His head throbbed. He would need another sedative to sleep tonight. "Up until very recently, there were only a few incidents of threats scrawled on the city walls and the defacing of a flag. All these small acts of vandalism bore the device of the crocodile god. And now, with the attempt on the king and the murder of his chief counselor, these people must be taken very seriously."

"Rumors of this secret society run throughout my country's long history," Prince Kamak said. "But there has been no word of them for decades. If they are who they say they are, they are absolutely ruthless and fear nothing, save their merciless god."

The ambassador, with Prince Kamak's help, then described the attack on the king in detail.

"And none of them were left alive?" said Porthos. "I would have liked to question one of them."

"None," said the ambassador.

"Do we know for certain they were Murian?" said Athos.

"Undoubtedly," said Kamak. "You know how difficult it is for foreigners to go unrecognized in Mur."

"But native traders are allowed in and are not so easily recognized," said Athos.

"True," Kamak said. "But two of them have been identified: the rebellious son of a saddler and the son of a widowed weaver. The families of both have been questioned fully and swear allegiance to the king. They know nothing of their sons' involvement with the sect."

"What I would like to know," said the ambassador, "is how a group apparently so well organized and strong could go unnoticed until now. And why *now*?"

"Pertinent questions," said Kamak. "I don't think I can answer with great authority, but I will venture an opinion, if I may. The legends of this ancient cult are as old as Mur itself. I recall rumors of their existence from the time of my father's grandfather. Of course, what they believe is absurd, worshiping a death god in the form of a human-dragon or were-crocodile of some sort. But apparently, through the years, they have been content to practice their superstitions peacefully and underground until now. Which leads to the second of your questions: Why now? I think that is somewhat easier. They hate what my father and I are doing to this country—modernizing it, building the dam—and they hate the outsiders who have come."

Prince Kamak glanced at the others in the room and continued, "Until a few days ago, my father and I agreed that if these 'crocodile people,' as he mockingly calls them, still existed at all, their numbers were few and their influence minimal. Clearly, my father and I were wrong in our assessment of the threat."

CHAPTER 21

A little before noon on the third day out from Marseille, they came in sight of Béjaïa. The harbor was a tenth the size of the one at Marseille, and Lincoln was struck by the dazzling whiteness of the buildings. The land, to his surprise, was neither desert nor flat. To the east and south were low rolling hills covered in scrub. To the west, a low table mountain overlooked the city.

Steaming into the harbor, he could make out the remains of the wall that once enclosed the city, defending it against not only Barbary pirates from the sea, but also marauding Bedouins by land. Many of the buildings didn't look so different from those in Marseille, which Lincoln found vaguely disappointing. Then, up the slope from shore, he saw a large onion-domed mosque, as if it had been put there to remind him that he was on exotic, foreign shores. Beyond the mosque and a little east stood the palace of the former sultan, which the colony's French governor now occupied. And everywhere, amid the buildings and lining the larger streets, rose stately palm trees. These appealed to Lincoln as much as anything. This was Africa, the great continent of adventure.

Lincoln and his friends were taken in the ship's yawl to the dock, which teemed with energetic hawkers of most every kind of merchandise imaginable. A squad of smartly uniformed Zouaves, recruited from the native population, made a feeble attempt to shield the disembarking passengers from the crowd. Lincoln had read everything he could find about the Zouaves. Though lacking the prestige of legionnaires or even of the regular French army, they were famous for their natty uniforms and sharp close-order drill—so much so that regiments from both sides in the War Between the States had patterned their uniforms after them, right down to the blousy pants, gaiters, and colorful sashes. On the dock, the Zouaves were outnumbered about fifty to one by the hawkers, who immediately waylaid Lincoln and his friends with myriad opportunities for the deal of a lifetime.

Most of them spoke French, some a kind of bastard Spanish, and some pidgin English, reflecting that before French rule, the Spanish and English flags had flown over Béjaïa. The local fashion seemed to be straw hats and long white muslin shirts with shabby old European waistcoats—apparently, they liked the pockets. They believed in the aggressive approach to selling their figs, raisins, dates, almonds, melons, straw hats like the ones they themselves wore, tobacco, beads, gold and silver jewelry, poultry, sashes of bright hues, silk cushions, leather pouches, pointy-toed slippers, and even baby crocodiles.

Johnny and Jake were not for dallying and wanted to secure transportation for their journey to Sidi Bel Abbès as soon as they could. Johnny asked one of the locals how to get there, slowly and loudly pronouncing "Sidi Bel Abbès." In answer, the man merely pointed inland, then went on trying to sell them an interest in a melon farm.

It was appreciably hotter on the land than it had been on the ship's deck. As they walked up from the dock and passed through the Moorish arched gate of the old city walls and into the bazaar, it grew hotter. The tightly packed souk, made up of small shops and booths and canvas awnings, teemed with a wide variety of life, about half of it human. It pulsed with a cacophony of haggling voices, the braying of donkeys, and the ungodly low, discordant groaning of camels with their necks outstretched.

Compared to the dock, few of the poorer residents worked the souk.

Rather, it was dominated by more prosperous merchants who wore fezzes of red felt, not the straw hats of the poorer class. The fez wearers were just as aggressive but tended to be better at communicating with foreigners—until it came to negotiating prices. Then their language skills seemed to break down.

Lincoln finally got a direct answer to where they might find transportation to Sidi Bel Abbès. They were directed to a camel trader who supposedly knew everything about travel, as well as a number of other services that Lincoln and his friends weren't interested in at the time.

They found the camel trader's booth. The prosperous middle-aged man who owned it could handle English well enough. After introducing himself as "your humble servant Aziz" and offering to buy Lincoln's rifle, he told them, "There are two options for going to Sidi Bel Abbès. A commercial coach escorted by a troop of Zouaves goes there twice a week, on Tuesdays and Saturdays. The escort is needed because the road to Sidi is a haunt for bandits and other vicious criminals. Seeing that today is Tuesday, you have missed the coach that left this morning.

"But I know also of a caravan leaving tomorrow morning. It, too, has an escort, but of the fiercest desert warriors—much better than the Zouaves, who are incompetent bastards of the French. The coach would take four days, the caravan six. But the land you would traverse is the most beautiful on Earth.

"The cost of the coach is five hundred francs each; the caravan, with each of you riding an excellent camel, is a hundred and fifty francs each. A mule is twenty francs cheaper. But if all three of you are going together, there will, of course, be a consideration."

The camel trader obviously had some interest in the caravan and also offered to arrange all aspects of the trip, including provisions. He would need a 20 percent deposit to secure their places.

"I'm for going native," said Jake, always keen to save a franc. "It'll give us a little time to get a feel for the country, acclimate a bit."

"When in Rome, ride as the Romans ride," Johnny said.

"Camelback sounds good to me," Lincoln said.

Once Jake had made arrangements for the trip—he managed to get the camels for the mule rate—the camel trader directed them to a hotel that he apparently had an interest in. After stowing their things in their rooms, Johnny and Jake headed next door to a canteen cooled by palm-leaf fans hung from the high ceiling, with cords tugged by two very skinny, very old men. Lincoln wanted to go exploring. He didn't care about the heat, which wasn't much worse than a South-Texas summer. On the way out, he stopped for a quick bite in the bar, where Johnny and Jake were on their second pitcher of sangria. As he was leaving, Johnny told him, "Keep a watch, 'cause there's hombres out there that make a living off unalert gringos."

By the time Lincoln got back to the souk, it was almost completely deserted for the North African version of a midday siesta. Three nearly naked children were scrounging through the debris that was left, in the hope of finding a few spilt raisins or dates or maybe even a dropped coin. When they saw Lincoln, they ran up to him and begged for a few sous. He gave them a franc each—a *hundred* sous—after which they gleefully ran away.

Lincoln wandered southwestward, where a big mosque with four minarets adorned the top of a hill. Walking on, he passed a smaller mosque and a large-domed Coptic church. Passing the smaller mosque, he saw what was unmistakably a group of Jews, wearing black hats and long black coats even in the heat of the day. About ten of them walked in a line past the mosque, all with their shoes in their hands.

Walking along in the sweltering heat, nearing the city's southern gate, he came upon a railroad bed under construction. Like the souk, the work site was abandoned for the midday siesta. But there was the newly laid track and the shimmering steel machinery, blistering to the touch. The sight disgusted him. This part of the world was also changing, though not as fast or as drastically as America. At least here it was slower and less efficient. In Sidi Bel Abbès, almost two hundred miles to the southwest, the march of progress would be even slower. And Mur, farther away, more remote, and cut off from the world for so long, would be more pristine yet.

The railroad's construction had required demolition of a section of the city wall where the tracks entered the city. But elsewhere, too, much of the wall was in shambles, sections of it toppled over, stones and bricks loose and fallen free from the ancient, lime mortar that had held them together.

A little farther west, the small mountain that he had noticed from the ship jutted precipitously up. It had a commanding view of the sea and the city, and, of course, Lincoln had to scale it. It took a while, and some sweat, to hike up via a series of switchbacks to the wooded area at the top. At its northern edge was a copse of cypress trees and some large boulders, which he climbed for the panoramic view. The city, with a clear outline of its dilapidated ancient wall, lay spread out below: the grand mosque, the palace, the souk, and, out in the harbor, the ship he had sailed in on and a score of sailing dhows. Rolling hills ran east and west, and to the south, the plain stretched to the horizon. He stood there, the view conjuring vivid thoughts of adventures to come. Then he recalled Johnny and Jake on their second pitcher of sangria in the canteen. Maybe it was best he got back.

CHAPTER 22

Picking his way down through the boulder field near the summit, Lincoln stopped to drink from a spring shaded by a cluster of cypress trees. Getting to his feet, he noticed a fresh set of footprints on the other side of the trees. Wondering who else could up there, he crossed the spring and followed the trail.

After perhaps two hundred yards, the footprints led to a tumble of huge loaf-shaped boulders. A narrow path twisted between the rocks. More curious than ever, Lincoln threaded his way through until he came to the mouth of a cave.

Standing just outside the opening, he called out, "I come as a friend. May I enter your cave?" He repeated the words in French.

After getting no reply, Lincoln took a few steps inside. At the far end of the chamber, on a rough wooden shelf, a half-dozen rush candles lit up the room. The cave was almost round, with a high ceiling. Straw mats were strewn on the ground around and beneath a low, wide table with a few books on it. Also on the table was a contraption that looked like a minia-ture Ferris wheel, but with three wheels, a smaller one inside a larger, inside a larger. One of the cave's walls was lined with plank shelves that held more books, an astrolabe, and a large hourglass, the sand having run through the neck to the lower bulb. A hearth was cut into the one of the walls, but it contained no fire or even ashes. And on the wall next to the fireplace hung a very old and battered shield. Still visible amid its many dents and scars, a mounted knight battled a dragon-like beast.

Lincoln walked over and had a closer look at the shield. Then he went to the shelves, where he lifted out a book bound in white vellum. The outer cover page bore a scene like that on the battered shield. Underneath the picture was some handwriting, now smeared beyond recognition. But inside the book, the text, written in an elegant Latin hand, was unmarred and quite legible. Having endured five years of Latin with his mother, Lincoln thought that with a little effort, he could decipher it.

As he was trying to parse the old Latin's second sentence, he heard a motion behind him and then a rock flew past his head and bounced off the wall above the bookshelf. Lincoln sprang about to see a very old man preparing to hurl another stone. "Hold on, please," said Lincoln, ducking and raising his forearm to shield his face. "Please, I come in peace! I was just admiring your book."

The old man lowered his throwing arm a degree. "With what now has time's fell hand thrust into my cave?" he said in a British accent, his arm still cocked with the stone in hand.

His advanced age notwithstanding, the old man was far from decrepit, and, with a rock at such a short distance, perhaps even dangerous. Moreover, he didn't appear to be altogether sane.

"Not 'time's fell hand,'" Lincoln parried, "but his whirligig."

The old man froze for a moment, then dropped his rock and roared in satisfaction, "He knows our Shakespeare!" And then, more softly, "Indeed, the whirligig of time!"

Lincoln had read various accounts of the marabouts, alleged holy men of North Africa and the Middle East. They lived hermetic lives in the deserts and mountains, where the heat and the seclusion were said to drive many of them mad. Lincoln wondered just how crazy this one was.

The old man threw back the hood of his muslin burnoose and took a few steps closer. Stroking his long gray beard, he inspected Lincoln more closely. "I seldom get visitors to my cave," he said. "And never one who knows his Shakespeare—at least, not human ones. For that matter, I don't often get to speak humans at all. You are human, then?"

"I believe I am, sir," Lincoln replied.

"And American?"

"Yes, they aren't mutually exclusive," Lincoln said, hoping to lighten the conversation.

"And how do you come to know the bard?"

"My mother is a schoolteacher."

After a few thoughtful moments, the old man said, "My book—you came to steal my book!"

"No, sir—is 'sir' how I should address you? Or 'Father,' or . . .?"

"Either will do, but to my book!"

"I didn't come to steal it, though I am interested in it—and your shield, as well. Are in you some kind of holy or knightly order? Is it the image of Saint George and the dragon?"

"Ah, would that it were Saint George," he said solemnly. Then, perking up, "Talk we will, but first, tea."

Not bothering to wait for a response from his visitor, the old man took from his shelf two cups and a pitcher, from which he poured some kind of liquid. "Please be seated," he said, and lowered himself to the straw mat at the table. With the aid of his hands, he crossed his legs. "I don't believe in chairs."

Lincoln sat down and tasted the drink. It was cold and tasted of mountain flowers. He looked around the room again and noticed an old sword leaning against the wall near the shield. He also felt how damp everything in the room was.

"What is this thing?" Lincoln said of the strange-looking wheel lying at one end of the table. He reached out as if to give it a spin.

"No, don't! It is extremely frangible. It is also very secret."

Lincoln withdrew his hand quickly. "Then will you tell me about the book and the shield?"

"You are going to Sidi Bel Abbès to join the Foreign Legion?"

"Yes, I am. How did you know?"

"You will then journey to ancient Mur."

"Have you been there?"

"It is where my former order is said to have been founded. Now it is a land of fable, ignorance, and superstition."

"So you took the vows of an order?"

"Futility, futility, oh, don't you see it is futile! The direction of the arrow cannot be changed. It may be slowed, but not changed." He again reverted to a deep, oratorical voice,

"Look on my works, ye Mighty, and despair!
Nothing beside remains. Round the decay
Of that colossal wreck, boundless and bare,
The lone and level sands stretch far away."

The old man took a deep breath before continuing, "They thought they could conquer but were conquered. The dragon's minion would not be thwarted. But, alas, through diligent study, I have learned to slow him."

"I'm not sure I understand what you're talking about."

"I will give you a hint." The old man chuckled, pointing a bony finger at the shelves. "See that glass? It used to take eight hours for the sand to fall through it. Precisely eight hours. I discovered that if I keep my cave extremely damp, I can slow it by fifty-one seconds. And that is not all I have discovered."

"You think you can slow up time by—"

The old man cut him off. "Do you know where you are right now? Tell me, do you know where you are?"

Lincoln tried to think of an appropriate answer, but the old man didn't wait for him to speak.

"I'll tell you where you are," he said, chuckling. "You are exactly thirty-six degrees, forty-two minutes north latitude, and I will show you why this is so important." He gingerly caressed the multiwheeled device sitting on the table. "This is a Waughton wheel, invented by the great medieval philosopher Silenus Waughton. Notice that now, when the wheels are not spinning, the red dots on each wheel align perfectly with the dots on the other two wheels."

Lincoln nodded.

The old man pushed on a lever attached to the device, and the three wheels began to spin. The smallest, about three inches in diameter, spun within the next larger one, about six inches in diameter, and these two wheels spun within the largest, some twelve inches across.

"They appear to be moving at the same speed, do they not?"

"Yes," Lincoln agreed.

The wheels slowed and stopped. The red dots were still perfectly aligned.

"They were not spinning at the same speed, though they appeared to be. But they couldn't have been, because the dots are still lined up. The larger wheels, having farther to go because of their greater circumferences, must have spun faster to keep the dots in line. And that proves the point."

"What point does it prove?"

The old man thought for a minute, looking bewildered. Then a light came into his eye. "Oh, yes, why I am here. It proves that the closer you are to the center, the slower time goes. And that is why I have taken my residence at exactly thirty-six degrees, forty-two minutes north latitude—the Waughtonian center, when one takes into account the shape and tilt of the Earth."

Lincoln nodded, trying to be polite.

"It is somewhat complicated. I am still working on the formulas to calculate the savings."

The old man did seem surprisingly healthy and spry for a man of his age.

"This is all very interesting," Lincoln said, "but I have to be going. Before I go, however, you mentioned that your former order was from Mur. I am on my way there. Is there anything I should know?"

"It is all there in the book that you were tempted to steal, which I give you on account of your courtesy and kindness. The order is *said* to have been founded there, over two millennia ago. But superstition and fable now blur the truth. They all were fools; Thanatos still prevails. No, no, no! You still don't understand!" he cried, leaping to his feet with sudden dexterity. "I have tried and tried. You can't kill it, can't get off it, can't get out of it! We are bound to it by 'adamantine chains and penal fire.'" Then, more calmly, "They delude themselves who think there is an exit other than through the jaws of Thanatos and into oblivion. Only I, as you have seen, have been able to thwart him.

Lincoln had by now concluded that the old man was daft. He rose and said politely, "I will think on these things, but I must be going. Thank you for your hospitality."

"But wait," the old man said, and shuffled to the bookshelf. He returned and handed Lincoln the white vellum-bound book with the image of the knight battling the dragon-like beast.

CHAPTER 23

On his way back from the mountain, still a block from the hotel, Lincoln heard a clamor and the whistles of the gendarmerie. Hurrying there, he saw a crowd of people pushing and shoving at the windows, trying to see what was happening inside the canteen adjoining the hotel.

Lincoln had an uneasy feeling that his friends must be the cause of the trouble. When he tried to go through the hotel's lobby entrance, it took some effort to get past the gawkers, but they backed away when they heard him saying, "*Les Américains! Je suis avec les Américains!*"

Then he came to a gendarme, who stopped him from going any farther. Behind the gendarme, the bar was a mess of broken chairs, tables, spilled drinks, and blood. Facedown on the floor was Johnny, hands cuffed behind his back, kicking, squirming, and bellowing beneath six gendarmes while two others shackled his feet. Jake was facedown on the floor too, but motionless. Blood trickled down the side of his face from a big red splotch on the back of his head. Two gendarmes were handcuffing him as well. Luckily, he didn't come to until seconds after they got his hands secured. Even so, he still managed to kick one and headbutt the other before the six more, having finally secured Johnny, gave assistance.

"Who were they fighting?" Lincoln asked the gendarme blocking his entry.

"These two threw them all out the windows, and they have been taken to hospital. Except the singer, who was unharmed and ran away."

"How many of them were there?"

"Eight or ten."

"Oh."

"And the singer's guitarist, the barman, and two waiters."

"May I go in? I'm a friend of theirs."

"No."

At this point, the gendarmes started walking their manacled prisoners out. Passing by Lincoln, Johnny slurred, "Gotta watch that dern sangria punch." Lincoln could smell it all over him.

Behind him Jake growled, not pronouncing his words too crisply either, "Forget about the punch. It was your dern appetite for that singer who was floozying all around."

"I didn't do nothing but wink at her," Johnny said. "Well, and comment admiringly on certain of her attributes. You didn't have to wallop the guitar player."

"I didn't like his looks—or what he said about Americans." Seeing Lincoln, Jake said, "Here's our pard! Did you scare us up any of them horned rats?"

At the jail, after considerable negotiation, Lincoln arranged to get an interview with his friends. It cost him ten francs. He also discovered that twenty more francs would get his friends a commodious private cell, a hot meal, and "excellent" medical attention. To this he agreed, having seen the wound on Jake's head. He also tried to find out what it would cost him to get his friends released. This, they told him, was impossible.

After waiting for over two hours, the jailer brought him into their cell. Set apart from the rest of the cells, it was apparently used for malefactors from the noble caste, or who at least had money. It was about twenty feet square, with two beds, a divan, two barred windows, and a curtained-off toilet in the corner. As Lincoln entered, Johnny and Jake were sitting on two chairs at a table in the center of the room, mulling over a piece of paper. Jake's head was bandaged, and both men looked as if they had been sprayed down with a fire hose.

"Well, it looks like you boys got the luxury suite," Lincoln said as the jailer left and locked the door.

"Yeah, in spite of all that *égalité, fraternité* blab, there ain't nobody like the French for respectin' the class system," Johnny said, deflated as flat champagne.

Jake said, "We let our side of the partnership down." He seemed more disgusted with himself than concerned over the bandage around his head, even though a little blood had seeped through.

"That dern sangria can make a man loco," Johnny said. "I warrant you, it ain't goin' to happen again."

"It sure ain't," said Jake. "I give my affidavit on it. 'Nuff said."

"As excuses go, an overabundance of sangria punch and floozy singers don't exactly hunt," Johnny said. "But like Jake says, it ain't goin' to happen again." He lifted the piece of paper. It had about ten lines of handwriting scrawled on it, and three places for signatures.

Johnny picked up a pencil from the table and signed the document. He handed it to Jake, who did the same. Jake then handed it to Lincoln and said, "We'll be needin' your signature right here."

"What am I signing?" Lincoln took the paper.

"A binding contract," Johnny said. "And you're the witness."

Lincoln read it over,

"Whereas the undersigned, Johnny Owens, IFKA Scott, and James Burns IFKA Jones, in regretfulness for the turpitude of their recent slippage, for the purpose of hardening our resolve, and for using the time we would ordinarily spend in carousing, getting drunk, and chasing floozies, for the said purpose of discovering wealth and related activities, do solemnly purpose, pledge, and commit to abstain from all manner of strong drink when females are in proximity, until we have either found our treasure, become rich, left the Foreign Legion, or become dead. Lager beer and diluted wine excepted. Signed and witnessed . . .”

“What does ‘IFKA’ stand for?” asked Lincoln.

“In the future known as,” said Johnny. “That was Jake’s idea, as we figured we needed to come up with our Legion names anyway, so we added ’em.”

“I was going to use Smith,” said Jake, “but you already took it. It was hard coming up with another, but I finally come up with Jones.”

“The sad part about it is,” said Johnny, as serious as a camp-meeting preacher, “we got the idea for it today in the bar, and today was to be the last hurrah.”

“Well, if this is what you want, I’ll sign it,” Lincoln said.

They nodded, and he signed the paper.

Then Jake said, “Don’t know how much we’re going to be needing it now, though.” He and Johnny looked glumly at each other, then at Lincoln.

“We shoulda’ done it in Marseille,” Johnny said, “but I guess it’s better late than never. It’s a sign of our true sorryfulness. Guess you ain’t heard what they’re doin’ with us.”

“No,” said Lincoln. He hadn’t seen his friends so down. “I tried to *baksheesh* your way out, but they wouldn’t take any amount of money.”

“Nah,” said Jake. “They got a deal with the Second Regiment.” He paused, looking even more miserable. “Me and Johnny are on our way to the island oven of march-or-die Madagascar.”

“How can they make you go against your will? You aren’t even in the Legion yet!” Lincoln was already annoyed at having had to wait so long to see his friends, and seeing them locked in a cell, even the luxury cell, compounded it. But hearing they were being shipped off to Madagascar with the Second Regiment set him off.

“They gave us a choice,” said Johnny. “We can either join up with the Second Regiment in Madagascar or we can go rot for five years in prison, and the prison they’ll send us to just happens to be in friendly old

Madagascar too. We've been in worse scrapes than this, though it's not one we'd prefer."

Still holding the signed contract, Lincoln paced a few steps around the cell, then came back to the table and handed it to Jake, who folded it and put it in the wallet where he kept the map. After a moment Lincoln said, "Then I guess it's the Second Regiment and Madagascar for me too."

"Nah, nah, you don't wanna do that," said Johnny. "It's not what you come here for, and there's no need for it."

"Son, you got your whole life ahead of you," said Jake. "We reckoned you'd offer, but . . ."

"Don't try to talk me out of it. As I recall, we're partners and we have a deal. So it's settled. It can't be much worse down there than a humid summer day in South Texas."

"I reckon it can," said Jake. "They don't have tsetse flies in South Texas."

"Nor the cast-off scum officers and noncoms of the world's worst armies," said Johnny.

"I don't care what they got," said Lincoln. "My minds made up."

"We figured it's what you'd say," said Johnny, "but we owed it to you to try and talk some sense into you."

"You know you'd do the same in a second."

"Me and Johnny are different," said Jake. "We're crusty ole cusses and can take it. And our plans can wait a spell; we ain't givin' up on 'em."

"Well, I can take it too. And when you do find your strike, you're going to need someone to keep you in line." Lincoln really didn't put much faith in the possibility of Johnny and Jake ever finding treasure, but he tried to be encouraging. "That contract I just witnessed, I believe, only applies up until you get rich. Afterward, if I'm not around, you're liable to go hog wild and blow it all in one day."

CHAPTER 24

At dinner the evening after Amanda Montier's arrival in Mur, Prince Kamak invited her and her tutor for a sunrise horseback ride outside the city gates. Amanda readily agreed when the prince proposed that they visit a site that would appeal to her interest in Murian history. And a sunrise on the Murian plain, he said, was beyond the power of words to describe. Accompanying them would be the German ambassador, Fräulein Zads, and her deputy, Colonel Hultz, both of whom had recently arrived in Mur, trying to salvage at least some trade considerations from the king.

Although Amanda's excitement had made sleep elusive, the sunrise as they trotted out of the city was indeed worth rising early to see. Not merely rosy fingered, dawn came as a wild, exultant man of fire, rising to run his race. The riders watched from a hill east of the city as the silent thunder of color roared on in variegated hues of purple, pink, and mauve.

But after they rode on and as the glory of the sunrise faded, so did Amanda's good humor. Who was this arrogant, large-boned German woman with the ridiculous fox-hunting hat, who spoke so condescendingly to her? And riding sidesaddle! Amanda's father had taken her to see Buffalo Bill's Wild West in Paris when she was twelve, and had even gotten an autographed picture. Since then, she had always prided herself on riding Western.

And she didn't like the fräulein's easy familiarity with Prince Kamak. Apparently, they had become acquainted when the prince was studying at university in Berlin. The fact that she wore an almost identical riding habit to Amanda's—except for that ludicrous hat—didn't help Amanda's mood either.

Riding southeast, they crossed a few miles of sandy plain until, out of the barrenness, a small palm-encircled oasis appeared. After dismounting and drinking from the spring, Kamak said to Amanda, "It is time that we proceed to the objective of our outing. I am sure you will find it most interesting."

"Yes indeed," said Amanda. "But I do hope you are planning to give us a tour of your temple excavations as well. Have you been able to confirm it as the temple built by your King Sol himself?"

"Mademoiselle," said Fräulein Zads, "I see you are one of those who have been besotted by the Murian fables. I am afraid that despite what you have read, you will find Mur rather more prosaic."

"Some of the stories I find credible, at least at their core," Amanda replied. "And in what I have seen here so far, there seems to be ample evidence." She had almost said, "from what I have *read*," but saw that she must choose her words carefully around this martinet.

"It appears, Your Highness," Fräulein Zads said, "that our young friend has a good share of the romantic imagination for which her country is so well known. Mademoiselle, the prince prides himself on being a scientist. Studying with the finest minds in Europe, he has indeed learned to discriminate between fact and fancy."

Professor Pleitan coughed, for he surely considered himself a leading member of the group Fräulein Zads had just mentioned. "I must say," he said with all the scholarly dignity he could muster, "in European academic circles, there is considerable variance of opinion. For instance, as far away as Tunis to the east, and Mauritania to the west, ancient references to the great King Sol appear. Moreover, I find the similarity in the names 'Mauritania' and 'Mur' compelling."

Finally, Fräulein Zads did not have an answer. She merely said, "*Proof*, I believe, is our topic, Professor, not speculation on primitive folk mythology."

"Prince Kamak," Amanda said, "I was seeking your opinion?"

"My dear mademoiselle," the prince said, "I am afraid I must confess skepticism. You must understand, if my country is to remain autonomous and survive through the land-grabbing, empire-building colonization by European powers, as well as all the other cataclysms that I fear this new century will bring, we must develop a sober, realistic outlook. We must see the legends for what they are: amusing stories from which we may draw inspiration, but not a foundation on which to build the future. I do believe that at some point in our history, a King Sol probably did exist, but I am afraid the legends attached to him are simply not credible. In that respect, he is perhaps not unlike England's King Arthur, or Saint George, who is claimed by a number of European cultures. That could easily account for the references to him that appear in other countries."

"So, then, it is not King Sol's treasure you are hoping to find in the temple?" Amanda asked. Prince Kamak was turning out to be almost as big a bore as Fräulein Zads.

"As a child, no one was more stirred than I by the stories of our supposed patriarch, but now what thrills my imagination more is the scientific approach to my country's history. I have pottery, arrowheads, and even parts of a sarcophagus from what could be the time of King Sol. I hope it is not too disappointing to you, but we have not found even a shard of evidence for his existence—or for his treasure."

"Well, I would still like to see what you have found," said Amanda.

"I am afraid that at this point," said Kamak, "it is off limits to all but professionals. As you might imagine, things of such antiquity are extremely fragile. At some later date, however, we hope to display them. But I do have something I am sure you will enjoy. It is another temple—or I should say, *tomb*—not far from here, that I am going to show you and that I hope will interest you greatly."

Amanda was unaccustomed to hearing *no*. Being told she couldn't see what Kamak was doing in the temple made her even more determined.

The recent Egyptian discoveries at Tell el-Amarna, in the tomb of Pharaoh Amenhotep IV, had verified what was long thought to be mere legend. King Sol and his treasure were what she had come to Mur to investigate, and she was not going to be so easily put off.

The party remounted and rode on for a couple of miles, toward what looked like a large mound at the base of a small mountain. As they came closer, an opening in the mound became visible, with some large square sandstone blocks extending into the remains of an arched entryway.

After dismounting and hobbling their horses, Prince Kamak took two small lanterns from his saddlebags. Just inside the opening, he lit the lanterns and handed one to Colonel Hultz. Despite the musty smell of dry clay and stone, a faint scent of flowers hung in the air.

A few steps inside, stairs carved out of stone led some thirty feet below the surface. After descending the stairs, they found themselves in a narrow corridor wide enough for two people to stand abreast, and high enough for a tall man with a crested helmet to walk through without stooping. After about fifty feet, the corridor opened into a circular chamber perhaps forty feet across.

"This tomb dates from centuries before the Ptolemies of Egypt," Kamak said, "perhaps 950 BC. We are now in the antechamber before the actual place where Queen Safali's sarcophagus once stood."

He lifted the lantern high above his head and motioned for Colonel Hultz to do the same. Then he slowly turned in a circle, casting light on the far reaches of the room. Across from them stood two fluted pillars bearing an ornate arch, marking the entrance to another room. All around the room, stone debris was scattered, showing that the floor's original covering had been ripped up. There were also barren patches on parts of the walls, where some kind of furniture or inlays had been violently removed. The undamaged parts of the walls were covered with a giant fresco, its colors barely faded, apparently telling a very old tale.

"They look more Greek than Egyptian," Amanda said, moving closer to study a pastoral tableau.

"Yes, but older than both and far more advanced," said Kamak, who came closer with his lantern.

Professor Pleitan studied the progress of the picture. "It is not Greek, though similar in some points of style."

"Do you catch the scent in here?" said Amanda, moving closer to sniff the wall. "When we entered, I thought I noticed the scent of jasmine. I believe it is coming from the fresco itself."

"Yes, jasmine and violet," Kamak said. "It is all part of the enchanting story told here. The scent was mixed with the pigment in the fresco. Apparently, the queen was partial to the fragrance."

"This looks like excerpts from Herodotus and Ovid," the professor said. "That looks like the story of Phaeton, and here, Arion and the Dolphins, and that looks like Orpheus's descent into the netherworld? But with notable differences."

"Yes, since they came before," said the prince. "These tales are so powerful and beautiful that derivations of them have captivated the imaginations of romantics for millennia. It is my opinion that a Murian poet gets the glory for having been their originator. Perhaps the original source of what we have from Herodotus and, centuries later, Ovid."

"And that would be glory indeed," said Amanda. "They are some of my favorites, especially Orpheus."

"Beautiful indeed, and to be ranked with the Germanic *Nibelungenlied* and the myths of Norse origin," Fräulein Zads interjected. "Wouldn't you agree, mademoiselle?

"I found Wagner's reworking of them, frankly, a bore," Amanda said.

"But of course, the French have not had their musical geniuses," said Fräulein Zads. "But we have our Mozarts, Beethovens, and—"

"If I may," Kamak broke in, "I will recount what you see here and also what we know of the history of this tomb."

"Please do," said Amanda. "I'll try not to interrupt."

"Fifty years ago, a goatherd, wandering in the area after a great sandstorm, discovered the tomb. It was, as it is now, barren of its original glittering baubles. The floor, once in pure gold leaf; segments of the wall; and the furniture, inlaid with all manner of precious ornaments, had been ravaged. We don't know in what epoch it was first molested—not long before we discovered it, or perhaps centuries before. It does not matter, though, for what they took is nothing compared to what they left behind: verifiable proof of Murian antiquity. As you noticed, Professor, the art can be scientifically proved to predate ancient Greece. This proves—and by my work, I will further prove—that my country is the oldest civilized culture on earth. Perhaps a millennium before Greece, at least centuries before the first dynasty of Egypt. And may I say, it is also my mission to see that my country survives for ages to come."

"Prince," said Amanda, abandoning her pledge not to interrupt, "I support your desires fully and I am sure my father and France do as well.

"I am sure we all, including my kaiser, desire the same," Fräulein Zads interjected. "Now, my prince, please go on with the tale."

"This fresco, as I mentioned," Prince Kamak said, "based on our analysis and of other artifacts found in the cave, dates back to somewhere between 1100 and 1000 BC, before the time of the Trojan War, before King David of the Hebrews, even before Pharaoh Amenemope. The story it tells outlines the mythical history of the founding of Mur, which happened perhaps a millennium earlier, and its legendary founder, King Sol the Great. This first sequence is indeed similar to the story of Phaeton as told by Ovid, with a number of variations. Here you see Phaeton . . ." Prince Kamak pointed his riding crop at the scene. "In our version, he is called Aton—as a boy, ridiculed by his friends for claiming that the sun god is his father. Then here he is on his trek to Mount Atlas, to seek confirmation from the god himself. Next, the god embraces his son, confirms his paternity, and as a token of his favor, vows to grant the boy a request.

"The boy, in overreaching hubris, asks to drive the sun god's chariot one day's journey across the sky. The god protests, citing the danger, but the boy holds him to his promise.

"The next sequence shows the boy mounting the sun's chariot, drawn by the sun god's four fiery, volatile stallions. Notice the musculature of the stallion—detail that is centuries ahead of other cultures. Then see here, as the chariot draws the already blazing sun with it from the east, the boy is already having trouble controlling the steeds. By the time it rises a few more leagues, it has already begun swerving violently off its normal, peaceful course through the heavens. The unmanaged horses swerve dangerously close to Earth, causing the sun to wreak devastation below. The intense heat scorches the earth, and the great deserts are formed.

"As the horses veer on a different course and the sun's chariot climbs to a great height in the heavens, the mountain snowcaps and glaciers are formed. But the wild swings of temperature below cause the surface of the earth to expand and shrink, and it groans and quakes and belches out volcanoes and catastrophic waves. The hours, days, months, and seasons that follow in the chariot's train go awry, and pandemonium is unleashed.

Prince Kamak walked a few steps over to the next panel of the mural. "Now we have our first sequence involving the Island of Mur, from which the legends say my country's name derives. The upheaval wrought by the sun's chariot has caused a great earthquake on the island. The times of peace and harmony are past, and the island is sinking into the sea. The island is doomed, and all have lost hope for survival—except for a young fisherman. He goes to the king and tells him that once, while far out at sea, he saw in the west, reaching up out of the horizon, a mountaintop. He offers to lead the king and the people to this new land, where Mur can resettle.

"The king equips the young fisherman with a sailing vessel and bids him find this new land, chart the way, and return before the island is gone. At this point, as you can see, the fresco is damaged. Some inlays of value have been ripped from the wall, and we are not sure of this segment of the story. It picks up here, where two dolphins lead the fisherman and the Murian ship to the new land.

"These two last series could indeed be the sources for a number of later myths," the prince continued, "including Ovid's version of Orpheus. In this one, the fisherman has now led his people inland, where he has been crowned King Sol of Mur and has married the old king's daughter. However, she soon dies and is carried away to the netherworld. Our fisher king cannot bear living without his love and descends after her. There, with his sword, Poema Logos, he does battle with the death god, Thanatos, who manifests as a man with the head and tail of a crocodile. The fisher king brings his bride back to Mur, where he rules with her in an age of peace and tranquility.

"This final sequence is somewhat difficult to explain. It seems to be a reiteration of the episode just told, but with Queen Safali and King Gno as the central characters. It shows the god of death on the loose again. Thanatos has now taken Queen Safali. King Gno, her husband, as you can see, also enters through a cave into the lower world and does battle with the death god, to bring back his lost love. But apparently, he is less successful since, in the fresco, he does not return, showing, perhaps, the natural progression of a culture's declining belief in the miraculous. This last sequence, with the recurring instances of more or less the same episode, in my studied opinion, also stresses the need for a figurative interpretation of the whole."

"I would like to ask a question," Amanda said.

"Yes, mademoiselle," said the prince. "I will do my best to answer, but as you can see, we have moved from my forte of science, into the realm of folklore, symbolism, and art history."

"What do you think was pictured directly beyond the crocodile monster?" Amanda asked.

"Thanatos is the god of death's name," Kamak reiterated.

"In the versions of the stories I have read," Amanda said, "the boats leaving Mur were filled with much of the island's riches. What do you think was right here"—Amanda pointed to the damaged area of the wall—"that Thanatos was guarding? This section is the most severely damaged of all the fresco. And if, as you said, it is because the inlays in the fresco were of gold and precious stones, could not those have been built into the story to represent the ancient treasure buried with King Sol? Could this not be another piece of evidence for the truth of the legend?"

"Doubtless, there were items of value inlaid here," said Kamak. "But surely, as in the rest of the fresco, the only credible interpretation is a purely symbolic one. Do you really think that a cataclysm on Earth was caused by the chariot of the sun going astray? Is it plausible to think that dolphins are of such intelligence, and so kindly toward us, that they would rescue a drowning man at sea? But on a symbolic level, it makes much more sense. Would not one pay all the riches and treasures of the world to defeat death? I think that is the proper interpretation."

Professor Pleitan walked up and examined closely the section of the fresco where the path leading from the cave down into the underworld came to a dark river. "There is an interesting difference," he said, "between this version of the hero's descent into Hades, and the Greek tales. The river looks almost like mud, and there is no ferryman to lead the dead across, and no Cerberus to guard the exit."

"It is the River Ubazapet," said Kamak. "I would suggest that those things in the Greek myths are later accretions. To the land of death, one needs no guide. And in our more austere version, Thanatos himself rules the way. I think this is the best representation of him over here, except for the damage to his eyes, which apparently had inlaid jewels—star sapphires, perhaps."

"And the worshippers of this Thanatos survive to this day?" asked Amanda. "And is it they who are responsible for the recent attempt on your father's life?"

"Unfortunately, superstition is even more rampant in my part of the world than in yours," said Kamak. "Though I have difficulty under-standing how they think they can placate death. But in answer to your question, there has arisen in our country a faction, whether sincere devotees of Thanatos or not, who are rabidly hostile to change."

"I hope you and your father are prepared to treat them with the utmost severity," said Fräulein Zads to the prince.

"I think you will find that my father does not hold in all respects with modern ideas of retributive justice. I could almost pity the leaders when they are apprehended. What is important and what these fanatics can't accept—and this is also the real metaphorical lesson of the fables—is that there will always be change, sometimes very difficult change. We must adapt. As applied to my country's current situation, if we don't adapt, we will end up sinking into the sea of modern European colonialism."

"May I ask one more question?" Amanda did not wait for permission. "If there once were great riches in this little room, where did they come from? Mur is not known for having gold and precious jewels as a natu-ral resource. If that is the case, is it not possible that the source of those riches is the Murian treasure that King Sol saved from the island? Where did they come from?"

"Mademoiselle, you draw your conclusion on a premise based on conjecture, not on empirical knowledge," said the prince. "What do you know of my country's natural resources? Perhaps my land is blessed with resources of which you are unaware."

"Can we get on with the tour?" said Fräulein Zads, anger flaring from her eyes.

Amanda didn't take offense at the prince's correcting of her logic. She simply didn't believe him. From her studies, she was convinced that the story of King Sol and his treasure had to be at least partly true. It might not be that he had brought it with him, as the tales told; he may have discovered it when he got here. And Kamak's suggestion—or veiled message?—about Mur possibly having great natural resources convinced her of it. She had to know what he had found in the temple he was exploring.

"Now," said Prince Kamak, "let's take a look at Queen Safali's and King Gno's burial place."

Leading them through the passage to the adjoining room, he raised his lantern and gasped.

"What is it?" said Amanda.

The prince picked up a bloody garment. "This robe belonged to Jaffar, my father's missing vizier."

CHAPTER 25

The next morning, Lincoln arose early. There was no Foreign Legion recruiting office in the city, and he must arrange for his own travel to Madagascar, first by ship to Alexandria, then overland to Aden, then aboard ship again for the six-hundred-mile sail from Aden to the island off the central coast of Africa. After seeing to what he could of these arrangements, he went to find Aziz, the camel trader, to get a refund of the 20 percent down payment they had paid for their journey to Sidi Bel Abbès.

It didn't take long to find Aziz. Lincoln almost bumped into him leaving the hotel. "I'm glad you're here," he said to Aziz, who was now wearing a colorful robe and turban. "I need to talk with you."

"And I you, my friend," replied Aziz, bowing slightly.

"I don't know if you've heard, but we need to get our deposit back for the trip to Sidi." Lincoln didn't stop to think why Aziz might have been looking for him. If he had, it would have made a lot more sense for Aziz to *avoid* seeing him.

"I am aware of the misfortune of your friends."

"Yeah, they're shipping them off to Madagascar this afternoon. And

I'll be going with them. To our regret, we won't be able to join your caravan. So we need our deposit back."

"As I stated, I am aware of, and deeply commiserate with you over the misfortune of your friends."

"Well, then, can we get our deposit back?"

"Perhaps, my young friend, you would do me the honor of walking with me away from the hotel. As the wise man says, 'the walls have ears.'" He put his arm through Lincoln's, and they began to walk.

"I am sure we will be able to come to an equitable arrangement," he went on. "But first, may I ask you a few questions?"

"Yes, feel free, but we really need to get our money back. Where we're going, we'll need every sou we have."

"Yes, I understand. Now, is it indeed your first preference to make the long and distasteful journey to that barbaric island where they are sending your friends?"

Lincoln stopped walking. "You need to understand one thing: where they go, I go; where I go, they go. We got a partnership."

"Yes, this is clearly my understanding. When I asked about your preference, I was asking for *all* of you—it is a grammatical weakness of your language that there is no difference in form between the second-person singular and plural. As you—the three of you—seemed intent on going to Sidi Bel Abbès, I was inquiring whether the three of you would still prefer that as your destination."

"Yes, but I don't think you understand. I don't know how you've heard about the trouble Johnny and Jake got into, but for them it's either Madagascar and the Second Regiment, or Madagascar and prison. It's Madagascar either way."

"I do believe I have quite a full understanding of the episode, and as its ramifications are not without impact on my interests, I have taken the liberty to inquire into the situation."

Lincoln, being from the American West, wasn't used to this circuitous route of getting to the point, but still trying to be polite he said, "I'm not sure where this trail is headed."

"Trail?"

"Perhaps you could speak more plainly."

"Would you and your friends still like to journey with the caravan to Sidi Bel Abbès?"

"Listen, by passing the guards a few francs, I was able to get my friends taken care of and put in a decent cell. But when I asked them what it would take to buy their way out of Madagascar, they told me it was impossible."

"As I said, this unfortunate episode is not without its potential effect on my interests, so I have inquired, perhaps a little more deeply than you, into the situation."

Lincoln stopped walking and freed his arm from Aziz's. "You're telling me there might be a way to arrange it so that my friends don't get sent to Madagascar?"

"I do think you are beginning to understand my 'trail.'"

"And what's it going to cost?"

"Of course, you will pay the rest of the agreed sum for your passage to Sidi."

"Of course."

"And . . ."

"And what?"

Aziz started walking again, and Lincoln hurried to catch up.

"It is against our honorable tradition to take advantage of a guest's misfortune."

"Yes?"

"Therefore, as this is a very expensive proceeding, there are two options."

"I'm all ears."

"All ears?"

"I'm listening. The two options?"

They stopped again, and Aziz turned toward Lincoln and spoke without looking into Lincoln's eyes. "It will cost an additional two thousand francs. As you know, this is a difficult situation, and many important people are concerned."

Lincoln gasped, "Two thousand francs!" About 1,100 US dollars. He was stunned by the amount. He had watched Jake negotiate a couple of times, and always, no matter what was initially proposed, Jake appeared flabbergasted by the audacity and injustice of the offer. But this amount was staggering, and it was nine hundred more francs than he had left, even before paying the balance of their caravan bill. Lincoln threw back his head in dismay and walked around in a small circle. "That's a boatload of money! It's more than we have—*way* more. What's the other option?"

"I am aware that this might seem an exorbitant amount, but I beg you to consider the many complications and individuals involved."

"What's the other option?"

"The other option, my friend," Aziz said, still not looking Lincoln in the eyes, "is that, knowing that this sum could be beyond your means, out of the goodness of my heart and as an admirer of excellent firearms, I will handle the whole transaction in exchange for your Winchester rifle. Of course, you would still pay what is owed for your caravan to Sidi."

Many times Lincoln had been offered substantial sums for his rifle. But it was his most precious possession and, other than his pocket watch, the only thing he still had of his father's. He would do almost anything not to part with it. He didn't say anything for at least a minute.

"Of course, you could still go to Sidi and leave your friends to Madagasc—"

"You would lose two fares to Sidi and have to return the deposits," said Lincoln.

"On cancellations, the policy is a 50 percent return of deposits."

Lincoln barely heard this. He was already agonizing over the prospect of parting with his rifle. After a moment, he said, "I could pay you eight hundred francs, and the rest in installments once we start drawing Legion pay. I would even pay interest."

"I am aware of the wages of *La Légion Étrangère*. And also the survival rate of a lowly legionnaire, even those not in Madagascar. Besides, it is beyond my humble means to extend such a loan. It still is possible for you and your friends to be in time for the caravan's departure this morning."

"You're sure they'll wait?"

"I can assure you they will wait."

As much as he valued his rifle, he knew that if it was the only way he could save his friends from Madagascar, he would have to give it up.

"It's back at the hotel," he said. "But there's no way I'm giving you the scabbard. It was the gift of a Comanche chief who was a friend of mine."

CHAPTER 26

On hearing of the discovery of his vizier's bloody robe, the king wanted to post a proclamation that anyone found to be associated with the cult of Thanatos would be tied naked on a nest of silver ants, then hanged upside down in the streets of the city. Ambassador Montier managed to dissuade him from making the public proclamation. Fear and unrest were already palpable in the city, and such a public edict would only add to it. The ambassador warned those who made the discovery not to discuss it with anyone except the Three, whom he sent, led by Kamak, to investigate the tomb. In another chamber, they found further evidence that it was the site where the vizier had been killed, and where some kind of ritual had taken place.

That afternoon, after returning from escorting the Three to the cave, the prince sat at his desk in his study. On the desktop was a large aerial photograph, taken from his hot-air balloon, of the temple he was excavating. At the moment, however, he wasn't studying the picture. His ear was pressed against a tube that came out of a secret compartment in the wall. The device allowed him to hear, reasonably well, most of the conversations that took place in the office of the French ambassador.

A knock sounded on the door. He put the cover on the device and hid it away. "Enter."

A servant came in and bowed. "My prince, the German ambassador is here."

"Show her in."

Fräulein Zads entered the room brusquely. She wore a tailored khaki suit, its jacket tightly fastened by a leather belt around her narrow waist, accentuating her voluptuous figure. Her head was uncovered, with her hair down to her shoulders and bangs in front, almost like a blond Cleopatra—a style the prince had told her he preferred.

She came in very agitated and started to speak, but the prince shushed her. Taking out the tube, he again put it to his ear. She paced the room for a few minutes until Kamak put away the device again.

"What is the matter, Fräulein? You look as if you had sat on the nest of silver ants that awaits the followers of Thanatos."

"I have wanted to speak with you privately since this morning," she said. "I think it was extremely unwise of you, even in levity, to mention 'natural resources' in the presence of that child and her tutor. They may not be the total fools they appear. I must ask you never to do that again. If the French were to have any inclination of what is at stake here, it would be a disaster. My kaiser has made a large investment in you and in these . . . excavations. And the political risk is even greater."

"And is not my risk the greatest of all? Please check yourself, Fräulein. I know exactly what I said."

"And we are behind schedule," she went on. "Our squadron is now off the coast. But as I have told you, they will not land the troops until you can assure us that the Legion battalion has left the fort."

"Great feats take time." He looked down at the temple photograph on his desk. "This temple, for instance, took twenty-seven years to build. Then the sands of the desert covered it for three millennia, burying it and the bounty that lies beneath it."

"And you're sure it is there?"

"Here is the report from yesterday." Kamak handed her a sheet of paper from his desk. As she looked over the paper, he said, "This discovery will make my country the richest nation in the hemisphere, and your kaiser will have his exclusive trading privileges."

"But what about the rest of the plan? We can't attack while the battalion is still in the fort."

"Yes, and now it is time that you sent the squadron the message to land. They need to be at the border in five days."

"How can you say that? You must be sure."

Kamak carefully rolled up the photograph and placed it in one of his desk drawers. He got up and walked to the office door and locked it.

"Yes, I am quite sure. The original plan of drawing them out through the threat of the slave traders is working brilliantly. The French ambassador is terribly concerned about them and has been in discussion about sending the column after them. It occurred to me that we may need something else to help him make the decision. I know now what that impetus will be."

"And what is that?"

"Did you know that when the ambassador's daughter was late in arriving from Sidi Bel Abbès, he feared she had been taken by the slave traders? He had given orders for the column to go after them shortly before she and the Three finally arrived."

"I was not aware of this."

"The mademoiselle's desire to explore my country's ruins will fit in perfectly with our plans. I think we'll whet her curiosity a little more."

Fräulein Zads smiled. "That little know-it-all deserves whatever she gets. I must admit, seeing her expression upon finding Jaffar's robe was *wunderbar*."

CHAPTER 27

The caravan did not come close to leaving at dawn. Shortly after Lincoln agreed to trade his rifle, Aziz had Johnny and Jake out of the jail, and two gendarmes had escorted them back to the hotel. With Lincoln, they grabbed their things and hurried to meet the caravan, which had assembled outside the city's southern gate. It seemed that Aziz had overstressed the need for celerity.

Lincoln had made Aziz promise not to tell Johnny and Jake what it had cost him to get them out of jail. When they asked him how he did it, Lincoln just said he tried some of the techniques he had seen Jake use in negotiating. But on their way to the caravan, it didn't take them long to notice that Lincoln wasn't packing his rifle. Lincoln said he had sold it just yesterday, as he had been planning to do all along. Johnny and Jake smelled the rat. They didn't say anything, just exchanged disgusted looks. Then Johnny said, "The debt will be repaid, my word on it." And Jake added, "And mine, if it's the last thing I do. 'Nuff said."

Outside the city walls, they first heard, then smelled, then saw the caravan. The camels stretched out their necks and groaned mightily, as if seeking to out-complain the mules.

The animals were arranged in a line about two hundred yards long.

At the rear were the twenty mules, all but one laden with canvas panniers strapped to their backs. Ahead of them were twenty pack camels, whose large wooden pack frames carried about three times the mules' burden. In front of these were ten camels, fine-looking taller beasts meant for riding and fitted with leather saddles of a sort. At the head of the caravan, in front of the riding camels, a dozen swarthy men were readying their fine Arabian steeds for the trek. Lincoln watched in fascination. The riders all wore black burnooses with hoods covering their heads. The color of their dress, according to Johnny, was a tribal thing. Beneath their robes, visible as they saddled their mounts, they wore leather belts with at least two ornate, curved *mouns*, small daggers with short, wide blades and jewel-encrusted hilts. In an elaborately worked metal sheath outside the robe, each man also carried a long, curved scimitar called a *yataghan*. They all had old long-barreled, Turkish-made, flintlock smoothbore guns strapped to their saddles. Though these firing pieces were old, they were not neglected. A few of the horsemen had old matchlock pistols stuffed in their belts.

"Brother," Johnny said, seeing the riders, "we must be going through some rough country if we need this bunch protecting us."

"What it cost the traders to hire those boys probably ain't a fraction of what all these goods are worth," said Jake. "I agree there must be more'n a few hostiles on the prairie, or they wouldn't need such numbers."

At this point, Aziz walked over to them. He had changed to less elegant clothing than when Lincoln met with him earlier that morning. "Greetings friends, you are welcome," he said. "I hope you were able to get a peaceful rest."

"Why don't you show us our mounts and let's get moving," Johnny said, apparently in no mood for chitchat.

"Always in a hurry," Aziz said. "But time is money, as I have heard it said from your countrymen. I will first have the pleasure of introducing you to the leader for your journey to Sidi."

He led them to a short, thick man wearing a white turban, embroidered with green and blue, and a gray robe over olive-green pants that could've been French army issue. Like the mounted guards, he had a leather belt but only one *moun*, though its scabbard and hilt were even more ornamented than the guards'. Also on his belt was a holster with a handgun—not an old one, but a modern Colt revolver.

"Abdulla Ahmed, please be introduced to your American travelers to Sidi Bel Abbès. They are warriors and mighty hunters, come to join the *La Légion Étrangère*," Aziz said, bowing and gesturing toward Abdulla, then to Lincoln and his companions.

Abdulla, with a quick and not altogether wholesome eye, made a summary assessment of the three Americans. He did a disinterested series of genuflections, touching first his forehead, then progressively down his body to his waist. "Your servant is honored with your company and will be pleased to deliver you to Sidi Bel Abbès, alive."

At this, Abdulla whistled, and when nothing immediately happened, he started hollering in Arabic. A young light-skinned boy in traditional Arab garb came running up, bowing repeatedly in contrition. Abdulla made a halfhearted show of thrashing him with a leather riding crop for his tardiness but then introduced him. "This is Gustave. He will show you to your camels, see to your packs, and be at your service until we reach Sidi. Be patient with him. He is an idiot, blessed of heaven, and speaks French as he is the bastard of a Frenchman and a whore."

"Now I take my leave of you," Aziz said, bowing again. "God open the gates of happiness to you, and may you have many male children."

At this, Aziz and Abdulla walked off together.

As soon as Gustave was alone with his new charges, he perked up considerably. "I have English too," he said, bowing, and then laughed out loud. "I am your manservant on the journey—very good manservant. I please you, you bonus me, if you please." He laughed again.

He led them to their mounts, the last in line of the riding camels. He then got to work explaining the basics of camel riding, from how to make the animal kneel for mounting and dismounting, to proper posture on the saddle (a kind of sidesaddle with one leg crossed under the other and around something like a large saddle horn), to trotting, to running, to how to doze without falling off. Every once in a while, Gustave would break out in a belly laugh about whatever he was talking about, then refocus on his instruction.

When he was done, he fed each of their mounts a handful of scrub and started laughing at the them. "Monsieur Camel has bad manners; see, he chews with his mouth sideways." He thought this especially funny.

Lincoln, Johnny, and Jake befriended their camels, feeding them a little brush. "Can't say they're handsome, exactly," said Johnny. "It's a long way down from this feller; I hope he's broke."

Gustave had finished securing their packs to their saddles and laughed. "Your camels are pearls of great price. I pick you good ones, *oui*? We ride forward once the caravan starts moving. I am a Frenchman and eat not the dust of peasants," he said, augmenting his comment with yet another laugh.

At that moment, a spate of braying and shouting burst out from the rear of the caravan. Above the noise of camels and donkeys, a voice could be heard speaking loud and fast. They turned to see who was making the disturbance.

"Well, I'll be a tobacky spittin steer," said Johnny. "I don't believe it!"

"Why? What'd you see?" said Jake, who, at about seven inches shorter than Johnny, couldn't see over the knot of people standing around the noise.

"I swear it's your old pal Tom Foote."

"Tom Foote! Don't say it!" said Jake with obvious concern. "What's that dern fool potwalloper doing here? A stretch to call him my *pal*, though, don't you think? *You're* the one almost married his sister."

"Barely escaped," said Johnny, "but he was even madder at you."

"And I had to educate him," said Jake, who had now gotten his camel to kneel so he could climb aboard and get a view of the situation. "That hasher's so cheap, he went for a donkey 'stead of a camel. Just like him. Crushing the poor brute too."

"Well, you didn't educate him good enough, 'cause he's here, and that's the sad truth. Let's lay low and we'll at least have some fun with him."

The crowd around him opened up to let a large man astride a donkey pass through. His beast was already packed, and he appeared ready for the journey. One of Abdulla Ahmed's servants led donkey and rider to the tail end of the group of donkeys that brought up the tail end of the caravan. A

few minutes later, after a great deal more noise and commotion, the caravan started its slow amble southwest to Sidi Bel Abbès.

Lincoln was curious to hear something about his new friends' old acquaintance. But where he was from, inquisitiveness into other people's business
wasn't considered a virtue, so he tried to restrain himself and not ask what
the story was with this man.

But despite his upbringing, Lincoln had always had trouble controlling
his curiosity about people he thought interesting. He often had to battle his
inclination to nose into what some strict constructionists might consider
other people's business. That someone of his companions' acquaintance—
and, apparently, more than a mere *passing* acquaintance—had just joined
the same caravan heading deep into North Africa was hard not to inquire
about.

On top of this, Johnny and Jake were men of experience who Lincoln
could learn from, and he liked hearing of their adventures. And it seemed
that a story came with the large man on the donkey, and he wanted to
hear it. But rather than be what might be considered rude, he didn't just
outright go asking a lot of questions—for a while anyway. But he was
about to burst the whole time.

Once the caravan got in stride, their pace quickened, and the train
stretched out over a quarter mile. When Gustave was sure the three of
them could handle their mounts, he loped ahead, in front of them, so
that their camels would follow his. "Sirs, follow me," he said. "We Europeans eat no dust of the desert's vermin," pronouncing the *v* as a *w* so that
it sounded like "wormin'." Their camels lurched out of the column and
jogged ahead of the other camels and about thirty feet behind the last
of the horse-mounted guard. There wasn't a lot less dust at this point in
the caravan, but Gustave was much happier now that his charges were at
the front of the camels. It was a matter of prestige, and whatever prestige
Gustave thought he had, he vigorously defended.

After a few miles of rocky desert, they crossed a mile or so of sand dunes, which Gustave assured them were nothing like the real dunes on the other side of Sidi Bel Abbès. Lincoln quickly settled into the camel's rhythmic sway from side to side, and the creak of the saddle.

After they had ridden a few miles, quite out of the blue Jake said, "Let's scare the grease out of that dough puncher."

"Might give 'im a heart attack," Johnny said, as if the conversation had been going on without a break.

"That'd be okay," Jake said. "Might slow him up a bit."

"Okay, we'll do it at our first stop," Johnny said. "We'll circle around and give 'im a hotfoot or something of the like."

Lincoln wanted to get brought into the conversation but wasn't sure how. He finally caught Johnny's attention and, with a little turn of his eyes and a twist of his head, tried to suggest that they let him in on whatever it was.

Johnny nudged his camel closer to Lincoln's. "It's a long story, pard, but you don't have to worry, your share of the treasure's intact. We'll figure a way to get rid of yon reprobate."

"I told you I'm not worried about the treasure," Lincoln said. "I'm just interested how an old friend of yours got on the same caravan as us, and why he's going to the same place as us."

"It's a tale of romance and treachery," Johnny said. He motioned back to Jake to ride up closer. "Me and Jake first met up with Tom Foote in Siam. This must have been around '86. We'd been doing some merchant marine work in the East Indies and, in our spare time, doing a little jewel importing and exporting, without the attendant formalities concerning duty, of course—which, in common parlance, is known as smuggling—to supplement our meager seaman's wages. About that time, we hear that the king of Siam is looking to raise himself an extension of his country's army, with a band of professionals. So, as me and Jake could be termed professionals, we volunteered to be at the king's service. The wages were decent, and it is true that at the time there were more rubies and sapphires in Siam than in any other country in Southeast Asia. Well, in that same army was yonder Tom Foote. He was the Special Auxiliary Brigade's head potwalloper. And he threw his weight around—which, as you've seen, is no paltry thing—quite effectively, what with the lofty position he held."

"He's the biggest dern liar on God's green earth," Jake said. "When we first met him—that was in Siam—I was telling him about this steer that was so smart it knew how to chew tobacky and spit, which was true. And he then tries to tell us about an Australian cow that had an ear for music—y'see, Tom puts on airs of being cultured—and claims that cow can sing as good as any Eye-talian. Course, part of the cowboy code—*American* cowboy code, anyway—is, you never accuse anyone good enough to tell you a story, of telling a lie . . ."

"No—you get even," Lincoln interjected.

"That's a fact, and I do believe I got even, but since I can't remember how, we'll just need to get even again, to make sure."

"Yes, Jake," said Johnny. "It will be perfectly appropriate. Tom's an Aussie, from Perth, and always claimed everything Aussie, like that special singing cow of his, left everything in the dust—and especially their women, which ain't altogether untrue. But he does have a knack for being where the doubloons are. Though I wouldn't trust him as far as I could throw him—and not even that far, 'cause I've had to throw him on occasion. Nothing compared to what Jake did to him, o' course, but that's a whole 'nother story."

The caravan was now moving at a comfortable pace. Four of Abdulla's men continually rode their horses up and down the length of the caravan to keep the column together and keep the slower animals from straggling. Every few minutes, Gustave would ride up and inquire about their comfort and their needs.

"Anyway," Johnny went on, "though we didn't really trust him and always had to have both eyes open around him, Tom Foote was a useful ally if you were a recruit in the Special Auxiliary Brigade of the king of Siam. We made out fairly decent there for two years, though we've got nothing to show for it now. Then things got hot and we needed to skedaddle, which we had a plan for.

"Problem was, old Tom Foote didn't exactly stay by the plan. He got away clean and easy, whereas Jake and me did so by the skin of our teeth, and no thanks to him. Well, about two years later, we run into him in a Shanghai hooch house. First thing, of course, is Jake trounced him. It was interesting to watch, he being about twice as big as Jake and not being what you'd call a pushover either. But then, after the fight was over, he wants to make it all up and tells us of his big plan and the new place where we have to get to, to make our fortune. His story was interesting, the way he told it. So Jake and me are willing to let bygones be bygones, and off we go with Tom in the guise of Australians, to join the Thirty-Fourth Punjab Rifles serving in North India, where, according to Tom, he had a lead on the whereabouts of the maharaja's lost treasure.

"Jake and me, we worked on our Australian, and pretty soon we got to where we could speak it, and we got to Bangalore, where we enlisted in the British army, with Tom leading the way. Well, after three long years, we had seen some interesting sights and fought some interesting battles, but we hadn't found any maharaja's treasure. The thing of it, though, was that after about nine months, Tom Foote disappeared on us. Well, me and Jake's been called a lot of things, but one thing we ain't, and that's deserters. So we stuck out our term, and when we got out, we went looking for Tom.

"We found him back in Australia, and of course, Jake thrashed him again, but this time not as bad. Tom is all sorry and has some excuse about his dying mother and wants to make it all up to us. So we say, *How?* And he says he doesn't know but he'll figure something out. But we did hang around those parts for a while, and I did make the acquaintance of Tom's younger sister, who had her attractions. Jake, on the other hand, happened to catch the eye of the lady Tom was wooin', Miss Myra Hostotler, and she his. Well, it wasn't long before old Tom wants us out of there and will do anything to get us to leave.

"Now, I ain't quite ready yet to settle down, and Tom's sister Molly knew it and wasn't too upset, 'cause we had our fun and remembrances. And Jake ain't ready for marrying either—he needs his orneriness to mellow a little—and so when we heard about an opportunity north of the Transvaal, we took off and left Tom, who swore he was settling down to married life. And that's the last we heard of Tom Foote, which was about five years ago. Back in those days, there had always been talk about the

Foreign Legion, but I don't think news of Mur had started to leak out yet. But the point is, we left him and he was about to get married and settle down. So it's a mystery what the man is doing here. It's a good sign and also a bad 'un. It's a good sign 'cause if it's worth his efforts to come, then he must have heard of some considerable opportunities. It's a bad sign because, well, because he's here and that's bad enough."

"Could be Tom didn't take to the married life," said Jake.

"Possible, but with his skills, he could find a lot more comfortable spots to hang his pots than the Sahara Desert."

"Potwalloper—he's a cook?" Lincoln asked.

"Oh, that's a good sign too," Johnny said. "He's a cook, all right, and whatever you might have to say about Tom Foote, wherever he's about, there's going to be good grub. He is master of the art, especially of the Siamese variety."

The caravan plodded along farther to the southwest till close to noon, then they came to a grove of palms with a spring of water in its midst. Here, Abdulla ordered a halt for a rest and their midday meal.

Johnny and Jake dismounted. "We'll be back soon, pard," said Jake. "If you could keep an eye on the gear, we'd be obliged."

As Lincoln was dismounting, Gustave came running up. He unloaded the camels and quickly set up a little lean-to for protection from the sun and windblown sand. Then he walked the camels to the spring to let them drink. Lincoln took a seat and wondered what kind of misery Johnny and Jake were going to inflict on their old friend—if that was the right word for him.

CHAPTER 28

Johnny and Jake circled around the oasis and came up on the far end of the caravan. They approached, hiding behind some trees and then in some scrubby acacia bushes. About forty feet away, under the shade of a big date palm, they saw Tom Foote. It seemed he hadn't paid for the caravan option that would have provided him meals and a servant, for he had pitched himself his own little sun-and-wind shield and was stirring three cook pots on his own little fire, occasionally dipping a wooden spoon in and tasting the contents. Even from where Johnny and Jake crouched in the bushes, they could catch the aroma of Siamese herbs wafting on the breeze.

"I think the situation calls for a change of plans," whispered Johnny.

Lincoln was reading a book, lounging in the shade of the lean-to that Gustave had made for them. Suddenly, first Jake and then Johnny came running back to their little campsite. Jake was carrying two pots, and Johnny one, both men taking great care, as if the pots contained some kind of precious elixir. Despite their efforts, a little had splashed over the side of two of the pots and exuded an aroma that Lincoln found altogether delightful.

"What do you boys have there?" Lincoln said. "I thought you were going to give your friend a hotfoot."

"After surveying the opportunity, we decided, due to conditions, to alter course and steal his lunch instead," Johnny said, taking the top off the pot he was carrying, and allowing more of the sumptuous aroma to escape. "And I'm dipped if we didn't catch him making his famous Siam curry, with chicken, peppers, mushrooms, and onions."

"He's an old scamp," Jake said, lifting the tops off his two pots, "but Tom Foote can cook. This here is his jasmine rice, and I don't know what's in this one, but it smells tasty."

Johnny took a look in the mystery pot and gave it a closer smell. "Mutton, garlic, and leeks. Oh, lots of garlic! What a flavor—almost singes the nose. It's the only way he's stayed alive all these years. Plenty of people have had it in for old Tom, but he's too valuable a resource to lose by way of ordinary vengeance. He's nothing less than a prodigy with a saucepan."

"Gustave is supposed to be bringing us our meal any minute," said Lincoln.

"That'd be a poor allocation of space in your belly, Smith," said Johnny. "Now, get your dish out. You're about to be eating as it's done in the palaces of the Orient."

All three of them got their plates out, and quickly. Johnny served them each ample scoops from the three pots. There was even enough for a third helping for Jake, who, though small, could pack it away.

"He made all this just for his lunch?" Lincoln said. He had a line of perspiration on his upper lip—not from the heat of the day, but from the peppers in the dishes.

"Never trust a skinny cook," said Johnny, sweating even more profusely than Lincoln. "And if that was the only rule for trusting a person, then you could trust Tom Foote without reservation, 'cause he can dern near out-eat Jake. Unfortunately, there's other factors to consider in trusting a man, 'sides his skill with the skillet. We best be keeping our eyes on old Tom. He's liable to be offended if he finds out we heisted his lunch."

Just as they were finishing their sumptuous repast, Gustave walked up with a pot of mutton and couscous. He looked quite pleased with himself and was understandably puzzled when both Lincoln and Johnny, with flushed and perspiring faces, waved him off. Jake, who was sweating even more than the other two, took a small helping. He savored it and said, "Not bad. Send my compliments to the chef, but that dog won't hunt in the same pack as Tom Foote."

Confused and deflated by his charges' rejection, Gustave tried to assure them that the meat really was mutton and not dog. His protestations continued until Johnny offered him fifty sous to run an errand, which he was willing and excited to do.

Johnny had him take the empty pots back to Tom, asking whether they belonged to him. He was to say he had found them with a pack of dogs on the other side of the meadow.

"Tell him one of the dogs was dead and another looked about halfway there," said Jake. "That'll make him madder than losing lunch would."

"Capital idea," said Johnny. "And, Gustave, make sure you don't mention us. We are his old friends and want to surprise him. Come back and tell us how he responds, and you'll get another fifty sous."

Jake made Gustave repeat his instructions three times before letting him go.

Not long afterward, Gustave came back. His intermittent laughter was even more frequent than usual. "Monsieur Foote, hee-hee, give me two francs to tell no one what happened. Says dogs must have been sick anyway. He said it will be our secret. He give me two francs, ha ha!"

Johnny said, "The old horse's ass is so vain, he thinks word of his vittles killing a dog could sully his reputation, so he wants to make sure it don't get out. I declare, the man's a marvel."

Johnny gave Gustave another fifty sous. The kid had made more in a half hour than he typically earned in a month.

CHAPTER 29

Not long after their lunch, Abdulla, accompanied by two of his black-clad guards, stopped by the campsite to find Johnny and Jake napping, and Lincoln trying to read from the book that the man on the mountain had given him. "They enjoyed their lunch," Lincoln said.

"We will be moving out soon," Abdulla said. "Tell your friends that from now on, utmost vigilance is necessary. We now enter the devil's domain."

The caravan got moving again, altering its heading from due south to southwest. As it got farther inland, the terrain turned to low rolling hills. At about three o'clock, the caravan began to ascend a small mountain range that stretched from the coast as far south as they could see. It would take two days to cross the mountains, then three more days through increasingly barren land to Sidi Bel Abbès, on the northern edge of the Sahara.

Johnny and Jake didn't give a lot of credence to Abdulla's warning. They had decided to lie low and not harass Tom Foote for the time being.

"I wasn't thinking Tom had brought his pots and herbs when I came up with the idea of hotfooting him," said Johnny. "Might be best just to let him discover us, or us come upon him 'naturally,' and then watch his reaction. I want to find out what the man knows, and stay on his good side for the time being. That he's on his way to Sidi now is no small item."

"Sure enough," said Jake. "And if we rile him too much, he might get stingy with his grub."

Late that afternoon, having ascended the mountains, the caravan stopped at a clearing about a half mile from a large forest of oak and cypress. A small river ran out of the forest and eventually down the western slope of the mountain. Abdulla commanded that the caravan camp by the river and passed word that all the travelers should stay well away from forest.

After Gustave set up their camp, he gathered what seemed an inordinate amount of wood. "You reckon it's goin' to snow tonight?" Johnny asked him. "Or you just tryin' to keep away the skeeters?" Johnny was only trying to make conversation. It might not have snowed there in a hundred years, for the mountains were only about two thousand feet high, and even at sunset there were only a few mosquitoes.

Gustave didn't respond with his usual loud guffaw. "Must have a big fire—keep away the ghost and his beast," he said.

Johnny and Lincoln tried to get him to elaborate on his concern, but he wouldn't say much more than, "Unholy forest. I'll keep a big fire all night and pray." He then crossed himself, went through what looked like some kind of Muslim genuflection—to hedge his bet, perhaps—made a few other arcane motions, and crossed himself again. He set up his bed so that the fire was between him and the forest.

Jake started to sense a palpable turn of mood in the caravan and set up his roll on the same side of the fire as Gustave. He also checked his pistol and put it under his blanket. When he was out of earshot, Johnny said to Lincoln, "Old Jake's the bravest man I know, 'cept when it comes to spirits and ghosts. It's best not to say nothing about it either. He can get kinda testy."

There wasn't a lot of conversation at dinner. They hadn't slept much the night before, were up before dawn, and had ridden all day. Jake went to bed soon after their dinner—more mutton and couscous—and Johnny nodded off a little later. Lincoln read a few pages of Herodotus, then also turned in.

When Lincoln first closed his eyes, he still felt the swaying of his camel. The swaying entered his dreams as the rolling of an old ship he was sailing in. Another ship hove into view bearing the skull and cross-bones. The pirate ship chasing him was manned by the swarthy guards of the caravan, and Abdulla was the pirate captain. The North African coast came into sight. If he could only reach land, he would be safe. He reached for his rifle to take it with him as he fled ashore, but it was gone. He looked and looked but couldn't find it.

Then he was in the old man's cave. But the old man's multiwheeled machine had grown huge. Lincoln saw himself hanging by his hands from the outer wheel, trying to drop to the next smaller wheel, where time was slower. But try as he might, he couldn't let go. He was stuck. Not only could he not drop to the lower wheel, he couldn't get off at all.

Then the terrible sound of camels rumbling and mules and horses whinnying entered his dream. After a moment of sleepy confusion, he awoke. The bedlam continued a minute more, then receded.

Gustave was frantically piling wood on the flames, and Jake was crouching behind the fire with his pistol out. Johnny was sitting up, also holding a pistol.

"The demon beast has come for his due," Gustave said, his voice trembling. "Last time, Abdulla angered him. Now we must leave mountain and go 'round. Abdulla is the great fool if we do not turn back."

The camels were still groaning loudly, the mules whinnying, and the donkeys braying, as a hint of gray lined the eastern horizon.

"I'm going forward to see what's afoot," said Lincoln. "I don't know about the camels, but those mules are riled like there's a puma come around."

"Don't know as they got puma here," said Johnny. "Most likely a lion—heard stories 'bout them further south that'd make your hair stand up. We'll keep watch of the camels and our goods."

When Lincoln got to Abdulla's tent, the gray on the horizon was turning to blue. A big campfire roared in front of the tent. Nearby, five of Abdulla's guards were holding the reins of twelve horses, including Abdulla's white mare. Six other guards, holding their old muskets, looked nervously out toward the forest. At the tent's opening, Abdulla was having a heated conversation with the leader of the guards. Abdulla was holding the rifle that, until last night, had belonged to Lincoln.

After a few moments, the leader of the guards left, went over to the men holding the horses, and began to speak with them. Without waiting for Lincoln to speak, Abdulla said to him, "They are very superstitious. With the light, they will calm down. But they will not spend another night on the mountain."

"What was it?" Lincoln said. "Some kind of lion?"

"They believe it is a jinni who dwells in a great demon beast. It took one of the mules. We will have to go back and cross the mountains at the southern pass."

"What do you mean, 'we will have to go back'? How much longer is that going to take?"

"Another five days' journey."

"What makes you think it was some kind of monster?"

"It is they who think that. I do not know what it is, but my men greatly fear it."

"You say it carried away one of the mules?"

"Are you not the American to whom this rifle once belonged?"

"Yeah, that was my rifle."

"It is the rifle of a great hunter, am I not correct?"

Lincoln didn't answer the question. He just said, "Can you show me where the mule was taken from?"

Abdulla looked up into the sky. "I do not give credence to the superstitions of my men, but perhaps we should first drink coffee and wait for a little more light."

As they drank the strong Arabian brew, which wasn't so different from the grainy "cowboy coffee" that a lot of the old westerners preferred, Abdulla told Lincoln about the jinni who was thought by some to inhabit the area, riding a great demon that took the shape of a man-eater of the forest. There had been many reported sightings, and the occasional animal carcass found. In the past year, Abdulla had started taking this route to Sidi Bel Abbès, because it was five days shorter than the more southerly route. Not until his last trip had there been any trouble. Then, in the middle of the night, while Abdulla was relieving himself, he thought he heard the panting of a beast in the darkness, and fired his rifle at it. There was no further incident, but the episode had excited his superstitious men. It was a matter of business to Abdulla. He needed his men on the rest of the journey, for there were other, quite real threats, which his men did not fear, like vicious Tuareg and Berber bandits.

When the dawn had fully broken, Abdulla, carrying Lincoln's rifle, walked Lincoln to where the guards' horses and mules had been tied up. The ground around the immediate vicinity was covered with hoof-prints of frightened animals. Lincoln searched outside the area and soon found a bloody trail leading toward the forest.

"What is your opinion?" Abdulla said to Lincoln, who was squatting down, examining a huge track.

"It's something awful big, all right. It looks like it was dragging the mule to here, then picked it up and ran away with it. Lotta blood—the thing went right for the throat. Can't imagine how big it has to be to carry off a mule. Maybe it *is* some kind of monster."

Abdulla looked at Lincoln with undisguised concern.

Lincoln stood up. "You say not going on through the mountains is going to cost you five days?"

"Yes. My men will go no farther with this beast running free."

"Five days—that's gotta be worth a pretty penny to you"

Abdulla screwed up his face. "Pretty . . . ?"

"A lot of money—five days'll put a dent in your profits."

"Yes! Oh, yes! Tell me, young hunter, can you slay it?"

"Well, I could give it a try. I'd need my rifle, of course. It'll take a buffalo gun to bring down something that big and nasty."

"Yes, of course."

"As I said, it's got to be worth something to you if I do get it. Make this a safe camp for all your future caravans."

"Yes, I will reward you handsomely."

"If I bring back the head of this thing, all I want is my rifle back."

At this, Abdulla threw up his arms as if amazed at the audacity of the offer. But Lincoln had learned a bit of the negotiator's art from watching and talking to Jake, who had said in most places around the world they wouldn't think of agreeing to a business transaction without wrangling.

After pacing around for some time in apparent agitation, Abdulla came back to face Lincoln. "I bought this rifle for five hundred francs. I couldn't possibly sell it to you for less than six hundred."

Aziz had said it would cost two thousand francs to bribe his friends out of the jail. That was a clearly a lie. Abdulla was probably lying too. But Lincoln didn't care; he wanted his rifle back. "I'll give you six hundred right now and I'll get that monster for you for another thousand." Saving the caravan five days had to be worth several times that much.

Abdulla paced around again, muttering to himself. Then he stopped and looked at Lincoln. "I accept your first offer: the monster for the rifle. If you are not back here by three o'clock with proof that you have killed the beast, the caravan must leave and go back down the mountain, and you will return my rifle. If you return after three, even with success, you will return the rifle. If you return before three, having killed the monster, I make you the peerless gift of the rifle, from one mighty hunter to another."

Lincoln pulled out his watch and checked the time. It was 6:27 a.m. He looked Abdulla in the eye and said, "You have a deal."

CHAPTER 30

Before Lincoln set out, he requested and received twenty more rounds of ammunition. Abdulla lent him a small rucksack provisioned with flatbread, dried mutton, and a canteen of water. He asked Abdulla to tell Johnny and Jake that he was off on a hunt—no more detail than that—and that he'd be back by three. He didn't want to offend them, but they would only slow him down.

As he was leaving, Abdulla said to him, "It is a forest of many mysteries. Be prudent."

The trail of the beast, which, Lincoln had decided, must be some sort of huge boar, was easy to follow—at first, anyway. It led deep into the forest, and the deeper he went, the denser the growth became.

A mile and a half in, he found a bloody patch of gray-haired skin on the ground. After another mile or so, the trail crossed a shallow creek. Thick underbrush lined the far side, broken by what looked almost like a tunnel where something big had crashed through the thicket. He knew the dangers of following a bear through dense growth, the bear waiting to attack until you were confined and distracted with trying to get through the brush. And getting through this thicket would take precious time, for there was at least fifty yards of it. Those acacias had nasty thorns too. He decided to circle around and try to pick up the trail just beyond the densest growth.

Traversing around, he found the thicket's end, on a steep, rocky slope. After the crest of this rise came a sheer drop-off into a heavily timbered canyon. It took him some time to pick his way down the slope, slipping several times on loose scree. At the bottom was another creek, this one narrower and shallower than the last. The bank on the other side was covered with another thick wall of thorny bushes.

He waded up and down the bank, looking for where the boar had come out of the creek. After going several hundred feet in both directions, he saw no tracks but did find a narrow trail leading up from the stream.

As it was the only way up from the creek, Lincoln climbed up the trail cautiously, holding his rifle ready. After about thirty feet, the ground leveled off and the forest began again. A couple hundred yards in, Lincoln saw a clearing in the forest and, in the clearing, the remains of a broken-down old hut. He approached the hut carefully, thinking that maybe some wild animal had taken up its abode there. With his rifle up, he kicked open the door. The inside was festooned with cobwebs and contained a ramshackle old table, an overturned chair, a few shelves, and a pallet for a bed. It appeared vacant of any human presence for quite some time.

As Lincoln turned to leave, he noticed what looked like the remains of a book on the floor beneath the shelves. He picked it up and brushed it off. Much of the book had been ripped apart by some animal, and only part of its white vellum jacket remained. But clearly discernible on the first page of the book was a picture of a mounted knight with a lance, battling some sort of dragon. With no time to dally, he tore the page from the book, put it in his pocket, and continued his pursuit.

Moving deeper into the forest, Lincoln picked up the trail of the big boar's tracks. Soon, another trail merged with the main path. And this trail was filled with cloven tracks of several other boars and possibly more, the smallest of which, according to the tracks, was the size of the largest boar he had encountered in the mountains of southwestern Texas. The big one might have a mate or even a harem of three or four sows. And these could be just as mean as the monstrous boar he was tracking, especially if they had a drift of little ones. He cocked his rifle.

The path dipped into a shallow wooded gully. Some fifty yards beyond, across a small creek, a large granite outcropping jutted out. The trail led toward a crevice that opened into what was likely the boar's den. Lincoln crept behind a cluster of rocks in front and slightly to the left of the opening. From this angle, he could see farther into the depths of the cave. Also, he didn't want a head-on shot of the boar. Animals with horns or tusks typically had hard skulls. The best shot was slightly from the side, through the upper shoulder, where the bullet would also pierce the heart or some other vital organ. And Lincoln didn't want to need more than a single shot. Whatever the creature was, it was likely huge and fast, and there could be a sow or two in the cave.

Now, how to roust the boar out of his cave? After the heavy meal of the mule, the boar could be sleeping. Lincoln wondered whether that could be to his advantage should the boar, like a human, need time to awaken fully. After waiting a few moments, he threw a good-size rock into the opening. Nothing happened for about five seconds. Then a reddish-brown sow charged out of the cave, to Lincoln's right. Its black face was uplifted, its open jaws baring lower tusks longer than his fingers. Though a sow, it was bigger than any boar Lincoln had ever seen. Should he take this one or not? Where was the big boar? He couldn't delay. He aimed and fired, hitting it through the neck, just above the shoulder. The sow crashed to the ground three paces from him.

Lincoln cocked his rifle, fixing his eyes on the opening of the cave and expecting the huge boar to come charging out at any moment. For seconds that seemed like minutes, nothing happened. Then, behind him, he heard the rustling of bushes and the clomping of heavy hooves.

As he spun around, a huge tusked boar bolted out of the forest on the same trail he had come in on. It was as big as a young buffalo, brown with a gray face and a black swath of wiry bristles down the ridge of its back. Lowering its head, it came at full tilt, ready to slash him with lower tusks the size of bowie knives. It was charging straight at him, so he didn't have the shoulder shot he wanted. The skull on this monster had to be as hard as oak.

As Lincoln aimed, the boar approached so close that Lincoln could see mucus spraying from its snout. Without thinking, he compensated for the rifle's problematic aim and fired.

The beast's head snapped down from the force of the bullet, its front legs collapsed, and the long snout plowed into the ground. It stopped so close to him that a thread of spittle from its mouth landed on Lincoln's shirtfront.

CHAPTER 31

Lincoln arrived back at the caravan at two, an hour before the time Abdulla had set to leave. As evidence of his kill, he brought the tusks of the big boar. He also cut out about twenty pounds of the sow's tenderloin. Wouldn't hurt to get on the good side of Tom Foote with a little gift.

He found the caravan arranged in circle, like a wagon train under attack. On hearing of the situation, Johnny and Jake had advised Abdulla of the tactic and then joined the guards patrolling the perimeter. In the process, they had encountered Tom Foote and acted as surprised and happy to see him as if he were a long-lost brother. They invited him to set up his shelter with theirs.

On seeing the giant tusks, the guards were almost as afraid of Lincoln as they were of the demon beast. To Gustave, he became a Perseus, returning victorious after slaying the Gorgon Medusa. Abdulla surrendered all claim to Lincoln's rifle without hesitation, saying he couldn't hit anything with it, anyway.

"Seems our pard's bite is a whole lot worse than his bark," Johnny said to Jake when Lincoln walked up. "We sure are glad you got your rifle back."

"We still owe you though," said Jake.

Johnny introduced Tom Foote to Lincoln, calling him "the most famous chef de cuisine on the seven seas." Tom almost blushed at the flattery and was delighted at the cut of tenderloin that Lincoln had brought.

Since they still had a few good hours of sunlight, the caravan got moving right away. They camped that night just a mile before beginning the descent down the mountain. Abdulla insisted they circle the caravan again.

While Johnny and Jake helped Abdulla, Lincoln managed to get Tom Foote talking, which wasn't difficult. "Yeah, I'm joining the Foreign Legion too," Tom said, "same as you and those friends o' yours. Got married a few years back, but it don't appear I'm cut out for the domesticated life." Moving closer to Lincoln, he lowered his voice. "But that ain't the real reason I'm joining. Last year, I was doing some merchant marining in Indochina. The French got a presence there, too, and a regiment of these Foreign Legion blokes was there. It was at their officers' club in old Saigon where I heard about Mur. And that's the place where a man interested in adventure and riches ought to be going. Ain't nobody had a chance to get in there and ransack the bloody place yet, like they did in Egypt.

"But here's the rub: them people are actually *European*. Could be the bloomin' lost ten tribes, or the remnants from Troy. That's my understanding of where the people of Mur come from, anyway."

Lincoln didn't bother to inform Tom that everything he had read about Mur put its founding at least a millennium before the Trojan War was fought or the ten lost tribes got lost.

"The point," Tom went on, "is, them Murians are smart 'cause they're Europeans, so you got to be smart dealing with 'em. But you stick with me and you'll be all right. Old Tom's been around a bit." Then he moved even closer and, in a conspiratorial tone, said, "Them details are only part of the story. The real rub is, there's heaps of treasure there, waiting to be plucked like fruit from a tree. Can you imagine that sawed-off runt Jake told me he was joining in the hope of collecting a herd of *horned rats*? I reckon him and Big John somehow got wind of the action too."

"That's not why I'm joining," Lincoln replied. "Can't say I'm much interested the treasure-finding business."

It took the caravan four more days to reach Sidi Bel Abbès. The closer they got, the hotter and dryer it became. Breaking camp in the predawn, they pushed hard to get to the city before the real heat of the last day. An hour before noon, when they reached the outpost, it was already one hundred and fifteen degrees in a camel's shadow—the only shade to be had.

The caravan stopped just outside the city walls. After saying their farewells to Abdulla and leaving Gustave with a sizable bonus, Lincoln, Johnny, and Jake, now with Tom Foote in tow, entered the town.

Lincoln's expectation that the farther he got into wilds of North Africa, the farther he would leave modernity behind him, got a bit of a jolt on his arrival. The town was only about fifty years old. Build on the Wadi Mékerra, it had grown out of a French military fort. Although the Foreign Legion now made up only a tenth of the population, the European influences were everywhere apparent. Even the city wall, with its four gates, looked new. The only thing he appreciated about the town was its souk, the local bazaar.

Then he got his first look at the French Foreign Legion.

CHAPTER 32

The outside of Legion Headquarters looked like a midsize nineteenth-century French hotel. Indeed, the legionnaire at the city gate who gave Lincoln directions had said, "You mean hotel to hell." He chuckled to himself when he said it.

The French tricolor and the Legion's own flag flew above the building, but the large double doors were locked. Four other hopeful enlistees were waiting outside the building: two Germans who had been with the caravan, a middle-aged Italian, and a young Swede whose white eyebrows glowed against his sunburned face. The Italian told them the office was closed for another ten minutes, until one o'clock.

At precisely one, a Legion corporal opened the doors from within and came outside. He looked the potential recruits over with evident distaste, muttered an oath in German, and then, in French, ordered them to come in and stand at attention.

They found themselves in a spotless room with two large wooden desks in the middle, and pine benches lining the wall opposite the desks. One of the desks was the corporal's. Behind the other, meticulously clean with four small stacks of paper arranged on its blotter, sat a chief sergeant. He didn't appear very absorbed in his work, for he spent most of his time looking at the recruits, also with unconcealed disgust. Behind the desks were three doors. One bore a placard reading Commandant de Brigade Brannon. Another door's placard read Capitaine Duvoe. The walls were covered with plaques, pictures of legionnaires, and framed letters of commendation.

After about three minutes, the chief sergeant, in the accented French of a non-native speaker, said, "Why you have come here, I cannot possibly imagine; neither do I want to know. You have been extremely foolish in coming. If you decide to join us, you will find this out soon enough. The enlistment period for a legionnaire is five years. Once you join, nothing but death will get you out. If you survive, fifteen years' honorable service earns a pension. In a few minutes, you will hear from Commandant de Brigade Brannon. You may sit at ease until then."

After another twenty minutes, the door marked Commandant opened, and the officer walked out, slightly dragging his right leg. The chief sergeant called, "Attention!" as he and the corporal sprang up and saluted sharply. The commandant saluted them back with his left arm. The empty right sleeve of his tunic was pinned neatly behind him.

The man's presence evoked awe and respect. Short, broad-shouldered but trim, not far past middle age, perhaps of Irish heritage. His face was ruddy from years of exposure to tropical sun, and his hair was close-cropped and gray, as was his goatee. With his one good eye, he gauged the caliber of those who stood before him. "Welcome, potential recruits," he finally said in French seasoned with the lilt of his warrior island. "Thank you for your interest in our army. You will follow me and you will clearly understand the journey upon which you are considering embarking."

The corporal opened the door without a name placard, and the commandant led the recruits through. They entered a large, immaculate room filled with all manner of Legion regalia. The walls were covered with medals, military ribbons and banners, famous weapons, battle and battalion flags, pictures of famous legionnaires wearing their decorations and medals, and a number of paintings depicting famous Legion battles. On pedestals sat the busts of famous legionnaires with inscriptions telling of their valiant deaths. Set apart in various sections of the room were nine sculpted marble or brass monuments to famous Legion battles, and display cases of spent bullets, broken and bloodied bayonets, and tattered, half-burnt battle flags.

The commandant gave the applicants a few moments to gape in awe at the historic artifacts around them. And Lincoln did exactly that. His imagination was inflamed with visions of battle and valor. But it was not only this that moved him. It was also the Legion's manifest loyalty in memorializing its fallen sons, and its tradition of courage and honor. All the applicants remained silent.

After a few more moments of silence, the commandant said, "The Foreign Legion is the most elite fighting force in the world. It remains so, in part, by telling potential recruits exactly what they can expect if they choose to join us, and also by our steadfast allegiance to our traditions. These," he said, pointing around the room, "are monuments to our most curious tradition, for they celebrate not victories but defeats, in which our men died valiantly rather than suffer ignominious surrender."

The commandant led the applicants to one of the monuments, a six-foot-high marble obelisk with a plaque on each of its sides, listing the names of the fallen. "This is from the Third Battle of Madagascar. Thirty men held off five hundred corsairs for ten days. When the Thirty's ammunition was spent, they charged with their bayonets. None survived."

After giving them a few minutes to inspect the monument, the commandant walked a few feet to the middle of the room. "Do your duty," he said, "and we don't care whether you were a prince or a poet, a saint or a scoundrel who stole the crown jewels. We don't care about your name, where you come from, or why you left. A superstition we cherish is that asking about one's past brings bad luck. So if you don't wish to die in your sleep, keep your past to yourself and let your fellow legionnaires do the same."

He strode to a small brass replica of a pagoda, mounted on a marble pedestal. "This is from our glorious storming of Sơn Tây in Tonkin. Before that charge, the battalion received its famous message from General de Négrier: 'You, Legionnaires, you are soldiers in order to die, and I am sending you where you can die.'" He paused, straightened himself, and said with great solemnity, "And die valiantly is what my brothers in arms did—all but five of us. I gave but a leg, an arm, and an eye. They gave their lives."

After letting the prospective recruits examine the memorial, he led them to the largest and most commanding of the monuments. In the center of the room stood an ornate pale-blue marble pedestal with a wooden hand resting on it. In a semicircle around it, on three slightly smaller pedestals of the same material, were the busts of three legionnaires. "This is from our grandest memory of all: the Battle of Camarón."

"I never knew they fought in Mexico," Lincoln mused, quietly but loud enough for the commandant to hear.

"Excuse me?" he said, apparently amazed that an applicant would have the temerity to speak in his presence.

"It wasn't anything," Lincoln said.

"Sixty-five men," the commandant went on, "held off two thousand Mexican troops until only six legionnaires remained. Led by one-handed Captain Henri d'Anjou, they fixed their bayonets and charged into the jaws of the Mexican army. This is all that remains of the captain." He picked up and showed them the captain's actual wooden hand. "D'Aanjou and two others died in the charge. The remaining three were severely wounded. The Mexican army honored their gallantry, releasing them when they had recovered. The Three from Camarón are legend in the Foreign Legion. If you choose to join our ranks, you will have the great privilege of serving with them in the country of Mur."

The commandant returned the hand to its pedestal. "If you choose to join, you'll be sent to Fort Flatters in Mur, where you will undergo your training. After six weeks, you will receive the white kepi and take on full rights, privileges, and responsibilities of a legionnaire, in the regiment guarding the dam that France has built for the king of Mur.

"I ask you to think hard if you want to spend the next five years where, if the heat and the weather, or the cafard or the Tsetse flies, or the dervishes don't kill you, and you do your duty, then you will have deserved the privilege to be called a Legionnaire. And remember this: the Legion does not surrender." He paused, taking time to look each recruit in the eye. "You have twenty-four hours to decide."

"I don't need twenty-four hours," Lincoln blurted out, quickly adding, "sir."

"It is regulations, in case you are drunk or temporarily out of your mind," the commandant thundered, plainly amazed that anyone should speak up twice in his presence.

CHAPTER 33

"Nothing we can do about it," said Johnny. "Those boys don't seem to have a whole lot o' flex in their regulations." He, Lincoln, Jake, and Tom Foote were standing in the street outside Legion Headquarters.

"I'm sure it's not as bad as he was making it out," said Lincoln.

"He's not realizing the quality of the crew he's dealing with here," said Jake. "Just trying to discourage the lowlifes, I imagine."

"What the bloke said is worth listening to," said Tom, whose army experience was a far cry from the hardships of the average foot soldier. "Five years! I wish there was another way to get into the bloody place."

"Well, I'm all for it," said Lincoln. "It's just what I was hoping for."

Tom looked at Lincoln as if he were out of his mind.

"What you worrying about, Tom?" said Johnny. "You'll more than likely end up cooking for the dern general while native girls fan you with palm fronds and feed you dates."

"If you think cooking for a bunch of stuck-up high-and-mighties is easy," Tom said, "you can just think again. I'd be out there pounding sand with you any day, but keeping the officers from getting grouchy over bad grub is a duty. Can you imagine that commandant on a sour stomach?"

"Could be some competition for you in this army," said Jake. "The

French are supposed to be good in the galley, not like your Britishers or Australians. Not that their cuisine is to my taste—their portions tend to be on the light side."

"I'll take the challenge," Tom said, "and don't you be lumping us Diggers so close with the British. We may share blood, but not taste buds."

"Tom's got nothing to worry about, from no Frenchy or anyone else," Johnny said, giving Jake a look that seemed to say he thought it unwise to goad Tom too much in such a sensitive area. If Tom did end up cook of the officers' mess, "friend of the cook" was a position of power.

"Well, I'm for heading to the hotel," Johnny went on, apparently desiring to get away from the touchy subject and out of the heat. The Legion sergeant had given them vouchers for rooms in a hotel two blocks away. "I could use a good bath and a snooze."

Jake and Tom Foote agreed, and the three of them set off for the hotel. Lincoln said he would come along after a while, but he wanted a look around the city first.

He lingered in front of the building, thinking about the commandant's speech and all the monuments. He was so excited, he didn't notice to the two native men standing in the shadows across the street, watching him.

Lincoln decided to go back inside. After the sergeant spat out some loud and not so elegant French oath asking him what he was doing back in the building, Lincoln asked him if he could look at the monuments again. The sergeant told him it took most recruits a least a few weeks in the desert before they got the insanity of *le cafard*, but apparently he had already got it. He added that if the young American idiot didn't get out in five seconds, he would be shot. Lincoln mumbled something back about not needing twenty-four hours to decide, then left and wandered off toward the bazaar.

What Johnny and Jake really wanted was to get free of Tom Foote and see what information they could uncover around town about the treasures of Mur. Once Tom joined them in the caravan, they had tried to stay clear of

the subject. When Tom had said, "So, any particular reason you chaps joining up with the Legion?" Johnny replied, "Oh, we're just lookin' for one last
adventure before we go and settle down in some homey hamlet on the prairie." Jake added, "We're interested in getting a look at the wildlife in these
parts. Hear they got some interesting critters they got nowhere else."

But Tom wasn't buying it. He had spoken openly to Lincoln about
the treasure and had repeatedly tried to draw Johnny and Jake out on the
subject. But they could be every bit as slippery with their answers as Tom.
They didn't need or want another partner in their enterprise.

The three of them checked into their hotel, and Johnny and Jake made
it plain they would be catching up on a little sleep. Tom said he might as
well do the same. After a few minutes, Johnny and Jake slipped out and
went off to the section of town where, according to the hotel clerk, they
would find several old antique and curiosity shops that often carried Murian
artifacts. Also in these shops were a few old and wise men who might have
some knowledge about the ancient country where they were going.

These shops were located on the far side of the bazaar, close to the city's
western gate. It was a five-minute walk through streets no more than six or
seven feet wide, with buildings crammed next to each other and two or three
stories high. In the narrow streets, at least, they were shaded from the sun.

They turned into the first shop they came to. The place had an assort-
ment of used goods and trinkets: sashes, silken cushions, leather tobacco
pouches, hunting bags of Moroccan leather with embroidered seams, gleam-
ing scimitars of Damascus steel, silver-hilted daggers inlaid with semiprecious
stones, leather knee boots, velvet slippers embroidered in gold and silver with
upturned toes, chechia caps worn by the Zouaves, and an array of various firearms, mostly old with long barrels and short wooden stocks. There were also
jewels and adornments, oil lamps large and small, and a few old books.

The proprietor of the shop approached them. A native in his midthir-
ties, he wore a long black beard, a white skull cap, and a long white muslin
shirt that came down past the knees of his white britches. "May I be of
assistance?" he asked in French, in a supercilious tone.

Jake was trying to figure out how, without drawing too much attention, he might bring up the subject of Mur. Johnny didn't like the guy, who

seemed like the sort who would try to sell him a one-horned goat and call it a unicorn.

"Is there something you are interested in?" the storekeeper asked.

They were still working out just how to broach the subject when Jake saw, in a glass cabinet, a set of miniature porcelain sheep. "Rodents—*horned* rodents," he said. "I was wondering if you got any horned rodents. Stuffed ones, I mean, though I wouldn't mind seeing one live. I've heard they're a species in this part of the world, and I—"

"No, my friend," the proprietor said, "those of the horned variety are exceedingly rare. On occasion, I come by one or two, but they are terribly expensive. If you are interested, I might be able to find one for you. Please tell me where you are staying, and I will contact you."

"We'll be at the Hotel St. Martin for one more night," Jake said. "The name is Jones."

"Very well," the proprietor said. "Is there anything else?"

"Well, yes," said Johnny. "We're looking for information you might have about where we're going to be stationed—especially old maps."

"You are interested in the lost treasures of Mur, as well?" said the shop-keeper.

"To some degree," said Johnny. "You get many inquiries on the subject?"

"On occasion. That gentleman over there was also inquiring," he said, pointing to a man in the adjoining room, whose back was toward them and who had a head so large it had to be Tom Foote. He had obviously been eavesdropping on their conversation.

"Ain't interested in Murian treasures, are you?" Tom said, coming out of the room and slapping his leg. "Do you think old Tom is such a fool not to see that you two were on the same trail as myself? Why, of course I knew."

"Well, maybe we are and maybe we ain't," said Jake. "I don't see how that's any business of yours at the moment."

"It makes no sense, mates, not to pool our resources," said Tom. "But perhaps we ought to take our parley elsewhere," he added, giving the two of them a wink, "if you get my meaning? Why don't we go catch ourselves a little fresh air?"

The three of them went outside and stood in the shade of the building. "What's on your mind, Tom?" said Johnny.

"First of all," Tom said, "that bloody shopkeeper's a crook if ever there was one. He tried to sell me a map that was about the worst fake I ever seen. Second of all, I heard you asking him about the horned rats. Well, some peddler tried to sell me one back in Béjaïa, and I confess I bought a mounted one, set up like a miniature big-game trophy—I know, contradiction in terms. And what did I discover in about two hours but that the horns were carved out of dog bone or something and stitched and glued onto the head of a stuffed wharf rat. I tell you, I went back to that blighter's booth in a hurry, but he'd packed up and skedaddled."

Johnny graced Jake with an I-told-you-so look, but when Jake got his sights set on something, they didn't get unset very easily, especially on the word of Tom Foote. "Don't mean nothing," Jake said. "Just 'cause he bought a counterfeit don't mean there ain't real ones about. Besides, our pard, Smith, read about 'em in a book."

"Well, suit yourself," said Tom. "My point is, I know your purpose for joining the Legion, and it's the same as mine, and it's a big job we're undertaking, especially as we're going to be doing it while soldierin' six days a week and sometimes seven. Now, I've acquired a lot of knowledge about Mur, and a map that I think's reliable, though you can't always be sure, 'cause there's a lot of fakes, like I just found out again in this shop. So don't you see, it just makes sense that we throw in together. There's bound to be treasure enough for the three of us."

Johnny motioned with his eyes to Jake, suggesting their need for a conference. They strode ten paces away. "He might have a point," Jake said. "If, 'cause of his cooking, he gets in good with the company commander, it could be valuable. It might affect our duties, and it would be good for the nutrition. And there's bound to be enough treasure for all of us. I say let's take it to Smith."

"I suppose you're right. There ain't a lot that goes around he don't know about, and his information usually is at least partially reliable. Still, it galls me just the same."

"There's something to what you're saying," Johnny said to Tom after they walked back to where he waited. "But we already got us a partner in young Smith, who's a solid man and able despite his years."

"Then it'll be the four of us," said Tom.

"I ain't opposed to the concept," said Johnny, "if it's okay with Smith."

"Me neither," said Jake, "but it ain't our call. We'll discuss it with our young pard."

"Okay, then, let's go find him," said Tom.

"Hold your horses," said Johnny. "Since we're here, we might as well look around these shops some."

There were three other shops on the street. In the first two, they found little of interest. Both shopkeepers claimed to know most everything there was to know about Mur, but the information would be expensive. One even gave them a glance at two maps—one of the supposed lost mines and another of lost temples. They were obvious fakes. They were nothing like the map Johnny and Jake had gotten from the German sergeant.

In the third and last shop, they had a different experience. Located at the end of the street, close to the city gate, it was smaller than the others and not as well lit. Inside, they found a boy of about fourteen behind the counter. The boy eyed them without saying anything. The room was loosely divided into three sections, one displaying old books, parchments, and pictures; another devoted to hookahs, narghiles, and tobacco in clay jars that filled several shelves; and a third section that held a modest collection of small statuary and figurines in brass, silver, and stone.

Tom and Johnny looked around the first section. Since all the books were in languages they couldn't read, nothing really caught their interest. Jake went immediately to the section with the statuary and sculptures. After a few minutes, Johnny and Tom came over to find him staring at a beautiful gold sculpture of a man in primitive armor fighting a dragon. The dragon, about thrice the man's size, didn't appear to be of the fire-breathing sort but looked more akin to some modern reptile. Looking around more closely, they found a number of other sculptures of the same theme.

"If I ain't mistaken," said Johnny, "these could be Murian. There's a story of some king there that fights a dragon."

"I think you're right," said Tom. "His name was King Sol. It was his treasure that's supposed to be the main hoard that was lost. Him fighting the dragon has something to do with their religion."

Seeing them looking at the sculptures, the boy walked up to them from behind the counter. When he still didn't say anything, Tom said, "Mur?"

The boy just stood eyeing them suspiciously.

"Mur?" Tom said again.

The boy still didn't answer.

"We are looking for information about Mur," said Tom in the bastard patois that he had learned in French Guinea. He held out a franc note. The boy didn't take the franc, but turned and walked back behind the counter and through a doorway blocked off by a hanging blanket.

"Talkative young fellow, ain't he?" said Jake.

"Maybe he just don't understand your lingo," said Johnny.

After a minute or so, the boy came back and motioned for them to follow him into the room behind the counter. On a cushion in the corner of the room sat a very old man, smoking a narghile. A few strands of wispy white hair hung from his head, and a long white beard came down to the middle of his chest. The light in the room was even dimmer than in the outer room. As the three of them came closer to the old man, they saw that both his eye sockets were empty.

"What do you seek in Mur?" the old man asked in French.

"We're on our way there with the Foreign Legion and was just wanting to find out what we could about the place," Tom said.

"You, too, seek her treasure. You are not aware of what you do."

"From what we hear, might not be any," said Johnny. "So don't see as there'd be any harm in taking a look. We're looking for clues that might aid our investigation."

The old man took a puff from the pipe and reclined his head on the wall behind him, letting the smoke trickle out of his crooked and toothless mouth. "Mur, the blessed and the damned. The treasure there is not the treasure you seek."

"Well, I guess we could settle for most any kind," Jake said.

"My grandfather is from the great city," said the boy, who had been standing next to the old man. "And I, too, have the blood of Mur."

"I advise you not to go," said the old man.

"And why's that, old man?" asked Tom Foote, walking toward him. The boy moved between the old man and Tom.

"There is violence and death in the streets. The followers of Thanatos arise. The French suppose they are a match for Thanatos. They are fools. And you are fools to go to Mur. Thanatos cannot be overcome."

"Well, if that's all you got for us," said Jake, "we're much obliged." A dare like this only hardened his resolve.

"He is a deceiver and devoid of mercy," the old man said.

"The warning's been noted," Johnny said. "We surely do appreciate your time." The boy led the three of them back into the main room.

"Thanks for letting us see your gramps," Johnny said, and handed the boy two francs.

This time, the boy took the money. "It is Thanatos who took his eyes," he said. "You would do well to listen to the wisdom of the ancients."

"That old codger," said Tom, standing with Johnny and Jake in the street outside the shop, "had one point I've been thinking about myself."

The sun now was almost directly overhead, and there was little shade to be found even in the narrow street. A hot breeze blew through the open gate in the city wall twenty feet away, which made it even hotter.

"What are you worryin' about?" Jake asked. "You think some dragon god is going to come along and rip out your eyes?"

"That ain't what I'm worryin' about, not with good partners like you two around to protect me."

"We ain't partners yet," said Jake. "We told you, till we talk it over with Smith."

"I know, I know, but what got me thinking is what that blighter back there in the Legion hall said. Five years in, and no way out except in a pine box. The old man said it, too, that we'd be fools to join up with the French army. I just wish there was another way we could get in."

"I don't see any way around it," Johnny said. "We gotta join to get in, and once we're in, how else we going to get out in less than five years?"

"Maybe there ain't no way 'round it," said Tom. "But I wish there was."

"Come tomorrow, it ain't going to be an issue anymore anyway," said Jake.

To the right of where they stood, the street led back the way they had come, through the marketplace. To the left, the street ended at the city's western gate, where a native man came through, leading a camel and four mules. Lying across the backs of the mules were four dead bodies. The man and the animals passed right in front of them, heading toward the center of town.

"Hold yourself up there, mate," Tom said to him, seeing from the style of the dead men's clothes and the color of their hair that they were European. "What happened to these poor blighters?"

The man stopped and looked his questioner up and down. Seeing that Tom was European, he replied, "A few miles from the Owasi oasis I found them, on my way back from Mur. They had been robbed—not by Tuaregs, or they would have been cut open and worse. Probably by whoever they hired to lead them to Mur. Do you know these men?"

Tom lifted up the heads of the dead men by the hair and looked at their faces. "Did you say they were on their way to Mur?"

"That is the only place they could have been going out in the desert," the man said.

"Did you find any of their papers?" asked Tom.

"In their bags are many papers. I do not read the English."

"I believe these are our brethren who we have been sent to find," said Tom. "I will need to look over their papers."

The camel driver nodded at the reasonable request. Tom then started going through the dead men's satchels, pulling out certain papers. Johnny and Jake looked on in disgust.

"Yes, our poor, dear countrymen—it is them," he said, after examining a number of their documents and putting four of them in his pocket. "Yes, our fellow Englishmen, from our newspaper, the *Manchester Guardian*.

"You have done our newspaper a great service in saving the bodies of our beloved comrades," Tom said to the camel driver. "We would like to pay you for your trouble." And here he pulled out a five-franc note and gave it to the man. "Please see that our comrades are buried. I will take charge of their papers and effects."

After the camel driver unloaded what was left of the dead men's belongings, he started off. But Tom called him back. "Do you indeed know well the route to Mur?"

"Yes, I am Murian and regularly come here to trade."

"And would you know a way to lead us there, in a way that we might avoid the fate that befell our dear friends?"

"First, the guides they hired were thieves and murderers. That was the only mistake they needed to make. But also, I would not advise taking mules or horses, but fast camels like my swift Filali," he said, pointing to the sleek-looking beast he had in tow. "If you are stout riders, I could get you there in two days. On occasion, I act as a guide across the desert."

"There would be a total of four of us going."

"I have access to more like Filali."

"Tom, you best not go making any commitments for us," said Johnny.

"Keep your knickers on," said Tom. "I ain't committing to anything yet, just priming the shot."

Tom fixed it that he would meet the camel driver at his hotel early the next morning and discuss an arrangement. Then the camel driver walked off toward the center of town, leading his camels and the four corpse-laden mules.

"They were newsmen, writing for some English paper," Tom said when the camel driver was out of earshot, "on their way to Mur to write up about it getting electricity and all. Don't you see, they let journalists in if they got papers, and now *we* got papers. We'll go in as English newsmen. It's just what we've been looking for."

CHAPTER 34

Lincoln was wandering through the bazaar of Sidi Bel Abbès. Walking slowly, his rifle slung over his shoulder, carrying his satchel, he was lost in a reverie. The bazaar was just as noisy but more rudimentary than the marketplace in Béjaïa, teeming with sights, sounds, and even smells he had never experienced before. From a street vendor, he bought a pocket bread filled with fresh grilled lamb, beans, and vegetables, all flavored with a delicious yogurt sauce. He ate it a few booths down while watching a snake charmer drone away on a reed pipe as a cobra slowly extended its length out of a basket. At another booth, a man and his son were selling small oil lamps like the ones he'd seen in picture books of *A Thousand and One Nights*. At another booth, he joined a crowd watching a frighteningly thin man, wearing only a loincloth, swallow a two-foot-long sword.

Lincoln's thoughts also ranged to the Legion and to the life he was about to embark on. The sergeant wasn't such a bad fellow, even if he had threatened to have Lincoln shot. He liked the man's directness. If this was a typical Legion noncom, it was fine with him. The sergeant was a guardian of the tradition, and not just anybody got to be part of that tradition. One had to earn it. Lincoln would be worthy and earn the respect of his fellow legionnaires. He wouldn't want it any other way. He didn't know what that tradition meant to others, but to him it had come to represent all that he longed for. "The Legion does not surrender"—the words were seared like great poetry into his soul. It was the code, and these people lived and, sometimes, died by it. Now he had one more day to wait and he would be part of the same noble tradition. He would be a legionnaire, and he, too, would never surrender.

Walking along, he came to the booth of a camel-and-horse trader. Three camels were hobbled behind the booth, and tied to a post in front were two splendid Arabian mares. He stopped to take a closer look at the animals. As he stood inspecting one of the horses, a young voice said, "Hey, Yank, maybe the mule they give you in the Foreign Legion not so good as my Khadidja, ey?"

Lincoln looked up to see a teenage boy giving him a big, toothy smile from across the booth. The boy walked up to Lincoln and looked him up and down.

"How do you know I'm joining the Legion?" Lincoln asked.

"They all come for the Legion. Or for treasure. But you look an honest hom-ber-rey," he said. "Maybe you are from Dodge City?"

"Close. I'm from Texas."

"Ah, Texas, the Lone Planet State of the Texas Rangers. I knew you were not a queenhorn."

"It's *greenhorn*, and it's the Lone *Star* State—not planet."

"I am Omar, a student of the American West, and have drunk long and deep from the springs of its literature." The boy pulled from the pocket of his robe two dime novels, *Wild Bill and the Dead Man's Hand* and *Cochise's Last Warpath*.

"I wouldn't believe everything you read in those books, kid," Lincoln said.

For a fleeting moment, the boy seemed perplexed at the statement. But Lincoln, sensing his confusion, added, "But some of them can be somewhat accurate."

The boy nodded as if he understood Lincoln, though he clearly didn't.

Across the way in a rug dealer's booth, two Arabs stood behind some hanging carpets, watching Lincoln.

"In the Legion," Omar said, "you will be stationed in Mur. My venerable uncle is the great camel-and-horse trader of the city. I go often there to visit and work. Perhaps you instruct me about the Old West and its ways, yes?"

"I don't think I'm going to be having a whole lot of spare time," said Lincoln.

"But then, now is not maybe the best time to join the Foreign Legion. Maybe we both go to the Indian Territory and fight the Dalton Gang."

"Why isn't it the best time to join the Legion?"

"In Mur, there is now violence and death. Thanatos and his followers don't like the French's dam. Unless you are a tough hom-ber-rey, you best stay here and teach me ways of west of the Pecos."

"It's *hombre*, and if you're going to curse, you might as well get it right—it's *the damn French*."

"No, no, it is the dam's electricity, up on the river. But King Suleiman, my noble kinsman, is not to be frightened by the people of the dragon."

"Well, maybe it'll get interesting there. That's okay by me."

"I hope you will not have a Big Little Horn, like your General Custer."

"Custer was a proud fool. And he was busted down to colonel."

"Did he not have fine weapons like your rifle?"

"His weapons weren't the problem."

"I would like to trade for your rifle and also for your spurs. They would fit well with my boots." Omar pointed down to show Lincoln the old and worn pair of Western boots he was wearing, which were at least two sizes too big for him. "And I also have this I traded from one of your countrymen last year." Omar displayed his US Seventh Cavalry belt and buckle, identical to Lincoln's.

"No thanks, not interested in trading. I got to get moving on." He started to walk away.

"Perhaps, we will meet in Mur, then, at my uncle's camel booth? And you will teach me more of hombres and the ways of the West, yes?"

"I'm sorry, but I doubt I'm going to have the time."

Walking on, he came to the last booth at that end of the bazaar. On a rug, amid various trinkets and cooking utensils, was a two-foot bronze figurine of a knight fighting a dragon. He squatted down to have a closer look. As he stood back up, a great force hit him from behind. Lincoln pitched forward on the ground, dropping his satchel.

After a few moments Lincoln regained consciousness and immediately realized his rifle and satchel were gone. He shook himself, got to his feet, and took off after the thieves.

At his booth, Omar saw two scraggly-looking Arab men running his way, carrying the young American frontiersman's fine rifle. He jumped out from behind the counter and tried to tackle the one carrying the rifle. Omar managed to knock him down, but the other man came back and whacked Omar over the head with the American's satchel. The two thieves ran off, up one of the lanes intersecting the main street of the bazaar.

Omar was still sprawled on the ground when Lincoln ran up. "They went up there," Omar said, pointing to the second lane on the left.

Lincoln didn't slow down, but ran up the lane. Omar jumped up and ran after him. Lincoln lost sight of them when they ran up another crowded alleyway, but saw them again as they broke out and turned down a different street. He ran after them, up a street that led to one of the city gates. The gate was open for the day's commerce, with the great expanse of open desert stretching beyond it. As Lincoln sprinted toward the gate, the two thieves, mounted on horses now, galloped away.

As Lincoln looked frantically about him for a way to give chase, Omar came running up, his too-large cowboy boots having slowed him some. "I am sorry, Yank," he said, breathing hard. "I should have warned you about thieves. They, too, liked your rifle."

"I have to get it back," said Lincoln. "It belonged to my father."

"I am afraid they will take your rifle and sell it to the Tuaregs or the slave traders," Omar said.

"Listen, kid, I need to borrow one of your horses. I have to get my rifle back!"

"They are not my horses. They belong to my uncle."

"I have to borrow one. I'll do anything."

"My uncle is not in the habit of lending his horses for chasing bandits through the desert."

"Come on, you have to help me. They're getting away!"

"They will be too far gone for you to catch them, even on an excellent horse."

"That's not an issue. I can track them."

This got the kid's interest. "Would you track them and produce an ambuscade, like an Apache, like the great Cochise?"

"I track Comanche. Apache tracking isn't beans to it."

"What is 'beans to it'?"

"Comanches were much better trackers than Apaches."

"You can track as the Comanche track?"

"Listen," Lincoln said, "you read many of those books you showed me?"

"I have fifty-three and have read each many times."

"Ever heard of Wes Smith? He was my father. I could show you some things those books don't even hint about."

"Marshal Wes Smith, the greatest shot in Texas!"

"He was a scout when he was young and learned tracking from Kit Carson. I could show you how."

Omar looked off in the distance, and Lincoln could see the gears turning. His imagination had just been fired with a flurry of wonderful images—visions of Omar, skilled tracker in the ways of the American Indian; Omar, scout and leader of troops; Omar, a hero of the Old West.

CHAPTER 35

The sun was still an hour above the horizon, and Lincoln and Omar had been in the saddle for almost three hours. Omar had secured two excellent Arabian mares from his uncle, under strict orders not to let them out of his sight.

Before setting out, Lincoln had sent a note to Johnny and Jake at the hotel. He had wrestled with what to say to them. He didn't want to tell them about his rifle, because they would want to help, which could throw off their plans. Omar was already more help than he wanted. Getting the rifle back was going to be tricky and probably dangerous, and he might not be back by morning. There was even the chance he might not make it back at all. He decided to tell them that something had come up that he hoped they would trust him about. He considered their offer of a partnership a great honor, but they weren't obligated to him in any way, and if he wasn't back by morning, they should go on without him. And although he would try, he couldn't promise he would be back.

Following the tracks of the thieves had been easy, and those tracks now led to a small oasis with the crumbled walls of a small ancient building adjoining it. Lincoln dismounted and looked at the tracks and some fresh horse droppings around the oasis. "They were here about an hour ago," Lincoln said. "We better slow up or we'll ride right up on top of them. We need to give our mounts a break, anyway."

"It is good to let them drink now," Omar said as they led their horses to the pool in the center of the Oasis. "But our Arabians are born for the desert and need not the water, or the rest that a Yankee palfrey requires."

"So you're an authority on American horseflesh?" Lincoln said.

"I have read it in my books. The horses of General Custer were no match for the mustangs of Sitting Bull. Is it not true?"

"Well, partly true. It wasn't only Indians who rode mustangs. I had one myself since I was kid." Lincoln dropped the reins to let his horse drink, and walked over to the ruins of the old limestone building. "So what was this?"

"All this land, to the edge of the desert, was once the domain of Mur. This was the ancient tomb of one of our minor kings. It was discovered many years ago."

"They find any of that treasure I keep hearing about?"

"No treasure was found here, but the mummies were in excellent condition. Perhaps the son of the great marshal comes here for other reasons than joining the Foreign Legion?"

"I didn't come looking for your old king's treasure, if that's what you mean."

"Many try to enter the country in search of it."

"The legends about your country are interesting. But I can't say I put a whole lot of stock in them." Lincoln walked back to the pool, knelt, and scooped a few mouthfuls of water.

"The legends are true," the boy said, following him to the pool. "My people come from a race who fled their island when it sank into the sea. Two dolphins led our ships to land, where we came and founded Mur. The ships carried great treasure, which was buried with King Sol after he died battling Thanatos, the crocodile god."

"You really *believe* all that?"

"The crocodile people do. They recently tried to kill our king."

"All my life, I wanted to get back to older times. Looks like I'm getting what I wanted."

Omar gave him an astounded look. "Fighting crazy worshippers of the god of the underworld is what you came here for?"

"No, but at least, it stirs my imagination." Lincoln walked back to the pond to retrieve his horse.

"I much prefer your American West with ban-did-oes, lawmen, and red Indians," Omar said, following him.

"It's all gone now," Lincoln said as he swung up into the saddle. "Even Buffalo Bill's turned into a dude businessman."

Omar quickly mounted. "But this is not what I have read in my books," he said, riding up next to Lincoln. "You must still teach me the ways of the Old West. We will be kicksides."

They rode on past dusk, and were thinking about stopping for the night when they caught the glare of a fire reflecting off the side of a sand dune a few miles ahead. A half mile from the fire, they dismounted and hobbled their horses. They went on foot until they came to a mound about fifty yards from the fire. At the top, lying prone, they peered over. Eight heavily armed turbaned men were sitting or standing around a large campfire. Behind the fire were three large goatskin tents, connected by covered passageways.

"Do you know who these guys are?" whispered Lincoln.

"Tuaregs—roaming mercenaries and slave traders. Are you sure they came here?"

"Do you doubt my tracking?"

The two men who stole Lincoln's rifle then walked out of the center tent, followed by a tall, broad-shouldered man. Wearing a black shirt buttoned to the neck, and blousy black pants, he wore no robe. In his thick belt were tucked two daggers and a revolver. And he was holding Lincoln's rifle.

"There they are," Lincoln said. "That's my rifle the big one's holding."

"This is not good," said Omar, dropping down below the crest of the mound. Lincoln scooted down below the crest as well. "They have sold your rifle to el-Krum. He is a man to be greatly feared."

"Don't worry. You can wait with the horses. If I'm not back in an hour, then you hightail it."

"Hightail it?"

"Take off as fast as you can and don't look back."

"But that is not proper. Doctor Holliday would not abandon his kickside. In the book—"

"You have to learn not to believe everything you read in those books."

A concerned look grew on Omar's face. He lowered his eyebrows and grabbed his chin. This seemed a difficult concept.

"It's called poetic license—you know, kind of a stretcher. The facts aren't what's important, anyway. It is the code."

"Yes, the code!" Omar brightened up. "Would Wild Bill Hickok abandon his kickside?"

"It's not the same."

"Would Wesley Smith, the greatest shot in Texas?"

"Okay, okay, but would you stop calling it *kickside*? It's *sidekick*, okay?"

From the tents below them, a timbrel and zills started tapping out a rhythm, and then a flute trilled an exotic, haunting melody. Lincoln and Omar edged back up the mound and looked over.

"El-Krum's harem have begun their dance," Omar said.

"He's got a harem? Okay, that might help." Lincoln slid back down below the dune's crest. "Here's what we'll do . . ."

In front of the camp, five Tuareg men-at-arms stood a little to the side of the entrance to the middle tent, peeking inside. Three harem girls danced before el-Krum and two of his lieutenants while another girl played the flute, and another beat a small hand drum.

Standing in the darkness at the rear of the central tent, Lincoln took the dagger from Omar's belt and cut a small slit in the fabric. He peeked inside. A large curtain hung down from the ceiling, blocking off a sleeping area from the main part of the tent. A kerosene lantern hanging from a tent pole was turned down low. No one was in the room.

He made the slit longer and slipped through it. A moment later, Omar followed him.

Inside the tent, the music was louder. Lincoln searched about the room for his rifle but found only a large bed of pillows and purple silk sheets, and a bag of clothes. Creeping to where the curtain abutted the wall of the tent, he peered around the edge. El-Krum and his men sat on plush cushions, their backs to him, about eight feet away, watching the dancers and smoking narghiles. To el-Krum's left and behind him, close to the heavy curtain that separated this tent from the next, was Lincoln's rifle. Omar peeked in, also.

Lincoln moved away from the curtain. Omar remained rooted there, mesmerized by the dance. Lincoln pulled on his sleeve, trying to get him to come away. Omar resisted for another moment, then both of them backed away from the curtain.

"It is the Dance of the Bumblebee!" Omar whispered. "I have never seen it before."

"Never mind that now. If we get into the next tent, I think I can reach my rifle."

"It is the harem tent."

"Yeah, I figured that. You think anyone else is in there?"

"The harem keeper, and possibly other women."

Lincoln went over to the bed and started wrapping himself in one of the sheets.

"What are you doing?" Omar said.

"We'll dress up like those girls."

"It is shameful for a warrior to dress as a woman."

"It's called *expediency*—standard practice in the West."

"Very well," Omar said with little enthusiasm, "but you must tell no one. My people do not understand the ways of the West."

After a few minutes, they had robed and veiled themselves in the sheets. In the dark, from a distance, they might conceivably pass for harem girls. Lincoln walked over to the curtain separating them from the harem tent and, pushing it slightly to the side, peeked in. The dimly lit room looked empty, though he couldn't see all the way to the back. He adjusted his veil, then nonchalantly walked in. Omar followed.

The flute and timbrel from the dance were still playing loudly. As Lincoln and Omar came in, they saw a robed and veiled woman walking with something in her hand, toward the corpulent, snoring mound that was the harem keeper. Seeing the two intruders, she turned her back and walked away.

Lincoln took a few steps toward her. Turning, she lunged at him with the dagger that she had been shielding behind her body. Lincoln caught the hand with the dagger and, putting his other hand over her mouth, pushed her to the tent floor and sat on her, holding her arms down with his knees. He didn't have to squeeze her wrist very hard to get her to release the dagger, but she chomped down hard on the hand covering her mouth. He almost cried out. Grabbing the dagger, he put it to her throat. Her jaw relaxed, and he extricated his bleeding hand. He shook his head, and the veil, already slipping, fell below his chin. "Sweetheart, if you make a sound or bite me again . . ."

With the dagger at her throat, he slowly pulled his hand away. She made an effort to free one hand from under Lincoln's knee, which he allowed. Then she defiantly pulled her veil down. It was not an Arab face, but European, with large sparkling eyes, even in the dim light of the tent, under raging fulsome eyebrows and a nose slightly Roman. "I'm not your sweetheart," she hissed, holding down her voice but not her outrage. "I am Amanda Montier."

Lincoln just continued to sit on her, bewildered and dazzled by her beauty. He had spoken to her in English and wasn't expecting a reply, hoping his threatening tone would be understood. With the loud trills of the flute, and the percussive banging on the timbrel, he wasn't sure he had heard her right, but it had sounded like French-accented English.

"What did you say?" he asked.

"I am Amanda Montier, daughter of the French ambassador to Mur. Now, if you don't want to create an international diplomatic incident, get off me at once."

"But . . . what are you *doing* here?" Lincoln asked. "And why are you dressed like that?"

"I've been kidnapped," she hissed back. "What's *your* excuse?"

Lincoln had forgotten what he was wearing. "Uh . . . I came to get my rifle. It's a long story, so just be quiet for now and I'll get you out of here."

"I demand to be taken to my father at once."

"Just be quiet," he said, getting off her and helping her up.

The harem keeper stirred and sat up. Lincoln and Omar turned away, adjusting their veils. The harem keeper stood up and walked toward them. Lincoln whirled about, putting a hand over his mouth, and the woman's dagger to his throat. The harem keeper's eyes nearly bulged out of his pudgy face.

"Make one peep, and I'll cut your balls off," Lincoln said to him in French.

"Idiot," the girl said. "He doesn't have any. How do you think he got the job?"

"What? Oh, right. Well, let's tie him up, then," Lincoln said.

Omar found three silk sashes among the clothes in the tent. Lincoln gagged and hogtied the plump and whimpering harem keeper. He was as helpless as a capsized tortoise.

Lincoln slashed a hole in the back of the tent, and the three of them squeezed out into the dark. Omar and the girl started off, but Lincoln just stood there.

"What are you doing?" said the girl. "Come on!"

He was thinking about his rifle, just a few feet from the curtain separating the two tents. Getting it was going to be dicey. He would be risking not only his life and Omar's, which was bad enough, but now he had this bratty French girl to think about—the ambassador's daughter, no less.

She got in front of Lincoln, a few inches from his face. "How *dare* you handle me that way! What kind of ruffian are you?"

"Okay, I'm sorry, but you were coming at me with a dern knife."

"You *sat* on me!"

"And you bit me! But I agree, it's no way to treat a girl, even if she's trying to give you rabies." He let out a long sigh.

"A *lady*," she said defiantly.

"Omar, take her to the horses. If I'm not there in five minutes, take off and ride as fast as you can to Sidi or Mur, whichever is closest."

"We are closer now to Mur," Omar said.

"Then ride there as fast as you can. Ride through the night if you have to."

"What are you talking about?" said the girl. "You don't mean you are leaving me!"

"Listen, I've got to get my rifle."

"What? That is the most unchivalrous thing I have ever heard of!"

Lincoln rolled his eyes, but the shot had hit its mark. If she had been a little nicer, he would have felt ashamed. "Omar," he said, "I'm going to have to save her rather than my rifle."

"A good woman or a good rifle," Omar said. "It is a difficult decision."

"I was just about to save myself," the girl said. "If your rifle's so important, I'll go get it."

He looked at her, not really entertaining the idea, but liking her spirit. Then he looked at Omar and said, "Maybe we ought to save those other women too."

"No! They are his wives! We need to get away from here—now!"

"Okay, you're right. Since I'm almost in the Legion now, I guess I better get her back to her daddy."

Amanda Montier didn't seem pleased with his words or the tone he spoke them in. But she said nothing. Lincoln grabbed her hand, and the three of them ran into the night.

Johnny and Jake didn't know what to make of Lincoln's letter. "You know it ain't that he's scared," said Jake. "Hearing 'bout all the hardships just made him want to join even more."

"Course not," said Johnny.

"Could he have found something even more miserable to do than join the Legion?" Jake wondered.

"Oh, some adventure must have come his way. That's got to be it. That's what the boy is looking for, adventure and a chance to get shot at. I only wish there was something we could do to help him avoid the latter."

But there wasn't. In the end, Johnny and Jake waited two extra days.

They would have waited longer, but what little money they had was running low. They must either enlist or succumb to Tom Foote's arguments about the advantages of going to Mur as "journalists," which Tom promised to finance. Tom said that if their friend turned up as a legionnaire, they would be free to join up then rather than leave him to face that fate alone. They finally agreed and, with the guide they had met, set out for Mur three days after Lincoln went missing—though without Tom Foote. The night before they left, the potwalloper had gotten himself stabbed by another Legion recruit, in a brawl in a Sidi nightclub. Johnny and Jake weren't there. They were keeping to their contract.

CHAPTER 36

Late the next afternoon, a crowd gathered in front of a second-story balcony of the Murian royal palace. An announcement had been made that King Suleiman would speak to his people that day. He was determined to show that in spite of his wound in the failed assassination attempt, he was undaunted by his enemies.

Inside the large room that opened onto the balcony, the Three from Camarón stood talking together. On the other side of the room, the king, his left arm in a sling, talked with Princess Salina, Prince Kamak, Fräulein Zads, and Colonel Hultz. Ambassador Montier was also in the group, though he looked distracted and was not adding to the conversation. Even after taking another sedative from the king's medicine man, he had hardly slept at all.

Various other Murian and foreign officials were in the room, waiting for the meal to be served after the ceremony. The Three from Camarón moved closer to the glass doors that opened onto the balcony. In a few moments, they would accompany the king as he presented himself to his people.

"He doesn't need to do this," Athos said to his two companions. "Not with the girl still missing." He especially didn't like that the king had over-ridden his order that a Legion guard be stationed in front of the palace. It had been pointless to try to talk him out of it.

"I daresay you'd do the same if you were he," Aramis said, "though I doubt you'd even let us go out on the balcony with you." The English legionnaire frequently chided Athos on his failure to follow his own guidance when it came to matters of personal safety. Some of the chances Athos took made it seem almost as if he *wanted* to die.

"Perhaps I should have volunteered to go out impersonating him," said Porthos. "Would I not look grand dressed in the robes of a king? We do share a similar noble appearance, don't you think?"

"No, no," said Aramis. "You're fatter, and he's much better looking."

Athos wasn't amused by his friends' attempts to lighten the mood. On top of all that had happened in recent days—the attempt on the king's life and the murder of his vizier—now Amanda Montier hadn't returned from yesterday morning's outing. He felt even more anxious about the ambassador's daughter than about the king's safety. Morose and melancholic by nature, today he wasn't at all in the mood for levity.

The Legion adjutant entered the room. After saluting the Three, he handed Athos a slip of paper.

Seeing the adjutant enter, Montier excused himself from the king's party and hurried over to the Three. "What is it? Have you any news?"

Athos took a deep breath and dismissed the adjutant, then handed the paper to Porthos.

"Is it news of my daughter?"

"They found her tutor's horse," Athos said.

"Yes. Anything else?"

"They found the tracks of twenty or more unshod horses leading from the ruins she was visiting. And her horse's tracks were with them."

"Is it the slave traders? Do we think it is el-Krum or whatever his name is?"

"They were riding in the direction of his camp," said Porthos. "I am afraid it must be."

The ambassador groaned and looked even worse than before. "She was not to ride more than five miles from the fort and not without a guard. That tutor of hers was useless. Those slavers have been plaguing us for long enough. How soon can Ruppert and the column be ready to go after them?"

"Ruppert and the column will leave at daybreak, and they'll find her and get her back," said Aramis.

"She'd got hold of an old map and couldn't wait to start exploring them. I saw no harm."

"If the column isn't back here within two days," Athos said, "I'm going after her myself. You two can continue to guard the king."

Outside, below the balcony, the crowd began to chant. "Suleiman! Suleiman! Suleiman!"

"Mur, bitter water of the desert," Omar said to Lincoln and Amanda. "The legends say its temple is older than the pyramids."

After riding through the night and much of the next day, Lincoln and Amanda on one horse, and Omar on the other had stopped on a bluff overlooking Mur. Lincoln was struck by the beauty of the ancient city with its thick stone wall, and the wooden gates with their elaborate pointed arches. Behind the walls, low sandstone buildings with terracotta roofs were shaded by many gently swaying date palms. Looming above these were several taller structures of white marble, with fluted pillars and large domed roofs. This was more like what Lincoln had hoped for: a place all but untouched by the modern world.

"It is splendid indeed," Lincoln said.

Just outside the city walls to the east were the bleached stone ruins of what must have been a large temple. But in this direction, the ancient aspect of the city was spoiled—for Lincoln, at least—by the presence of two motor trucks parked outside the ruins.

"What are those things doing over there?" Lincoln asked. "I thought I would be getting *away* from machines."

"They belong to Prince Kamak's German archaeologist friends," Amanda replied.

"He's looking for the lost treasure too?"

"No," she said. "The temple was discovered five years ago, but the tomb and treasure have not been found. He's cataloging artifacts. He's a scientific bore and is not interested in the legends."

"Well, aren't you the authority!" said Lincoln.

"She is correct," said Omar. "Prince Kamak is happy to find ancient pottery. And she is also correct that the prince is a very uninteresting man. He will not make a great king like his noble father."

"Doesn't sound like you're too fond of him either."

"Would you two quit blabbing and take me to my father?" said Amanda.

"You know, you could show a little gratitude for us rescuing you," Lincoln said. "I'm starting to have second thoughts about not saving my rifle."

"I was rescuing *myself* when you barged into the tent. I would have . . ."

"Look! Legionnaires are coming," Omar said. Three legionnaires had ridden out of city gate and were heading their way.

"Thank goodness," Amanda said. She kicked the horse she and Lincoln were on, and it dashed off toward the legionnaires.

"I am Amanda Montier," Amanda said to the lieutenant leading the patrol. "I've escaped from terrible brigands who tried to kidnap me. I do not know what they have done to Pierre, my tutor, but I fear for him."

Though Lincoln and Omar had shed their robes when they left el-Krum's tents, Amanda still wore hers. The lieutenant and his men didn't quite know what to think of her appearance.

"We saved her from the slave traders, sir," Lincoln said.

"Excellent work," said the lieutenant. "We've all been in a big stir about her."

"I'll have you know I was in the process of saving myself when this ruffian—"

"Sir, she's a little out of her mind," said Lincoln. "She hasn't had a lot of sleep. You'll have to pardon her rudeness."

"Not at all," he replied. "We're elated that she's safe. I'll escort you back to the ambassador myself."

After passing through the city's southern gate, they dismounted.

Omar said, "It is time that I leave you, my friends. Another uncle's booths are just down this street. I must return these horses there and send word to my uncle in Sidi that they are safely returned."

"Omar, won't you come to the palace with us and meet my father?" Amanda said. "I am sure he would want to personally thank you and reward you for your brave service to me."

"I must now see my uncle. The only reward I seek is what my kickside has promised me. Remember our deal, Yank. You must give me two more lessons in tracking the way of the Comanche."

"I will personally see that he fulfills his promise," Amanda said.

"I'll remember," Lincoln said. "And thanks, you're a real natural. I'll come see you once I find out what the Legion will have me doing."

"Omar, I, too, thank you," Amanda said. "I wouldn't have made it without you. If there is ever anything I can do for you, please let me know."

Omar gave a slight bow and, taking his and Lincoln's horses by the reins, hustled up the street.

Farther into the city, Lincoln, Amanda, and the lieutenant, who had also dismounted, turned up a cross street and nearly bumped into two bodies hanging by their necks from a pole stuck in the ground. Naked from the waist up, their chests were tattooed with the image of a human body with the head and tail of a writhing crocodile. Amanda shrieked and turned away into the Lincoln's arms.

"They were part of the assassination attempt last week," the lieutenant said. "Murian justice is swift, severe, and public."

They walked on and came to another cross street. Up ahead, they could hear the chant of "Suleiman! Suleiman!" from a crowd gathering in front of a palatial marble building.

As they walked up to the rear of the crowd, which stretched some fifty yards from the palace, the large double doors on the second-floor balcony opened. Two scimitar-carrying guards stepped out and stood at the doors. After them, three legionnaire majors walked out and took positions on the balcony, where they could watch the crowd below. The Legion lieutenant standing with Lincoln and Amanda snapped to attention.

"Who are they?" Lincoln asked.

"They are the Three from Camarón, the pride of our Legion. I have the honor of being under their command."

"They are great friends of mine," Amanda said, "and gallant gentlemen. None of them would have sat on me, even while assisting in my escape."

"What should have I done—let you stab me?" Lincoln was irritable as well after the all-night ride. "And I don't weigh that much, anyway."

Amanda didn't bother to answer. Out of the balcony doors walked King Suleiman. He had taken off his sling, and his left arm hung down at his side. Seeing him, the crowd gave a collective gasp and started chanting his name faster and louder. Walking to the balustrade, he wore the determined look of a leader who loved his people and was honored by the loyalty they showed him.

He lifted his right arm to quiet the crowd, and their chanting died down.

Suddenly, a high-pitched tremolo broke out from somewhere in the crowd. Toward the front, two men threw off their robes, revealing drawn scimitars. The crowd fell back from them as they charged toward the balcony, leading the way for a third man running behind them. This man also shrugged off his robe. In his right hand, he carried something dark and metal, a grapefruit-size sphere with a burning fuse.

The lieutenant and Lincoln tried to push their way through the crowd but made little progress. At the front of the crowd, the two men with the scimitars hacked down three palace guards stationed below the balcony. The three legionnaires on the balcony, having drawn their pistols, were trying to get a clear shot at the charging dervishes. They fired several shots, and the two running in front fell to the ground. The dervish with the bomb kept coming. The dark and burly legionnaire fired at him and hit him in the chest, just as he hurled the bomb in a high arc toward the balcony.

The tall legionnaire pushed the king down and covered him with his body. Just as the bomb was reaching the top of its arc, the third legionnaire, with the graying beard, aimed his revolver and fired twice. To Lincoln's astonishment, the bomb landed on the balcony, almost at the king's feet . . . and did nothing. The fuse had been shot off. The legionnaire shoved the revolver back into its holster, then he and the others quickly helped the king back into the palace.

CHAPTER 37

"There, there, dear, everything is going to be all right now," Ambassador Montier said to his daughter. The Legion lieutenant had escorted Amanda and Lincoln into the ambassador's office in the palace. "We will find the professor, I assure you."

"You're still going to let me continue with my investigations, aren't you?" Amanda said through her tears.

"You must never leave the palace again, not without an armed guard," the ambassador said. "Never. You must promise me now."

Amanda released her father from her embrace and backed away a few steps. "But I may go out with an escort?"

"No more than three miles from the city, and only with the armed escort that I appoint." The ambassador turned his attention to Lincoln, standing a few feet away. "Now, monsieur, may I say how deeply indebted I am to you for rescuing my daughter." He shook Lincoln's hand, placing his other hand on top of Lincoln's.

"I could have rescued myself," Amanda said, "but he did help. He is American and his name is Smith."

"Indeed, this is splendid service, monsieur Smith. You've saved us sending the battalion after Amanda. You are aware these are trying times here, and we must be wise with our resources."

"I've come to join the Legion, sir. It was my duty."

"Saving me was merely a *duty*?" Amanda said, taking a threatening step toward Lincoln. "I knew you were no gentleman."

"Please excuse her," said the ambassador. "When she's tired, she says things she doesn't mean."

"Actually, sir, she's right. It was indeed my duty, but also my pleasure, to save her."

"Ah, you're as silly as she is."

Ambassador Montier took a few steps around the room, deep in thought. "Monsieur Smith, you have shown courage, capacity, and initiative, and I like that. I'd like to give you a special assignment, if you're willing."

"I'll do my best, sir."

"Good. Now, you both need rest. Smith, you'll stay at the hotel until arrangements can be made for you here at the palace."

"What's he going to be doing here?" Amanda grumped.

"Since you two get along so well and since you've lost your tutor, Monsieur Smith, disguised as your new one, will be your personal bodyguard."

"Father, that is absurd! He probably can't even read, and I must continue my studies and investigations."

"Oh, to blazes with your treasure hunting! We can't spare a man from the fort, and you must be protected. No one but the Three and us will know that he isn't a real tutor."

"Sir, all due respect, but I didn't come here to nursemaid a schoolgirl."

"And I'm not to be nursemaided either. And don't call me a schoolgirl."

"I'll hear no more of it," the ambassador said. "The issue is closed."

Amanda stormed out of the room and bumped into a legionnaire who was just entering. It was the man who earlier shot fuse from the bomb.

"Major Athos, I want you to meet Monsieur Smith," the ambassador said as Athos approached.

"It's an honor to meet you, sir. That was quite a shot you made today," said Lincoln, reaching out his hand. Athos didn't take it.

"The doctors have looked over King Suleiman," Athos said to the ambassador, as if Lincoln were not even there. "He is as defiant as ever—refuses to make any changes in the schedule."

Lincoln either didn't notice Athos's rebuff or wasn't discouraged by it. "Sir, the stories I have heard of you and your friends are inspiring. And that was an amazing shot today."

"He is the stubbornest man in existence," Montier said of the king, also ignoring Lincoln.

"At least, we have a few days before the ceremony at the dam," Athos said.

"Yes," said Montier. "Oh, yes, Monsieur Smith was the one responsible for rescuing Amanda. He's agreed to be her bodyguard, disguised as her tutor."

"I didn't actually agree—"

"I had heard about the rescue, sir," Athos said, cutting Lincoln off. "I would have liked to be consulted. We don't need another wet-behind-the-ears kid to look after around here."

"Who are you calling wet behind the ears?" Lincoln demanded.

"Nonsense," said the ambassador. "Smith has demonstrated courage and ingenuity, and I am not burdening the battalion with my daughter's protection."

"Yes, sir," Athos said, obviously not pleased with the decision.

"Now, Major, please show Monsieur Smith to the adjutant, who will see about his quarters and kit."

"Smith—*that's* original," Athos said to Lincoln as they walked down the hallway to the adjutant's office.

"Just because I'm young, doesn't mean I'm green."

"Oh, you're green all right. Green as a spring turd."

"Maybe I don't like working with greenhorns any more than you do."

"Watch who you're talking to, kid."

"It's *whom*, not *who*," said Lincoln.

Athos stopped and glared at the arrogant youngster. He hadn't had his English corrected in a long time. He started to get angry, then just shook his head in annoyance. "You just better keep that girl—and yourself—out of any more trouble. Is that clear enough?"

"Another failure!" Fräulein Zads said to Prince Kamak. She had just entered his office, where she found him reviewing paperwork at his desk. "And on top of that, the girl has escaped. The Legion column is no longer leaving in the morning."

"Yes, but what a shooting exhibition!"

"This is no time for humor. With those legionnaires always at his side, your father is invulnerable."

"I assure you, not invulnerable, but I agree with you. We must focus our attention on them. As a matter of fact, I've already planned a little something for this afternoon."

"Good. But what about the Legion column?"

"You are correct. The column was to go after her and the slavers in the morning. We will have to take the girl again."

"She will now be guarded."

"Yes. Montier has appointed the young American to be her bodyguard, disguised as her tutor." Kamak and Zads both laughed.

"My dear," she said, "I am sorry for my irritability, but the waiting is getting to my nerves."

"I understand, but we must continue to follow the plan," Kamak said, standing up. "Now, a little diversion ought to do you good. Come, it's been a long day. I would like to show you something." He led Fräulein Zads to the back of his office, where he twisted the base of a lamp next to the daybed. A soft grinding noise began behind the tapestry on the wall. Kamak pulled back the tapestry to reveal a door that was opening. He and Zads walked through the door. Kamak stopped and drew the tapestry back across the opening, then twisted a torch bracket just inside the room, and the door closed.

A few minutes later, they walked into the central area of an underground temple. The large, high-ceiled room had a thirty-foot-wide river running through its center—effectively, a moat separating a large gallery area, opposite Kamak and Zads, from the shrine area. On the gallery side were three doors, about twenty feet apart. On the shrine side of the moat was a large brass altar. Above the altar was a huge bronze idol of the crocodile god. Hanging from the idol, suspended by his hands, was a well-fed middle-aged Frenchman. Smoke curled upward from the altar, and the man kicked and jerked on the rope from which he hung.

"The girl's tutor!" said Fräulein Zads.

"Yes," said Kamak. "I have doubled his dose. His hallucinations shall begin shortly."

About twenty feet below and to the left of the door that Kamak and Zads had entered through was a large cave, from which ran the underground river that filled the moat. Barring the mouth of the cave was a portcullis-style gate. Behind it teemed twenty or more adult crocodiles.

Prince Kamak motioned to a dervish standing on the bank next to the cave. The dervish cranked a wheel, and the portcullis rose above the cave's mouth. The crocodiles swarmed out toward the idol, and began snapping at the Frenchman's feet, which were just out of their jaw's reach.

The Frenchman screamed and tried to keep his feet out of reach of the jaws snapping below him. Then, through the scaly reptilian mass, a huge croc pushed its way directly below the Frenchman. The great beast lunged and snapped but couldn't quite reach him. The Frenchman screamed, then fainted into silence.

CHAPTER 38

The hotel where Lincoln was to stay until his palace accommodations could be arranged had at one time been a harem. It had belonged to an earlier king's brother, whose residence at the palace was not large enough for his passel of wives and concubines. The building was a three-story affair with high ceilings and marble floors. On the ground floor, the lobby was separated from the adjacent rooms and restaurant by archways lined with miniature palms. Behind one of these arches, Aramis and Porthos watched as Lincoln checked into the hotel.

"You are in room 217," the fez-wearing clerk behind the counter said to Lincoln. "An attendant will assist you with your bath, which is down the hall on the left."

"Thanks," Lincoln said, "but I can bathe myself." He picked up the bundle of new clothes he had received from the legionnaire adjutant and walked off down the hall.

Porthos and Aramis stepped out from behind the archway. "That is he," said Aramis. "They say he saved the girl from slave traders. He doesn't look like too bad a chap."

Porthos grinned. "If he's to serve with us, we'll give the whelp our own little test and see the stuff he's made of."

Lincoln entered the bathing chamber. On one side of the room were three large tubs, and on the other side a stove heating large pots of water. An attendant, who had been dozing in a chair, stood up and offered Lincoln assistance, which he curtly declined.

A while later, as Lincoln was soaking in his bath, the door of the room flew open, and Porthos marched in, cheerfully humming to himself. When he noticed Lincoln in the tub, his mood quickly changed. "What is that carcass doing in my tub?" he demanded of the attendant.

The attendant looked confused. "Why, taking a bath, sir."

Recognizing the man as one of the Three from Camarón, Lincoln decided not to take his comments personally. "That's okay," he said. "I was just getting out, anyway." He got out of the bath and started drying himself with a large towel.

"Never mind," Porthos said to the attendant. "Fill up another for me, and put some flower water in it. That tub will have to be burned—it's the only way to quell the stench of an American." The attendant started to fill a different tub as Porthos began taking off his boots. Now Lincoln was starting to take it personally.

"And have his towel also burned," Porthos said.

"Listen," Lincoln said to the burly legionnaire, "do you have something against Americans?"

Porthos didn't reply but just took off his other boot.

"I asked you if you have something against Americans," Lincoln said.

"Are you speaking to me?" Porthos said, standing up and unbuttoning his shirt. "You insolent, young pile of camel droppings?"

"As a matter of fact, I am, and where I'm from, a man expects a reply, you . . . you wormy old buffalo chip."

Porthos reached down, as if arranging his boots, then sprang at Lincoln with a dagger in one hand, pushing him against the wall with the other. Amazed at the legionnaire's temper, Lincoln raised his arms, causing his towel to drop.

"How dare you speak to me like that," Porthos said, "you slime of a toad!"

"If I'm toad's slime, you're a cow pie."

"*Cow pie?* You hyena's whelp."

"Don't speak about my mother," Lincoln said, still pressed up against the wall.

"Oh, a thousand pardons," said Porthos, apparently remembering the touchy nature of Americans' sensibilities surrounding their mothers. "The offense was unintentional. I did not mean to deprecate your honorable mother along with you, you capon."

"Then you're the . . . the teats on a mule."

Porthos could not help chuckling. He released Lincoln from against the wall. "Teats on a mule, is it? I think I might like you, but I must kill you anyway. Let me see, I am busy now, but we shall meet at six o'clock, behind the hotel, with swords."

"All right, six o'clock it is, behind the hotel," replied Lincoln. "But I don't have a sword; I haven't been issued my weapons yet."

"One must do the best he can with the tools he has," said Porthos, looking down at Lincoln's naked front. "You can borrow my second's blade. And don't be late. Teats on a mule—huh!"

Dressed in his new clothes, Lincoln walked down the second-floor hallway, looking at his key and then at the signs on the hotel room doors. Not having slept the night before, and after his bath and his encounter with Porthos, he was sleepy and even more irritable. The Murian script on the key and the doors was unintelligible to Lincoln, and he couldn't figure out which of the rooms was 217. He was trying to find the room with markings identical to those on his key, but they all looked about the same to him.

Suddenly, Aramis burst out of the room that Lincoln was just passing and held him at sword point against the wall. "What is the meaning of this?" Aramis said. "Who sent you?"

"I'm only looking for my room. I can't read Murian." Lincoln showed him the writing on his door key.

"I don't care about that, you bloody little cur." Aramis pressed his blade closer to Lincoln's chest.

"I'm not a cur. I'm American, and don't try me—I'm tired and liable to erupt."

"Are you *mad*? I can see you're a bloody American, you lump of carrion."

"I'm just getting the hang of the etiquette around here, not that I mind it, you wart on a toad."

Aramis lowered his sword. "Wart on a toad? Original!" he said. "Tonight at six, behind the hotel."

"I already have an engagement there at six."

"Don't try to evade me. Have you no honor?"

"Okay, at six, then, behind the hotel, with swords."

Aramis raised his sword again to Lincoln's chest. "And tell no one of our meeting, or I will not kill you quickly." He pulled away his sword and started back into his room, but Lincoln put his foot in the door as Aramis was closing it.

"What are you doing, whelp?" Aramis said, glaring at Lincoln. "You truly must be mad."

"Could you please tell me which of these rooms is 217?"

Once Lincoln finally found his room, he fell asleep with his clothes still on. An odd menagerie of images flitted through his dreams: the crocodile god, monstrous camel-eating tsetse flies, toads, fertile mules with teats, and gigantic legionnaires flailing at him with swords. And then, from deep in his sleep, he remembered his appointments. He sprang up from his bed and looked around for a clock, but there was none. He pulled his pocket watch out and saw that it was 6:01 p.m. He looked out his window overlooking the courtyard in the back of the hotel. Aramis and Porthos were walking into the courtyard.

Lincoln caught some movement and realized they were not alone. Behind them crept several hooded figures. They stopped and took cover some thirty paces from the courtyard.

Lincoln looked around his room for something to use as a weapon.

The curtain on his window was hung on an iron rod. He pulled it down and shucked the curtain off it.

Porthos and Aramis had taken off their jackets and holsters, laid them aside, and were leisurely practicing sword thrusts. "I don't know why Athos couldn't see the fun in this," Porthos said.

"Lads like the American set him in a funk," Aramis said.

Hearing a clamor from a second-story window across the courtyard, they both looked up in time to see a body leap out, holding a curtain rod. Lincoln crashed down on the wooden bins below, smashing them and making a huge racket. Aramis and Porthos stared in amazement. "The lad is absolutely out of his mind!" Porthos said.

"Somewhat given to histrionic display, I must say," said Aramis, "but at least he's here."

Dazed from his landing, Lincoln staggered up from the debris of the bins, trying to stand. "You're late," Aramis said as if that were the most unusual thing about his arrival.

"Sorry. I know it's bad form being late to a duel."

"Well, at least you're here," Aramis said. "Now, I'll have at you first. I can't remember the last American I killed, and my British soul still resents the rebellion on the colonies."

"My friend," said Porthos, "I must claim prior right. You may have whatever is left of him."

"You've been followed," Lincoln said, coming toward them. "At any moment, I fear an ambuscade."

While Lincoln's warning was registering, four scimitar-wielding dervishes ran out from cover from the side of the alley.

"Behind you!" Lincoln cried out.

Porthos and Aramis spun around. The dervishes were thirty feet away, between them and their pistols. The two legionnaires backed up, preparing to defend themselves with their swords. "Two against four," said Porthos. "Could be worse."

Aramis and Porthos charged the attacking dervishes with their swords. Then four more dervishes ran out from the other side of the courtyard. "And now it is!" said Aramis.

Lincoln ran up and whacked one of the attackers over the head with his curtain rod, knocking him unconscious. "Three against seven," he said.

"You're liable to get hurt, boy," Porthos said to Lincoln.

"Don't call me 'boy,'" Lincoln said, as he flailed away with his curtain rod at another dervish. He parried a few blows from his enemy's yataghan, then feinted and whacked him in the side of the head. The dervish dropped to his knees, then fell on his face.

"I think he is erupting," said Aramis, who, in an elegant combination of parries and thrusts, blocked an attacker's sword strokes and then impaled him through the chest. "Cambridge Fencing Society, class of '75."

Porthos, in a flurry of sword strokes, ran one of his attackers through. "That I learned from the sheikh of Aqaba."

The two fighting Lincoln attacked with renewed energy. He blocked their blows, then, spinning, impaled a dervish with the sword of his fallen comrade. "Bronco Buck Burke's Wild West, '99," he said.

The other dervish came on him afresh. Lincoln backed up a few steps and tripped over the body of the assassin he had just slain. As the dervish advanced, sword raised to strike, around the corner of the building came Athos. Drawing his pistol, he shot the attacker dead. The one dervish still standing turned and fled.

One of the fallen assailants got up, trying to flee. As the Three and Lincoln ran to him, the one who ran reappeared and threw a dagger at him, hitting him in the chest.

Lincoln and Porthos ran after the dervish who had thrown the knife, while Athos and Aramis hurried to attend to the dervish who had been hit. Perhaps, they could get something useful out of him.

A few minutes later, Lincoln and Porthos jogged back. "We lost him in the bazaar," Porthos said, breathing hard. "I wouldn't let the boy go after him."

Lincoln said, "Don't call me 'boy' . . . uh, sir."

With the toe of his boot, Athos pushed open one of the dead men's robes. Tattooed on his chest was the image of the crocodile god.

CHAPTER 39

"The trick they pulled on you last night was beastly," Amanda said to Lincoln. "It almost got you all killed, but you behaved gallantly, as you did when you aided my escape." She offered her hand to Lincoln, which he shook, holding back his amusement.

They were sitting at a table in the French embassy's section of the palace. In front of her was a stack of books that she had assembled for their first "tutoring" session. They were supposed to have these sessions every morning, five days a week, to keep up the pretense that Lincoln was her new tutor.

"I don't hold it against them," he said. "They were just having some fun, trying to test my mettle a little."

"Yes, but you acted bravely, and you impressed the Three—Aramis and Porthos, anyway. I respect their opinion, though they think you are something of a lunatic. But at least they said you're *their* type of lunatic."

"I've never been accused of being normal."

She took the second book from the stack and opened it on the table. "Now, since we have to spend this time together anyway, and since you have something of an adventurous spirit, I've decided to tutor you on a little Murian history. It's fascinating, and if you can follow it, I think you'll enjoy it."

"You're going to tutor me?"

"I know, ridiculous, isn't it? But I have set out to discover everything I can about Mur's past, and have become rather an expert about it. Can you read, Mr. Smith?"

Lincoln studied her face. She was serious. "I like pictures," he said.

"Well, maybe we should look at this map, then. It's really just one big picture." She took out a map from the opened book and scooted closer.

"So *you're* looking for the treasure too?"

"Very good. Learning is such a joy. This is written in Latin. I'll translate it and print it in English for you. If you apply yourself, I'll have you reading some basic things in no time at all."

"Will you?"

"Yes, I will."

"So what does it say?" asked Lincoln.

"My Latin is not the best, but I think it says, 'The Lost Treasure of King Sol.'"

"Actually, it says, 'The Palace of Sol: Finished by Manu, Second King of Mur, in the Seventh Year of His Reign.'" Lincoln's face was the picture of innocence.

"How . . . ? What . . . ?" She stiffened, folding her arms. "That was most ungentlemanly of you, letting me go on thinking you couldn't read."

"And that was most condescending of you, treating me like some kind of uneducated simpleton."

"I didn't say you were simple; I just assumed, you being from the ranks *and* an American."

"That's not condescending?"

"Well, maybe a little."

"I'm sorry if I embarrassed you. My mother is a schoolteacher. She even made me go to college till I was expelled for blowing up a chemistry lab—accidentally. I'm not good with machines."

"I loathe modern inventions," she said, unfolding her arms.

"I loathe modern *everything*, especially trains."

"Oh, to have been born in an earlier age!" she said.

"At least before 1830."

"At least before the Revolution—ours, not yours."

"They weren't that far apart."

"That's true. Further back, during the Renaissance, or at the time of Charlemagne!"

"Yeah, or Coeur de Lion or King Arthur."

Their unguarded gaze into each other's eyes was interrupted by a knock on the door. Amanda folded up her map and tucked it back into the book. "Come in; the door is open," she said.

Ambassador Montier entered the room and gave an approving nod to the stack of books between them. "After lunch," he said, "Prince Kamak and I are visiting the dam in preparation for the ceremony. We thought you two might enjoy accompanying us."

"Thank you," said Amanda, "but Mr. Smith and I have plans to go for a ride."

"Very well, but remember what I said. No more than three miles from the city, and Monsieur Smith is to accompany you at all times."

"Didn't you say five miles?"

"Smith, three miles."

"Three miles, sir."

When her father had gone, she took out the map again and spread it before them on the table.

"You really believe in this treasure stuff, don't you?" Lincoln asked.

"Oh, I do, and I so want to be the one who discovers it before it is stolen. For the Murian people, to preserve their heritage, and also to prove the skeptics like my father and Prince Kamak wrong. Of course, there is a law in Mur that whoever discovers ancient treasures is entitled to a 10 percent bounty. I wouldn't accept it, of course. I would just like to preserve their wonderful heritage and have the great honor of being the one who discovered it, like Captain Bouchard finding the Rosetta Stone. He was a friend of my grandfather, who was also an archaeologist."

Lincoln smiled at Amanda. "Well, I guess that's as good a reason as any." He pulled the map closer and looked it over in detail. "There's a big section missing from here, but according to this, modern Mur is built on the ruins of an ancient city. Here is the old palace, and this was the temple proper. It says here, it was started early in the reign of King Sol but wasn't finished until the seventh year of King Manu. According to this, way over here is the tomb of King Sol and the treasure vault. And there is an entrance here, through these caves west of the city. I don't know, though. I hear there are a lot of fake maps going around."

"Is it less than three miles?"

"Right about that."

"Good," said Amanda. "We'll go this afternoon."

"I don't know about this map," he said. "There's a lot of bogus stuff floating around from people trying to profit off treasure hunters."

"True, but even if we don't find anything, it will be a lovely ride."

Prince Kamak was down in the temple, at the cave of the crocodiles. Standing on the ledge next to the lowered gate, he was supervising three black-robed men who were cutting slabs of raw mutton and throwing them over the gate to the crocodiles.

"There you are," said Fräulein Zads, coming through a secret passage leading from the palace. "I suppose you are aware the outcome of last night?"

"Just a moment," said Kamak. "Spread it out and don't overfeed them," he said to the men. "I want them hungry. There, that's enough." He walked up to where the fräulein stood.

"You are aware of what happened to your incompetent men last night?"

"Of course I am aware. I knew of it fifteen minutes after it happened." He walked down the passage toward the idol, where the unconscious Frenchman was now bound to the base of the altar. "Untie him and place him on the altar," he ordered the dervishes.

"It was another failure," Zads said, following Kamak. "How am I to account to my superiors for this? We cannot tolerate failure."

"We had two of them in our grasp," Prince Kamak said. "It was that insane American who spoiled it."

"Our army has now landed," said the fräulein. "They will arrive in the mountains to the north of the dam late tomorrow."

"I've told you, these things must be handled delicately," Kamak said. "The assassination of a ruler in this part of the world can set off tribal disputes for the throne lasting for generations. But even so, there is nothing to get alarmed about. Every attack by my crocodile men works to our purpose. The panic is spreading in the city. And when I deliver my people from this menace, I will have their complete devotion."

The dervishes laid the unconscious Frenchman on the altar, and Kamak came up and took his pulse. Then he grabbed him by the chin and shook him a little, and the Frenchman mumbled incoherently.

"You are fortunate he is still alive," said Zads.

"I know what I'm doing. He will be released outside the city walls. The stir he will cause will be quite amusing."

"El-Krum is waiting. When can I tell him we will deliver the girl?"

"The girl will still be taken today. While her father and I visit the dam, she will go treasure hunting again. Tell him to be ready and not to lose her this time."

The fräulein gave a wry smile. "Sometimes, I think you enjoy this ruse a little too much."

"There is a certain irony in using silly legends to my purpose, though I must admit I am intrigued by these beasts." Kamak turned to look at the crocodiles, which were still milling behind the portcullis, eager for more meat. "I wonder how long they've actually been breeding down here."

CHAPTER 40

Just after noon Lincoln and Amanda rode out through the western gate of the city. It was a hot day, the Murian sky unsullied by a single cloud. Lincoln was unfazed by the heat, even in the French woolen suit the ambassador was making him wear. Amanda wasn't as comfortable, but she wouldn't dream of waiting for the cool of the afternoon. She wanted as much time as possible to explore the cave depicted in the map.

A mile or so out from the city, they were startled by a whooping noise behind them. A rider was galloping toward them. Lincoln pulled out the Mauser pistol he had been issued and moved his horse in front of Amanda's. When the rider got closer, he laughed and put it away. It was Omar, doing his version of a Sioux battle charge.

"Hey, Yank, you look as a dude of the city," Omar said.

"He looks just fine in that suit, Omar," Amanda said, "and don't you tell him otherwise."

"Yes, Your Highness," Omar said, still unclear on the finer points of civil rank and title. "He looks just like a queenhorn."

"It's *greenhorn,* and hold your tongue; I'm already getting enough of that from everyone else. I'm suffering for a reason."

"He's only obeying orders, Omar," Amanda said. "Don't you make fun of him."

"Yeah, I'm supposed to be looking out for 'Her Highness' here."

"Please don't call me that either," Amanda said to Lincoln. "And you do look like a dude."

"Have I not done well? I tracked you as the Comanche tracks, as you instructed, and I found your trail. I still have two lessons yet, but after one I do well, yes?"

"Like I said, you're a natural. But what did you ride out for?"

"Oh, yes, my uncle humbly asks you to pay a hundred sous for the cost of returning the rental horses back to Sidi Bel Abbès."

"A hundred sous?" Lincoln said.

"Yes, for each. That is ten francs. My cousin will make the trip. I will stay in Mur for my lessons."

"That is more than reasonable, Omar," said Amanda. "I will pay. What is your uncle's name? I will have it sent to his booth."

"His name Kamil and is well-known in the bazaar. He desired three hundred sous, but I achieve a bargain for my friend. Now, I must return to my uncle's booth before he cut my pay." Omar turned his horse and galloped off.

Twenty minutes later, Lincoln and Amanda hobbled their horses below a sandstone escarpment that jutted out of the hills southwest of the city. A steep trail led up through the rocks. About seventy feet up the trail, a series of caves became visible.

They came to a level area before the mouth of one of the smaller caves. Lincoln pulled out the map from his shirt pocket and studied it closely. "This is the one," he said. "With the mouth about four feet high, looks like egg." He took off his rucksack, which Amanda had packed with things she thought would be useful for the expedition. Digging through it, he pulled out a rope, a leather case that looked as if it could hold three cigars, a three-inch-long metal tube, and, at the bottom of sack, a small kerosene lantern.

After inspecting the lantern, he picked up the leather case. "What's in here?" he asked, opening it.

"Oh, you should be careful with that. There's three half-sticks of dynamite in there, in case we need to blast through something."

"Dynamite! Are you telling me I've been riding with a bunch of dynamite strapped to my back?"

"Oh, you needn't worry; it can't go off without a detonator or a lit fuse. I got it from the engineers who are building the dam."

"In one hundred and ten degrees, that's comforting. What's this," Lincoln opened the small metal container.

"Matches. The container is waterproof."

"You plan on going for a swim?"

"You never know what you might need. The legend says that the original temple was built next to an underground river, full of crocodiles."

"Great. If we find any crocodiles, we can blow them up with dynamite."

Lincoln lit the lantern and put the match container in his pocket. He slipped the rucksack back on and picked up the lantern, and the two of them crawled through the entrance of the cave.

After the first five feet, the cave opened into a large room. They walked deeper inside, seeing nothing interesting.

"So why are you so sure the legends about King Sol and his treasure are true?" Lincoln asked.

"For one thing, the Thanatos cult," Amanda said. "It is said that King Sol died opposing them. Supposedly, he and his treasure were buried in a secret chamber so they would never be defiled by the presence of the crocodile god. That cult is still around today, and if it's true that the cult opposed him, shouldn't the rest of the legend also be true?"

"Well, not necessarily—"

Just then a bevy of bats flew at them from deep inside the cave. Amanda shrieked, and both of them ducked. After the bats passed, as Lincoln straightened up, he noticed the remnants of fresh footprints. He started walking again but very slowly, studying the ground as he moved.

"What's so interesting?" Amanda asked.

"Where did you get the map?" he asked.

"I have a contact in the city who supplies me with information about ancient Mur."

"Stop!" Lincoln drew his pistol.

"What's the matter?"

"*Shh!* There are tracks in here someone recently tried to cover up." He inched forward, holding his lantern high. They took a few more small steps forward, and the lantern's light revealed a pit, square in the middle of the path. Lincoln peered over the edge. It was close to ten feet deep with sheer sides.

A faint noise came from behind them, like someone kicking a loose pebble. They turned and listened. Footsteps were coming toward them.

Lincoln dug into his pack and pulled out the rope. Tying one end around a large rock, he dropped the rest into the pit, then tossed dirt and gravel over the section of exposed rope.

Toward the front of the cave, two black-robed dervishes, one carrying a lantern, crept forward with scimitars drawn. A woman's loud scream sent them rushing toward the pit.

They peered over the edge, looking to confirm that their trap had worked. As they looked over the edge, Lincoln fired twice. One man fell back onto the ground. The other, hit in the chest, staggered at the edge of the pit. Lincoln, standing in the loop he had knotted into the rope, reached up from the pit, grabbed his leg, and yanked him over the edge. He bumped off the side before hitting the bottom.

Taking his foot out of the loop, Lincoln inched his way up, hooked one heel over the edge of the pit, and pulled himself out. Then Amanda stood up from behind the rock, and they hurried out of the cave.

Once outside, something hard and heavy slammed into the back of his head, and then everything went blank.

He woke up gasping. His head throbbed. He was lying on top of a body—the dervish he had shot and yanked into the pit. As his breath returned, he pieced together what had happened. Outside the cave, someone had blindsided him, knocking him unconscious. Then they had thrown him into the pit, which, luckily, was only about ten feet deep. It could have been much worse.

He was about to yell for Amanda but stopped himself. Finding the rope, he shinnied up it and again pulled himself over the lip. It was oddly dark, with only a few cracks of light coming through the cave's mouth. Someone had blocked the opening with a large boulder. He tried it from several angles, but it wouldn't budge. A moment later he took off his rucksack, lit a match from Amanda's canister, and started rummaging through the sack.

The two dervishes reached the bottom of the trail, where their leader sat astride one of the horses, with Amanda, hands bound, mounted in front of him. Their other four horses were tied up next to Lincoln and Amanda's mounts. One man unhobbled Lincoln and Amanda's horses and slapped them both on the rump, sending them running.

Then an explosion behind them shook the ground. Through a cloud of dust and smoke, out of a hole the blast had blown in the top of the cave, Lincoln came crawling out.

The dervish with Amanda galloped away. The other two scattered the two extra horses, mounted up, and took off at a canter.

Taking risky leaps, Lincoln bounded down the escarpment. A few feet below him, two dervishes were riding by. With no time to weigh options, he leaped off the ledge, hitting one of the riders from the side and knocking him off his horse as the other rode away.

The man whom Lincoln had unhorsed stood up to draw his scimitar. Lincoln tackled him and, grabbing the dagger from his belt, buried it between the dervish's ribs.

Wiping the dagger on the dying man's robe, he clamped the blade in his teeth. Then he grabbed the dervish's scimitar, leaped on his horse, and set off at a dead run.

Riding hell-for-leather, in two minutes he had caught up with the other rider. As Lincoln came alongside, the dervish slashed at him, but he warded off the blows with the dead man's scimitar. The dervish then slashed at Lincoln's horse, causing it to shy and tumble forward. Lincoln dropped his scimitar and leaped off, grabbing the mane of the dervish's horse.

In one of the riding tricks he had routinely performed in the Wild West show, Lincoln hung on to the neck of the horse, bouncing his feet off the ground and swinging over to the left side, making it more difficult for the dervish to reach him with the scimitar. Then, hooking his right heel over the horse's back, he grabbed the pommel in his right hand, took the dagger from his teeth, and stabbed the other rider in the groin. With a howl of pain, the dervish slumped away from Lincoln, dropping the scimitar. Lincoln then stabbed the dervish in the belly and pushed him off the horse. He slid onto the saddle and raced on.

The dervish with Amanda was still a quarter mile ahead. He approached a gully, where he slowed to ride down one side and up the other. Out of the gully, he started picking up speed again.

Lincoln never slowed his horse. Instead of carefully negotiating the gully, he gave his mount more rein and a light kick in the flanks, and it leaped, landing smoothly on the other side. He was now only a hundred yards behind.

Amanda was astride the horse, just behind the withers and in front of the dervish, and though she was light, the added weight made it easier for Lincoln to close the gap. The dervish drew his scimitar and swung. Lincoln ducked and leaned to the side, and the blow struck his saddle. Lincoln partially lost his balance and dropped three lengths behind. He spurred his horse, and as he started catching up again, he took the dagger out of his mouth and held it in his right hand, coming up on their left.

Amanda, slouching in front of the dervish, straightened up violently, smacking him in the face with the back of her head. The dervish jerked backward, falling off the horse onto the dagger held in Lincoln's outstretched hand. Lincoln let go of the dagger and the dervish who was impaled on it, and the body tumbled to the ground.

Coming up ahead was a wider, deeper gully with a small stream running through it. Amanda, still riding in front of the saddle and unable to grasp the flying reins with her bound hands, clung to the horse's mane, just trying to stay on.

Lincoln spurred his horse ahead and, almost to the gully, rode up and grabbed her with one arm. He gave the reins a tug, and the horse stopped short, but Amanda couldn't brace for the stop. Lincoln must either let her go or fly off with her.

They flew. Over the horse's neck, over the lip of the gully, and into the water below.

They sat in the cool, shallow water, catching their breath. Amanda looked at Lincoln and tried to smile. He responded with something like a groan.

Up the river about three miles was a military fort, and about three miles farther upstream, where the river ran out of a canyon in the hills, was the dam the French were building for King Suleiman.

"So that's the dam up there these crocodile people are so stirred up about?" Lincoln finally said.

"Yes," said Amanda. "And that's Fort Flatters, where you'd be stationed if you hadn't the good fortune of being my bodyguard."

Lincoln heaved a sigh, unsure how much more good fortune he could survive.

CHAPTER 41

"Sir, I'll make a full report of the incident," Lincoln said to Ambassador Montier. At Lincoln's insistence, he and Amanda had come to report their run-in with the dervishes.

"It wasn't that big an issue, Father," Amanda said. She was trying to get Lincoln to tone down what he was saying. She didn't want to get her explorations any more restricted than they already were. "We were more or less in control of the situation at all times."

"Yes, I'll want a detailed report, Smith," said the ambassador. "And until I say otherwise, I don't want Amanda going out beyond the city walls. Not even with you."

"No, Father," she said. "I can't stand being confined."

"You'll both come to the dam dedication ceremony, day after tomorrow—with the full guard contingent, of course. But other than that, Smith, no travel outside the city walls. Am I clear?"

"I understand, sir," said Lincoln.

"Very good then," the ambassador said. "Your room in the palace is ready now. You should transfer your things here as soon as possible."

A knock came on the door, and the ambassador called out, "Enter."

Athos walked into the room, looking even graver than usual. "A word with you, Ambassador?" he said. "In private."

"Yes, of course. Amanda and monsieur Smith, could you please excuse us?"

"You can stay," Athos said to Lincoln.

With an insolent toss of her head, Amanda left the room.

"Miss Montier's tutor has been found," Athos said after Amanda had left. "He's alive, but she shouldn't see him in his condition. He's been tortured and is raving out of his mind."

Prince Kamak and Fräulein Zads were in Kamak's office, ear to ear at the listening tube. Prince Kamak pulled the device away and restrained himself from slamming it down on the desk. He put the cover over the earpiece and put it away in its secret compartment.

"Perhaps the American is not such easy game after all," Fräulein Zads said.

"Incompetence!" stormed Prince Kamak. "It surrounds me!"

"What are you going to do if the Legion column is not gone when your father goes to the ceremony? The column must be gone!"

"Tell el-Krum to wait and that his patience will be rewarded. Just one more day."

"Are you sure your way is best?" She gave him a coy look. "Perhaps a subtler approach would be in order."

"What do you mean?"

"Perhaps I could distract the young American. He is somewhat attractive, in a primitive sort of way."

"Don't be a fool. I already know what I am going to do. He won't be coming back from his hotel."

Approaching the door of the infirmary, Athos, Ambassador Montier, and Lincoln heard a man's shrieking. Entering, they saw a legion doctor, along with Porthos and Aramis, standing at the side of a bed. Strapped in the bed was Amanda's tutor, twisting and jerking in semiconscious convulsions. "Ah! Ah!" the tutor screamed. "No, get them away! . . . Get them away—no!"

"I've given him a sedative," the doctor said. "It's starting to take effect. You should have heard him a few minutes ago."

"Will he live?" asked the ambassador.

"Physically, other than exhaustion and dehydration, there are no major injuries. But like the others, he's been drugged and tortured and has been the victim of a similar ritual. They are not trying to kill these people."

"Ah! . . . Ah! Get it away, get it away!" screamed the tutor. He jerked and twisted, then abruptly passed out.

"What does he think is trying to get him?" Lincoln asked.

"He's been raving about . . . well, about being attacked by hordes of crocodiles and by a giant wraith of some sort."

"He is out of his mind," said the ambassador.

"Undoubtedly," the doctor replied. "The nearest crocodiles are in the Nile, fifteen hundred miles away."

"But a giant crocodile wraith!" said the ambassador. "That's delirium talking."

"With due respect, sir," Porthos said, "perhaps there's more here than is at first apparent."

"I suppose, then, you believe in this crocodile god," said the ambassador. "And perhaps in magic lanterns and flying carpets? In the name of St. Denis, Porthos, this is the twentieth century!"

"No, Monsieur Ambassador, this is Mur."

Leaving the infirmary, Lincoln stopped off at the adjutant's office to inquire whether a couple of new Legion recruits named Jones and Scott had recently come from Sidi Bel Abbès. The adjutant thought this humorous and told Lincoln that they typically had four or five recruits each month named Jones or Scott. Lincoln refined his question, asking if one very tall American and another rather short one had come. To this, the adjutant told Lincoln he didn't have time to keep track of all the flotsam and riffraff that trickled in from all over the world. After a little more persistence, Lincoln finally got out of him that only two Italians and a Greek had come from Sidi in the past few days.

Thinking that Omar seemed to know a lot about what was happening in Mur, he decided to ask him to scare up whatever information he could about Jones and Smith. He would have liked to go and talk to Omar right then. But it was getting late in the afternoon, and there was an embassy dinner that night, where he must make a showing as Miss Montier's new tutor. He needed first to move his things from the hotel to his room in the palace. The next morning, before their studies, he would see Omar and set him on the task.

Lincoln walked into his hotel room. He was in a good mood. Though things weren't working out precisely as he had expected, they weren't going all that badly. He wasn't actually *in* the Foreign Legion yet, but he felt confident that his service to the ambassador would help in that regard. Other than his concern for Johnny and Jake, he was far from displeased. And he felt confident they would show up sooner or later.

From what he had heard, ordinarily it could take a recruit a number of years even to make corporal, let alone sergeant. And he might get through his whole five-year hitch without ever becoming an officer. He hoped that with the work he was doing for the ambassador, he could get a promotion quickly, maybe even a commission. And he was already getting to work with the Three from Camarón. They were crusty old warhorses, especially the one called Athos. But in time, he might even earn their respect. And there was the French girl. He hadn't thought women like her still existed.

As he cleared his few things out of the armoire and stuffed them into his new satchel, he was thinking grand thoughts of leading charges against bands of Tuareg brigands. When he had emptied the armoire, he took the satchel over to the dresser and dumped the top drawer's contents into it.

But as he shut the drawer, he heard a faint hiss. He rattled the drawer again and listened. There it was again.

He moved to the side of the dresser and slid the second drawer open a few inches. The head of a snake arose out of its depth. He slammed the door, catching its head and a few inches of its neck fast in the nearly closed drawer. The snake's head spread out into, what Lincoln saw, was a cobra's intricately patterned hood. The thing squirmed and hissed, but its head was held fast. "Huh, they aren't any quicker than rattlers," he said aloud.

He had handled rattlesnakes many times in Texas. How different could a cobra be? He grasped the creature high up on the back of its neck with his thumb, bottom two fingers, and palm of his hand, and with his middle and index fingers he pushed down hard and controlled its head. With the toe of his boot he slid farther open the drawer, enough for him to grab the snake's four-foot-long body halfway in the middle. He walked to the window, which had apparently been left open by whoever left the snake. On the ground below lay the screen and a few feet to the side, some garbage bins. And trying to conceal himself was a native man crouching behind the bins. Lincoln tossed the snake out the window, and a moment later he heard a horrified scream.

Ducking under the window shade, he flung the snake so that it just cleared the ash can. A horrified scream rang out as he was closing the window.

Carrying his satchel, Lincoln walked into his new room in the palace and was surprised to see Athos, getting dressed in a formal Legion uniform.

"You're my roommate?" Lincoln asked.

"Now the ambassador wants *us* staying in the palace too," Athos growled. "I lost the toss."

He appeared no happier than Lincoln about the arrangement.

"I'd be careful opening those drawers," Lincoln said. "I just found a snake in one of mine back at the hotel."

"You're quite a magnet for trouble," replied Athos. "Maybe I'll sleep in the ambassador's office."

"You know," Lincoln said, putting down the satchel, "maybe we should at least make an effort to get along. I'm not as green as you think—and we're both Americans, you know."

"Listen, kid, I joined the Legion a long time ago to get away from America and Americans. Maybe that's why I don't like you."

"Well, then, I suppose I'll just stay clear of you, and you can do the same."

Lincoln turned and started unpacking his things.

Athos took a large bladed knife out of the drawer and slid it into a sheath strapped to his calf. As he pulled his pant leg down, a knock came on the door.

"It's open," said Athos.

Aramis walked into the room. "The reception is starting soon," he said. "The ambassador would like to see us before it begins.

CHAPTER 42

When Lincoln, in a French-cut suit he was not at all comfortable in, entered the reception, the room was already crowded with various dignitaries. On a bandstand in a corner of the room, a chamber orchestra, provided by the French delegation, was playing a Chopin concerto. At the other end of the room, a long buffet table held a lavish array of finger sandwiches, skewers of lamb and taro root, and other French and Algerian delicacies.

Prince Kamak was standing and talking with his father, Princess Salina, Amanda, Fräulein Zads, and Colonel Hultz. As Lincoln entered, he caught the look on Prince Kamak's face, the flash of surprise, followed by thinly veiled wrath. Ambassador Montier, standing with the Three from Camarón, left them and led Lincoln over to introduce him to the king and the rest of his group.

When Fräulein Zads offered Lincoln her hand, she held his for an uncomfortably long moment while gracing him with a voluptuous smile. He could feel Amanda's scorn for the attention Fräulein Zads was showing him. Without excusing herself, she took Princess Salina by the arm and walked off to where Athos, Porthos, and Aramis were talking among themselves. He also noticed the way Porthos took and kissed the princess's hand when Amanda introduced them.

On being introduced to the king, Lincoln had an uncomfortable moment. He wasn't sure of the proper protocol for showing respect, especially as an American meeting royalty. He certainly wasn't going to genuflect or kiss Suleiman's ring. But the king's mere presence exuded dignity and authority and deserved respect. The king perhaps sensed Lincoln's dilemma, and extended his hand for Lincoln to shake. "I understand the American penchant for egalitarianism," the king said. "It's a lot of camel dung, of course. Men are not equal, but that inequality is not by birth, but by merit. And from what Montier tells me, you have shown considerable merit— especially for an academic." Here the king gave a hearty laugh. "Now, if you will excuse us, the ambassador and I need a word in private. Please enjoy the delicacies of our table."

Lincoln wandered over to Amanda, who was still talking with Salina and the Three. But when he arrived, Amanda left abruptly, so he decided to get something at the buffet table.

"I hope your arrangements in the palace are acceptable, Mr. Smith," Prince Kamak said, walking up as Lincoln helped himself to sliced cucumbers and goat cheese.

"Thank you, they're fine," Lincoln replied. "And how was your visit to the dam?"

"Uneventful. But since my father insists on going through with the dedication ceremony, I think it wise to see that adequate security is in place."

"I understand," said Lincoln, whose eye Fräulein Zads had now caught from across the room.

"Of course, you will be joining us tonight after the reception?" Kamak asked.

"Excuse me?" said Lincoln, a little disconcerted from the looks Fräulein Zads was giving him.

"The king has planned a little Murian—how should I say it?—exotic entertainment. I believe you will find it interesting."

Zads made eyes at him again, and he noticed Amanda, looking on with disapproval.

"That sounds intriguing," Lincoln said to the prince. "I am quite interested in your country's history. I understand that the excavation at the temple outside the city is your project."

The prince gave him a cold smile. "A few associates from the University of Berlin and I have found some interesting artifacts, but they would be of little interest except to the professional."

"So you aren't one of those believers in the famous lost tomb and treasure?"

"I'm afraid, Mr. Smith, that ancient folklore is not an interest of mine. Scientific archaeology, on the other hand, has always fascinated me."

"Yes, I noticed some of your equipment and that floating machine."

"Ah, the balloon! With it, we are able to make precise aerial drawings that aid us in our diggings."

"I would be interested in taking a look sometime," Lincoln said. He had hoped that Fräulein Zads was trying to catch someone else's attention or had some kind of eye trouble, but behind him was only the floral centerpiece on a buffet table.

"I am afraid the temple is off limits to all but professional scholars," Prince Kamak said. "Artifacts of such antiquity are ever so fragile."

Lincoln watched Amanda watching Fräulein Zads watch him. Then her eyes met his, giving him a look that could have withered granite, before she stalked out to the balcony.

"Perhaps at a later time, then, Your Highness. But now, if you would excuse me, I must see to my student."

"Perhaps," the prince said as Lincoln walked away. "And don't forget the entertainment later."

As Lincoln walked out onto the balcony, Amanda turned away and walked to the railing.

"Is everything all right?" Lincoln asked. "Have you recovered from this morning?"

"I'm quite all right," Amanda said, with her back still toward him.

"Are you sure there's nothing the matter?"

"Yes. Can't you see? I'm fine."

"You don't seem fine."

Amanda turned around, in tears. "It's just that I was beginning to think you were different and actually did believe in those things you talk about," she said, blotting her tears on a hankie and trying to get her composure before she went back into the banquet hall.

"What? Are you talking about the German ambassador? I don't know anything about her. She must have a problem with her eyes." Lincoln held his hands out, palms up. "I could care less about her."

The oil lamps in the room where the post-reception entertainment was being held were turned down low. Colorfully patterned carpets, set about with abundant bolsters and pillows to recline on, covered the floor. Tapestries, colorful like the carpets but thinner and lighter, draped the walls and ceiling. Occasionally, a slight gust of warm wind through the open widows would cause the lamps to flicker and shadows to dance on the walls. Indeed, the room had the look and feel of a sheikh's desert tent, which was the point, after all.

To the king's right sat Ambassador Montier, Porthos, Aramis, and a few other dignitaries. To his left was a vacant space, and next to this sat Lincoln and then Athos. In front of each place, servants were setting up large hookahs and filling their bowls with pungent tobacco that filled the room with its fragrance even before the first bowl was lit.

"Do you smoke, Mr. Smith?" the king asked Lincoln. "What has the poet said? 'My breath is rank, my health doth flee; but fatter I'd grow without the tawny weed.'" The king and the ambassador were quite amused with the lines.

"I used to chew a little when I was younger," Lincoln replied.

"Chew?" said the king. "I've never thought of it, but I shall have to try. This is the finest of our Murian leaf. We take great pride in it."

A servant was now packing the bowl of the hookah in front of Lincoln with shredded golden-brown tobacco. "Maybe you should pass," Athos said. "This stuff isn't for beginners."

Lincoln's immediate reaction to Athos's suggestion was stubborn determination to try the stuff no matter what. He'd show Athos. As the servant put a match to the bowl, he took a couple of puffs. Though he made a heroic effort not to cough, he had drawn too deeply to avoid it. After a moment, he recovered and took another puff. "It's flavorful, quite flavorful."

"Now, where is that son of mine?" the king said after exhaling a cloud of smoke. "We'll wait only a few more minutes."

Lincoln took a few more jaunty puffs on his pipe.

"Mr. Smith, I saw you talking with him earlier," the king said.

"Yes, I was asking him about his diggings in the temple."

"That must have been a dull conversation. He measures our heritage by a few shards of broken pottery. Doubtless a product of his decadent European education."

"Thanatos, this god your King Sol was to have battled—I believe it's the Greek word for death?" said Lincoln.

"And the Greek word comes from the Sanskrit, from which our language derives," said the king.

"Many cultures have myths of a hero battling a dragon that represents death," Lincoln said. He was getting a little woozy from the strong tobacco. "It doesn't take much imagination to see how a dragon might resemble a crocodile."

"The existence of similar myths does not detract from its essential truth," the king said. "It rather confirms it and, moreover, points to the true occurrence from which the other stories descend."

"Then you believe the legends are true?"

"Ah, here he is!" the king said as Kamak entered the room. "What I believe is not important. What I know is that my great ancestor has already bestowed on his people a treasure that no man or monster will ever take away."

"Father, have you been enchanting our friends with stories of dragons and treasures?" Kamak said, sitting down between the king and Lincoln.

"And you almost missed the dance." The king clapped his hands. A flute, timbrels, and some kind of stringed instrument started playing an arabesque. Then, from behind a screen in the front of the room, five lithe, female dancers entered, moving in rhythm to the music.

They wore brightly colored, blousy silk pants banded at the ankles, and silk blouses, low-cut and short-sleeved. Accentuating their narrow waists were short velvet bodices adorned with jewels, sequins, and gold coins and reaching from just below their breasts to above their bare navels. Covering their shoulders were silk shawls, whose ends were attached to their wrists with bracelets, giving an almost winglike effect. Their bracelets, anklets, necklaces, earrings, and headbands were all of gold and adorned with jewels and gold coins. Only the lower portions of their faces were veiled, in see-through silk, allowing a full view of bewitching kohl-accented eyes.

They started their dance in front of the king, swaying seductively to the music. After a few moments, the middle dancer moved slowly and gracefully forward. She pressed her hands together over her head and began a sinuous swaying back and forth.

"It's the dance of the Bumblebee," Lincoln said, feeling a little dizzy from the tobacco.

"Be quiet!" said Athos.

"He is correct," said the king. "You indeed are an able scholar, Smith."

"I told you, I'm not as green as you think," Lincoln murmured to Athos, who didn't reply.

After a few minutes, Prince Kamak gave a look to one of the servants, who came over and began refilling Lincoln's hookah. The servant put a match to the pipe, and Lincoln puffed.

As the dance continued, Lincoln felt dizzier, then way beyond dizzy. The lights and shadows in the room started doing tricks on him, the lights pulsating, the shadows of the dancers elongating and shrinking and taking on strange shapes. The faces nearest him started bulging and throbbing to the rhythm of the music. The dancers became more like adders than bees, their bodies leaving wakes of color in the air as they moved.

The music and laughter and voices all merged together, as did the faces of the dancers.

"*Is the tobacco to your liking, Mr. Smith?*" he thought he heard Prince Kamak ask. The words ended in a strange cackling laughter.

"Are you all right, kid?" It sounded like Athos, speaking in a well.

"The dragon . . . the dragon . . ." Was that the king, or was he imagining it?

The music caught his attention again. It was pleasant and peaceful. Then everything again began pulsating and stretching to the rhythm of the timbrels.

Lincoln took a couple of deep breaths, trying to clear his brain. The dancers and the room seemed to return to normal. After a moment, just as he began to think he had regained control, the atmosphere in the room began weighing down on him, and his ears began to hurt, as if he were deep underwater. The dancers' eyes, mottled yellow-green, had vertical slit pupils and no irises, and their jaws grew long and toothy as scaly tails slashed behind them.

Lincoln staggered up and reeled out of the room. Trying to keep his balance, he staggered down the hall, looking for a quiet place to gather his wits. Coming to a door, he pushed it open and tottered through, only to find himself in the midst of fluttering multicolored silk, sweet fragrances, and high-pitched shrieks. A fat face loomed in front of him and pushed him out of the room, and he stumbled on down the hall.

He entered another room. Inside, it was dark and quiet. The door opened behind him. He could vaguely sense someone moving toward him, hands reaching out.

Athos grabbed him. He turned him around, shook him, and patted him on the face a few times. Lincoln came back to semiconsciousness.

"You're green, all right," said Athos.

"I'm *not* a greenhorn," Lincoln slurred.

"I didn't call you one. I just said you're *green*."

"What was that stuff?"

"I told you it wasn't for beginners. Come on, you've had enough for the night, I'll take you back to our room."

CHAPTER 43

After taking some deep breaths on the balcony, Lincoln walked back into his room. Athos handed him a glass of water, and he drank it down. He felt almost himself again.

"Must be something I ate."

"Yeah, okay. You sure you're all right?

Lincoln stopped for a moment, turning his head to listen. "What's that noise?"

"You might be hearing things for a while."

"No. Can't you hear that clinking?"

"I don't hear any noise."

"I have very sensitive hearing. It's one of the reasons I hate machines."

"Yeah, I bet you do. You get some sleep. I'm going to check on the king."

"There's that sound again. Where have I heard that before?" Lincoln walked toward the open door of the balcony. "It's like I've heard it in my sleep before."

"Do you want this?" Athos said, lifting his revolver out of its holster.

"Thanks anyway for the offer. I have one."

"Better get married to it. I'll be back after a while." Athos turned and headed for the door.

"And, Major . . ."

"What?"

"Thanks."

"Yeah. Just listen to me next time. I didn't do too well with that stuff the first time I tried it either."

Lincoln walked out on the balcony again and breathed deeply, feeling almost back to normal. Below the balcony, he heard a rustling in the bushes. He leaned over the railing, trying to see what was causing the noise. The low palm bushes were stirring as a dark shape moved between the fronds. He ran back into the room and returned to the railing, pistol in hand. The shape had gone out of sight. He put the pistol in his belt and climbed over the balcony and down the passion fruit trellis against the side of the palace.

Following quietly in the direction of the rustling fronds, he saw a hooded man stand up out of the bushes below one of the balconies. In the room behind the balcony, a light moved to the door, and the door opened. Princess Salina came out.

As Lincoln drew his pistol, the man threw back his hood. It was Porthos. Lincoln stopped and crouched back down, watching and wondering.

Below the balcony, looking at Salina, Porthos called softly, "My dearest Hurrem, bringer of my joy, I am emperor of the world by being a beggar at your door."

Leaning over the balcony, Salina replied, "Gentle breeze, tell my love that like the nightingale, I sigh and pine away without him. The hand of grief pierces my heart with its painful arrow."

Then Porthos, nimble as a cat, scampered up the trellis and vaulted over the balcony, into Salina's arms.

Lincoln watched for a moment as they left the balcony, then he started creeping back toward his own room. Two balconies down, he saw someone at the railing who also had been watching Salina and Porthos. Amanda's face rose above the railing.

Lincoln heard footsteps walking his way. He dropped deep in the bushes, and Amanda ducked below the rail, as two palace guards walked by.

When they were past, Lincoln came under Amanda's balcony and tossed a pebble up. Getting no response, he tossed another. Amanda's head peered over the rail. Lincoln spoke softly up to her, trying to imitate Porthos's style, "Away to my lady, gentle breeze; send tidings of an aching breast."

He stuck his head out from behind the palm fronds.

"Are you are crazy?" she whispered back. "There are guards all over this place. If you don't get out of here, I'll call them. Now, *go!*"

"I have to explain to you, there's nothing between me and that awful German woman."

"We'll talk about it tomorrow. Now, leave. You're going to get us both in trouble." She turned to go back into her room.

Lincoln started up the trellis. "I won't leave if you're still angry with me," he said, leaning out to see her.

He felt and heard the snap as the trellis broke, and he fell six feet to the ground. Amanda heard him fall and ran back to railing. He was sprawled on the ground, apparently unconscious. She climbed down the other side of the trellis and knelt beside him, lifting his head as he groaned and mumbled incoherently.

"Oh, Mr. Smith!" she said. "Please be all right!"

"What tongue can her perfections tell," Lincoln, with eyes closed, murmured between groans.

"Oh, Smith, are you all right? You're delirious!"

"Whose eyes below her fulsome brows, before their light the angels bow; oh, not away . . ." On he babbled.

"You must get up!" Amanda said.

"And I, for her, would death beguile if she would grant the slightest smile," he said, and opened his eyes in a not very delirious way.

"Why, you!" she said, letting his head drop and hit the ground.

They heard the noise of the guards coming their way.

"We mustn't be seen like this," Amanda whispered. They got up and hid in the bushes, where Lincoln put his arms around her, sheltering her from the prickly fronds. She resisted at first, though not very strenuously. When the pair of guards had passed, he didn't let her go.

"I am different," Lincoln said.

"What?"

"I *am* different. You said I'm not, but I'm not like most men."

"Obviously! Now, let me go."

Lincoln loosened his hold on her but didn't fully let go, which seemed satisfactory. "Oh, why can't there be more men like Porthos?" she said.

"Yeah, wasn't that gaudy? I saw you watching the old lizard and Salina."

Amanda tried to slap him, but he caught her hand. "How dare you! Let go of me . . . You mustn't tell a soul about them."

"I'll honor the sanctity of their love."

"Good. Now, release me!"

"I've played the fool," he said, dropping his arms and letting her go.

"You *are* the fool."

He looked her solemnly in the eyes. He started to bow down on one knee. She pulled him back up and seemed to have a hard time keeping from smiling. "Don't be a buffoon."

"The knights of old used to do it."

"I don't want a man bowing to me. At first thought, anyway. You could be bowing to me on the outside and your heart could still be with that horrid, bossy German."

"My heart's not with her." He looked amorously into her eyes again. She couldn't help smiling back.

"I'll raise a monument to this night of bliss," he said, smiling and looking her deep in the eyes, "and enshrine the memory with a stolen kiss." Then he tried to kiss her. She slapped him squarely, but he kissed her anyway. She resisted for a moment, then let him. Not a long kiss, but neither a short one. Lincoln gave out a muffled noise that was something between a wolf's howl and an Indian's war whoop.

"Shh!" Amanda said.

A few moments later, Lincoln stuck his head above the fronds, looking about them. He and Amanda then hurried to her trellis, where he helped her up. Then he ran off toward his own balcony.

Lincoln walked into his room from the balcony. After closing the door, he belted out another Comanche war whoop and heaved a sigh of love. Hearing a whisper of movement behind him, he turned as a hooded figure lunged at him with a dagger. Lincoln just managed to block the blow and wrestled the attacker to the ground. Holding the hand with the dagger, he banged it against one of the iron legs of the bed, and the knife clattered on the tile floor. The hooded attacker reached over and grabbed the brass chamber pot and slammed it over Lincoln's head, causing him to let go, then dashed out of the room.

Lincoln came running out of the room and raced down the hall after him. As he ran, a door flew open, and he smashed into it, falling to the floor.

"What is going on out there?" Amanda said, stepping out into the hall.

The hooded assailant had disappeared around the corner. She walked around the open door and saw Lincoln lying flat on the floor. "Oh, no, you don't. I'm not falling for that trick twice in the same night."

She walked back into her room and shut the door.

CHAPTER 44

The next morning, Amanda and Lincoln sat silently across from each other in the palace library. Pretending to be reading, they each held a book in front of their faces. Amanda lowered hers slightly, trying to steal a look at Lincoln. He lowered his, revealing a major lump on his forehead. She gave a pacifying sort of smile, and he mustered up something approaching a smile.

"Speaking of monuments," she said, "it looks as if I have raised one of my own—on your forehead. I really am terribly sorry. Perhaps, we should try to start over."

Lincoln put his hand to the bump. "I liked where we were last night—about ten minutes before you opened that door.

"Some of those verses you used were quite good. Did you make them up yourself?"

"Some of it was Spenser; some was mine. I guess Porthos kind of inspired me."

"You will be all right, won't you?"

"I'm fine. Heck, growing up where I did, I used to get one of these or a black eye most every week."

"What was the American frontier really like?" she said. "Was it grand and dangerous?"

"I was too young and missed most of it, but my father was one of the greatest lawmen of the time. By the time I grew up, it had all changed. I didn't fit in. All I ever wanted was to be like my father."

"Your father must have been a fine and brave man."

"My mother used to say that men like him were a dying breed, whose code of behavior you could trace back to the times of King Arthur and Charlemagne."

"But the breed has not yet died."

"Yeah, but against grease-leaking, fire-belching, noisy machinery that crams the equivalent of twenty horses into a single motorcar, what chance do they have? And then there's the bankers and the politicians!"

"I don't think they are really the problem."

"Yeah. Maybe those are just the symptoms, and the disease is something else. On my way here, I met this strange, crazy hermit who lived in a cave on a mountain. He didn't have much of it right, but maybe he had something. He was convinced he'd discovered the real problem. He had spent the last fifty years trying to slow time. How can you fight the onslaught of time and the changes it brings? Maybe he wasn't so crazy after all."

"He sounds like a lunatic to me."

"But it's true. Finally, time wins. It's like that character in Shakespeare says: in the end, it's all 'mere oblivion.'"

Amanda thought for a moment. In a way, what Lincoln was saying made sense. But the pessimism it displayed contradicted her experience, and not only her experience, but also the experience of every sane—or at least, happy—person she had ever known. "You don't seem like it, but you're really a pessimist."

This took Lincoln aback. "I'm not a pessimist."

"If you truly believe what you're saying, then you are."

"Maybe I'm more of a pessimistic optimist. Or an optimistic pessimist."

"The Legion never surrenders," she said. "Do you know the saying? It's the motto of the Foreign Legion? That's pure optimism."

"I know and appreciate that saying more than you can imagine."

"Well, it seems to me, that is exactly what you're doing: surrendering."

"I haven't surrendered. Maybe I've just retreated a little." But he didn't like the thought of retreat any more than that of surrender. "Maybe I'm just . . . just regrouping."

"Mr. Smith, you are a perfect case of a person's reality and experience contradicting his philosophy."

Lincoln appeared to be thinking this one over.

"You silly goose," she said, "don't you see? The problem isn't machines and politicians. And bankers can be useful if they're honest. Your quest is just different. You have your evil knights to fight, you even have your own bandidos and desperados, as your father had. You just need the imagination to see them."

"I was always told I had an overactive imagination."

"Hardly! You don't have *enough* of one."

Later that afternoon, Omar was returning from his midday meal at his grandmother's house when he passed a house with three horses tied up in front. They were fine-looking horses, and since horses were his profession, he stopped and looked at them. Standing in front of the house were two unpleasant-looking robed men. Seeing Omar, they sneered, sending him the message to keep moving.

Before he turned to go, something caught his eye. Peeking out from the saddle scabbard on one of the horses was a rifle stock of dark wood. He looked at the men again and called out, "Very fine animals," then got another quick glance at the rifle. Engraved on the buttstock was a large cursive *WS*. He waved at the men and walked on.

Prince Kamak had been pacing the floor of his office for much of the day. Tomorrow afternoon, at the dedication ceremony for the dam, the culmination of his plan was to take place. But the Legion regiment was still in Fort Flatters. He had to lure them out of the fort, marching south, where el-Krum and his warriors would annihilate them.

The young American had become more than an irritant. He had managed to escape, however clumsily, from every snare Kamak set for him. On hearing of last night's failure, the prince's first response had been fury. But he had overcome his emotion with reason and analysis, the kind of systematic, detailed thinking he had learned in his German education.

By the time Fräulein Zads arrived in his office, he was confident in the solution, having written up a detailed plan for it, including any possible mishaps and contingencies. The key element, the initial taking of the French girl, he would not entrust to anyone. He would do it himself.

"El-Krum has arrived," said Fräulein Zads, who, though German, was not good at masking her emotions. "I meet with him tonight. What can I tell him?" Sitting down at a chess table, she picked up a knight and gripped it.

"Tell him we will deliver the girl, and to have the ambush in place."

"How are you going to take her? That American doesn't let her out of his sight."

"I will dispose of him and take the girl at the same time."

"When? Do you realize what will happen if the Legion regiment has not left the fort?"

"Early tomorrow, you and Hultz will take her by motorcar to the pass."

"This must succeed," Zads replied. "Even the combined forces of el-Krum and our battalion will not suffice if the Legion is still in the fort.

"I am handling the disposal of Smith and the taking of the girl personally. Tell el-Krum you will have her at the rendezvous point before noon. Make sure he is ready, with his cannons primed. I don't want one legionnaire left alive."

Lincoln and Amanda came out of the palace library and walked down the hall toward their rooms. They stopped in front of her door and silently gazed into each other's eyes. Lincoln gently took her hand, and they moved closer to each other.

"See you tonight." She squeezed his hand and entered her room. Lincoln stayed at the door for a few seconds, then turned and bumped into Athos, Porthos, and Aramis, who were walking down the hall.

"I see you're carrying out your charge—with diligence," Athos said. "Don't let your judgment get clouded by frivolous emotion."

"Don't worry, I'll do my duty," replied Lincoln. He walked on and entered his room, but instead of closing the door behind him, he left it slightly ajar and listened.

"Really, old boy," Aramis said as they walked on, "perhaps you ought not be so hard on the lad."

"I think you see a little too much of yourself in him," Porthos said.

"I was nice to him last night," Athos replied. Then he walked off ahead of the other two.

When Lincoln entered his room, he saw a folded piece of paper lying on his pillow. After reading it, he checked his pistol, put it back in his belt, and left the room.

CHAPTER 45

The note Lincoln found in his room read, *Powwow needed pronto at booth of your kickside's uncle.* It wasn't difficult for Lincoln to find Omar's uncle's booth. The first person he asked knew precisely where Kamil, the horse-and-camel trader, conducted business.

When Lincoln arrived, Omar was in the back, inspecting a camel. Seeing Lincoln, he brought a finger to his lips, for the booth was crowded with customers and attendants.

Omar approached Lincoln and asked whether he might interest the American in a Méhari racing camel. Lincoln walked with Omar to the back of the booth, where they positioned themselves on the far side of a camel and started inspecting its teeth.

"In front of the house," Omar said. "It was on his horse, in front of the house."

"Wait a second, start over. What did you see?"

"I saw your rifle on el-Krum's horse, in front of a house not far from my honorable grandmother's house."

"Are you sure it was el-Krum's horse?"

"Am I a queenhorn? In fact, I am not sure it was his horse, but I recognized the two guards. They were also with him at his camp. And I am sure it was your rifle—the initials were on the stock. The guards saw me and made me leave."

"Omar, that's great work!"

"I came back from a different direction and spied on the house. A man left, and I followed this man to the gates of the palace, where he gave a note to a blond woman."

"What did the woman look like?"

"She was tall and blond, with large . . . What do you call them?"

"Never mind. I know who she is."

"Perhaps they are setting up a powwow?"

"A powwow. Yeah, I think you're right. Okay. Is there any way you can get back and keep watching the house?"

"The house is being watched now. I have a cousin who also wants to learn the ways of the American West."

"How did you get the note into my room?"

"Was my note not excellent?"

"Yes, nice and cryptic."

"I wrote it and gave it to my cousin who works in the palace who is also interested in the—"

"You—all of you—must be very careful and not trust anyone. There are surely spies in the palace. I almost bit the dust there last night."

"Why would you chew dust in the palace, where food is plentiful?"

"No, no, it's a Western phrase, like 'got his chips cashed in' or 'got his ticket punched.'"

Omar looked confused.

"I almost got *killed* in the palace, is what it means. Some hostile attacked me. The point is, be careful. Next time you need to send me a message, just send the single code word *powwow*, and I'll meet you here as soon as I can."

On his way back to the palace, Lincoln saw Athos walking down a side street. His back was to Lincoln, and he carried two large bags. What was Athos doing alone in this poorer part of the city? Lincoln was heading back to the palace to tell Athos what he had heard from Omar, and here the man was. So he decided to follow him.

Farther down the street, Athos stopped at a gate outside a courtyard where children were playing. Lincoln kept back on the other side of the street, hiding behind some bushes, watching him. Athos rang a bell at the gate. An old woman came out and greeted him. The children in the courtyard saw Athos and ran and embraced him. He handed one of the bags to the woman, and from the other bag he distributed gifts to the children. They received the gifts and ran back to their games. The old woman gratefully shook Athos's hand with both of hers, and he turned and walked back the way he had come. Lincoln kept himself hidden until Athos had gone.

A couple of streets away, Lincoln saw him sitting at a table at an outdoor café. He had a drink in front of him that didn't look like coffee, and he seemed to be brooding over it.

Lincoln walked up to the table. Athos looked up, startled. "Mind if I sit down?" Lincoln asked.

Athos took a swallow from his tumbler and, with his boot, pushed out the chair across from him.

"What are you doing out here?" Athos said as Lincoln sat down.

"I just had a meeting with my friend Omar. He had some important news."

Athos did not seem impressed and took another swallow of his drink.

"What are you doing out here?" Lincoln asked.

"Not your business."

"I saw you at the orphanage."

Athos looked up at Lincoln; Lincoln didn't look away.

"So what?" He finished off his drink and looked around. Catching the waiter's eye, he motioned for another drink. "Well, what did he tell you?" Athos finally said. "What did the kid say?"

"El-Krum is hiding in the city. And Omar saw him send a message to the German ambassador."

"Fräulein Zads?" Athos scowled. "I've never trusted her for a minute."

"What are we going to do?"

"Do? We're going to do our jobs and try to keep another bloody war from breaking out."

Lincoln looked at Athos, trying to understand him.

"You got a lot to learn, kid. I don't know why you joined the Legion, but whatever you're running from or trying to find, it's just as bleak here as everywhere else. You oughta go home while you still got a chance."

"You should use *have* instead of *got*; it's preferred," Lincoln said. After a pause, he added, "And what are you running from or looking for?"

Athos quickly grabbed Lincoln by his shirtfront. Drawing his knife from the sheath on his leg, he put it to his throat. After a moment, he let him go and slid back down into his chair, slamming the big bowie knife on the table but leaving his hand on the hilt. "What I'm looking for, I'm not going to find. You're lucky it's me you said that to. Another legionnaire would have slit your throat."

"Maybe I *am* learning a few things," Lincoln said, noticing the knife, then looking up.

"Yeah, for instance?"

"I don't know. I have to think about it for a while."

The waiter came and set down another drink in front of Athos. Athos picked up the drink with the hand that was on the knife. The waiter, picking up Athos's empty glass, knocked the knife onto the floor. Athos brushed the waiter aside, mumbling something, and picked it up and put it back in its sheath.

After a moment, Lincoln added, "The problem is, we don't have any poets anymore. I've been listening to the prose of the moderns instead of the poets of old. If no one ever read any old books, there wouldn't have been a Renaissance. It's not the Legion that I came here to find, it's the *poetry* of the Legion."

"You're as crazy as a mad steer on locoweed!"

"At least I'm happy. I think."

Athos grunted a laugh. "Well, then what are you going to do about Fräulein Zads?"

"Me? What do you mean, 'what am I going to do'? What do you want me to do?"

"You seem to have all the answers."

"I never said that."

"If you want my advice, I suggest we don't let on we know about her and el-Krum. There's nothing we can do at this point, anyway. We got—we *have*—to find out what she's up to."

"I agree," Lincoln said. "I wonder where Prince Kamak stands with all this."

CHAPTER 46

Just after sunset two hooded figures walked up to the house where Omar had earlier seen Lincoln's rifle. A guard came out of the shadows at the side of the house and opened the door for them. The two figures pulled back their hoods and entered the house. From across the street, crouched behind an acacia tree, Omar didn't recognize her male companion, but he did recognize the tall, blond, voluptuously built woman he seen at the palace gate.

Inside the house, through the open doors on the second-floor balcony, Omar could see four men reclining at a low, broad table, eating from a large plate of fruit. When Fräulein Zads and Colonel Hultz came in the room, none other than el-Krum licked his fingers clean and got to his feet. He offered the plate to the fräulein and then to the officer, both of whom declined. He gave the plate back to his men, who had not arisen.

Omar climbed up the acacia tree that shaded the adjacent house, and hopped from the tree onto that house's roof. He sneaked across the roof to its edge and jumped across to the building Fräulein Zads had just entered. He knelt for a moment, listening to make sure he had not been heard. Then he crawled to the front edge of the roof, directly above the open balcony doors. He lay down prone on the roof, putting his ear over the edge, trying to catch the conversation in the room below.

He heard a female voice say, "I assure you, the prince's plan will not fail. Mur and the German Reich will forge an alliance that will be the most powerful force on the continent."

Then a male voice with accents of a desert tribe said, "And then what will this alliance's next conquest be?"

"Let us concern ourselves with the matter at hand," the woman said. "Then we can discuss these things. We will bring the girl, and the Legion will follow. Make sure you are ready."

Omar rose up and slipped away. At the edge of the building, he hopped across to the next roof. But he pushed off on a loose tile, which made him slip and come up short on his jump. The loose tile fell into the shrubbery, and Omar barely reached the other roof, catching its edge with his hands. He hung on for a few moments, then the tiles he was hanging on gave way, and he crashed into the pomegranate bushes below.

The guards at the corners of the house heard the crash and ran toward it. Inside, Fräulein Zads, el-Krum, and the others heard it as well. "Find out what that was!" Fräulein Zads ordered Colonel Hultz.

"You go, as well," el-Krum said in Arabic to his three men.

At the back of the house, Omar got up and saw the two guards running toward him. He took off in the opposite direction. Coming to a fence, he vaulted over it and ran through a side door of the next house.

He burst into a room where five men lounged on pillows, smoking water pipes. They were so startled at seeing Omar that they just sat there and did nothing. Omar looked around and, seeing a stairway at the far end of the room, dashed up it. He heard his pursuers coming as he ran up the stairs.

Omar came out on the roof of the building, ran across it, and jumped to the roof of the next building. Running to the only room on the roof, he threw open the door and burst in. Inside, a belly dancer was swaying before a man on a low divan. The dancer shrieked and covered herself. Without pausing, Omar ran through the room and into the hallway. At the end, a stairway led down to where music was playing.

Omar burst out of one of the rooms in the hall and ran back through the room with the belly dancer, who had started to sway again. Without stopping, he dashed through the room, out the door, onto the roof—and into the arms of the German colonel.

El-Krum was reclining at the low table, and Fräulein Zads was nervously pacing the floor, when Colonel Hultz returned, followed by el-Krum's three men, dragging Omar. "He claims he a poor orphan," said Colonel Hultz.

"Yes, I was only looking for a few scraps of food," Omar whined.

El-Krum arose and walked over to Omar. He grabbed and squeezed his face, looking him over, head to foot.

"Little thief, what need have you of these?" he asked, kicking Omar's Western-style riding boots.

"My name is Omar, and I work for my uncle, a trader of camels and horses."

"He's the boy who helped the American rescue the French girl," said Fräulein Zads, walking up and inspecting Omar. "We heard the ambassador and his daughter talking about him. Take him to the temple. I must go the reception, but I want you to find out what he knows."

CHAPTER 47

Dressed in his French suit again, Lincoln stood alone before a window of the palace library. Tomorrow afternoon was the dedication ceremony at the dam, and tonight there was a reception at the palace, celebrating the event. He could hear the noise from it building in the reception hall on the floor below.

Amanda, dressed in a blue taffeta evening gown with a sash in the colors of the French flag, entered the room. "There you are," she said. "The reception has started. The Germans are putting on the entertainment and will be offended if we aren't there when it begins."

"I was just coming," Lincoln said. "I just needed some time to think things over."

Amanda's countenance dropped, though she tried to hide it. "Oh, okay." She raised her chin, losing her smile. "If that's the way it is, I understand."

He saw that she had misunderstood him. "There's one thing I don't need any time to think about, though," he said, approaching her with a roguish gleam in his eye.

She took a step backward. "All right, all right, I believe you. But what are you so concerned about?"

"I've had some important news," he said, backing off a few steps. "I saw Omar today. He saw el-Krum in the city, and the guy is in cahoots with the Germans."

Amanda gave him a puzzled look. "What are these cahoots?"

"Omar saw one of el-Krum's men take a message to Fräulein Zads. It seems the Germans are in league with el-Krum in some way. The question is, what are they up to? Could there be a link between him and the crocodile people? And what about Kamak? He went to school in Germany, didn't he?"

"You really think the prince is conspiring with them? All he cares about is digging up that old temple."

"He stands in line for the throne, doesn't he?"

"But Suleiman is his father! You aren't suggesting . . ." Amanda cut herself off, looking more concerned than ever.

Lincoln walked back over to the library window. "Do you ever hear a clinking noise at night? I could swear I hear it sometimes, and I've heard that kind of sound before; I just can't place it."

"I think I may have heard something before. Could be a number of things, like work they're doing on the palace." She turned away and started toward the door. "Really, we should get to the reception. We'll raise a scandal if we're not there soon."

"Just one other thing," Lincoln said, walking fast to catch up. "Why won't Kamak let anyone in the temple except his 'specialists'—his German friends he studied archaeology with? Maybe he's found something important in there. Maybe he's even found the treasure."

"If it matters," she said, correcting him, "he didn't study archaeology, he studied geology."

"Geology! Are you sure of that?"

"Oh yes, quite sure. He's bored me with the topic on several occasions, droning on about minerals and ores."

After thinking for a moment, Lincoln said, "And some of that stuff is valuable."

"You aren't suggesting?" Amanda said.

"I need to find out," Lincoln replied. "I'll meet you at the reception in a few minutes. I forgot something in my room."

"What?"

"I want my pistol, just in case."

Mounted on a table in the middle of the reception hall was a large model of the dam the French had built for the Murians. The room was filled with even more people than had attended the previous night's reception, as a caravan had arrived in Mur earlier in the day. When Lincoln and Amanda entered the room, the orchestra was playing a French minuet. The Three from Camarón were chatting with Princess Salina and the wife of the British ambassador. King Suleiman, Ambassador Montier, and the British ambassador were talking to two other men, one appreciably taller than the other, whose backs were to the room's entryway. Even seeing them only from behind, Lincoln immediately recognized his friends and partners, Johnny and Jake.

Lincoln couldn't imagine under what circumstances they had arrived in Mur and were guests at the reception, especially dressed in business suits as they were. But he could be sure those circumstances were irregular, to say the least. He and Amanda walked up to the group they were standing in, and Lincoln, completely ignoring Johnny and Jake, bowed to the king and then greeted the ambassador. After a few cordial niceties, the king walked away to another group standing by the buffet table.

Lincoln, feeling a bit odd in the presence of his unacknowledged friends, said, "Mr. Ambassador, I don't believe that Amanda or I have had the pleasure of meeting these gentlemen."

"Why, of course," said the ambassador. "Amanda and monsieur Smith, may I present to you monsieur Walcott and monsieur Huntley from the *Manchester Guardian*, here do a story on the dam for their British readership."

Amanda acknowledged them with a slight bow of her head, and Lincoln, trying hold back his amazement, shook hands. In what sounded to him like Australian English, Mr. Walcott and Mr. Huntley were delighted to make their acquaintance.

After a suitable bit of chitchat, Johnny and Jake excused themselves and walked over to the buffet table. A short while later, Lincoln did the same. He picked up a plate and helped himself to some broiled lamb, then wandered over to where Johnny and Jake stood alone, enjoying the repast.

"Well, it ain't beef," Jake said, taking a bite of the roasted lamb, "but somewhat well prepared."

Johnny chimed in. "Not exactly sure what they are, but I like the spices."

"I'm not even going to ask," Lincoln said, "but I'm glad you're here safe. Where's Tom?"

"The blighter's still in Sidi, in the hospital," Jake said. "It was the pact that saved us."

"What happened?" Lincoln asked, breaking his promise of seconds ago.

"We got your letter and didn't know what to do," Johnny said. "Then we got hold of some journalists' papers who had some bad luck on the way here. We waited two extra days for you, and it didn't look so good for you. So we became journalists—coincidentally, with the same names as the two recently defunct newsmen. Figured we'd have freer run of the place for our prospecting. Actually, it was Tom's idea, but the night before we left, he decides he's going to lay one on, seein' as he won't have the opportunity again for some time. Well, me and Jake declined going out with him because of the pact, and lo, but Tom goes off and aggrieves some local by having too much firewater in him. The old bloke got himself gut-stabbed."

"If Tom had to get stuck around here, I reckon Sidi's the best place for it," Jake added. "He ain't dead, but he'll be invalided for a spell. Left it for me and John to carry out the newspaper reportin'. How's our accents?"

"Yeah, we're trying to hold off talkin' too much," said Johnny.

"That's probably a good idea."

"And what about you?" said Jake. "You don't look like you're joined up. As John said, we didn't know if you was kilt or what. But we're still ready to enlist if you're in."

"I'm not in yet," Lincoln replied after swallowing a bite of shawarma. "I'm the ambassador's daughter's bodyguard, disguised as her tutor. It's complicated. I'll tell you about it later. But I'm glad you're here. There's trouble brewing, so keep your eyes and ears open."

Seeing Amanda and Prince Kamak approach, Johnny and Jake took a sudden interest in someone across the crowded room.

"Mr. Smith," said Prince Kamak, "Mademoiselle Montier tells me her studies have taken an interesting turn since you took over and that you are a scholar of penetrating insight."

"Your Highness is kind to say so," said Lincoln, "but I am learning as much from the mademoiselle as she is from me. She is a formidable scholar herself."

Prince Kamak bowed slightly, acknowledging the compliment to Amanda. "I must compliment the French in their technical achievement," he said to her. "Tomorrow, this palace will be lighted by electric lamps."

"I understand the Germans were also considered to build the dam," Lincoln said.

"One of life's dilemmas," said the prince. "French technique or German efficiency. It appears my father's choice was justified."

"Yes, of course," said Lincoln.

"After reflection, Mr. Smith," the prince said, "it appears I was quite ungenerous to deny a fellow scholar a look at my findings in the temple. Are you still interested in seeing our discoveries?"

"Yes, we are!" Amanda blurted. "We'd love to see what you've found."

"Why yes, thank you," Lincoln said, flashing Amanda a cold look. "I would very much enjoy seeing your discoveries."

"Then I insist you let me give you and the mademoiselle a personal tour of the dig. Tomorrow morning? But we'd have to do it early, before the work begins—say, eight o'clock, if that is convenient? That would also give us plenty of time before the ceremony."

"We'll look forward to the tour in place of our morning lessons," Lincoln said.

"Very well, then. Tomorrow at eight o'clock." Kamak dipped his head slightly and walked off.

"See, he's not so secretive after all," said Amanda.

"I don't know. A rattlesnake drools all over its prey just before swallowing it whole."

Amanda grimaced.

"Do you know why the king really chose France instead of the Germans to build the dam?" Lincoln asked.

"My father boasts that it was his negotiating, but I happen to know one reason was that the Germans demanded exclusive trading rights that Suleiman was unwilling to give."

"Trading rights—does that mean exporting as well as importing?"

"Both, I suppose. But Mur has nothing of great value to export, unless the legends about the mines are really true."

Lincoln set his jaw. "Do you know where Kamak's office is?"

"His suite is on the second floor, down the far end of the hall, first room around the corner. Why?"

"Before we go with him on any tour of his temple, I need to find out more about what he's up to there."

At the other end of the room, one of the French officials clapped his hands, and the orchestra struck up a tune in a minor key, with a sultry North African air. A blond woman dressed in luxurious Murian robes ambled out on the dais and began singing in German, then in Murian.

While everyone's attention was on the singer, Lincoln stepped out of the ballroom.

CHAPTER 48

The door to Prince Kamak's office was locked.

At the end of hall was a large window. Opening it, he looked out at the balcony attached to Kamak's room. There was no way he could get to it from the window. He would have to get to the ground, then climb up to the balcony a good fifteen feet above.

There had recently been some refurbishing of the palace, and the vine-laden trellises that hung on most of the outer walls had been torn down and lay heaped in piles below. A narrow ditch, freshly filled in, ran from the wall under Kamak's room to the wall that enclosed the palace park. And from where the ditch intersected the palace, a metal casing six inches wide ran up along the wall to a corbel at the side of Kamak's balcony. Lincoln wondered what it was for—something to do with the prince's activity in the temple, perhaps. He also wondered whether it would hold his weight.

Hanging from the ledge under the window, he dropped to the ground, where a pile of vines cushioned his fall. He examined the casing below Kamak's balcony. It was fastened to the wall with masonry bolts every three feet or so. They looked secure enough to hold him. He began climbing up, using the bolts as footholds.

Two-thirds of the way up, the upper bolts pulled out of the stone. The tin casing started folding, and Lincoln began to fall. But as the casing gave way, the thick rubber-insulated wire behind it remained. Lincoln managed to grab hold and stopped his fall. He had seen electrical power lines before.

He pulled himself up onto the balcony and entered through the double glass doors. The half-moon shining through the doors gave some light, though less toward the front of the room. He lit his match from the waterproof container Amanda had given him. Along the tapestry-covered right wall were a velvet divan and a couple of elaborately carved chairs. Toward the front of the room was a large desk and, on it, a kerosene lamp. He struck another match and lit the lamp.

Looking through the drawers, he found a packet of aerial drawings of the temple. As he studied them, a muffled sound of turning gears came from the wall. He quickly put the drawings back, blew out the light, and crouched behind the divan.

The noise of the gears slowed. Peeking around the corner of the divan, he saw rays of light shine from behind the tapestry. The mechanical noise stopped, and the tapestry slid to the side.

From an open panel in the wall, walked Colonel Hultz. A torch on the wall behind him revealed a narrow chamber. He did something to the lamp on the wall next to the opening, and the panel closed. Hultz pulled back the tapestry over the wall and then went out the front door into the palace corridor.

In the reception hall, before an enrapt audience, the singer was coming to the end of her song. She stepped off the dais, sauntered up to the king, and finished off the song with an elaborate bow.

The king clapped enthusiastically, and most of the audience followed his example. Fräulein Zads and Prince Kamak, standing behind him, clapped perfunctorily.

As the applause died away, Colonel Hultz entered the room. The fräu-lein excused herself and walked over to where he stood alone, near the door.

Amanda, having noticed Hultz enter the room, watched Fräulein Zads's reaction to whatever he told her. As Hultz was leaving, Zads immediately went to Prince Kamak, who was talking with his father and a German dignitary. She whispered something to Kamak, and the two of them excused themselves from the group to speak alone. Moments after this, when their attention was away from the door, Amanda left the room.

Standing before the wall where Colonel Hultz had come out, Lincoln pulled aside the tapestry. He felt around the wall, looking for the seam where the door had opened. He tried pressing and twisting different parts of the lamp that Hultz had used to close the door, but nothing happened. As he continued fiddling with the lamp, he heard a key being inserted in the office door. He pulled back the tapestry and scampered back behind the divan.

Colonel Hultz entered the room again and went directly to the wall. He pulled back the tapestry, then twisted the base of the lamp, and the panel opened. Stepping inside the passage, he pulled the tapestry across the opening, blocking Lincoln's view of whatever he did to make the door close.

Amanda had followed Hultz and saw him go into Kamak's office. Believing Lincoln to be in the room, she racked her brain over what to do. She put her ear to the door but heard nothing. Finally, she just decided to knock on the door. If Hultz answered, she could say she was looking for Prince Kamak.

Suddenly, the door swung open, and Lincoln and Amanda stood face to face.

"Are you all right?" she said. "I saw Colonel Hultz come in here."

"Shh!" He pulled her inside and shut the door. "I was just coming to give Athos a message. Now you can give it to him. There's a secret passage in here. I saw Hultz come out of it, and he just went through it again."

"Show it to me."

"It's here, but you have to go and tell Athos." He led her to the tapestry and pulled it back.

"Let me see it first."

"I think you just turn this." Lincoln twisted the lamp's base. Again came that grinding noise he'd heard before, and the secret door opened. The torch was still burning inside in its wall sconce. They took a couple of steps into the passage.

"You saw Colonel Hultz go in here? He came into the reception and told Fräulein Zads something that looked very important. She went immediately to Prince Kamak. Then Hultz left, and I followed him because I thought he'd catch you in here."

"Well, thanks. That was brave of you. But you have to go. I want you to tell Athos what you've seen and that I've followed Hultz down the passage. And if I'm not back in two hours—"

"I'm not letting you go by yourself. I'm going with you!"

"No, you are not! This is going to be dangerous, but we have to find out where this passage goes and what they're up to. Now, go back and tell Athos what I told you."

"*You* go back and tell Athos."

"You must go. I'm responsible for your safety."

"I'm going with you."

"This is not a negotiation. Someone has to tell Athos about this, just in case."

Footsteps sounded out in the corridor. Two voices were talking. Then came the metallic click of a key being inserted into the lock.

They heard the door open. There was no time to hide in the room. From inside the passage, Lincoln slid the tapestry back into place and looked desperately around him for the device to close the door. He tried fiddling with the sconce that held the torch, but nothing happened. Footsteps were coming through the room, straight at them. Lincoln grabbed Amanda's hand, and they ran deeper into the passage.

Prince Kamak and Fräulein Zads walked up to the tapestry, and Kamak pulled it back. Both were startled to see the secret door open.

"The colonel is becoming careless," the prince said. "Or . . . ?"

"He would never be so sloppy," Zads replied.

"Was the tutor in the room before we left?"

"I saw him when he and the girl entered the ballroom, but I don't recall seeing him after that."

Kamak walked back to his desk and took a pistol out of a drawer. "Come," he said, and they entered the chamber.

CHAPTER 49

A few steps down the passage, Lincoln and Amanda came to a narrow stairway that spiraled downward into darkness. Lincoln grabbed the torch from its sconce at the top of the stairs, and they hurried down as quietly as they could. After descending what must have been five or six stories, the stairway ended at a long, narrow, curving corridor that was already lit by kerosene torches every forty feet or so. Above them came the sound of the hidden door closing. They hurried down the passage in front of them, which declined at a rather steep angle, taking them deeper underground.

After a hundred yards or so, they slowed up, catching their breath and listening. Footsteps echoed on the stairs behind them. In front of them, more clearly than Lincoln had heard before, was the clanking noise.

"There's that sound again," he whispered.

"Yes, but what's so important about it?"

"I have it! I knew I'd heard it before."

"What is it?" Amanda asked.

"Shh!" Lincoln said as the footsteps in the corridor behind them grew louder. He grabbed Amanda's hand, and they hurried farther down the passage.

They slowed up again after another hundred yards and listened, for the footsteps but also for Hultz in front of them. "We better slow down and go softly," Lincoln whispered. "We don't want to get too close to Hultz. We need a place to hide."

Soon, the passage led them into a circular room perhaps thirty feet in diameter. On the opposite side from where they entered, the corridor continued. Around the periphery of the room stood perhaps a dozen ancient-looking ornate upright coffins, with the images of men and women engraved on their fronts.

"What is this?" asked Amanda.

"It must be part of a great underground temple or tomb," Lincoln whispered. "Or maybe even an underground city." He walked to one of the coffins and tried to force it open.

"What are you doing?" Amanda said. "Isn't it bad luck to disturb—"

Lincoln turned away from the coffin, listening. "There's someone coming." He grabbed Amanda's hand, and they scurried out the far end of the chamber. Stopping in the lighted passageway beyond, Lincoln extinguished the first three kerosene torches in their wall brackets and waited.

A few minutes later, Prince Kamak, holding a pistol, took a cautious step into the mausoleum room. Moments later, Fräulein Zads came up behind him. She reached into her coat pocket and pulled out a small revolver. After listening for a few moments, they walked into the middle of the room.

They poked around, and Prince Kamak looked behind a couple of the coffins.

Then, apparently satisfied that no one was hiding there, he and Fräulein Zads walked toward the passage on the far side. They didn't put their guns away.

Lincoln and Amanda raced silently down the darkened passage. They paused to listen. He heard faint voices ahead of them. He turned to listen for Kamak and Zads behind them.

"They're coming," he murmured, "and they're not that far behind us."

"What are we going to do," Amanda said.

He caught the edge of panic in her voice. "Shh!" he whispered. "We need to hide in one of those branches off the main passage. There was one not that far back."

"They're dark—how do we know what's in them?"

"We don't," Lincoln whispered, "but there are people ahead of us too." He took Amanda's hand again and started back up the passage.

After about fifty feet, they came to a hallway that cut through the main corridor. Lincoln hesitated, unable to see more than a few yards. Choosing the opening to the right, he felt along the rock wall, leading Amanda into the darkness.

"This is far enough," Lincoln whispered when they had gone about twenty feet in. "Be real quiet; don't hardly breathe."

The footsteps in the main passageway grew louder and then began to trail off. After about three minutes, Lincoln whispered, "Do you hear that?"

"What? I heard them walking," Amanda said.

"Not that—that whirring sound."

"No . . . well, maybe."

Lincoln paused for a moment, thinking. At last, he said, "Now I think I understand. Come on, we have the advantage—*we're* following *them*." He grabbed Amanda's hand again, and they went back to the main passageway, turned left, and quietly followed the footfalls ahead.

Lincoln and Amanda cautiously edged up to where the secret passageway ended at a large brass door that had been left ajar. Through the doorway, they could hear voices. Lincoln peeked through and saw that a flight of stairs descended to the floor of what looked like an ancient temple. The stairs were cut directly into the bedrock and ended at a forking path. One fork immediately led to a drawbridge of sorts, spanning a small stream. The other path led to a strange-looking altar, over which loomed a monstrous bronze image with the body of a man and the head and tail of a crocodile. At the base of this strange idol, Colonel Hultz, Prince Kamak, and Fräulein Zads, accompanied by six dervishes, stood facing a live body, suspended by the hands from the idol's huge jaws, six feet off the ground. It was Omar.

Lincoln turned back into the corridor to Amanda, who had been trying to peek through the door. "They've got Omar down there, hanging from a huge idol."

They heard Colonel Hultz's voice. "Tell me why you were spying on the fräulein and me, or I will feed you to the crocodiles."

"Please, sir, I was not spying," Omar said. "I was only playing a game with my friends."

"The little swine lies," said Fräulein Zads.

"What has he said?" Prince Kamak asked. "I want to know everything."

"He is now saying he was playing with his friends," said Hultz. "Before this, he said he was looking for food."

Lincoln and Amanda scooted back into the corridor. "I have to do something to save him," Lincoln said.

"Now I hear that sound you've been hearing," Amanda whispered. "What is so important about it?"

"Take a whiff. Smell it?"

Amanda sniffed the air, trying to place the smell. "What is it?"

"I can see why the Germans would be so eager for exclusive trading rights. But it gives me an idea." He peeked back through the doorway.

He looked down the steps to where the path branched left, toward the idol, and right, across the drawbridge. At the beginning of the drawbridge, a steep bank led down to the stream that the drawbridge spanned. On that bank, slightly under the drawbridge, one could not be seen from the area around the idol.

Kamak said, "Tell me the truth, and you will not be hurt. If you don't, you will die a slow and painful death."

Lincoln whispered in Amanda's ear, "I'm going down. I have a plan."

"Then I'm going too," said Amanda.

"This is no time for an argument."

"Then don't argue."

"Fine, then, follow me."

At the idol, Omar pleaded, "I am a loyal subject of you, my prince, and your father, the king."

"Tell me why you were spying on the fräulein's meeting," Kamak said. He and his party stood with their backs to the stairs.

"I told you, I don't know anything," said Omar.

At the doorway above, Lincoln whispered, "Come on, follow me." They sneaked through the doorway and down the stairs. At the bottom, they hopped over a low wall on the bank of the river, where it ran under the drawbridge. They crouched below the bridge. Suddenly, behind them they heard what sounded like the banging of an iron gate. Turning to look upstream, they saw a portcullis-like gate blocking the mouth of a large cave, and through it they could see movement. It took several seconds for them to realize that they were staring at a mass of live crocodiles milling behind the gate. Amanda almost shrieked, and Lincoln put a cautionary hand over her mouth.

"Don't worry," he whispered. "That gate looks pretty strong."

"They grow hungry," Kamak said, turning toward the cave. "This is your last chance."

"Colonel, did you fail to close the hidden door when you came down?" Fräulein Zads said.

"Of course not," Hultz replied. "I would never be so negligent."

"It was open when we came into the room," Zads said. "And Smith was not at the reception."

"What do you know about this?" snarled Prince Kamak. "We know you are friends with the American. We know you provided the horses to help him free Mademoiselle Montier."

"I don't know anything!" cried Omar.

"We would have run into him if he tried to go back up," Zads said.

"He may have found one of the other corridors," said Kamak. "We must find him—now." He, Fräulein Zads, Colonel Hultz, and the six dervishes walked to the drawbridge, leaving Omar hanging from the idol.

On the drawbridge, they stopped, facing Omar, a few feet above where Lincoln and Amanda were hiding. Lincoln drew his pistol.

"You have been extremely unwise," Kamak said to Omar. "Now you will save me the price of at least two goats by feeding my pets."

Lincoln swung up onto the drawbridge and, grabbing Fräulein Zads from behind, put his pistol to her head. "Okay, the plan just changed."

They all spun around, the dervishes going for their swords. Lincoln cocked his pistol.

"No one move," Kamak commanded. "Put your swords away."

"Send someone to untie the kid—now!" Lincoln said as Amanda climbed up on the drawbridge.

"Mr. Smith, you don't strike me as a man who would kill an unarmed woman."

Dragging Zads with him, Lincoln moved closer to Kamak.

"Colonel, put your gun to the girl's head," Prince Kamak ordered. As Colonel Hultz started for his pistol, Lincoln, in quick movement, let go of Fräulein Zads and grabbed Kamak, putting his gun to the prince's head. With his other hand, he took Kamak's gun and pointed it at the others.

"You're right, I couldn't kill an unarmed woman. But you, not a problem. And now I have at least one bullet for each of you, and as you saw, I can make them count. Now, do what I say or *you'll* be dinner for your lovely pets. Colonel, gently lay your gun down."

Hultz complied.

"You don't know what you're doing," said Prince Kamak. "What I am doing is for Mur's benefit, bringing it out of centuries of barbarism."

"Yeah, you've been real civilized so far," said Lincoln.

"He's bluffing," said Fräulein Zads.

Lincoln thumbed back the hammer of the prince's pistol. "Do you want to call me?"

"Do what he says," Kamak said.

"Amanda, pick up the colonel's gun," Lincoln said as he backed away with Prince Kamak off the end of the drawbridge, toward the door they had entered through.

Amanda, standing a few feet from Fräulein Zads, bent down to pick up the pistol.

In a sudden movement, Fräulein Zads had Amanda by the hair and was holding a small revolver to her head. "Now, Mr. Smith, I enjoy poker too," the fräulein said.

"A Mexican standoff!" Omar called out, still hanging from the idol.

"Be quiet, Omar," Lincoln said.

"Hilda, don't do anything rash," Kamak said.

"Mr. Smith?" said Zads. "I call you."

Lincoln put down his pistol and let Kamak go. Prince Kamak and Colonel Hultz picked up their guns, and the dervishes again drew their scimitars.

"Oh, her German insolence—isn't it charming!" Kamak said.

Then he said something to the dervishes, and two of them stepped toward Amanda. But Lincoln snatched up a burning torch from an iron ring on the drawbridge.

"Now it's my turn to call," Lincoln said, holding the torch high above the water.

"What are you doing?" Kamak said, almost laughing. "Are you out of your mind?"

"Worse. I'm from Texas, where it used to be quiet and peaceful across the plains, until they started bringing in machines—machines that made lots of noise."

"You have five seconds to drop the torch," Kamak said.

"And the noise those machines made is just like the noise I've been hearing here. You aren't hunting for artifacts or even for buried treasure."

"Is that right?" said Kamak.

"Yeah. You've found oil."

After a pause, Kamak said, "Very perceptive, Mr. Smith. You could also have mentioned my ruse of the crocodile cult so that when I destroy it, I'll have my people's undying devotion and loyalty."

"I knew it was a fraud; I just hadn't figured out how it all fit together. It's all up, anyway. I have you exactly where I want you."

"You're starting to become tedious. Get to the point."

"You know that if there's oil down here, then that water has to be full of it. And if I torch it, this place is going to blaze up before you can say *Tom Jefferson*."

"Oh, Mr. Smith, your imagination is sublime, though not quite accurate. Try as we might to find this river's source, all we know is that it flows from the west. All our wells are to the east—*downstream*. There's not a drop of oil in that water."

"You're bluffing," said Lincoln.

Kamak barked a command, and after hesitating a moment, the two dervishes advanced toward Amanda.

Lincoln tossed the torch into the river. It hissed and went out at once.

Amanda tried to resist, and Lincoln moved to help her, only to find four scimitars pointed at his chest.

"Fräulein, take the mademoiselle to el-Krum tonight. Smith has saved us the trouble of snatching her in the morning." Zads, Hultz, and the two dervishes holding Amanda moved off the drawbridge and deeper into the temple. Prince Kamak spoke to the other four dervishes and then turned to Lincoln. "I'm sorry, where are my manners? I just told them to hang you from the idol with the boy and to make sure they put you in reach of my pets."

The four dervishes with scimitars out nudged Lincoln toward the idol. Kamak turned the device that raised the drawbridge. After tying Lincoln's hands with one end of a rope, the ranking dervish, a man whose facial scars curled his upper lip into a sort of perpetually sad smile, threw the other end over the top of the crocodile idol's four-foot jaws. They pulled it tight so that Lincoln was suspended a yard off the ground, his feet even with Omar's. Then they hitched the rope's end to the idol's tail, leaving Lincoln and Omar dangling within easy reach of the crocodiles, should they be let into the moat.

Amanda kicked and squirmed and yelled a variety of creative French names at them as they dragged her away.

"Amanda, don't give up," cried Lincoln. "The Legion column will come after you before morning."

"Quite observant, Mr. Smith," Kamak said. "We've needed to be rid of the Legion all along, but it has been impossible while they remain holed up in Fort Flatters. When they go after her now, they shall receive a most unwelcome surprise. The girl will become a unique addition to el-Krum's harem."

Prince Kamak and the four dervishes walked up the stairs leading to the secret passage. They went inside, and Kamak stopped just inside the door. Turning and facing Lincoln, he said, "With the Legion out of the way, getting to that foolish old man will finally be quite simple."

"He's your father!" said Lincoln.

"Just another impediment to progress, Mr. Smith. But enough chit-chat. It is time for you to meet my pets."

Kamak motioned to the dervishes, who began cranking a lever inside the passage. The portcullis in front of the cave began to rise, and some two dozen crocodiles began swimming through the opening, toward the idol.

"I've had them skip a few meals lately and are quite famished," Kamak said. "The large one, I am especially fond of. He probably won't even share you with the others. Do you know what I call him just for fun? Thanatos. Goodbye, Mr. Smith. Or, as I believe they are fond of saying in Texas, happy trails."

The large brass door where Kamak had been standing slammed, followed by the sound of the bolt being shot.

In the moat, eighty feet away and closing, the crocodiles swam toward Lincoln and Omar.

CHAPTER 50

Lincoln swung and jerked on the rope that held him suspended from the crocodile idol, trying to topple it. But the giant bronze casting must have weighed two tons. It didn't budge.

Lincoln twisted around and faced Omar. "Try to hang still," he said. Then he wrapped his legs around Omar, taking his weight off his own rope. Then, grasping the rope that Omar hung by, he pulled himself over and proceeded to use Omar as a ladder. Omar groaned at the hard riding heels of Lincoln's boots digging into his shoulders. Lincoln's hands were now only three feet from the grinning bronze jaws.

"Hurry!" Omar said. "They are almost here!"

Stepping on Omar's head, Lincoln could almost reach the idol's lower jaw. With his hands tied together, it was difficult pulling himself up the rope. But by squeezing the rope between his ankles so he wouldn't slip back down, then grabbing farther up the rope, he could go about eight inches on a pull. After four pulls, he got his hands over the idol's head. Then it was a simple matter of hooking one heel over the snout and swinging over to straddle the jaws. The first of the crocodiles were clambering out of the water and onto the bank, only a few yards away from Omar.

Lincoln leaned over and, grabbing the rope Omar hung by, began swinging it. Two crocodiles of middling size had now scrabbled onto the bank, and one lunged at Omar, snapping at the swinging feet. It missed by several inches, but if it were to use more of its tail to push off the ground, or if a bigger croc should try, it would not be pretty. On the next swing, Omar helped Lincoln by jackknifing his body to add momentum. He also lifted his feet on the downswing to keep clear of the jaws. Swinging the kid like a pendulum, Lincoln could pull in only a few inches at a time. Still, each pass brought Omar a little farther up and out of reach of the snapping jaws.

Then a huge beast heaved itself out of the moat. It simply climbed over its smaller brethren. Swinging past, Omar kicked it on the tip of the snout, but this only focused its attention on the live meat swinging above.

"Yank! You must hurry!" cried Omar.

"Kick your feet up and get upside down!" Lincoln yelled.

At first, Omar could swing his feet only up to chest level. But on his next try, he got them above his head and hooked his ankle around the rope. The big croc lunged, and the jaws closed on air a foot below his head.

Lincoln leaned over and grabbed Omar by the foot. The oversize boot was so loose, it almost came off, but Lincoln squeezed through the leather and clamped down on his ankle. Scooting backward on the idol's head, he pulled Omar up feetfirst, high enough that Omar could reach up and embrace the snout. After a minute or two working together, they managed to get Omar astride the bronze jaws. They sat there facing each other, exhausted.

"Your boots are so dern big and floppy, I almost dropped you," Lincoln said, catching his breath. "Here, untie my hands."

"I would have surely chewed the dirt," Omar said as he untied Lincoln's hands.

"Yeah, that was close," Lincoln said. "We both almost bit the dust all right."

"That big croc is very mean," Omar said as they watched the mass of hungry creatures below them.

"I'm sorry I got you into this," Lincoln said after he had untied Omar's hands.

"I will forgive you the moment you get me out of here. What do you think Wild Bill would do?"

"I'm thinking Marshal Hickok didn't have a lot of experience with crocodiles back in Kansas."

After an uncomfortable hour of sitting atop the idol, waiting in vain for the crocodiles swarming below to go back to their cave, Lincoln's patience had run out. The crocs hadn't left and didn't appear interested in doing so, what with fresh meat so tantalizingly close.

The twofold objective was simple enough: get down and don't get eaten. The cold bronze under his backside wasn't getting any softer, and it began to seem as if any action was better than not doing anything.

"You think they feed those birds to the crocs," Lincoln asked, turning and pointing to the two cages full of doves up the bank behind the altar.

"Crocodiles eat flesh of any kind, doves and humans, Omar said. "I saw them break the wings of several and throw them into the cave."

"Did the crocs chase them?"

"What I saw through the bars of the gate was not a beauteous sight."

Lincoln looked around the large, high-ceiled room. The river-moat flowed from the crocodile cave some eighty feet to his left and disappeared under the temple wall to his right. The cave's mouth, about ten feet wide and twenty high, was open, its ten-foot-high portcullis gate suspended four feet above the water by a rope running up the front of the cave. The small drawbridge, about halfway between the idol and the cave, was still secured upright, with its hinge on the nave side of the river. Other than on the other side of the moat, there was scarcely anywhere they could go to be out of the crocodiles' reach. And getting down and across the moat, then up the steep embankment and over the retaining wall, without being caught by the crocodiles, would be next to impossible.

"We have to try something," said Lincoln. "What do you have in your pockets?"

"Nothing but this," Omar said, pulling from the back of his pants a paperback book with a two-tone picture of a few unhorsed US cavalry soldiers being swarmed by mounted Indians. *Custer's Last Stand* was printed across the front of the book.

"How appropriate," Lincoln said, taking the book and ripping out a few pages.

"What are you doing? You are ruining my book."

Lincoln pulled out his waterproof match container and stuffed the pages into it. Then he took out his watch and looked at it. It still ticked away. He handed it to Omar. "Hold this for me. I don't want to get it wet."

"What are you going to do?" asked Omar.

Lincoln looked over his shoulder at the dove cages. Set about five feet apart, they were cubes of wire mesh and sheet metal, on three-foot-high stone frames. He looked at the cave again, measuring the distance. "I'm going to burn off the rope holding that gate up," he said, scooting to the back of the idol's head. "Maybe there's a way out through the cave. With the gate down, it'll keep the crocodiles away—at least, it'll be safer than here."

"But how are you going to get there without being eaten?"

"I'm going to try and distract them with the doves, then swim for it."

Lincoln eased himself down to the idol's shoulders. The bank sloping up behind the huge casting was now about eight feet below him. He sprang off the idol, hit the bank, and scrambled up. Several of the crocodiles noticed and started after him.

Opening one of the birds' cages, he rattled and shook it violently. The doves started flying out, and the crocs coming after Lincoln twisted and snapped at them as they flew over. The fleeing doves also got the attention of the crocodiles still beneath the idol, but the big croc stared at Lincoln for a moment, then started toward him and the cages. Lincoln quickly moved to the other cage and freed the doves there too.

Even after the distraction of the doves, several crocodiles were almost up to the top of the bank. Lincoln rocked the second empty cage back and forth and pushed it off its platform. It tumbled down the bank, coming to rest a few feet into the water. As soon as it stopped, he bounded down the bank in four strides. Without losing speed, he sprang off the cage and dived into the moat. He was swimming furiously as he hit the water.

As Lincoln ran from the bank, the big croc tried to twist its heavy body and swing its mighty head around to snap him up. It didn't miss by much. It took off after Lincoln, quickly picking up speed. It was running fast by the time it got to the water. Hitting the water with deadly focus, it started closing the gap.

Swimming frantically, Lincoln was about ten feet from the mouth of the cave, the huge croc only about twenty feet behind him. Reaching the entrance, Lincoln scissors kicked, lunging upward out of the water, trying to grab the lowest bar of the gate, about four feet above his head. He touched the bottom rail but didn't get enough purchase to hold on. The giant crocodile was about eight feet away. Lincoln kicked and stroked again, this time getting his hand on the rail. He grabbed hold with his other hand and pulled himself up on the cave side of the gate. The giant croc was almost to him when, to Lincoln's startled surprise, the gate came crashing down into the water.

The monstrous croc smashed into the iron bars of the fallen gate.

"Yank, are you all right?" cried Omar, still sitting on top of the idol.

"That was close," said Lincoln from the water on the far side of the gate. His extra weight had caused the old, frayed rope holding up the gate to snap, and he had just managed to push himself inside the cave as the gate came crashing down. Catching his breath, he shook the gate to make sure it was secure. It was reasonably stable, its base stuck in the mud at the moat's bottom. Then the big croc, swimming in an arc in front of the cave, rammed the gate with its snout.

"Yank, are you okay?" Omar called out again.

"I'm okay," Lincoln answered, wading in the water inside the cave. "Just give me a minute."

Behind him, a few small waves rippled his way. "This water has to come from somewhere," he said.

The V of ripples behind him grew in speed and size.

"Yes, it must," Omar said, "but what should I do?"

"Just stay there. I'm going to try and find its source."

"Behind you!" yelled Omar.

Lincoln darted a glance over his shoulder—three feet behind him, another crocodile lunged.

Over the thrashing of water and the banging of the gate, Omar's voice cried out. "Yank? *Yank?*"

As the thrashing died down, Lincoln clung to the top of the portcullis, about five feet out of the water, dripping and trying to calm himself. A crocodile was now circling beneath him inside the gate; on the other side, the big croc still milled around.

"I'm okay, but I've had about enough of these overgrown lizards," Lincoln said, looking up at the two-foot-long spike extensions of the vertical bars on the gate's top. He tried bending one of the spikes, which were about a half inch in diameter. He found that if he put all his weight on it, the extension started to bend where it joined the upper horizontal bar of the gate. He began heaving it back and forth. The bar finally began to weaken and, after more bends, snapped. He held out the broken-off bar— effectively a pointed spike two feet long.

"This fella here is about to get a headache," he said, looking at the crocodile circling below.

He waited for the creature to glide below him. When its head was directly beneath him, with the spike with both hands, he jumped off the gate, driving the pointed end through the top of the crocodile's head. The beast kicked and flailed as Lincoln drove the shaft deep into its brain, until it finally went still.

CHAPTER 51

As the eastern sky was just showing hints of pink, a topless motorcar, preceded by four dervish horsemen, drove south across the Murian plain. Colonel Hultz drove, with Fräulein Zads and Amanda in the back seat. Amanda had tried to escape three times as they were leaving the temple. Now she was gagged, her hands and feet bound.

"It will be a glorious morning, my dear mademoiselle," said Fräulein Zads. "But I imagine you will get used to mornings in the desert, since that is where all of them will be for the rest of your life."

Amanda spat out a flurry of invective. Though the words were muffled by the gag in her mouth, their intent was not difficult to construe.

"Oh, come now, dearie, it won't be all that bad. There will be other women, who will keep him occupied some of the time. Then, of course, I hear those other wives and concubines can be quite catty."

Amanda let loose with another torrent of muffled verbal abuse.

"By now, that good-looking American of yours is being digested by the prince's pets. You would not believe what those beasts can do to a piece of meat."

Even with her hands tied in front of her, and her ankles bound together, Amanda attacked Fräulein Zads, walloping her in the head with her bound hands and then trying to jump on her. Colonel Hultz pulled the car to a stop and, reaching across to the back seat, succeeded in pulling Amanda off the fräulein, though not without getting smacked a few times himself. This time, before he started driving again, he tied her hands and feet tightly to the metal seat brace in front of her. After trussing her up so she could barely move, Hultz got back in the car, and they proceeded farther into the Murian desert.

It was Princess Salina who first missed Amanda the night before, toward the end of the reception. And when the mademoiselle could not be found, it was quickly noticed that her tutor was also missing. Prince Kamak reported that he had heard the mademoiselle talking to Mr. Smith about another treasure map she had got her hands on, and that he had seen them leaving together about halfway through the reception.

Then word reached the ambassador that the Murian guard at the south gate of the city had been slain, and close to his body, the tricolor sash Amanda had worn at the reception was found.

Ambassador Montier held a consultation with the Three from Camarón and Colonel Ruppert, ranking officer of the battalion at Fort Flatters. The Three volunteered to go after Amanda and Smith. But Colonel Ruppert argued that a greater force was needed to pursue el-Krum and his mercenary force, which was known to comprise upward of two hundred men. The Legion had intelligence reports of them moving to the south; therefore, they would pose no threat to the dam or the dedication ceremony. He strongly recommended, however, that the ceremony be canceled. If it could not be canceled, the Three, along with a small contingent of legionnaires and royal guards, should be ample protection at the ceremony.

The postponement of the ceremony at the dam, the ambassador said, was a political impossibility for King Suleiman. If it appeared that the king's enemies were strong enough to force a major change of plans, the effect on the population, already in a state of near panic, could be disastrous.

The gates of Fort Flatters opened moments after sunrise, and the column of legionnaires, led by five officers on horseback, marched out in double time. Because it would slow their march, they were not bringing any heavy weaponry other than two of the fort's four Maxim guns. Mounted on caissons and pulled by mules, they brought up the rear of the column. The Maxims, bought from the British, could shoot two hundred .50-caliber rounds a minute.

The column alternated twenty minutes of double-time march with twenty minutes at normal pace. Three hours before sunrise, Colonel Ruppert had sent out scouts, one of whom had already returned with news of a large mass of men and horses sixteen miles to the south. Within forty minutes of receiving the report, the Legion column was on its way.

Beyond its mouth the cave of the crocodiles opened to perhaps forty feet in breadth. Farther in, it was much deeper and had a gentle current. As Lincoln swam underwater toward the back of the cave, through the murk he could see a coffin, a part of a broken portico with fluted columns and an ornate capital, pieces of broken statues, and other debris. The closer he got to the rear of the cave, the more strongly he felt the flow of water coming toward him.

"What are you doing?" Omar called out, still on the top of the idol, when Lincoln came up for air.

"I'm trying to follow the source of this water. This cave must have been some kind of palace room. An earthquake or something must have caused this river to flood it. This water is coming from somewhere. Maybe I can find where."

The big croc slammed into the gate again.

"What about me?" Omar said.

"Just sit tight. We're going to get out of here."

"I will try to. Please watch out for more crocodiles."

"I'm pretty sure that was the only one this side of the gate."

After taking a couple of deep breaths, he submerged and swam toward the back of the cave. At the back, the water shallowed to only about eight feet, and in the dim, hazy light he came upon a large pile of rocks that blocked him from going any farther. But he could feel a steady flow of water coming through the rocks. He came up for air again. "I think I might have something," Lincoln called out to Omar.

"Tell me, Yank. What?"

"I don't know. Maybe a way out."

After several more dives, Lincoln had pulled away enough rocks to clear a small opening in what perhaps was once a hallway. After a few more, he had cleared the way enough to let him fit through the opening. After surfacing once more for air, he swam through.

A few feet into the opening, it had become totally dark. He swam a few more feet, where the flow of water, only barely felt before, grew considerably stronger. He turned back and went up for air once more.

"I've found where the water is coming from," he called out to Omar. "This time, I'm going to follow it as far as I can go."

"Please come back and don't leave me here," Omar pleaded.

Lincoln didn't answer. Taking three deep breaths, he submerged and, swimming hard, entered the opening again. As he progressed, the passage grew not only darker but narrower. In a few more yards, he could no longer swim but had to crawl, pulling himself along by the rock that closed in around him. He couldn't hold his breath much longer and if he didn't find some kind of opening soon, he would have to go back. After a few more seconds of crawling, the bottom dropped away and the rock opened up in all directions. He swam desperately upward. Lungs almost bursting, his head broke the surface of the water, and he gasped for air in the pitch darkness.

He swam slowly forward, and after a few strokes his feet touched the bottom. Then, wading forward, he banged his shin against something very hard. He roared—as much a release of tension as a response to pain.

After letting his hands dry off, he pulled a match from Amanda's watertight container and struck it. In the light, he saw that he had bumped into one of two large dolphin statues that were partly submerged in the water. The match went out, but before it did, he got the impression that the statues were of gold.

He struck another match. Behind the dolphins, which were about eight feet apart, was a raised platform, only the lower part of which was submerged. On the platform, inlaid with gold and jewels, were two large stone thrones.

Omar was still sitting atop the idol, growing more anxious every minute. He lifted his head from watching the milling crocodiles beneath him to see the big crocodile bash into the gate again, this time breaking a hole in it.

Colonel Hultz drove the motorcar up a rise and onto a low mountain pass. From out of the rocks rose el-Krum's warriors. On either side of the dirt road were at least fifty men and a Maxim gun, and on the crest of the pass were two cannons. Hultz drove over the crest, where another fifty of el-Krum's men waited. The car turned off the road and stopped before a tent that Amanda was already familiar with.

Colonel Hultz and Fräulein Zads got out of the car and walked to the tent. They found el-Krum having his breakfast of gruel mixed with dates and honey. "You must have the girl," said el-Krum. "I assume she did that to you?" He nodded at the swollen lump below the fräulein's eye.

"She did worse to one of the dervishes, she knocked out two of his teeth," Fräulein Zads said. "She's tied up in the motorcar."

"Your rider reported that the column left at daybreak," el-Krum said. Then he turned to one of his men. "Take thirty men and ride down the plane. Leave a track that the Legion will be sure to see."

Two minutes later Amin entered the room. He did not greet or even acknowledge the two Germans.

"Take thirty men and ride down the plain," said el-Krum. "Leave a track that the Legion will be sure to see. And make sure you cover any of the tracks that our careless friends have made on their way up here. The French are stupid, but we don't need them seeing motorcar tracks."

"We will leave by a different route," Colonel Hultz said, clearly embarrassed by the blunder.

"I don't want one of them left alive," said Fräulein Zads.

CHAPTER 52

Lincoln stood on the raised platform next to the thrones. He had already made two torches by wrapping pieces of a curtain that hung behind the thrones around the metal shaft of a spear, and was making a third. To the side of the thrones, which, after closer inspection, were not stone but white gold, he had found not only a number of ancient spears, but also swords, battle-axes, helmets, shields, and other weapons. He wedged a torch between the arm and back of one of the thrones and lit it. Carrying the two other torches, he investigated the front part of the throne room. After a few minutes, he walked to the back of room, where, behind another curtain, stood a long stone table. On it were a number of musical instruments, more weapons, a candelabra, and an ancient hourglass whose sands had run out millennia before. Next to the table was a door.

Lincoln leaned one of his torches against the table and picked up a spear. Holding a torch in his left hand and the spear in his right, he approached the door. He pushed the heavy wooden door with the point of the spear, and instead of opening, the door crashed to the ground. Lincoln jumped back and let his fright subside.

At the entrance to the cave, the huge crocodile slammed into the gate again, further widening the hole it had already made. It circled again and drove its head into the hole. This lunge carried it through, up to its shoulders. It struggled and squirmed and, whipping its tail and body back and forth, managed to press its way through the opening.

On top of the idol, Omar saw the big crocodile break through the gate. He started hollering as loud as he could, until his voice gave out.

After his thumping heart slowed, Lincoln pushed the fallen door out of the doorway and entered the room. He found himself in what had to be an ancient mausoleum. Two large and beautifully engraved marble sarcophagi sat in the middle of the room. Behind them was a marble monument of a man with a sword and shield, fighting a crocodile-like monster. Lining the walls of the room, on either side of the monument, six large chests overflowed with gold and jewels.

Lincoln went to one of the chests and sank the shaft of his torch in the treasure, fixing it upright. Still holding a spear in his right hand, he buried his other hand in the treasure and let the gold coins and jewels trickle out. He picked up a large ruby the size of a walnut and brought it up to his eye. Peering through it, its translucence turned everything red. He put the ruby in his pants pocket.

Out in the throne room, the still water before the thrones rippled and broke as the giant crocodile's snout surfaced between the dolphin statues.

Lincoln was now standing between the two sarcophagi. On top of one was the beautiful jeweled effigy of a woman wearing a crown; on the other was a man's effigy—less ornate, but also elaborately sculpted. He, too, wore a crown, and held a long, straight-bladed sword, the wide cross guard of its hilt on his chest, the blade reaching down past his knees.

After laying his spear on the ground, Lincoln strained to push the heavy stone top off the king's coffin. Once he got it dislodged, he was able to slide the top off but could not keep it from crashing to the ground.

Inside lay the remains of a body wrapped in a frayed and worm-eaten burial cloth. A real sword rested on the remains of its body, in the same position as on the outside of the sarcophagus. Unlike its copy, the hilt and eight-inch cross guard were inlaid with diamonds and other precious stones.

Outside in the throne room, the giant crocodile crawled out of the water, past the thrones, and toward the open doorway of the mausoleum.

Lincoln stood between the two sarcophagi, holding the sword by its rusted blade with both hands, looking up at the gorgeous hilt. The jewels refracted the flickering light into a multitude of variegated hues.

Behind him, the giant crocodile entered the room. Seeing its quarry at last, it lunged toward him.

In the reflection of the sword blade, Lincoln saw a sudden movement behind him. Diving behind the queen's sarcophagus, he barely avoided the huge, chomping jaws. The furious crocodile knocked the sarcophagus onto its side. Lincoln backed around the heavy stone casket, trying to keep it between him and the beast.

The crocodile came around the corner of the sarcophagus. Lincoln was still holding the sword by its blade, now with one hand. With his hand a few inches below the hilt, it almost looked like someone brandishing a cross to ward off a vampire.

The crocodile caught a flicker of its reflection in the blade. It stopped and tilted its head, then lunged at Lincoln again. Lincoln jumped around the end of the sarcophagus, and the crocodile plowed into it. Still holding the sword by its blade, Lincoln smashed the crocodile on the head with the pommel. It seemed only to further enrage the beast.

The crocodile started climbing over the sarcophagus. Lincoln backed up and, taking the sword by the hilt, jabbed the point at the croc, keeping it at bay. It lunged again, and he thrust the sword into its gaping mouth. The crocodile chomped down, snapping half the blade off.

Holding what remained of the sword, Lincoln jumped back—and tripped over his spear. With its prey on the ground, the crocodile moved in. It took a couple of steps and lunged, opening it jaws to chomp down an easy meal.

Lincoln grabbed what was left of the sword, and as the jaws were coming at him, he jammed the sword vertically into its open mouth, wedging the two-foot length of steel deep inside, holding the jaws open. The crocodile writhed in fury, trying to free its jaws, but the more it tried to clamp down on the sword, the faster it held.

Still on the ground, Lincoln grabbed the spear he had tripped over and thrust it up through the open jaws, through its brain, and out the top of its skull. As the crocodile writhed about, its huge tail smacking into the king's sarcophagus and then upending the table where one of the treasure chests sat, Lincoln held fast to the spear, twisting it in the creature's brain. Finally, the animal fell still. When Lincoln was sure it was dead, he collapsed amid the gold, rubies, diamonds, sapphires, and other jewels scattered across the floor.

PART FOUR

CHAPTER 53

Omar still sat atop the crocodile idol, with the mass of hungry reptiles milling beneath him. "Please come back, please hurry," he mumbled to himself.

In the crocodile cave, ripples moved on the water from deep inside. Lincoln surfaced, wearing a helmet with a spiked crest. Holding a spear in one hand, he sidestroked toward the gate, on the lookout for any other crocodiles that may have gotten through. At the gate, he climbed to the top and called out to Omar, "I'm back."

"The big croc has broken through. I was very fearful for your life."

"Yeah, I ran into him. He's a little more open-minded now."

"What do you mean?"

"Thanatos is dead."

"What are you wearing?"

"Protection in case any other crocs got through the gate. I found the throne room—and the treasure."

"You found the treasure?"

"And maybe the bodies of King Sol and his queen."

"And the treasure was there?"

"Tons of it. Now, keep those guys' attention. I'm going up to see if I can get to the other side of the moat."

"I will try." Omar leaned and waved his hands, calling out to the crocodiles, making a lot of noise. Lincoln leaped off the gate and swam up to the far bank, twenty feet away. Running out of the shallow water, he then climbed up the steep six-foot embankment, using his spear as a crutch to keep from slipping down its muddy sides. Getting to the top without the crocodiles noticing him, he jumped the retaining wall and found himself in the middle of the temple's main sanctuary.

"Yank, that is well for you, but what about me?"

"I've read about soldiers in Egypt who used to gamble on who could run across a river on the backs of crocs. I'll get their attention, then—"

"'There is no wisdom in gambling,' the wise man has said."

"I am serious, Omar. I have read about it."

"Was it a book of fact or fiction?"

"I can't remember."

"You told me not to believe all I read in books—I've already gotten myself into enough trouble from books."

"I'll get their attention; then you jump down on the dove cage." Lincoln jumped over the wall and took a few steps down the embankment. He threw his helmet into the river and started yelling at the crocodiles, which started moving toward him. Omar slid down the back of the idol, ran down the bank, and jumped on the dove cage.

More than twenty crocodiles were now crossing toward Lincoln, their backs making something that, with imagination and a great deal of faith, could function as a bridge.

"Come on!" Lincoln urged. "You can do it."

Omar hesitated. Then, with a loud *aaaahhh*, he made a running leap off the cage and onto the back of a crocodile, then onto another, then another. As he ran from back to back, the crocodile he had just stepped on snapped at him, but by then he was gone to the next. He reached the bank, where Lincoln tugged him up the bank, and pulled him over the wall, then followed him over.

"Aaaahhh!" Omar yelled, trying to calm himself.

Lincoln patted him on the back. "Good job. That was amazing. By the way, I just remembered—it was fiction!"

Omar didn't seem amused.

"I wonder how long we've been down here," Lincoln said. "Here, let me have my watch back, please."

Omar handed it to him. "It's stopped. Did I damage it?"

"No. It's old and kind of sensitive sometimes. Come on, we have to get Amanda back and warn the Legion." They started running off, but seeing the three different passageways that exited from that side of the temple, they stopped. They looked at each other, then up at the door across the moat. They looked at each other again.

"I am not walking on crocodiles again."

"The door's bolted," Lincoln said. "If it weren't, we could let down the drawbridge."

"I do not know which to take," said Omar, looking at the three passageways again.

Lincoln decided that the middle passage made the most sense. He took a torch from one of the iron brackets mounted beside each passage. Then, spear in one hand and torch in the other, he trotted off through the middle opening, with Omar hard on his heels.

Three minutes later, Lincoln and Omar ran back into the temple area they had just left, but through the passageway that was on their right when they started off. They turned around and looked at the three passageways again. This time, they chose the left passage.

A few minutes later, they were back in the temple, this time arriving through the middle passage. "Come on," said Lincoln, and they ran off through the passage on the far right—the one they had come back through the first time.

Not long after, they ran back into the temple through the passage on the left. They turned and looked at the openings.

"It must be some sort of a maze," said Lincoln.

"The ancient Murians were skilled mathematicians and delighted in such puzzles," said Omar. "They called them labyrinths. I have read of some that had combinations of turns in the many thousands."

"Yeah, I've read about 'em too," Lincoln said. "Maybe this is why Kamak has that flying machine: to try and map the labyrinth."

"What are we going to do?"

"In the story I know, the guy tied a thread to the opening when he went in, so he could follow it back out."

"That will not work for us."

"I know; I'm just thinking," Lincoln looked around the room for something to trigger an idea. Two more dovecotes stood next to the back wall by the three passageways. He looked around again.

"The doves! The doves are all gone and haven't come back," he said. "Where did they go? The crocs didn't get any of them, did they?"

"I do not think so," said Omar. "They have flown the croup."

"That's right, they've flown away. They must know how to get out of here." Lincoln went over to one of the dovecotes, opened the door, and took out a dove. He tossed it in the air, letting it fly away. It immediately flew through the middle passage. Lincoln did the same with two more doves. Both flew away through the middle opening.

About ten minutes later, none of the doves had returned. "They know the way out," said Lincoln. "I don't know how, if they actually remember the way or they can just sense it, but they know how to get out. We just have to figure a way to follow them."

"But they fly too fast to follow. If we carried enough of them with us, perhaps . . ."

"No," Lincoln interrupted. "We could tie a thread to one of their feet and then follow it that way. We just need a thread."

"The rope," said Omar, pointing at the pull for the drawbridge. "It is made of many threads of the hemp woven together. There is a rope maker close to my uncle's booth in Sidi Bel Abbès."

Lincoln took his spear and began sawing with the edge against the rope. The heavy bridge faltered and slammed down as the rope gave way. Lincoln then cut other end free from where it was attached on the far side of the bridge. They now had about fifty feet of one-inch-thick rope woven from some fifty thin strands of light hemp. He and Omar went to work unraveling the strands.

It took them over an hour to put together a thin, light, and reasonably strong coil of string that was close to two hundred feet long. After attaching one end of the cord to a dove's foot, Lincoln would let out the coil as the dove flew away. Omar would carry an extra dove in case the first got off the cord.

Lincoln freed the birds from both cages except for two, which he handed to Omar. With Omar holding it, he secured the end of the cord around one of the doves' feet. He readied his coil, letting out some slack, and prepared to let out more as the dove flew away. They walked to the middle passageway.

"Okay, let him go," said Lincoln, and Omar tossed the dove gently in the air.

It flew away, dipping slightly in its flight, flapping its wings harder to stay aloft, but still making its way down the passage. It flew stronger after a few feet of getting used to the cord.

Lincoln ran behind it, letting out the cord, giving the bird plenty of slack. Omar followed as fast as he could, carrying the spare dove under one arm, and the torch in his other hand. He had tried to carry Lincoln's spear too, but quickly abandoned it. Carrying the dove and the torch already slowed him enough and he didn't want to get left behind.

CHAPTER 54

At the head of the Legion column, Colonel Ruppert saw two of his scouts riding hard at them. He ordered his first lieutenant to halt, and the lieutenant gave the signal and called out the order. The column had been marching due south since dawn, toward where the first scout party had reported seeing el-Krum's camp. El-Krum could take any of several routes through the passes off the Murian plateau, and the colonel had sent more scouts to figure out which.

The scouts reported that they had found the trail of many riders heading toward the westernmost route down the plateau. They estimated the riders were not more than an hour's hard march ahead. The colonel ordered a double-time pace.

At 11 a.m., the king's party left the gates of Mur on its way to the dedication ceremony for the dam. Athos, Porthos, Aramis, and four other mounted legionnaires rode in front. The king's Daimler came next in the caravan, followed by six mounted Murian guards, then six horse-drawn carriages. In the back seat of the motorcar were the king, Prince Kamak, and Ambassador

Montier. Murian officials rode in two of the carriages, and in the other four were various dignitaries and journalists from those European countries that were allowed to attend. The German delegation had sent Kamak a note that morning, so he said, that Ambassador Zads was not feeling well and would not be attending. The British newspapermen who had recently arrived in the city, though expected, had not been there at departure time. And the king wasn't in a mood to delay.

The party left the city heading northwest toward the river. After five miles they veered due north along the river road that led up the canyon where the new dam was to be dedicated. The few legionnaires still manning Fort Flatters let out a cheer as the caravan passed the fort a half mile or so away.

Lincoln and Omar had been following the dove for over an hour. Twice, Lincoln's coil of rope thread had run out, forcing him to hold the thread taut to keep the dove from flying away. They caught up with it and rewound the coil. Finally, following the cord, they turned a corner, and a dim speck of light appeared up ahead. "Omar, lower the torch," Lincoln said. As they walked farther along, the light grew stronger. They found the dove just outside a small aperture above a rock slide. The thread holding its leg was snagged in the rocks. Omar let his dove go, and Lincoln, giving the dove that had led them a kiss on its head, untied it, and it flew away.

They cleared away the rocks until the opening was big enough for a person to crawl through. Lincoln stuck his head out and looked into a narrow gully about fifty yards from the temple's front opening.

After crawling out, they crouched in the gully. The hydrogen-filled balloon hung low in the air above the front of the temple. From where they stood, they could see only a few feet into the ruins. Just inside, two Germans in khaki sat on a barricade of sandbags. Behind the sandbags was something covered by a tarpaulin.

"What time do you think it is?" Lincoln asked, looking at how far the sun had climbed in the sky.

"A little before midday," Omar said.

"If the column left around dawn, they've at least a five-hour start on us."

"Even with my uncle's fastest racing camels we could not catch them," said Omar. "We would need a magic carpet."

Lincoln looked up into the sky. "Okay, then, a magic carpet it is."

They crept along the gully, staying low. The temple entrance was a dozen steps away, the guards just inside, shading themselves from the hot midday sun. Thirty feet in front of the entrance, the balloon's six-foot square wicker basket was secured to the ground by four ropes fastened to large pegs.

With all the nonchalance of a clueless sightseer, Omar walked out in the open and over to the balloon's basket. Within a few seconds, the two guards saw him and started yelling in German.

As the two men came out of the entrance to confront Omar, Lincoln slipped up behind and tapped one of them on the shoulder, then met his turning face with an elbow. The German was knocked off his feet and wouldn't be getting up soon. The other guard dashed off toward the temple's entrance. Lincoln ran after him and tackled him just before the entrance. Omar started untying the ropes that tethered the balloon to the ground.

The German got up and tried to kick Lincoln before he could stand, missing his face but catching him in the shoulder. Hollering in German, the guard made it to the sandbags in the temple's entrance and ripped off the tarpaulin, revealing a machine gun. As he swung the gun around and pulled back the cocking mechanism, Lincoln dived over the sandbags, catching him solidly on the chin with his shoulder and knocking him over. Lincoln jumped on him and hit him on either side of the jaw with a left-right combination, and the German fell back, unconscious.

Omar was in the balloon's basket with three of the ropes untied when Lincoln chugged up, hefting the machine gun and an armload of cartridge belts. The balloon's basket was tilting radically toward the corner still tethered to the ground. "Hurry!" Omar called, moving around, trying to balance the tilting basket.

Lincoln threw the cartridge belts into the basket and then lifted the gun's barrel up to Omar, who was trying to level the basket with his weight. Leaning over the side, he grabbed the heavy weapon and pulled it in. The extra weight of the gun and Omar's leaning ripped the last peg from the ground. The balloon started to rise. Omar scrambled, trying to figure out how to stop its rising.

Lincoln tried to grab onto the bottom of the basket as it floated up past his head, but there was nothing to hold on to.

As the balloon rose higher, two other Germans ran out of the temple. Lincoln grabbed a tether rope dangling from a corner of the basket and started floating upward with the balloon. One of his pursuers reached him just in time to get a boot in the face. As the balloon floated higher into the sky, Lincoln shinnied up the rope, and Omar helped him into the basket.

Immediately, Lincoln started fiddling with the knobs and levers on the liquid-petroleum propeller engine that enabled the balloon to move horizontally. The three-bladed propeller was attached to a metal tiller, which could be swung around at different angles to control the balloon's horizontal direction. Lincoln pulled one of the levers, and the balloon dropped abruptly. He let go at once, and they both fell back, grabbing the sides of the wicker basket. When the balloon stabilized, Omar shouldered Lincoln away from the controls. After a few moments of Omar's tinkering, the balloon rose. He twisted a knob, and it surged forward, quickly picking up speed.

"Okay, good," said Lincoln, "but we've got to be careful how much you push it. Kamak says the balloon is full of hydrogen, and that stuff is pretty volatile."

"What does *volatile* mean?" asked Omar.

"It means it could blow up."

Athos, Porthos, and Aramis rode at the front of the caravan. Close behind them in the motorcar were King Suleiman, Ambassador Montier, and Prince Kamak, then six carriages of dignitaries, and twenty or so Murian cavalry at the rear. As they were passing Fort Flatters on the dirt road up to the dam, Athos said to Aramis and Porthos, who were riding close by, "Ruppert and the column left at daybreak. They should be nearing the camp where el-Krum was last spotted."

"Yes. Montier ordered him to take the whole regiment," said Aramis. "There are only fifteen men left behind, manning the fort."

"Our reports are that he and his men were seen yesterday," Porthos added. "If they were doubling back, they would have been seen."

Two hundred feet in the air, Omar was still sorting out the balloon's propeller system. "Have you figured it out yet?" asked Lincoln. "You have to make it go faster."

"If you let in the gas faster than the engine can burn it, it will stall the engine," Omar said. "If you stall the engine, we lose our ability to steer the balloon."

"You have to find our maximum speed."

"We could also run out of fuel, or it is possible it could explode."

"You have to get more speed out of this thing." Despite his aversion to mechanical things, he felt like tinkering with the thing himself. "If we don't catch the Legion before the ambush, they'll get slaughtered. And el-Krum will get away with Amanda."

Omar hesitated as if muttering a prayer, then cranked a valve. The balloon surged forward, picking up speed.

CHAPTER 55

The front of the Legion column reached the narrow mountain pass that descended down from the Murian plateau. When half the column had marched in, an enfilading crossfire of machine guns opened up on them and annihilated all but a few men at the rear of the column. Two Krupp cannons bombarded the ends of the column, and from the rocks, two hundred rifles opened up a withering fire.

Colonel Ruppert and all but one of the officers at the head of the column were killed in the first volley from the Maxim guns. The remaining officer, Lieutenant Levrey, whose horse had been shot from under him, ran back and forth issuing orders. About half the column—forty men—managed to reform in a defensive position fifty yards from the pass and tried to return fire. Then another fifty of el-Krum's army rode over the hill.

As el-Krum's men closed around the Legion's position, no one, in what remained of the column, had to give the next order. If the legionnaires tried to retreat back down the pass, they would be in open desert for over a mile, where they would first be pummeled by the cannon and rifle fire and then run down by mounted dervishes. But retreat was not considered. Surrender would land the survivors in the slave markets of Timbuktu and the Levant. But that wasn't an option either, for the simple reason that the Legion didn't surrender. To a man, even the wounded, they fixed bayonets. At Lieutenant Levrey's command, they charged.

In the hills northwest of Mur, Johnny and Jake dismounted from their horses. Hot and irritable, they sat down on some boulders. After taking swigs from their canteens, Johnny pulled out the map they had purchased from the German sergeant in Cairo.

The map was giving them problems. It had led them up an old trail six miles east of the river, then up a narrow, winding trail in the hills north of the dam. They had been following the trail west for five miles and had not a seen a trace of anything that suggested even a borax mine, much less a diamond mine.

"According to how I read this thing," Johnny said, "we shoulda' come on the mine three miles ago."

"Well, maybe these folks measure distances different than us," said Jake. "Or maybe the map ain't got its proportions right."

Jake got up and walked to where the trail overlooked the land below. He could see the parts of the river that wound down through the mountain, and beyond the desert plain below.

"Maybe they don't got their proportions right," said Johnny, "but this place just don't look like diamond or ruby country to me. It don't look nothin' like it did in Burma."

"Now, that's intelligent. Burma's tropical jungle, and here we're in high desert. Of course it looks different."

"That's not what I mean," said Johnny. "I mean it just don't look like land where there's apt to be precious jewels. It don't look like South Africa either."

"It don't look like South Africa, 'cause it ain't. The whole dern continent is between us and South Africa."

"That's not what I'm trying to say. It's that this place don't have a *feel* for jewels—gold, maybe, but not jewels."

"So now you have a built-in treasure finder? Why, your hide's so thick, you could be sitting on a *cactus* and wouldn't know it, never mind a diamond mine."

"That's got nothin' to do with it. I'm startin' to have my doubts about this map of yours."

"What do you mean this map of *mine?*" Jake said. "It's just as much yours as mine."

"Yeah, but I'm getting a feeling that it ain't no more promising than those horned rats you wanted to go and spend good money on, just because you read about 'em in a book."

"Well, I still ain't convinced there *ain't* any horned rats around here; they could be just hard to find, and just because we ain't found one don't mean a thing. Just 'cause you never seen a polar bear don't mean there ain't any."

"Just don't go spending any of our money trying to find one. Now, let's move on—might as well see where the flamin' thing leads to, anyway." Johnny got up and mounted his horse. "Who knows? Maybe it ain't a map to a diamond mine, but to the dern Fountain of Youth."

From three hundred feet in the air, Lincoln and Omar could see the remains of the battle—the fallen bodies, the craters and smoke from cannon shells, the tracks and dust of hundreds of horses and men. As the balloon drew closer, Lincoln's heart sank. Most of the Legion column had been annihilated.

El-Krum's army came into view. At the rear of the column, some forty mounted dervishes led horse-drawn caissons bearing two cannons and four machine guns. In front of them were thirty legionnaires—all that remained of the Legion column. Leading them were another forty dervishes and, at the head of the column, a rider leading another horse, ridden by a female.

"We need to get a little lower," Lincoln said. "Just above the hills, so we don't get noticed till we cross the pass. Then we'll swoop down on them fast and blast them with the machine gun."

The balloon flew to about a hundred yards behind and two hundred feet above el-Krum and his men. Lincoln finished loading the machine gun with a belt of ammunition. He hefted the machine gun and rested it on the rail of the balloon's basket. "Okay," he said, "take us in."

Omar cranked two of the engine's dials, and they quickly accelerated and dropped in altitude toward the rear of the column. At thirty yards away, Lincoln opened fire. The dervishes were taken wholly by surprise, and before they realized where it was coming from, Lincoln had raked up through half the column. The dervishes began fleeing in disarray as Lincoln kept firing on them. Then he aimed at the core of the army, in front of where the legionnaires had been marching. The legionnaires had already broken away and were picking up the rifles of fallen dervishes and opening fire on their captors.

Lincoln loaded another belt of ammunition into the gun and continued shooting up the column, until the dervishes who remained alive were fleeing in chaos. Up in front, Amanda kicked her horse and broke away from el-Krum. After getting control of his rearing mount, the bandit chief rode after her.

"Over there," Lincoln said, pointing to Amanda and her pursuer. "Just get me a little closer."

Omar pulled the rudder toward him, making the balloon surge to its right. As el-Krum closed in on Amanda, Lincoln took aim. At fifty yards, he fired, missing el-Krum but tearing up the ground in front of him, causing his horse to rear and pitch him off.

El-Krum got up, ran to his horse, and pulled Lincoln's buffalo rifle from his saddle.

"That no-good buzzard's got my rifle! Hold steady."

El-Krum cocked the rifle and brought it up to his shoulder.

"Hurry up, Yank!" Omar said. "Shoot him!"

"It shoots low and right."

"He's had time to learn that."

El-Krum fired the rifle, and a bullet ripped through the lower left part of the balloon's basket.

"Told ya," Lincoln said, then squeezed off a burst of fire. This time when el-Krum fell, he didn't get up.

The surviving legionnaires by now had finished off most of el-Krum's army, though twenty or so had managed to ride off. Omar had lowered the balloon close enough to the ground for a half-dozen legionnaires to grab the ropes hanging from it. Unable to find anything else to secure the ropes to, they tied them to one of the cannons that el-Krum's men had abandoned.

Not far from the balloon, Lincoln was holding his rifle in one hand, and Amanda with the other as she shed tears of relief punctuated with words of rage at el-Krum and Fräulein Zads.

A legionnaire sergeant ran up to Lincoln and saluted him. "I am Sergeant Bellini," he said. "Our last officer was killed in our charge. I am the ranking noncommissioned officer still standing. Shall we go after the rest of those fiends?"

"There's going to be an attack on the king at the dam this afternoon!" Amanda said.

"Take as many men as you can find mounts for," Lincoln said to Sergeant Bellini, "and ride as fast as you can to the dam. The king and the Three have to be warned."

"We'll be lucky to get there by sunset," said the sergeant.

"Do the best you can," said Lincoln. He kissed Amanda and started for the balloon. After a few steps, he stopped and turned toward her. "Well, are you coming?"

Now that he had invited her, she hesitated. "We're going in *that*?"

"It's just a balloon," he said.

"I'm afraid of heights."

"It could come crashing down any minute," Omar said. "It is very unstable."

"It looks like we're going to have to learn to live with these things," Lincoln said.

"If you're going, then so am I," she said.

"At least we'll be together," Lincoln said.

"I truly do not understand the ways of your people," Omar said.

Lincoln placed his rifle in the balloon's basket, then helped Amanda in. A legionnaire brought up three belts of ammunition salvaged from their own maxim gun and handed them to Lincoln. Lincoln hopped in. The legionnaires untied the tethers from the dead horse, and the basket floated upward as Omar started the engine and turned some knobs on the control panel. The propeller whirred, and they sailed off toward the dam.

CHAPTER 56

Johnny and Jake were even hotter and grumpier than before. They were now walking their horses. Even Jake was starting to lose faith in their map. They had followed it for another three miles, on a mainly western heading. The trail was often narrow and had many steep, uphill switchbacks followed by similar sections downhill. "This trail reminds me of the one I used to take to a secret fishing hole in Montanee," Jake said.

"What good was it being secret?" Johnny was in even a worse mood than Jake. "As I recall, you were about the worst fisherman in the territory. You just don't have the patience for it, 'cause you can't sweet-talk a fish onto the hook like you do women. Whereas with me and fish, it's a battle of the minds."

"Now, that'd be quite a battle, what with your evenly matched intelligences, you and a fish. But you're the one who suggested—"

All of a sudden, both men stopped walking. The trail they were on converged with another, much broader trail coming from below them. It was full of fresh horse tracks.

"There musta' been a small army come through here not more'n a couple of hours ago," Jake said.

"A whole herd of 'em—at least thirty or forty," Johnny said. "And these horses ain't shod."

"What's that many riders doing up here?"

"Well, I doubt they're looking for diamonds. They rode mostly in twos. Don't appear to be any mule tracks either."

"Well, it's clear they ain't miners," said Jake. "Maybe bandits. Maybe they're on their way to their hideout, where they stash their loot."

"Like with Ali Baba. And that's where they stashed all the horned rats too. That's why you can't find none."

"If I find one of 'em, I swear, if it weren't so valuable, I'd make you eat it."

"Ha! If you found one, I'd be happy to."

"I'll remember that."

"Well, I guess we'd best be seeing what these fellers are up to. We best watch our step; there's a passel of 'em."

On the deck at the top of the dam, Ambassador Montier spoke at a small lectern in front of three rows of seated guests. King Suleiman sat in the front row, along with Prince Kamak and a few high Murian officials. In the second row were dignitaries from the other European embassies, and in the back were a handful of French engineers and Athos, Porthos, and Aramis. A photographer was taking pictures. Montier didn't seem in any great hurry to finish his speech, and the Three, especially Athos, kept looking around, probably missing half of what was being said.

"They might be thieves too, but there's no doubt they ain't up to no good," said Johnny.

He and Jake were now perched on a crag two hundred feet above and just east of the dam. Below them, they could see the gathering where the French ambassador was making his speech. And they also saw, concealed in a ravine a couple of hundred yards upstream, the band of riders they had been following. Dark-robed and hooded, they were armed with rifles and various long blades.

Johnny and Jake had followed their trail for another mile or so until they first came upon their horses, being watched by four dervishes a quarter mile farther up the ravine. Then, staying higher up on the ridge, they had moved closer to the dam, to where they were now, where they had a prime view of what was unfolding below: the ceremony on the dam's deck, the legionnaires and king's guards waiting by the motorcar and carriages on the dirt road, and the dervishes hiding in the ravine upstream, flanking the dirt road.

"Well," said Jake, "what do you think? I count fifty of 'em. Against us, with the thirteen legionnaires and guards, it'd be a tossup. It's the king and all the other noises that's the real problem."

"Yeah, agreed," said Johnny. "Protecting the king and his entourage would hinder our tactics. I wish we had more'n just these sidearms."

"I imagine they're going to wait until they come off the dam before they attack," Jake said. "That the sensible thing. Too much cover on the dam. They could hold 'em off for hours up there. What's the plan?"

"I don't know, maybe we should just try a page from the Legion's book."

Ambassador Montier finished his speech to perfunctory applause. He invited King Suleiman to the lectern, where, before sitting down, he posed with the king for another five minutes of picture taking. King Suleiman, like an ancient king of a similar name, thought it wise to limit one's words. He thanked the French but also declared that his country would remain autonomous, chart its own destiny, and be highly selective in what it borrowed from modern European culture. Mur would find a proper balance of the new with the old.

His speech received more generous applause than the ambassador's. Ambassador Montier got up, and he and the king walked over to a switch box on the wall of the dam's deck. The switch box had a gold ribbon tied in a bow around it, and two French engineers stood beside it. One of them handed a large pair of snips to the French ambassador, who in turn tried to give the shears to the king. Suleiman waved him off, then drew his dagger and sliced the ribbon.

One of the engineers opened the switch box and showed the king a lever. After pausing for another picture, the king pulled down the lever. There was a sound of clanking machinery, and after a few moments, three electric lights, secured on a platform above the deck, flickered and began to shine. The entourage gave its most enthusiastic applause of the day. The king and the ambassador stayed on the deck for more pictures, and all but the Murian and French members of the party headed off to their carriages.

Amanda had quickly gotten past her fear of heights. They were sailing at about five hundred feet, where the breeze was blowing in the direction they wanted to go. Lincoln gave her the tiller so he could help Omar get more speed out of the engine.

"Let me try?" Lincoln said.

Omar looked to Amanda, no doubt hoping she would say something to keep Lincoln away from the controls. Instead, she let go of the tiller and tried to get at the knobs and levers herself. Omar moved in front of her, and the balloon started veering to the southwest.

"The machine is very hot," he said. "I am afraid it will seize up. And someone needs to steer."

"We had this thing going faster before," Lincoln said.

"There is more weight in it now," Omar replied. "If we can gain another two hundred feet altitude, I think the wind will help us more."

"The king and my father's lives are at stake," Amanda said.

Omar gave them a dubious look and gradually dialed one of the knobs. The engine coughed and sputtered, then surged forward.

The king was still up on the dam, getting detailed explanations of how the penstock, turbines, generators, and other parts of the huge machine did their magic. Most of the party had departed an hour ago, and now only the king's Murian and French entourage were left. Ambassador Montier waited with the king. Bored with the whole hydroelectrical discussion, he wasn't listening, or understanding anything the chief engineer said. Kamak and the Murian entourage stood a few feet away. Beyond them, the Three from Camarón were also ready for the lecture to end. Down on the dirt road, near the eastern end of the dam, the Murian and Legion escort waited with the two remaining carriages and the motorcar. The king's driver had already started the Daimler's engine.

Walking their horses, Johnny and Jake had traversed across the mountain and dropped down to a position below the dam. Behind them, a mile to the south, the pass led down to Fort Flatters and Mur. Ahead of them, around a bend just to the north, were the motorcar and carriages. Three hundred yards farther up, in the gully just beyond the dam, the dervishes lay in wait, ready to attack once the king came off the dam.

Johnny and Jake's plan was plan was simple, relying on audacity, noise, and the element of surprise. They would charge up the gully past the dam and drive the dervishes back up the canyon. Then, while the dervishes were trying to regroup, they would hold them off long enough for the king's party to make a run for the fort, and take out at least six or eight dervishes in the process. Then they would turn and hightail it themselves. They had considered trying to alert the king's party, but that would just sow confusion, bring on the attack, and maybe even get them shot.

The king and Ambassador Montier were still on the deck when Johnny and Jake charged. Their first hazard was the armed escort waiting by the motorcar. By the time the guards recovered from seeing two men in European garb racing up the gully, firing their pistols and waving their arms for others to follow, and kicking up as much dust as they could, they were past them.

Athos came running off the deck to see two riders chasing a horde of black-cloaked men up the canyon. He quickly sized up at least part of the situation and started giving orders. "Load them up and get them out of here!" he hollered to Porthos and Aramis, who were already herding the king and the ambassador off the dam. Athos mounted his horse and galloped up the gully.

After hustling the king, Ambassador Montier, and Kamak into the Daimler, and the Murian entourage into the carriages, Aramis led the way down the road while Porthos rode behind.

Johnny and Jake had driven the dervishes back close to where their horses were being held. The dervishes had taken cover behind large boulders and mounds of shale scattered about the upper part of the ravine. They had begun returning fire when Athos arrived. He rode, shooting down three of them who had risen from behind cover.

"What in the hell is going on?" he asked, recognizing the two journalists he had briefly met at the reception.

"They were planning a surprise party for you," Johnny said. He drew down on another dervish, and his pistol clicked, out of cartridges.

"I'm out too," said Jake. "I suggest we skedaddle." As if in confirmation, the return fire on their position grew hotter.

Athos emptied his gun, hitting two more dervishes, and the three of them turned and raced off. After they had gone a hundred yards or so, still at full gallop, Athos reloaded his pistol.

"Man's spent some time on a horse," Jake said, riding abreast of Johnny as they, too, reloaded.

Toward the end of the canyon road, they caught up with the motorcar, carriages, and other riders. A little farther down, the road emptied out from the canyon and widened as the terrain leveled out. Emerging from the canyon, they ran almost straight into another band of forty mounted dervishes heading up the canyon.

The dervishes were even more surprised than the king's party. Aramis, riding at the front of the party, took advantage of the confusion to shoot three. Athos and Porthos rode to the front and started shooting. The dervishes, carrying only rifles and no sidearms, could not respond quickly and so veered away to the east. As Aramis and Porthos, joined now by Johnny and Jake, and the four Legion guards kept firing at the retreating fighters, Athos led the motorcar, the king's mounted guards flanking it, and the carriages off the dirt road, toward the fort three miles distant. Between them and the fort was only barren plain.

The dervishes had regrouped enough to start returning fire. A legionnaire's horse was hit and fell, and as the legionnaire struggled to free himself, a spray of blood shot out the back of his head and he lay still. Another of the king's guards went down nearby. Then, out of the canyon, rode the first of the band whom Johnny and Jake had driven up the canyon. Aramis and Porthos fired at them, slowing them up, but thirty more were riding up not far behind.

"We have to get to the fort!" Aramis yelled.

Turning about, he, Porthos, the two Americans, and the three legionnaires chased after the royal party toward the fort, across flat and unprotected ground a mile or more away.

Inside the motorcar, King Suleiman had drawn a pistol and was leaning over the side of the car, trying to get a clear shot at the dervishes galloping not far behind the legionnaires and Johnny and Jake. Ambassador Montier had ducked, trying to take cover in the back seat. Prince Kamak was crouched on the floor in front.

As they neared the fort, a cannon shell exploded a few feet in front of the motorcar. Shrapnel hit in several places, with the sharp *ting* of rending metal, making the driver swerve to a stop. Automatic fire ripped up the ground in front of the Daimler. A squad of twenty German soldiers had wheeled out a cannon from behind a bluff, drawing attention away from the machine gun tucked in the cleft between two boulders.

"*Dummkopf! Nicht das Auto!*" the German officer ordered. "*Vielleicht ist der Prinz dort drin!*" The machine gun then ripped apart the two carriages, killing all inside, while rifle fire from the Germans downed all but one of the king's guards.

The king jumped out of the car and emptied his pistol at the Germans. Ducking behind the car, he reloaded, then mounted one of the horses from a fallen guard and started firing again.

"How many men are left in the fort?" the ambassador called out from the car to Athos, who was still mounted and firing away.

Then a boom and a puff of smoke came from the wall of the fort. A second later, the German machine gun exploded.

"Fifteen," Athos said. "We have to run for it."

Another explosion blew a sizable gap in the German line, mangling a half-dozen soldiers.

Meanwhile, the dervishes from the canyon had joined with the Germans. They advanced at a gallop on the remnant of the king's party.

"To the fort, NOW!" Athos commanded.

As the dervishes came on, a cannonball exploded in their vanguard, obliterating those riding in front. The rest pulled up abreast of the Germans.

Another cannon blast from the fort landed in the midst of the Germans. The fort's gate opened, and eight legionnaires ran out and set up a firing line fifty yards before the gate. With the legionnaires keeping the Germans and dervishes pinned down, Ambassador Montier and Prince Kamak ran out of the car. Montier swung up behind Johnny onto his horse, and Kamak vaulted up onto Jake's and held on as they raced off toward the fort. The king, already mounted, stayed behind, firing at the dervishes. Athos rode to the motorcar to retrieve the driver but found him dead with a bullet hole in his head.

A cannonball from the Germans exploded close to the legionnaires' firing line. Athos couldn't see the result at first, but as the dust settled, he could see pieces of at least three legionnaires on the ground. Still firing away from behind the car, Porthos was grazed by a bullet to the side of his neck. He slumped over the pommel for a few moments, then rose again firing his pistol, a bloody kerchief wrapped around his wound.

"Take off," Athos said. "I'll get the king."

Aramis and Porthos fired one more volley, turned their horses, and raced off to the fort. The king, with something of the battle rage on him, was wheeling his mount and firing away at the dervishes.

"Your Highness," Athos said, trying to stay low in his saddle while reloading his pistol. "NOW!"

The king, with a wild, fierce look in his eye, tried to fire one more shot, but his pistol was empty. Muttering an oath, he jammed it back into his belt, turned, and rode off toward the fort. As he rode, a rifle bullet hit in the shoulder. Slumping over the neck of his horse, he teetered in the saddle.

Athos raced up alongside the king, holstered his gun, and pulled him onto his own horse as more rifle fire zipped past them. As they approached the heavy wooden gate, two of the legionnaires covering them went down.

Athos galloped into the fort, carrying the king across his saddle. The remaining three legionnaires in the firing line turned and ran in behind them as two men shut the gate.

CHAPTER 57

Omar was having more trouble with the balloon's propulsion device. The engine was missing and sputtering, and they were losing speed and altitude.

"What's the matter with it?" Lincoln asked.

"It has overheated," Omar said, "and the engine is almost out of fuel. I do not think we can go on much longer."

"Isn't there anything we can do?" asked Amanda.

"Get rid of excess weight, and get out and push," Omar said.

Lincoln looked around and then started throwing out the sandbags used for ballast. The balloon continued to lose forward speed.

"We aren't going to make it," cried Omar.

Below, they saw a plume of dust moving north, the direction they were going.

"It's Fräulein Zads!" Amanda said.

"Well, we're going to have to borrow her buggy," Lincoln said.

Inside the topless motorcar, Colonel Hultz was behind the wheel, and Fräulein Zads sat beside him. Hearing the balloon's engine sputter, the fräulein turned and saw the balloon fifty feet behind them. As Lincoln picked up his buffalo rifle, she fired a pistol at them, ripping a hole in the canvas envelope. Hydrogen rushed out, and the balloon began zigzagging out of control as it sank. Amanda and Omar dived to the floor of the wildly swinging basket, and Lincoln set down his rifle and held on.

Outside the walls of the fort, three more squads of German infantry had joined the remaining dervishes and German troops. They had formed a battle line five hundred feet in front of the fort's only gate and had just wheeled up six more cannons into firing position. A flash and a boom came from one of the cannons, and a moment later, one of the eight cannon emplacements on the parapet of the fort exploded, killing the two legionnaires stationed there.

There was another boom, and another cannon on the parapet exploded, along with two more legionnaires. Still alive were six legionnaires who had been manning the fort, three of the king's escort, a Murian guard, the king, the ambassador, the Three from Camarón, Johnny, and Jake. The king and Porthos were wounded, though Porthos less severely.

After carrying the king up onto the parapet, Athos, Porthos, and Aramis huddled at a gun embrasure, discussing what could be done. In front of the fort, they could see the Germans building their battle line. Fifty more dervishes had now joined the line, extending it the entire width of the fort.

"There's at least a hundred and twenty of them," Porthos said.

"And fifteen of us left who can shoot," said Aramis.

"If our ammunition holds, we have a chance," Porthos said.

"The problem's going to be their damn cannons," Athos said.

Johnny and Jake ran up the stairs with one of the legionnaires, who had taken them into the armory and equipped them with rifles and bandoliers of ammunition.

"I don't know what you were doing up that canyon—or want to know," Athos said. "But it's a good thing you were there."

"It was bold, the two of you charging the whole lot of them," said Porthos.

"We was planning on joining up with y'all, anyway," said Johnny. "We just got around to it sooner than we expected. I'm Johnny and this is Jake. We've been in our share of warm spots before. This'n looks particular so."

"We're glad you happened by," said Aramis, drawing a bead on a German cannoneer. He took the shot, and the gunner fell across the breech of the cannon. "Getting away from the dam might have been a trifle more unsettling."

Then the German cannons fired a six-shot salvo. On the fort wall, all took cover behind the parapet. Four of the balls went high, missing the fort entirely. The other two hit the wall, one landing a few feet from one of the two remaining machine-gun emplacements, demolishing the gun and the legionnaire who manned it.

Then, from the battle line, a squad of German riflemen marched toward the fort.

"Fire when they're at sixty yards," Athos ordered. "And make it count."

The deflated balloon hung tangled in the fronds of a tall palm in the middle of an oasis. Out from the oasis galloped a camel with Lincoln astride, in one hand its reins and his rifle, in the other a stick with which he urged on the beast.

When Lincoln was within three camel lengths of the motorcar, Fräulein Zads fired at him again, then Colonel Hultz turned and fired. Lincoln aimed the rifle with one hand and squeezed off a round. Hultz's body slumped against the steering wheel, and the car swerved sharply to the left, though it didn't stop. Leaning over across the dead colonel, Fräulein Zads opened the door and pushed his limp body out. The body rolled with the car's forward momentum, bumping over rocks until it hung up in a thicket of desert scrub. Fräulein Zads slid into driver's seat and stomped on the accelerator.

Lincoln rode alongside the moving car and jumped in. Fräulein Zads clawed and scratched at him, and as he tried to ward her off, the motorcar swerved out of control. It spun around in a half circle and stopped short when the front wheels hit a shallow but steep depression, causing Lincoln to fly out over the windshield. He landed, stunned, in front of the car.

Fräulein Zads got out of the car and approached Lincoln, pointing her pistol at him. He looked up at her, his face full of dirt.

"Now, Mr. Smith," the fräulein said, "what is the expression? *Adios!*"

Lincoln, still on the ground, looked at the German ambassador with an amused expression. Then the blow from the heavy black-oak rifle stock smacking her in the back of the head sent her sprawling unconscious almost on top of him. Behind where she had been a moment before stood Amanda, holding Lincoln's rifle like a croquet mallet.

As Lincoln untangled himself from the German woman, Amanda, with a gleam in her eye, said, "It'll teach her to keep away from my beau."

Behind Amanda were two other camels, one of which had Omar on it, with the machine gun strapped to the back of its saddle. A short distance behind them, three irate travelers came running and shouting for the camels that Lincoln and his friends had hastily commandeered.

Amanda ran up to Lincoln, who was getting up.

"Thanks," he said, "but be careful with that rifle. It's one of the few things I got left of my pa's."

"Come on, Omar," Amanda said. "We'll take the car."

Omar hopped off the camel and quickly loaded the machine gun and the three remaining belts of ammunition into the back seat.

"I can't drive this thing," Lincoln said.

"Nor can I, Yank," said Omar. "I have had enough of machines for my lifetime."

"It can't be that difficult," Amanda said, getting behind the wheel as Lincoln and Omar hopped in. "I've been watching how they do it." She shifted the car and, looking over her shoulder, accelerated, expecting the car to back up. Instead, it lurched forward, clearing the shallow depression. She shifted again, and it lurched ahead even faster, over a sizable bump.

"What was that?" Amanda asked.

"It was only fräulein," Omar said.

Amanda shifted the car again, and they darted forward down the road.

CHAPTER 58

On the wall of the fort, smoke billowed from the emplacements where five of the six cannons had been mounted. Only nine fighting men were still alive. Athos, Porthos, Aramis, Johnny, and Jake were on the parapet with rifles. Two legionnaires were at the embrasure for the one remaining cannon. The third legionnaire and the last remaining Murian guard manned the last Maxim gun. In a corner of the parapet, the king had fallen into a swoon as Ambassador Montier tried to stanch the bleeding of his shoulder wound. Prince Kamak was with them, keeping his head down.

The Germans' three working cannons fired another salvo, and a wave of some sixty dervishes and Germans charged the fort. The defenders on the parapet fired at them desperately. The Maxim gun raked the attackers, but rifle fire hit the legionnaire and the Murian manning the gun. Then a cannonball exploded on the wall just in front of the last cannon, destroying the gun and killing one of the two legionnaires manning it.

"Get on that Maxim!" Athos yelled to the legionnaire who had survived the blast. The legionnaire got up and staggered over to the gun and reloaded it.

Twenty attackers made it to within a few yards of the fort as rifle fire from the German line thudded against the top of the wall, kicking up splinters of wood. Four men swung ropes with grappling hooks over the walls. Johnny and Jake let them climb most of the way up, then hacked the ropes away with Legion sabers.

Porthos slogged up the steps to the parapet, carrying a keg of gunpowder under each arm. Athos ran over and took one of the kegs from him. He lit a fuse on the keg, waited several seconds, and tossed it over the wall. It exploded, killing or otherwise incapacitating eight attackers. He and Porthos moved over to a nearby battlement, where Athos lit the fuse on the keg Porthos held. After smiling and reciting a line of poetry that Athos didn't understand, Porthos heaved it over the parapet, blowing up all but three of the remaining attackers. They turned and fled toward their battle line. They still had a dozen steps to go when Athos and Aramis brought them down with rifle shots.

Porthos headed back down to the magazine to fetch more kegs of powder. Two or three seconds after he left, a German cannonball exploded on the wall, right where he had just been. "That wild man has unnatural luck," said Aramis.

"Yeah," said Athos, looking out over the wall, where the German and dervish lines had ceased fire and were reforming out of rifle shot from the fort.

"Will they attack again?" the ambassador called out to Athos.

"They'll be back," said Athos. "bet on it. In the meantime, we've got to take out those cannons."

"There's still forty kegs of powder left," Porthos said, coming back onto the parapet with two more kegs. "I'll take 'em out."

"No, I'll go," Aramis said.

The king was still unconscious but breathing regularly after Ambassador Montier bandaged his shoulder and apparently stopped the bleeding. The ambassador and Prince Kamak sat silently by him. Athos looked around the parapet. Only he, Porthos, Aramis, the two "newsmen," and the legionnaire manning the Maxim gun were still at the embrasures. "The three of us will go," Athos said. "Two of us have to get through."

"Yes, the three of us shall go," Porthos said. "But first, give me a hand."

He went over to one of the dead legionnaires a few feet from him. Heaving the corpse into a sitting position, he propped it upright in an embrasure. He straightened the dead man's kepi on his head, then snugged his rifle against his shoulder, with his other arm on top of it. Athos and Aramis started doing the same, propping up dead legionnaires in empty embrasures. From a distance, it looked as if the fort were still manned by a good number of able-bodied soldiers.

When they were finished, Athos said to the legionnaire at the Maxim gun, "You'll keep them honest when we charge."

Johnny approached Athos after positioning another fallen legionnaire's rifle. "Me and Jake would count it a privilege to ride with you," he said. "If we're goin' down, I can't think of better company."

"Expresses my thoughts perfectly," said Jake.

"We need you here to cover us," Athos said. "Put up as big a show as you can. We need them to think there's still a lot of us left."

"Ambassador," Athos said, "you're gonna have to man the gate."

"I can do that," Montier answered. "But we need you to make it back. Consider it a direct order."

"Sir, I assure you that is our intention," Aramis said. Then, to the legionnaire at the Maxim gun, he said, "Corporal, keep your eye on their battle line. We would like a moment between three old friends."

The Three from Camarón walked a few feet away to a corner of the parapet. Aramis handed a cigar to Athos and Porthos, keeping one for himself. He lit their cigars, then his own, and pulled a metal flask from his hip pocket. "To you, my friends," he said, lifting the flask. "What is left of my fortune is willed to the orphanages. Ah, to have seen England again. Perhaps they have forgotten me by now. But—no regrets!" He drank and passed the flask to Porthos.

"The Legion has been good to us, and, I trust, we to the Legion," Porthos said. "You, my friends, have been more than brothers. I would have liked to bid Salina adieu. But I have no regrets!" Porthos raised the flask to Aramis. "For the supply of fine tobacco and cognac." And then to Athos, he said, "And to the man I did not think could be killed." Porthos took a drink and handed the flask to Athos.

Athos held it, looking away. After a few moments, he looked back and said, "It has been my honor and privilege to serve with you as comrades in arms. But more than that, you are true friends. True brothers, my only family. To you, the wild, uncrowned prince of the desert," he said, toasting Porthos. "And to you, the Robin Hood of jewel thieves." He raised the flask to Aramis.

Then he paused again, not finding the words for what he wanted to say. "They couldn't kill me, because, I guess, I was already dead," he finally said. "I've been feeling sorry for myself for so long, and just when I start to see . . . Guess you got to be alive to get killed. Now, let's go get those bastards, and the hell with regrets."

He took a swig from the flask and gave it back to Aramis, who flung it away. The three of them went down the parapet stairs to the storeroom.

Minutes later, they emerged, each carrying a keg of gunpowder. They mounted their horses. "You ready, son?" Athos said to the legionnaire on the machine gun, who saluted. He looked up at Johnny and Jake, and they saluted too.

Each holding a keg of powder under one arm, they lit the fuses with their cigars.

"Now!" Athos said to Ambassador Montier at the gate. The ambassador opened the gate, and the Three from Camarón charged out of the fort.

The battle line of dervishes and German soldiers was caught off guard. Several dervishes even started retreating when they saw the three legionnaires charging toward them, with the machine-gun and rifle fire from the fort supporting them. The German colonel in the line tried to maintain discipline and direct concentrated fire at the Three, but the covering fire from the fort kept the firing line pinned down until the Three were within fifty yards.

Then the cover fire stopped. With the king unconscious, Ambassador Montier down at the gate, and all other eyes on the battle line, Prince Kamak had shot the legionnaire firing the Maxim gun, the shot's noise unheard amid all the other gunfire. Kamak quickly returned his pistol to his pocket and pretended to be attending his father.

With the cessation of the covering fire, the battle line started firing again at the Three, who were bent over their horses' necks and riding low in the saddle, straight at the cannons. Jake ran from his place on the parapet to man the Maxim gun. As he was running, a cannonball exploded within a few feet of the gun, blowing it apart and knocking Jake to the floor of the parapet.

Johnny shot as fast as he could to give the Three some cover. He was the only one still shooting from the fort.

Forty yards from the cannons, a bullet took Aramis's kepi off his head, along with a small strip of his scalp. Another bullet hit him in the calf. Yet another struck Athos's saddle, and his horse began to bleed. But neither man slowed his charge. More bullets chewed up the ground all around them. Then, to the Three's astonishment, a whole swath of dervishes and German soldiers dropped where they stood. The sound of automatic gunfire grew as the firing line fell silent once more.

Athos glanced southward at the startling sight of a motorcar roaring toward the battle. It was Amanda at the wheel, and Smith blazing away in the back seat at the enemy line with a machine gun. Nearing the battle line, Amanda swung the car so that it ran parallel to the line, and Lincoln continued to spray it with the machine gun. Any Germans or dervishes who hadn't been shot yet took cover against the barrage. And Athos, Porthos, and Aramis closed in on the three cannons.

At twenty yards, the Three veered off, each toward one of the cannons. At about ten yards, their fuses having almost burned down, they shoved their powder kegs by the guns and swerved away from the battle line.

The motorcar continued to pound the battle line with machine-gun fire. Then three explosions almost simultaneously shook the ground, and a large cloud of smoke billowed in front of the battle line.

Out of the smoke burst three horsemen and the motorcar. From the back of the car, machine-gun fire continued to pummel the decimated enemy line.

When Johnny saw the Three and the motorcar racing toward the fort, he ran down and helped Ambassador Montier pull open the gate. As he did so, Jake was getting up from where he had lain on the parapet.

"Well, hope you had a good nap," said Johnny. "Now how about lending a hand?"

"Damn," said Jake, "I wasn't restin'! I had my lights knocked out. Hey, I see we ain't dead yet!"

"It is, though I'm a little less dead than you. And now we got Smith here, and he has a *machine gun.*"

Once the Three and the motorcar were inside the fort, the ambassador and Johnny closed and barred the gate. The Three hopped off their horses and ran up the parapet to assess the damage they had done. Amanda and Lincoln jumped out of the car, and Amanda ran to embrace her father. Johnny and Jake greeted Lincoln with a hearty welcome.

"Is the king all right?" Amanda asked.

"That Kamak is a coat-turning, back-stabbing, country-betraying polecat." Lincoln said, breaking away from Jake's handshake. They all turned and looked up on the parapet. Prince Kamak was gone.

The king was leaning on his good arm. "He went over the wall," he rasped. "My only son is a traitor."

Athos, Porthos, and Aramis looked over the wall and saw Kamak, legging it almost to the battle line. They raised their rifles, but gunfire hit the embrasures, forcing them to take cover. When they looked up again, Kamak had reached the line.

Everyone still breathing at the fort was up on the parapet. Athos, taking command, had Lincoln and Omar set up their machine gun in one of the embrasures. He had the ambassador and Amanda seeing to the king, who insisted that he be allowed to take up a rifle. Porthos, Aramis, Johnny, and Jake each had several rifles loaded and ready for a renewed attack.

"Kamak will enlighten them about what numbers we actually have left," Porthos said.

"How much ammunition do you have?" Athos asked Lincoln.

"Two belts," said Lincoln, who had already loaded one into the gun.

"I doubt we can hold off another attack," Aramis said.

"When my bullets are gone, they will face my bayonet," Porthos said, fixing the blade to his rifle.

"More of them are coming up," Athos said, seeing thirty new Germans join the battle line.

"And they've got two more damn cannons," Aramis said.

"Damn, that's it!" Lincoln said, stepping away from the machine gun. "How much gunpowder's left?"

"About thirty kegs," said Porthos. "Not sure how we could use it against an army that size."

"Well, there's still some fight left in me," said Amanda, picking up a rifle.

"Come on, Omar," Lincoln said. He and Omar ran down the stairs. A few moments later, they came out of the magazine carrying kegs of gunpowder and loading them into the motorcar.

"What are you *doing*!" Amanda called out from the parapet.

"There are at least a hundred people out there waiting to kill you," Ambassador Montier said. "And they have two cannons."

"We aren't going that way," Lincoln said as he and Omar made another trip into the magazine. "We're going up to the dam."

"Athos, would you get control of him?" the ambassador said.

But the Three were looking at one another and nodding. "He's right, let's give him a hand," Athos said to Porthos and Aramis. Then he commanded Johnny and Jake, "Man the machine gun until we're ready." The Three ran down the stairs and helped Lincoln and Omar load the powder kegs into the motorcar.

At the enemy battle line, gunners were cranking the two new cannons to the proper elevation. This time, riflemen guarded the artillery against a possible charge from the fort. Prince Kamak stood next to three German officers, giving them instructions.

He looked at his watch and said, "In two minutes, the squad should be in place at the rear of the fort."

"Open fire in two minutes," the German commander ordered the cannoneers.

At the back wall of the fort, where there was no gate and no watch being kept, five black-robed men dismounted. They threw ropes with grappling hooks up the wall and began to shinny up.

As the first man reached the parapet, the section in front of him exploded, sending up a cloud of smoke, shards and splinters of wall, and pieces of him and his comrades.

Out of the dust and smoke, moving carefully over the rubble drove the motorcar, with Amanda at the wheel. The king and the ambassador rode in the back seat, followed on horseback by Lincoln, Omar, Johnny, Jake, and the Three. When they were finally clear of the rubble that had been the fort's east wall, Amanda opened up the throttle and roared off up the road to the dam.

At the battle line, they heard the prodigious boom and saw the cloud of smoke and dust rise from behind the fort. Prince Kamak felt a surge of optimism. It appeared that some dire calamity had befallen the defenders—an errant spark in their powder magazine, perhaps. As he was deciding how to work this bit of serendipity to his advantage, a dervish rider galloped up to him and the German officers and jumped off his horse. "They are trying to escape up the canyon," said the rider.

"After them!" Kamak shouted. "We can trap them in the canyon!"

CHAPTER 59

A mile below the dam, Athos pulled up his horse. "Go on!" he shouted to the others. "I'll catch up." Then he turned and headed back down the canyon. Lincoln and Omar pulled up their horses and followed him.

They rode fifty yards back down to a rise. A mile away, they could see sixty flowing black robes on horseback, and behind them, fifty German infantry moving at double time.

Athos fired his pistol in the air and yelled, "Come on, you lily-livered, four-flushin', bushwhackin' sons of perdition!"

Then Omar started hollering, as well. "Aa-a-a-hoo-o-o, children of calamity, sons of donkeys and toothless camels! Come and reap the whirlwind!"

Even Athos chuckled over the kid's attempt at invective. "Come on!" he said. "They're coming, and fast." The three of them turned their horses and raced back up the narrow canyon road toward the dam.

At the dam Ambassador Montier, Amanda, and Omar helped the king up the canyon's side, to a sheltered position in the rocks above the dam, where

Johnny and Jake had set up the machine gun. The Three, Lincoln, and Omar were unloading the kegs of gunpowder that they had wedged between the seats and strapped onto the motorcar's fenders, running boards, and hood. Soon, they had all sixteen kegs stacked in the storeroom on the dam.

"I'll set the charge," Lincoln said when they had stowed the last of the kegs.

"Go ahead," Athos said to Porthos and Aramis. "I'll give him a hand."

With his knife, Lincoln punched a hole in one of the kegs and poured a thick line of gunpowder from the storeroom to a spot on the dam's deck. Then he went into the storeroom again, rolled out a large empty barrel, and pushed it against the storeroom door to prop it open.

"Go. I'll be right behind you," Lincoln said to Athos. "I have to get my rifle out of the car."

As Lincoln grabbed his rifle from the back seat floor, rifle rounds kicked up the dirt at his feet, and one went through the fender beside him. He zigzagged from the car, across the deck, with bullets flying around him. Then, from above, rifle and machine-gun fire poured down on the dervishes and Germans who had gathered in the now-dry bed where the dammed river once flowed. When Lincoln had made it up to the barricade in the rocks, the firing stopped. In the riverbed a hundred yards below, Kamak and the rest of his army had arrived to join the force already there.

After a few moments, a German officer next to Kamak raised a white flag and stood up. "You cannot escape," Kamak called out, also standing up. "Give us the king, and the rest of you will go free. Otherwise, it is certain death for all of you."

"The Legion doesn't surrender," Lincoln called down, "and neither do I! You have ten seconds to lay down your guns. This is your only warning."

Kamak ducked behind the riverbank, and his army immediately started shooting. Lincoln picked up his rifle and trained it on the little pile of gunpowder on the dam's top deck.

As he was taking aim, Athos demanded, "Where did you get that rifle?"

"I thought legionnaires weren't supposed to ask personal questions," Lincoln answered, not looking at Athos.

"I said where did you get that rifle?"

"Quiet, all right? I'm concentrating. This rifle is tricky. It shoots—"

"Low and to the right," Athos said. Lincoln was so startled, he jerked the trigger and badly missed the shot. He turned and stared at Athos.

Several dervishes were making their way up closer to the dam, and the rest of Kamak's men opened fire again. Everyone up in the rocks was getting nervous. "Let me see that rifle," Athos said, reaching for it.

Lincoln numbly handed it to him. "That rifle's custom made," Lincoln said. "Someone who doesn't know it couldn't hit a barn from inside it."

Athos aimed the rifle and fired. The bullet hit the concrete below the pile of gunpowder, sparking it and igniting the line of powder leading into the storeroom. Lincoln and Athos turned and stared at each other as the powder burned toward the open doorway.

"Only one person besides me could have made that shot with that rifle," Lincoln said.

"Where did you get this?" Athos said.

They looked at each other, dumbfounded. Below, the line of gunpowder burned closer to the storeroom.

"That rifle was my father's," Lincoln said.

"Then . . ." Athos gave up trying to talk and just looked at Lincoln.

"You are the famous Wesley Smith, greatest shot in Texas?" Omar gasped.

"It's stopped!" Amanda shouted. "It's gone out!"

Lincoln looked, and indeed, the line of gunpowder had fizzled out just outside the storage room's open door. He turned and ran down toward the deck. Porthos, Aramis, Johnny, and Jake poured down covering machine-gun and rifle fire. Athos sprang up and ran after him.

Lincoln came backing out of the dam's storeroom onto the deck of the dam pouring a much thicker line of gunpowder. Bullets flew at him from below, and now three dervishes had crawled up onto the deck. Rifle fire from above killed one of them. Then Athos, with a pistol in each hand, ran out on the deck and blasted the other two. Lincoln continued pouring the line of powder.

"You're Lincoln? My *son*?"

ALL THE COWBOYS AIN'T GONE

"You sure can shoot, just like they said."

"I thought you were dead! And your mother?"

"She never remarried. Raised me to always do what would have made you proud."

Another black-robed man crept onto the deck, armed with a long, curved yataghan. Athos shot him, and he fell over the dam into the stream below.

Lincoln finished pouring the line. Then he ran into the storeroom and rolled out another of the wooden kegs. He also rolled out the keg holding the storeroom door open and brought it to the edge of the deck. Then, as his friends above tried to hold down the gunfire from Kamak's army, he ran off to the end of the dam. He came back in a few moments, carrying three large rocks. Bullets were pinging and ricocheting off the concrete around them.

"Now what are you doing?" Athos said.

"Ballast. It's something Frenchy told me about. He's been riding barrels over Niagara Falls."

"Frenchy LeBeau! Okay, get in, I'll light the fuse." Athos fired his pistol, lighting the line of gunpowder just outside the doorway of the storeroom. It burned heavily through the doorway. Lincoln stood in one of the barrels, holding its top.

"You know the reason I wanted to join the Legion was to—" Lincoln started to say, but Athos cut him off.

"Just get in. You talk as much as your mother." Athos took the wooden lid from him, pushed him down in the barrel, and secured the top.

More gunfire was hitting the deck now, and twenty or more dervishes had crawled up within forty feet. Fire from above hit two of them and sent the rest to cover.

Athos pushed the barrel Lincoln was in into the small flow of water that the dam released. He jumped into the other barrel and pulled the lid tight. From inside, he rocked the barrel, and it fell over and rolled off the deck into the water.

As ten dervishes climbed up on the deck, the dam erupted in a great explosion. For a few moments after the blast, there was silence. Then the

338 JOHN J. JACOBSON

main structure of the dam started cracking. The cracks grew, and water started pouring through. The structure suddenly crumbled, and the water held back above the dam tore through in a great torrent. It swamped everything in its path—what remained of the dam, the barrels, the dervishes just below the deck, and the rest of Kamak's army in the riverbed below.

Ten minutes or so later, the torrent had subsided. Toward the base of the canyon, one of the barrels popped up out of the flood and washed close to the bank. The barrel's top came off, and Lincoln struggled out, coughing and spitting up water. He crawled up the bank and fell facedown on the ground.

In the river, a section of the wooden storeroom's wall floated against the bank. An arm clung to it, and a head broke the water's roiling brown surface. Prince Kamak looked around him and saw Lincoln lying on the bank. Crawling out of the water, he pulled a dagger from his belt and staggered toward the oblivious Lincoln.

Forty feet past where Lincoln lay, Athos watched from beneath the tilted lid of his barrel, which had fetched up in a small eddy. Seeing the prince approach, dagger in hand, on Lincoln's blind side, Athos rose from the barrel, aimed his pistol, and squeezed the trigger. But the mechanism was so fouled with river silt that it misfired.

"You. You ruined everything," Kamak said, raising the dagger.

Lincoln whipped his head around and tried to scoot backward. He got his forearm up in time to block the dagger thrust to his neck, taking a deep cut in his shoulder. Kamak raised the blade again.

Athos already had the bowie knife out of his boot. It flashed through the air and sank hilt deep in the prince's neck. Kamak feebly grasped at it and fell dead on the ground beside Lincoln.

CHAPTER 60

Three days after what became known in Murian history as the great flood, the only one in Murian history, a large crowd had gathered in front of the king's palace. They had been chanting for some time, and seeing the door on the second-floor balcony open, they chanted faster and louder. Out onto the balcony walked two Murian guards, who stood by the large double doors. Then out walked the Three from Camarón, drawing a loud cheer. After a few moments, King Suleiman walked out unassisted. The crowd roared. He raised an arm, giving the people his blessing. He didn't bother trying to silence them.

Later, in the reception room, Ambassador Montier, Amanda, Princess Salina, Lincoln with his arm in a sling, Omar, and Porthos stood exchanging small talk. On a chain around her neck, Amanda wore the large ruby that Lincoln had taken from the treasure. A few feet away at the buffet table, Johnny and Jake were filling up their plates with roast mutton, vegetables, and couscous.

"It weren't quite what we was expecting," Johnny said. "But I got, as our friends from Camarón like to say, no regrets."

"Nope, I reckon not," said Jake. "With the rocks the king gave us, I'd say we got enough to buy up a stake a quarter the size of Montanee."

"It ought to do for a sizable herd of beeves," Johnny said. "A few horses and beeves, Jake—they're reliable, there's demand for them, and they *exist*."

"You never know what might turn up."

"Like what?"

"Like . . ." Jake paused. "Polar bears."

Ambassador Montier walked over to Athos, who was getting himself a drink at the punch bowl. "Now, Major," he said, "I would like to continue our discussion of the morning."

"Sir, I understand you wanting to get a man like my Lincoln for your daughter, but he isn't marrying anybody until he finishes his schooling. If young people are going to thrive in this world, they must be equipped."

Lincoln and Amanda weren't *trying* to eavesdrop, but they were standing only a few feet away, and Athos had a strong, deep voice. They walked right over to their fathers.

"Wait a minute," Lincoln began. "I don't think this is any of your—"

"Mind your manners, son," Athos said.

"I quite agree with you, Major," said the ambassador, "the match would meet with my approval, but not till after she goes back to Paris to finish her education."

"Father!" Amanda protested. "You have no right to—"

"Hush, child," said the ambassador.

"And, of course," said Athos, "we'll have to work out the dowry. I believe it's a tradition worth preserving."

Now it was not only Amanda and Lincoln but also Montier who took umbrage. "What era do you suppose we are living in, Major? The Dark Ages?"

The king approached. "A word with you, Mr. Ambassador," he said.

As they walked away, the king put his good arm through the ambassador's arm.

"How may I be of service, Your Highness?" the ambassador said.

"About the rebuilding of the dam," the king said.

"It could be arranged," said Montier after a moment's thought. "We would, of course, need to agree on just a few minor considerations."

"Absolutely not!" the king boomed. "We'll have no foreign inter-ference. But," he added in a softer tone, "if you were also to include a railroad, we would certainly entertain your offer."

Not wishing to overhear any more of other people's conversations, Lincoln and Amanda walked out on the balcony. The sun was vanish-ing behind the mountains in the southwest, and the crowd below had broken up. This time, Lincoln didn't need to steal his kiss. Leaning back against the rail, he felt a tiny pinprick to his backside. Startled, he turned in time to see a small rodent scamper away along the balcony rail. In the dimming light, he could have sworn he saw, growing out of its head, tiny two-inch horns.

THE END

ACKNOWLEDGMENTS

My mother was the most creative person I have ever known. Among her artistic prowesses, she was a professional fashion designer, accomplished painter, and fabulous cook. Watching her cook is how I came to my under-standing of creativity. She would take a portion of this, some of those, a splash of that, a pinch or two of a few other things, swirl it around, let it stew, then give it a taste to see what she had, or what else might be needed. Disraeli used the term "combinations" for putting together creative endeavors like this.

The books and authors inspiring or influencing the stew of this book are too many to list, but for a few of the most immediate ones: the adventure stories of Walter Scott, Dumas (the elder), H. Rider Haggard, Stevenson, and P. C. Wren's tales of the French Foreign Legion. Going further back, Ovid's Metamorphoses, the legends of St. George questing the Dragon, and even a few of the Medieval courtly love romances. As for the theme of "Time's Scythe" (as Shakespeare puts it), it is one of the major themes of the great poets (see his Sonnet 73). As for my attempt, in places, to capture the melancholy mood of inexorable time, I know of nothing greater than "Lonesome Dove."